THE GENERAL'S GOLD

LYNDEE WALKER

BRUCE ROBERT COFFIN

SEVERN RIVER
PUBLISHING

Severn River Publishing
www.SevernRiverBooks.com

This is a work of fiction. Names, characters, businesses, places, events and incidents are either the products of the author's imagination or used in a fictitious manner. Any resemblance to actual persons, living or dead, or actual events is purely coincidental.

ISBN: 978-1-64875-589-7 (Paperback)

ALSO BY THE AUTHORS

The Turner and Mosley Files

The General's Gold

The Cardinal's Curse

The Pirate's Secret

BY LYNDEE WALKER

The Faith McClellan Series

The Nichelle Clarke Series

Never miss a new release!

To find out more about the authors and their books, visit

severnriverbooks.com

To my real-life Avery, thank you for taking me on the greatest adventure of my life when you made me a mom.

"Adventure is worthwhile in itself."
— Amelia Earhart

PROLOGUE

Stuart Whittenstrom kept watch from the bow of one of three dories while handpicked members of his ship's two-hundred-man crew struggled with the heavy trunks. The deafening boom of cannon fire fueled their need to expedite the mission. Even under the cover of darkness, the young lieutenant recognized the tonal difference between the six-pounders on board their Continental Brigantine and the more devastating nine-pounders carried by the enemy. As the men hoisted the chained and padlocked containers over the dories' gunwales, he worried how long their captain would be able to stave off the threat.

Whittenstrom's ship had broken from a line of colonial navy vessels in the hopes that the pursuing British frigate would follow the group, but their captain's plan had failed. Like a wolf hunting easy prey, the Royal Navy ship had turned and followed them up the channel.

With the trunks preloaded into the dories, the captain had put Whittenstrom in charge and launched the small boats on a last-ditch mission to complete delivery. The trunks, a dozen in all, were to be carried through the woods to the horse-drawn wagon awaiting them. Once loaded, the entire cargo would be taken to another location, one that only the captain knew, and secreted away for later retrieval. Whittenstrom had inquired of his captain the specific contents of the trunks, but the captain would only say, "highly valued objects."

At the behest of his superiors, Whittenstrom had scouted this area for several weeks before locating a suitable place to transfer the precious cargo for delivery to its final destination. Though he was reasonably sure of their position, he couldn't be positive. Conditions had been far more favorable when he had reconnoitered the area. There hadn't even been any fog, let alone enemy fire.

Though the captain had not divulged the trunks' contents, their burdensome weight—it took three strong men to carry each one—suggested riches beyond imagining. *Maybe riches enough to turn the tide on this war*, Whittenstrom thought as the last trunk slid toward the water in the arms of a young petty officer, before two others reached in to share the load.

An abnormally loud report emitted from one of the enemy cannons, immediately followed by the all-too-familiar shrill near-whistle of a rapidly approaching projectile.

"Get down!" Whittenstrom shouted.

The cannonball split the air in two, passing directly overhead before harmlessly splashing into the river less than fifty yards away. Whittenstrom had no way of knowing if the shot was random fire from the channel, or if the British frigate had drawn closer and was now targeting them. Launched at a slightly different angle, the cannonball would have demolished at least one of their small craft, killing many of them as a bonus.

No matter, he thought. If they didn't get their freight to shore in the next few moments, a quick death at the hands of the enemy might be the most merciful outcome for all of them. A far better fate, certainly, than that of the gallows.

His men quickly regained their footing and surrounded their charges like pallbearers. Each crew of three hoisted their trunks once again and trudged toward the rocky shore, grunting and groaning as they struggled with the awkward loads.

"Put your backs into it," Whittenstrom called.

One by one, the procession of men carrying trunks disappeared into the woods. The young lieutenant began to believe they might make it before being overrun by the British.

Toward the back of the small, strange parade, one of the containers listed dangerously to one side, the midshipman on the falling corner looking over his shoulder for another cannonball with wide eyes. Whittenstrom could read the terror even in the moonlight. Whittenstrom leapt from the bow of the dory into the shallow water. Gripping his weapon in one hand, he grabbed hold of the trunk with the other. Muskets opened fire from the opposite shore. The rounds ricocheted off nearby rocks and punched through the dark canopy of trees ahead of them.

"Step lively, man," Whittenstrom offered the frightened midshipman a smile he knew couldn't possibly look sincere. "Many hands make light work, and safety is right ahead." Another few yards and they'd be concealed by heavy summer foliage and the Spanish moss hanging from the trees. The midshipman nodded, and their group nearly caught up to the one in front of them.

As they reached the forest's edge, another volley of musket fire erupted from the darkness at their flank. The midshipman's head evaporated in a spray of blood and bone and Whittenstrom barely swallowed a scream. The midshipman's body folded to the ground, his hand still gripping the chest, adding his dead weight to the load. As the trunk crashed into the dirt, the two petty officers let go and scattered, provoking another half dozen men in the closest groups to desert alongside them. Two dove into the river while the other four sprinted into the woods. Whittenstrom yelled for them to return, but his voice was drowned out by the sounds of war.

1

Avery Turner felt the blade of the knife pressed against her throat. Clamped around her bicep, her assailant's other hand squeezed like a vise.

"Come on, Avery," her broker's shrill voice emanated through the Bluetooth earbuds. "Hold or sell? We have millions hanging in the balance here, and Twitter is on fire over these lawsuit rumors."

Avery drove her right foot into the attacker's instep, and the back of her head into his chin. The well-practiced maneuver stunned the man, loosening his grip. Before he could recover, she spun to her left, driving an elbow to the side of his head. Reaching up with her right hand, she grasped onto the wrist holding the knife and twisted. Using her hips as a cantilever, she pulled, flipping the man over her body and onto the floor.

"I have millions hanging in the balance," Avery said. "Not you. And I am holding." She dropped to her knees, delivering a final elbow strike to the supine man's solar plexus before knocking the weapon out of his reach.

Barely winded, Avery continued, "Panic selling in the technology industry is a fool's game, Bob. An hour from now, Twitter will move on to some celebrity breakup or political scandal—social media isn't real life, that's why I don't waste time on it."

"But—"

"But nothing. We hold. The shares will rebound."

The shares had better rebound, she thought. Because she couldn't afford it if they didn't. But Bob didn't need to know that. Avery pressed the button behind her ear, disconnecting the call before her overanxious stockbroker could protest further. Hopping to her feet, she regarded her assistant, Harrison, lying on the mat. Dressed in gray sweats, a maroon padded vest, and matching sparring helmet, he looked like a cross between the victim of a boxing TKO and a Teenage Mutant Ninja Turtle.

Harrison groaned. "You know you're gonna make me an old man before my time, Ave."

"You *are* an old man," Avery said as she reached down to help him to his feet.

"My knees are killing me."

"Nothing to do with me. That's from you chasing down murderers for two and a half decades."

"Um, almost three, thank you. And I didn't take this cushy retirement gig just to have you torture me."

Avery grinned at his dramatics. "I gave you a mat to land on."

She turned and padded barefoot across the cool polished marble foyer floor, past the twenty-foot-tall Corinthian columns to a chic iron bistro cart. Placed atop the cart by her housekeeper, Dorothy, was a silver coffee carafe, a bowl of fresh cut fruit, and several of Harrison's favorite pastries. Though she signed Dorothy's paychecks, Avery wasn't sure the woman could name her favorite pastry—cinnamon-sugar croissants—if pressed. But she had made a quick study of expertise in Harrison's favorite foods. Not that he understood the gesture, but it made Avery smile, which she needed after the call with Bob.

Avery popped a chunk of watermelon into her mouth before pouring two cups of coffee, one black and one with skim milk and Splenda. She handed the black coffee to her sweaty assistant.

Harrison plopped down on an iron chair beside the cart. Holding his padded helmet in one hand and coffee in the other, he gestured toward Avery's mug. "My doctor says water is healthier following a workout."

"But water doesn't have caffeine," Avery countered.

"You've had three cups already."

Stretching her back, Avery caught a glimpse of Harrison's hand hovering above a raspberry Danish.

"Did your doctor have any thoughts on sweets?"

He grumbled something unintelligible before grabbing a chunk of honeydew from the bowl.

You can *teach an old dog*, she thought as she headed back to the mat to begin her cooldown routine.

"The stock will rebound," Harrison said, grabbing a Danish and pretending not to notice when Avery shook her head.

"Let's hope so," she said. "Before Bob has a stroke. And since when did you become so market savvy, Harry?"

Avery sat facing a two-story wall of windows, legs ninety degrees from one another. Reaching one hand over the other, she stretched toward one foot at a time. She gazed through the glass past the perfectly manicured landscape surrounding her sparkling blue Olympic-sized swimming pool to the ocean beyond. The prospect of early retirement and financial independence had been exhilarating initially. Now here she was, less than a year later, living in her dream home on an island in the Keys, completely bored with her life. She wanted—no, needed—some adventure. Something to get the creative juices flowing again.

As if on cue, an aging, but serviceable, salt-stained white speedboat glided up beside her deep-water dock. *Carter.*

She jumped to her feet and ran across the foyer toward the sweeping, curved double staircase.

"Where are you going?" Harrison said.

"Diving," she hollered over her shoulder as she mounted the steps two at a time. "Carter is here early."

Less than five minutes later, Avery sauntered across the emerald grass toward the concrete dock where Carter Mosley was busy inspecting equipment. She carried her fins in one hand and dive bag in the other.

Carter, already in predive mode, checked mental boxes, along with tank gauges and regulators. Avery took her time walking the length of the dock, reluctant to break his concentration since she had only recently learned to tell a regulator from a rabbitfish. Though she had completed her adventure diver certification, she deferred to Carter's much more extensive experience when they went diving together. He looked up as she approached the boat.

"You don't mind that I'm early?" he asked.

"I've been inside too much already this morning," Avery said. "It's a truly marvelous day out here."

"Most days are. That's why I love it here."

"He said, until hurricane season." Taking the hand he offered, Avery climbed aboard.

Carter waved a hand. "Storms are part of life everywhere. But here, we get way more perfect days than storms. You ready for an adventure?"

You have no idea, Avery thought. "Does this mean you're finally going to tell me where we're headed?"

Carter shook his head. "It's a surprise."

"Not so much as a hint?"

"Nope," Carter said as he turned away and began to stow their gear in the hold. "I will tell you it's the deepest dive you've done yet. And that you'll have a wonderful time. Trust me."

For some reason she couldn't put a finger on, Avery did trust him. "As much as I appreciate you teaching me to dive, you really should let me pay you for the lessons."

Carter stood upright and turned to face her. "I don't need your money, Avery. But I appreciate your friendship."

Carter's boat, *The Deuce*, which he claimed to have named after an old friend, was a worn but seaworthy craft. With its white fiberglass hull, trimmed in chrome and teak wood, *The Deuce* reminded Avery of Harrison: crusty but capable.

Her phone buzzed, and she glanced down and silenced the call from her attorney's office. Nope—talk of life-altering lawsuits and falsified reports she'd had nothing to do with weren't ruining her perfect afternoon. She paid the lawyers enough to handle things on their own.

Avery raised her sunglasses up onto her sun-bronzed forehead and peered over the weathered gunwale into the water. A brightly colored school of fish darted through the sunbeams below the surface just above the sandy bottom. She smiled and inhaled deeply. The warm sun on her skin combined with the scent of salty ocean air relaxed her. It was the reason she had come to live on the island in the first place. She reached up and slid the Ray-Bans back down across the bridge of her nose before settling back against the faded blue cushions to watch Carter work.

"Can I ask you something?" Avery said.

"As long as it has nothing to do with where I'm taking you." He pulled the lines in and eased the throttle up, moving away from the dock into the open water.

"Okay, how deep can you go?" Avery raised her voice over the hum of the engine and the rush of the wind.

"The answer to that depends on whether or not we're still talking about water." He arched one eyebrow and grinned.

Avery rolled her eyes. "I forgot who I was talking to for a minute there. Let me rephrase the question, Mr. Mosley: What is the deepest scuba, seawater," she hit those two words hard, "dive you've ever done?"

"Touché, Miss Turner. Let's see, the textbook answer is that with my level of training and experience I'm required to stay above 146 feet. And I'm certified to instruct TecRec diving to that depth."

"But you've gone deeper, haven't you?"

"I plead the fifth, your honor," Carter said with a grin.

"So, no diver can go farther than 145 feet down?" Avery said.

"It's not that simple, and you have to remember that the limits on each certification are about personal responsibility—it's not like there are scuba police waiting below to write you a ticket. The limit for recreational diving is 130 feet, which may be conservative, but diving is definitely a realm where it's better to be safe, because being sorry can make you the guest of honor at a funeral. Anything below 130 is technical diving, which requires special training and sometimes different gas mixtures." Carter pointed to their gear. "For rec diving, our tanks only have compressed air inside. Go too deep with that and you risk what they call nitrogen narcosis. It's like being drunk, but not in a fun way."

Carter waved at a passing pleasure boat and Avery followed suit.

"Can I ask you another question?" Avery said.

"Maybe I should be charging you after all. Pop quizzes were never my strong suit." Carter pulled his sunglasses down the bridge of his nose and winked. "Sure, go ahead."

"Why do you insist on using this boat? I've seen your other one. It looks brand new."

"That's because it *is* new."

"Then why *The Deuce*?"

"I don't know. It's just comfortable. Familiar." He ran a hand across the chrome wheel. "Besides, she's been with me since the beginning."

"But wouldn't the newer boat look better to your paying customers?"

Carter laughed. "I'll let you in on a little secret, Avery. People tip better when they think you're destitute."

"Fair point."

Though Avery had only known Carter for several weeks, she had already grown fond of his easygoing demeanor, his laugh, and his smile. She enjoyed having him around.

A year into her high society lifestyle, Avery still felt like an outsider. She wasn't an islander—more like an uninvited guest who had crashed the party of the gilded elite. In a way, she supposed she had. Avery hadn't come from money, far from it. But her current wealth was well known, and, as a result, she was invited and expected to show up at various fundraisers and openings.

Which is how she met Carter—she'd been hanging out in a fern-shrouded patio corner under a large palm tree at a museum benefit, sipping the melting ice from her margarita while people-watching a crowd of the island's most affluent residents, when Carter, attired in the same simple tuxedo as the rest of the waitstaff, popped his head around the tree and handed her a fresh, salt-rimmed glass.

"You've been nursing the dregs of that drink for what has to be six months by now," he'd said. "The bartender insisted I bring you another."

"Weren't you the bartender?"

"I'm extremely good at insisting. You need anything else?"

"I'm set now, thank you," she'd said. "Just reluctant to give up such a good hiding place."

"I see. Hiding from anything interesting?"

"Like what?"

"I don't know. How about the FBI?"

Avery had laughed at the absurdity of the question. "Nothing so sordid, I'm afraid."

"What then?"

She lifted her drink toward the crowd. "How about mindless cocktail chatter and endless chains of fake smiles for selfies that will be all over the special pocket of hell that is social media before we even leave here tonight?"

"Can't say I blame you there." Carter had taken her response as an invitation to join her, proclaiming himself "off duty for the remainder of the evening."

"What do you have against social media?" he'd asked, his eyebrows disappearing into his hairline as Avery had recited her usual speech on how frivolous and too-often harmful she found the simpering smiles and staged, filtered photos.

"I will never download an app, look at a video, or open an account," she'd finished with a smile. "I'd much rather talk to real people live and in person."

He'd spent the next two hours making her laugh with irreverent comments about the guests, many of whom he seemed to know quite well for a waiter, interspersed with stories about scuba diving, which he seemed to take very seriously. Avery gathered from his stories that he gave lessons.

"So, are you supplementing your diving income via the island's service industry?" Avery had asked.

Carter had laughed at her question. "Why would I do that?"

"Maybe to be closer to your passion."

Carter had leaned in close to her and lowered his voice. "Don't tell anyone, but I only agreed to serve drinks tonight to help out a friend of mine."

"And who would that be?" she'd asked, scanning the crowd.

"MaryAnn Everly, the museum director," Carter had said, pointing out a striking blond woman who turned to wave at them.

"Wow, helping her must be an awful chore." Avery had hidden a smirk behind her glass.

"It's a sacrifice I'm willing to make."

"For the sake of friendship."

"Of course."

Several drinks and so many laughs her sides ached later, Avery asked about diving lessons. Since that night, she'd figured out quickly why Carter loved it so much and was pretty sure she had made her first island friend, too.

The sound of the boat's engine throttling back pulled Avery from her reverie.

"We're here," Carter said as he killed the engine and dropped anchor.

Avery looked around at nothing but ocean. "Where's here?"

He waved her up to the bow and pointed into the waves.

Squinting against the glare, she peered into the crystal blue depths where something darker began to materialize.

"What's down there?" she asked, thinking it might be a reef.

Carter winked as he passed her the dive bag containing her gear. "You ready to see your first shipwreck?"

2

Carter grinned at Avery's unbridled excitement. Her reaction to diving a wreck was everything he had hoped it would be.

"Is it a Spanish galleon full of lost treasure?" Avery asked breathlessly as she struggled into her wet suit.

"You'll have to wait and see."

"How old is it?" Avery said. "What's it called?"

Carter laughed at her enthusiasm.

"This is so cool, Carter. I can't wait."

Avery slipped into her fins and then rinsed out her face mask and rechecked the gauges on her air tank.

"Why are there no other divers out here?" she said as she scanned the area.

"I'm surprised we're alone, but it's still early in the day," Carter said. "All the tourists seem to be diving the *Tigershark* lately, about ten miles that way." He pointed east. "So it may stay quiet here."

"Can we swim inside the wreck?"

"There's a lot more to swimming inside a submerged vessel than you think. You aren't ready for that, Avery. But we can explore it from the outside."

Avery pulled on her mask and adjusted the straps.

"The depth we'll be diving is about fifty feet," Carter said. "On the way back to the surface we'll do the standard three-minute safety stop at fifteen feet, okay?"

Avery nodded.

"Now, remember all the things I've taught you. Diving a shipwreck is a little different than exploring the ocean floor. You'll need to stay right with me. Watch for sharp metal. Keep an eye on your gauges. When you see the reading approaching 750 PSI we'll start for the surface, okay? You ready?"

Avery gave him two very enthusiastic thumbs up.

Carter felt her excitement as he positioned his own mask and regulator into place.

Like synchronized swimmers, they flipped backward over the side of the boat and into the sea. The warm, clear water enveloped them, blocking out the wind, the waves, and the cries of the gulls. Sunlight passing through seawater cast everything in a greenish hue.

It was always like this, he thought. Each time he dove it was like entering another world. Though he enjoyed skydiving, too, Carter never felt more at home than when he was underwater. Especially when the dive was for pleasure.

He quickly reestablished visual contact with Avery. She made an "O" with the thumb and index finger of her right hand, the universal okay signal. Carter pointed in the direction of the wreck then gestured for her to stay right beside him. He kept his pace slow as they descended, making it easier for her to keep up while helping her to conserve her air. He knew her excitement could cause her to burn through the tank more quickly.

Avery was still an inexperienced diver, but she had picked up scuba diving faster than anyone he had ever taught. He watched her closely for signs of distress or fear, but she appeared completely at home in their surroundings. Even through her mask he saw the childlike wonder in her eyes. She paused a moment to point out a pair of large blue and gold angelfish, then made a heart sign with her hands. He smiled around his regulator. Her exuberance was contagious.

Carter pointed toward the hulking outline of the sunken freighter directly below them. He loved diving the wreck of *Isabella's Dream*, mostly because it had been responsible for him earning his first million by posting dive videos to Instagram. What had started out as a fun way to document his dives had exploded into a head-spinning wave of endorsement requests, agents, and entertainment lawyers. A celebrity fashion guru had taken notice of him, reposting a video of Carter and his former diving partner, Jeff, as they explored the ship. Carter had awoken the next morning with a half million new followers, most of whom were hoping to see photos of exotic sunken treasure. It had been a life-changing moment.

As Carter knew all too well, American Revolution–era treasure was often nothing more than fine silks and refined sugar. Treasure of the day to be sure, but hardly the heady stuff of legend. His rabid new followers wanted to see galleons, silver, gold bullion, and treasure maps. The very things that led to fevered and dangerous quests, often turning friend into foe.

The difficulties with hunting for anything that old were many. The main issue was that the ships of the eighteenth and nineteenth centuries had been constructed almost entirely from wood. Submerged in the warm waters off the Florida coast, wood quickly begins to break down. Combined with several centuries worth of hurricanes, most of the ancient wrecks had been reduced to nothing more than fields of rubble. Even the few wooden wrecks that had managed to partially survive beneath the ocean floor began to decay rapidly once they were discovered.

Seasonal hurricanes and tidal patterns completely altered the underwater landscape, too. The shifting ocean sands were equally capable of concealing or exposing long-lost vessels. Shipwrecks located and charted one year might be lost beneath the ocean floor the next. Despite the exhaustive research that went into finding the older wrecks, Carter knew it often came down to nothing more than a matter of luck and timing. Instead of focusing on the protected wrecks, Carter limited his searches to vessels of the more recently lost variety.

As they neared *Isabella's Dream*, he glanced over at Avery. She was right beside him. He could tell by the number of bubbles that the excitement was causing her to burn up more air than normal. He tapped his left index and middle fingers to the palm of his right hand, the signal for her to check her tank gauge. She nodded and complied, flashing an "okay" sign. Using their legs to propel themselves forward, they glided onward.

The freighter had settled onto her port side, partially submerged in silt as if the receding tide had left it grounded. Carter kept a close eye on Avery as they swam above the remnants of coral-encrusted deck railing. The bridge, formerly used by crew members to navigate across the Atlantic, was now nothing more than a rusted, windowless protrusion covered in red algae and barnacles.

Carter removed the flashlight from his belt then signaled Avery to do the same. They illuminated the interior of the bridge. Schools of smaller fish moved through the beams of light. Carter directed his light toward the floor, causing something to bolt away from them, stirring up a cloud of sediment in the process. A moment later, a large crab appeared from the murk before quickly scrambling under the rusted remains of a control panel. Seeing remnants of the control room covered in underwater growth, both plant and animal, always reminded him of an abandoned house where sheets had been draped over everything.

Avery shook her head in awe as she gestured with both arms at the entire room. She pantomimed snapping a photo then held her hands up in frustration at forgetting to bring a camera. Carter unclipped a small under-water camera from his dive belt then handed it to her. He steadied his lamp on the bridge as she snapped a half dozen photos. She returned his camera, then touched her regulator with two fingers, the universal sign for gratitude.

They moved away from the bridge along the side of the ship. Not wanting Avery to be surprised by a sudden encounter with a nurse shark, hammerhead, or something more aggressive like a barracuda or a territo-rial moray eel, Carter kept his eyes peeled as they swam above the exposed starboard side of the wreck. Schools of silver fish darted in and out of holes in the hull.

Carter snapped several photos of Avery before he reattached the camera to his belt, then checked his air. It was time for them to surface. He pointed to his regulator, then gave a thumbs up. Avery nodded her under-standing and followed him from the wreck.

They ascended slowly while Avery continued to stare down at the wreck as if she was afraid it might disappear. At fifteen feet he signaled to her to stop. As they treaded water beneath the brightly lit ocean surface, he watched her hold her position in the water column like she'd been diving for years and not weeks.

The moment she surfaced and peeled off her mask, Avery launched into a verbal recounting of everything they had seen—an hour's worth of bottled-up conversation poured out.

"Oh my God, Carter. That was incredible. I feel like we just traveled back in time. Like I could almost see the crew manning the bridge." Avery grinned as she flopped onto the blue-cushioned bench and squeezed water out of her hair.

She kept talking, and Carter nodded and smiled as he removed his wet suit and toweled off. His attention, however, had been divided since they'd first surfaced by another vessel bobbing up and down as it passed at a crawl about a hundred feet off their port side. Unusual, since they were not anchored near any of the normal underwater attractions, and because he had been flying the red and white diver down flag. As a matter of safety and courtesy, most boat pilots kept far away from active dive boats.

The boat was a small cuddy cabin with twin outboards. Carter couldn't help but be suspicious of the lone man moving about the deck of the other boat. He wasn't fishing. Wasn't diving. In fact, he didn't appear to be engaged in any type of typical boating activity.

Not wanting to alarm Avery, Carter kept it to himself, but continued to monitor. He moved toward the controls where he kept a pair of binoculars within easy reach.

Avery paused a moment, her face reddening. "I'm babbling, aren't I?"

"Maybe a little. I take it you enjoyed *Isabella's Dream*?"

"Enjoyed it? When can we go back?" Avery's eyes shone bright with the same kind of joy Carter had felt himself after his first dive.

He smiled at her excitement. "I was thinking you might like to check out a different wreck in a few days."

"Would I ever."

"I wasn't sure how you'd adapt to diving around a large wreck like that. Some people get nervous."

"Why? There's nothing scary about it."

"Well, sharks can be a bit scary when you're not expecting to see one,"

Carter said as he began to hoist the anchor. "Sometimes they'll hang out around wrecks for the food opportunities."

Avery placed her hands on her hips. "If I can manage the Armani-clad sharks of Wall Street, I can certainly handle whatever might be lurking down there."

Before he could reply, Avery's cell rang.

"Excuse me a moment." She rolled her eyes. "I've got to take this. My broker doesn't seem to understand the word 'no'."

As Carter waved for her to go ahead, a flash of reflected sunlight caught his eye. He grabbed the binoculars, then focused them directly on the other craft. The man held something in his hand that looked suspiciously like a high-end camera, but he lowered it so quickly that Carter couldn't be sure. The man waved at Carter, then moved quickly toward the controls of his own vessel.

"Look, Bob, you need to trust me. I—what? Yes, this is Avery Turner. No, I'm sorry, Detective. I-I thought you were someone else."

Carter's attention returned to Avery in time to witness her expression morph from annoyed to deeply troubled.

"Excuse me?" Avery said. "No, that can't be right. I'm planning to visit him in Maine next week."

Concerned, Carter tried to decipher the subject of the call, difficult to do from only one side. But one thing was unmistakable: the heartache in Avery's voice.

"I understand. No, that won't be necessary. I'll come to you."

Carter glanced back in time to see the other boat accelerating away from them at a good clip. Everything about the guy was wrong. Was he just watching them? Or looking to steal something? Either way, his mere presence had every hair on Carter's arms standing straight up.

"I'll be there as soon as I can, Detective. No, I don't care. I'll be there by midnight. And I want to see the scene. Can you please text me your information and the address?"

Carter could see the tears brimming in Avery's wide brown eyes as she ended the call.

"What is it?" he said.

"A friend of mine is dead."

"I'm sorry, Avery."

She nodded. "I have to get to New England. The police say they found him dead in a motel on the southside of Boston." Her tears spilled over before she slipped her sunglasses on.

Carter didn't know what to say.

"I'll take you home," was the best he could muster.

"Thank you." Avery sniffled as a tear slipped from behind her Ray-Bans.

He fired up the engine and turned the boat toward Avery's island home. Pushing the throttle harder than he normally would, he glanced back at her. She sat stoically, staring off into the distance. She was grieving, the excitement of her first shipwreck dive now a distant memory.

3

Avery sprinted through the French doors into the sunroom. She called out to Harrison in a voice so shrill with emotion that he nearly tripped hurrying down the stairs.

"What's wrong?" Harrison said. "It's that Carter guy, isn't it? I told you I didn't trust him, Ave."

Avery waved one hand. She knew well that Harrison thought Carter was some sort of gold digger playing a long game, and he knew well that she disagreed. She didn't have the capacity to revisit that argument right then. "No, it's not Carter. It's Mark."

"Mark? What about him?"

"The police said he . . . they say he's dead." Her eyes filled again.

"What? Which police? Slow down and tell me exactly what happened."

Mark Hawkins had been Avery's mentor, friend, and more. She and Mark had simultaneously retired from the tech industry more than a year ago, a feat made possible by Avery's invention of a reservation app, which Mark had bankrolled. Subsequently, a German technology company purchased the app—along with Mark's company—for a whopping twelve point two billion dollars.

"This detective from Boston called my cell phone and said Mark had my contact information on him. I guess since he has no next of kin, they needed to notify someone. That's how this works, right? The police have to notify someone?"

"Did they say what happened?" Harrison said.

"Only that he was at a motel in South Boston. Why would Mark be at a motel anywhere?" Avery's lower lip quivered, and Harrison put an arm around her shoulders.

"What's this detective's name?"

"Burke. Albert Burke. Here, I'll forward you his text." Avery wiped her eyes and tapped her phone screen, pulling up a photo of Burke's business card. Reading over her shoulder, Harrison sighed and put two fingers to his chin.

"What?" Avery twisted her neck to look up at him.

"Nothing." Harrison stared at his sneakers.

"That's not 'nothing' face, Harry." Avery stepped out from under his arm. "I've known you my whole life, and you have 'something' face. What did I miss?"

Harrison sighed, pulling out his own phone and opening her text with the forwarded card image. "This. The card says Burke is a DVD detective."

"So?" Avery blinked, her face blank. "I'm not sure what that means, but since the vast majority of video stores went under twenty years ago, I'm pretty sure he's not guarding the local Blockbuster. Why does that make you look like," she waved a hand, more tears welling, "like that?"

"DVD in metro PDs is the Drugs and Vice Division," Harrison said. "Your mother and I worked homicide our whole careers, so you'd have no reason to know that, but . . . a DVD guy at a death scene calling a number he found on the victim isn't looking for next of kin. That means it's an overdose and he's trying to find the dealer."

Avery shook her head. "We're going to Boston, Harry."

"What? When? Why?"

Avery ran up the stairs. "As soon as you can, get Marco ready to fly. Because Mark didn't do that. Mark *wouldn't* do that."

"Where are you going?"

"I gotta shower and pack. Call Marco and tell him to get the plane ready, please."

Grumbling, Harrison pulled out his phone to place a call to Avery's private pilot. "An hour be enough time?" he called after Avery.

"Plenty," she hollered from the second-floor hallway.

Closing the door to her bedroom, Avery went directly to her walk-in closet. She heard Harrison's baritone voice as it carried up from the foyer directly below. He recited the motel address that Detective Burke had provided to someone on the other end of the line.

"We should be there by eleven thirty tonight," Harrison said.

Avery wondered who he could be talking to that would care about the motel address. Certainly not Marco. A car service, perhaps? She dismissed the thought as she wriggled out of the bathing suit and discarded it onto the tile floor. Scanning the closet racks, she grabbed a pair of light blue cotton shorts and a matching blouse. She hurried to the en suite and turned on the shower. As she stepped inside, she couldn't help but wonder how fast her jet could really go.

The City of Miami's lights twinkled to life in the distance as Avery's Gulfstream lifted off from the private airstrip on Key West. A violent chain of thunderstorms passing through from the Gulf of Mexico had delayed their departure, and Avery still saw the occasional bolt of lightning dance across the horizon.

Flying alongside a peach-indigo sunset, the G650ER climbed smoothly into the evening sky. Admittedly, the jet with its brushed leather seats, plush carpeting, and mahogany trim was an excess, but necessary given the amount of globetrotting she planned to do. And, as it turned out, despite the aircraft's enormous price tag, it hardly made a dent in her share of billions.

Avery settled into the cream-colored leather reclining seat, absently fiddling with the scalloped hem of her cotton shorts as she stared through the window. Dark, ominous clouds dominated the eastern horizon. As usual her mind was already working the problem, even as she attempted to wrap her head around Mark's sudden death.

She was vaguely aware of Harrison speaking to someone on the phone and then conversing with Marco. Sympathetic to the grief she was feeling, both men spoke in hushed tones. Avery turned her head to look as Harrison approached.

"How're you holding up, Ave?" he said as his eyes focused on one of Avery's legs bouncing up and down.

She changed her position, trying to stop the nervous twitch. "I'm okay. What does Marco say?"

"He said it looks like the storm front has stalled in the northeast from Providence to Concord."

"Meaning?"

"We'll be forced to land in Hartford if the current weather holds."

Avery sighed and returned to window gazing, her leg bouncing. "Who were you speaking with on the phone?"

"I took the liberty of booking us a car," Harrison said.

"Rental?"

"Weren't any. Too many commercial flights diverted by the storm."

"What then?"

"Scored us a Town Car and a driver," he said proudly.

Avery nodded but said nothing.

"I had to haggle with the guy," Harrison said. "Paid twice the going rate. Probably bumped someone, too, but we've got a car. And someone who knows the area."

"Thanks," she said absently.

Harrison departed. He returned as they reached cruising altitude.

"Here," he said, handing her a glass of bourbon. "Thought you could use it."

Avery pushed the glass away.

"You gotta calm down, Ave. Let's take this one step at a time."

"I am calm," she snapped. "And you didn't hear his voice. Mark was so excited about showing me the inn. This makes no sense."

Harrison sat down in the seat beside her and tried a softer approach. "I know it doesn't. But the truth is, people rarely do what you'd expect. Most hide their personal demons and struggles quite well. Hell, if I had a dollar for every suicide during my career that shocked a family member, I'd have my own plane."

"Suicide?" she snapped. "Who said anything about suicide?"

"I didn't mean to imply that Mark intentionally overdosed, I'm just saying it is something to consider."

She didn't respond.

"If Val was still alive, she'd tell you the same thing."

Avery whipped her head around at the mention of her mother, ready to light into him, but the sincerity in Harrison's expression defused her and she said nothing.

"She was always so proud of you, Ave."

"I miss her so much, Harry," Avery said, the tears threatening to return. Jesus, she hated this. That feeling of helplessness. She had wept more in the past few hours than she had in the past five years.

"Me too, kiddo. Me too."

Harrison and Avery's mother, Valerie, had been partners on the police force in New York for almost two decades. Dubbed by their peers as the "dynamic duo," Harry and Val had put away more murderers than any other detective team in the department's history. They had grown closer than some married couples.

Avery considered Harrison more of an uncle than a paid assistant. Having grown up around him, she couldn't remember a time when Harry hadn't been a part of her life.

"You know she used to keep a file folder of all your drawings," Harrison said. "All the crazy contraptions you invented when you were growing up. She always said you were destined for greatness."

"Shoot for the moon," Avery said, her lips formed into a tight smile as she recalled her mother's words. "If you miss, at least you'll land among the stars."

Harrison chuckled and waved a hand at their plush surroundings. "I'd say you hit the moon dead center, Ave."

"I'm glad I dragged you away from police work, Harry," she said after a moment.

"So am I. It wasn't the same after Val died. Besides, you saved me from some crappy security gig. Can you imagine this body in a friggin' polyester suit coat?"

Avery laughed, wiping away her tears with the back of her hand. "What kind of suit coat?"

"Huh?" Harrison asked as confusion creased his brow.

"I thought we agreed to break you of street language. You know it doesn't fly in the corporate world."

Harrison patted the back of her hand. "Consider me a work in progress."

Avery's attention returned to the window as the sun slipped below the horizon. It had taken months, a few lessons in nuance, and a scary close call for her to convince Harrison to leave police work—his pension wasn't enough to retire on with rent in New York climbing faster than kudzu vines in July, and he'd been insulted by Avery's offer to buy him a house in the country where he could collect dogs to his heart's content and live out his days on his pension in peace. But after an armed robbery pursuit gone wrong had torn his ACL when he dove to avoid a bullet, he'd grown amenable to taking a job as her assistant, which she swore to him she'd been going to hire someone far less competent to do anyway. Breaking him of talking like a homicide cop in front of her wealthy new peers was proving a challenge, but Avery Turner was nothing if not persistent. Stars dotted the sky outside, her eyes growing heavy. It had been a long day, and it was far from over. Physically tired from the dive and emotionally spent with the news about Mark, she felt herself slipping toward exhaustion. She looked back at Harrison. "Any chance I could still get that drink?"

Harrison jumped to his feet and grabbed the glass, handing it to her like a waiter. "M'lady."

"Thank you, Harry."

Harrison gave her a wink. "Now, if there's nothing else, I promised Marco a great war story."

Avery took a sizable swallow of bourbon, the warmth spreading slowly from her stomach to the tips of her fingers. She leaned her head back into the soft leather and closed her eyes.

"Why Mark?" she mumbled.

4

"You sure you folks want to go—there?" Their driver's dark eyes widened in the rear-view mirror as the Town Car picked up speed and merged onto the rain-soaked highway. "That's not a very safe area. There're nicer places nearby."

"We're sure," Harrison said. "Just drive the car, okay, buddy?"

Avery settled back, resting her head on Harrison's shoulder as she listened to the cadence of the windshield wipers. She was not sure of anything at this point, aside from turning down Detective Burke's offer to meet them at the precinct. She knew it would have been a waste of time. No, she needed to see for herself where Mark's life had ended. And how.

I'm finally doing what I was meant to do, Avery. The memory of Mark's voice still resonated inside her head. His last words to her were filled with excitement and promise. She had been every bit as excited to see Mark as she was the old New England inn he had spent the better part of a year—and a sizeable chunk of his cut from the sale—rehabbing into a luxury oceanside resort. But beyond that, Avery had wanted to see if there was still a chance that whatever had simmered between them during the years they had worked together might still be viable. She hadn't ever wanted to admit to herself that she was in love with Mark Hawkins—she'd always worried he might see her as a silly girl with a crush, and clearly the one time he'd kissed her had mattered way more to her than it had to him. But she'd wondered often in the past year if things would be different between them now. If she could finally have what she'd wanted for so long. Now she would never know.

As she shut her eyes, she heard the privacy glass going up and the driver muttering something about it being their dime.

Lightning flashed in the distance. A gust of wind tugged at Avery's hair, pulling several strands free from the messy bun atop her head and whipping them across her face. She stared at the bright yellow crime scene tape fluttering against the front of the building. Harrison placed a comforting hand on her back and nodded to the uniformed officer standing at the entrance to the room.

The motel was every bit as unsavory as their driver had implied. The parking lot was a battlefield of cracked asphalt and broken glass. Weeds sprouted from the cement walkway that ran the length of the property connecting each unit. The screen door on unit eleven, Mark's unit, hung askew by a single rusted hinge. Next to the door a single light fixture flickered as if it might burn out any second. This was not a place Mark Hawkins would have stayed. At least not the man Avery knew. Not for any reason.

"You've finished with the scene?" Harrison said.

"Hours ago," Detective Burke said. "I only held it as a favor to you." Burke turned to Avery. "You're more than welcome to step inside, Ms. Turner. If you want to, that is."

She looked up at Harrison, eyes wide. "Mark's not still in there, is he?"

Harrison shook his head. "No, Ave. His body would be with the coroner by now. You know you don't have to do this, right?"

Her attention returned to the door. "I do, Harry. I need to make sense of this, or I'll never be able to move on."

Harrison sighed. "All right."

At a nod from Burke, the uniformed officer pulled down the tape crisscrossing the door, opened the unit and flicked on the inside light, illuminating the room.

Burke gestured to Avery. "Whenever you're ready."

"You want me to come with you?" Harrison said.

"I want to do this myself."

Avery steeled herself before stepping through the doorway. The inside of the room was even smaller than it had appeared from the parking lot. The furnishings were dingy and dated, as if the motel's patrons were more apt to pay by the hour than avail themselves of longer stays. The matching beige carpet and bedspread were threadbare and stained. Avery could not imagine spending one minute more than necessary in a place such as this.

Burke hadn't mentioned how long Mark had been here before his body was discovered. Thankfully, the only odors assaulting Avery's olfactory receptors were those emanating from an ancient window air conditioner and the musty room. Her eyes moved about the space, pausing on the rumpled bedding. The bed appeared to have been slept in, though she could no more picture Mark sleeping there than she could see him checking in. None of this made sense.

Without turning around, Avery asked how Mark died.

"Overdose," Burke replied matter-of-factly.

"What, specifically?" Harrison said.

"This is an open investigation," Burke said. "We don't just give out details to just anyone."

Harrison cut in before Avery could. "We aren't just anyone. I was on the job at least twice as long as you, Detective. And as for Avery, the only one of us who actually knew Mark, she was in Florida with me when this happened. How about a little professional courtesy?"

Burke let out a long sigh of frustration before responding. "Based solely on the traces we found in the room, we believe it may have been Percocet laced with Fentanyl. But we're awaiting the results of Mr. Hawkins's autopsy."

"Mark never used drugs," Avery said. "In all the time I knew him, he never even drank a beer. He had a back injury from playing basketball in college that caused spasms occasionally, and even that he fought with Advil and magnesium supplements."

"Back injury, huh?" Burke nodded like she'd just confirmed his every suspicion.

"You heard the part about the Advil, too, right?" Avery asked.

"People do change, Ms. Turner," Burke said. "When was the last time you saw him?"

Avery turned toward the detective and gave him her most menacing scowl. She slammed the inside door closed, shutting out Harrison and the two Boston police officers.

Avery knew that Burke was partially right. Much could change in a person's life during the span of a year. And it had been that long since they'd seen each other. The enormous amount of money they had netted from the app sale had dramatically altered everything from their addresses to their social circles. But Percocet? And Fentanyl? She didn't buy it for a second. Mark's mantra had always been "my body, my temple." He'd never want to risk clouding what he had jokingly referred to as his creative brain, to the point that he suffered through back spasms with vitamins and over-the-counter meds and the occasional wince during a business meeting.

Avery couldn't believe Mark would have turned to narcotics so close to the opening of his inn.

She moved to the center of the room and slowly turned. "Taking in your surroundings" was what her mother had called it. A beat-up dresser stood against the long wall opposite the bed, each of its drawers in various stages of hanging open. A couple of cheaply framed and faded prints hung askew against the water-stained wallpaper. It was obvious that the detectives, or crime scene people, had been thorough in their search of the room. If there had been something to find, it was likely that they already had. Besides, Avery had absolutely no idea what she was looking for.

She moved toward the bathroom and switched on the light. The tiny room smelled strongly of cigarettes, cheap air freshener, and an unpleasant unidentifiable odor not masked by the air freshener. The room had one small window. She attempted to open it but found that it would only go up about three inches before it stuck. Judging by the window's nicotine-stained frame, the room's previous occupants had routinely availed themselves of the space as a place to smoke. She nearly succumbed to nervous laughter as she wondered who would care. The wall-mounted porcelain sink was hanging at a precarious angle as if someone heavy had been leaning on it. Mismatched blue towels hung from chrome rods between the sink and the grungy walk-in shower stall. The toilet was the tankless indus-trial variety, meaning there was no place to hide anything.

Avery returned to the bedroom to take a closer look. The unit's walls were thin, and she could hear Harrison talking with Burke and the uniformed officer outside. Twisting up her face with disgust, she knelt and peered beneath the bed. Nothing there save for a couple of dust bunnies the size of kittens. Lifting the bed covers produced nothing. To the left of the bed stood a scarred and battered nightstand and lamp. Avery pulled open the nightstand drawer. The only thing inside was a tattered copy of Gideon's Bible. She picked up the Bible and fanned through its pages, but nothing fell out. As she tossed it back into the drawer, she wondered whether Mark, or any of the room's other lost souls, ever found solace within its pages. She started to push the drawer closed, then stopped. Recalling one of Marks's habits of hiding passwords, she reached up and slid her fingers along the underside of the drawer until she encountered a small piece of paper. Before she could do more than retrieve it, there was a rap at the front door, and it swung open.

"How are we doing in here?" Burke said. It was obvious that he was trying to get her to hurry up.

"Fine," Avery said as she quickly slid the scrap of paper into a pocket, then stood. "I'm finished in here."

"Did you find whatever you were looking for?"

"You mean answers?" Avery asked as she brushed past him. "No, Detec-tive. I didn't."

5

Carter Mosley picked up the gold-rimmed Pilsner glass left behind by the home's previous renters and poured himself another Heineken. After taking a healthy gulp of the cold beer, he returned to the living room and sat down at his desk. He swiped across the touch screen, unlocking his computer. He needed to finish editing the dive video for tomorrow's post, but thoughts of Avery kept swirling through his head. He opened a text message, then dragged several of the photographs Avery had shot aboard Isabella's Dream into the message box. He stared at the blinking cursor for a long while trying to think of something clever to say. At last, he typed: *Hope u r okay, wherever u r. Thought these might make u smile.*

He took another drink while repeatedly tapping the backspace button on his phone until the second line of text disappeared. Staring at the blinking cursor for a full minute, he retyped the words and hit the send arrow before he could change his mind.

He waited to see if Avery would reply. She didn't, but an email from the bank popped up in the top right corner of his screen, the subject line making him queasy with déjà vu. Low account balance? Carter hadn't had to worry about money in nearly two years.

He clicked it, sighing when he saw it wasn't about his account, but his brother Brady's. When Carter accidentally landed in the lap of luxury, one of the first things he did was set up accounts for his baby brother and their cousin, Lena. They'd shared everything from ice cream to chicken pox growing up, so why not this, too? Not that he could afford to send them riding off into the proverbial sunset, but a few hundred grand each had been intended to offer security and a little luxury, too, if they wanted.

Lena had paid off her house and set up college and activity accounts for both her kids—and still thanked Carter with the occasional batch of home-baked cookies. That was a win—Lena's DNA had come complete with grandmomma's culinary talent.

Carter picked up his phone and clicked her name in his favorites list.

"Hang o—" she said by way of hello, most of the "on" swallowed by a scream. A cat yowled over the sound of glass breaking.

"Everything okay, Lee?" Carter stood, his voice going up half an octave.

"Sophie Ann, what did I tell you about practicing your archery in the house?" Lena screeched so loudly Carter pulled the phone away from his head as he laughed.

"Sorry Carter, the inmates are taking over the asylum here. Again," Lena said, a door closing behind her.

"Archery? I thought Sophie was going to be a champion jockey?"

"That was last week. Before she stormed out when they told her to use a riding crop on the horse."

"She didn't want to hurt it," Carter said.

"Correct. But killing my ancient cat with a bow and arrow is apparently collateral damage." Carter could practically hear her dark eyes rolling. "Anyway. What's up?"

"Wondering if you've heard from Brady lately." Carter slid back onto the barstool and toyed with his beer glass.

"Does that mean you haven't? Is he still mad at you for what you said about his restaurant?"

"Brady has always been able to hold a grudge longer than a job or a girlfriend."

Lena laughed until she ran out of air. "Pot, let me introduce you to Kettle."

"Yeah, yeah," Carter said. "I wasn't trying to hurt his feelings, you know."

"He said his dream was to own a restaurant, and you told him he can't cook."

"What he said was that he planned to sink every dime I gave him into a waterfront restaurant on Miami Beach while appointing himself, who has never so much as waited tables, head chef and menu designer. And for the record, almost burning the house down trying to make frozen waffles, or losing his eyebrows in that unfortunate turkey fryer incident and leaving us with frozen pot pies for Thanksgiving dinner—those things said he can't cook. It's not like I made it up to tick him off."

"Call your brother, Carter," she said. "He's just miffed because you've always been his hero and he wants to make you proud. Did you see the review in the *Herald*? He could use his hero right now."

"How'd you get so wise without getting old?"

"Just blessed, I guess."

Carter smiled. "Good luck keeping everyone there out of the ER until my favorite rug rat finds a new obsession."

"I'm going to need it."

Carter heard another crash in the background as he ended the call.

Opening a text, he found Brady's name—had he really not heard from his baby brother since Christmas? He hadn't realized that much time had passed. He started typing. *Hey little B, can you spare a table for your favorite bro Saturday night? Been too long.*

Carter had indeed seen the review in the *Herald*. Dismal was a kind word for it, and Brady had been open for six months, so it wasn't like he was working out first-week kinks. Carter wouldn't brave the food, but drinks, maybe dessert, and showing up could go a long way toward mending Brady's injured pride.

Like Lena had said for months now, Carter gave Brady the money. It was a gift. If Brady lost every penny on a dream he didn't have the skill to pull off or the sense to hire help with . . . well, it was his penny to lose.

His phone buzzed. Brady.

I know the bank is probably bugging you, but I have it all under control, C. That critic had a cold, we didn't get a fair review.

Carter shook his head. *Are they going to print a retraction?*

Brady replied almost instantly. *Don't need them to. I'm reimagining our menu. Brady has it all under control. Skip Saturday, come in next week after we launch the new stuff, see for yourself. Miss you.*

That was a big thing for Brady to admit. Carter smiled. *Try and stop me,* he typed. *Keep me posted on how it's going.*

Will do. I got the bank handled, they held a check I took them Monday. But it's good now.

The bubbles kept bouncing at the bottom of the screen.

Thanks for checking on me.

Anytime. Night Little B.

Carter put the phone down, and his attention returned to editing the dive video. Using state-of-the-art software, he muffled the distracting sound of a speedboat passing overhead. Next, he cut approximately ten minutes from the long swim sequence at the start of the video. Nobody wanted to see that stuff anymore. Carter's fans preferred getting right into the action. He had learned that to succeed in the world of video social media, one must give the viewers what they want, and in the murky world of shipwreck diving, the viewers loved historical elements and tales of treasure. They simply couldn't get enough. He slid his thousand-dollar Neumann TLM 103 microphone into position, cleared his throat with another swig of beer, then began recording the voiceover narration.

The sunken ship in this video was a 1970s-era freighter that had gone down in a hurricane on its way from Colombia to Haiti. Carter recapped the details, taken from newspaper archives and his go-to online maritime database, before turning the story to the combination safe listed on the ship's manifest. Its contents were conveniently absent from all known documentation.

Having made a study of the region's history and politics, Carter knew that the owner of the shipping company had hidden ties to Columbian drug lord Pablo Escobar, leader of the Medellin Cartel. And Carter would bet his beachfront McMansion that the safe in question had contained drug proceeds in need of laundering. An oversized load.

After editing the exploration segment of the freighter video down to twenty minutes, he continued his voiceover. He pointed out old Coke bottles in the galley and a crate of broken statues and other handmade goods likely destined for Haitian tourist shops, before narrating a tour of the captain's quarters. He amplified the point that the captain's safe was nowhere to be found as his viewers simply couldn't get enough treasure talk. The more mysterious the better. He spent a few moments speculating that the safe might have been transferred to a lifeboat before the ship sank, and possibly subsequently moved to another vessel. Or that members of the crew might have intentionally sunk the lifeboat, and the safe, far away from where the freighter went down to avoid detection, marking its location for later retrieval by divers. He had read about both scenarios commonly employed by maritime narcos.

Carter finished the narration with his trademark closing comments, meant as a cute warning to future treasure hunters.

"Remember, folks, if you're searching for real treasure, history is a far more likely discovery than gold. Dive safely, my friends."

After saving and backing up the file, he checked his overflowing direct messaging box. Carter didn't reply often, but he usually made a habit of at least scrolling through the comments to get a feel for what people were saying. There were five hundred and ten more votes for the "Jacques Cousteau meets Investigation Discovery" comparison of his videos. This was his favorite description, probably because his agent had been in negotiations for months with the Discovery Channel about developing a show for their streaming service. The idea initially appealed to him, but as time passed, Carter began to worry about network oversight and the general insanity that might accompany a television show. He had already made more money than he ever dreamt possible, thanks to the online advertising deals. And with a highly skilled and trustworthy crew of three at his beck and call, why would he want to add a rigid shooting schedule, a producer, and a team of writers to his life? Would he be forced to give up the skydiving classes he taught? Did he really want to give up creative control just to let a bunch of television nerds order him around every day? It was a question he had begun to ask himself regularly.

The additional money would be nice, but would it be worth it? Perhaps. It might save Brady's restaurant long enough to convince him to hire actual restaurant experts to run it, anyway.

He made a quick trip into the kitchen to top off his glass, then headed out onto the deck. The night air was warm and inviting. He plopped down onto a cushioned recliner without bothering to turn on the outside lights. Carter liked the dark. Sitting there alone while listening to the surf calmed him. As he sipped the Heineken, his mind drifted back to Escobar's missing safe. Had Carlos sent men to recover it, or had someone else risked trying to locate it? There were no records of the safe having been recovered, but as Carter knew too well, a drug kingpin's proceeds were not the kind of salvage anyone reported, no matter what international law decreed. One thing remained certain: an increasing number of shady characters now populated the lucrative sport of treasure hunting. And some were far more dangerous than the sharks he had warned Avery about.

He wondered how Avery was coping with the loss of her friend. It was obvious from her reaction earlier that Mark Hawkins had been more than just her employer. Carter wondered what she was doing right that very minute. He slid the cell from his pocket and checked to see if she had responded to his earlier message. Nothing. He hoped she was okay. He finished off the beer in one long gulp, then set the empty glass on the deck beside him.

He laid back and allowed his eyes to close. As he drifted off to sleep, he thought about how lucky he was now. His life was uncomplicated. He only worried about chasing the next shipwreck and keeping his online followers happy. Diving kept him busy and out of trouble. Most of the time.

6

Samael scrolled through the images on the iPad sent to him via secure email. The dark-haired young woman depicted in the surveillance photographs was quite different from what he had conjured in his mind. Avery Turner looked more like a sorority girl enjoying spring break than a worthy adversary, but Samael had long ago learned how appearances can deceive. He traced a fingernail across an enlarged shot of her face as he considered his options.

He returned the tablet to his desk, then walked to the window and gazed out at the Atlantic Ocean.

Apart from the tailored three-piece Armani suit, Samael's appearance was disarmingly plain. He looked every bit the well-groomed boardroom executive, effectively camouflaging all his deadly skills. Even the expressionless nature of his handsome face gave nothing away. He wondered if Ms. Avery Turner might be such a chameleon. Perhaps there was more to her than met the eye.

"You were saying?" Samael asked, speaking through his Bluetooth device to the man on the other end of the call.

"You met Ms. Turner at a fundraiser several years ago," the man repeated.

"I don't recall."

"No reason you should. She was a nobody at the time."

"And now?"

"Now her resources are substantial."

"And she is closely connected to Mark Hawkins?"

"Connected, but I don't yet know how closely."

"What are the chances Ms. Turner knows where the diary is located?" Samael said.

"It can't be a coincidence that she just recently took up scuba diving," the man said.

Samael didn't believe in coincidence. "I don't like failure. Losing Hawkins before he could assist us with the diary was an absolute failure in my view. I don't want to make the same mistake with Ms. Turner."

"I'll take care of it."

"No, we will."

Avery paced the lot near Harrison and the Boston cops.

"Well?" Detective Burke said.

"Well, what?" Avery snapped.

"Are you satisfied?"

"No, Detective, I am not. I cannot bring myself to believe that Mark killed himself with drugs, accidentally or otherwise. It's more than out of character, it's flat unimaginable."

"We found zero evidence of foul play."

"Really? How did he rent the room?"

"We spoke to the desk clerk. He rented the room himself."

"And you're just gonna take the clerk's word for it?"

"We checked the front desk video, Mark was alone."

"And the parking lot video?"

"There aren't any cameras covering the lot or the rooms, Ms. Turner."

"Where's his vehicle?" Avery asked.

"We towed it and inventoried it."

"What about his cell phone? Did you locate that?"

"We didn't."

Avery glanced at Harrison. "Mark never went anywhere without his phone."

"He may have intentionally left it at his residence." Burke shrugged. "There's a chance he didn't want anyone to know where he was."

Harrison spoke up. "You mentioned finding a note with Avery's contact info. May we see it?"

"Certainly," Burke said as he unlocked his cell phone and held it up for them to see.

"The original is back at the office, but I've got a picture of it here."

Avery studied the image. Printed on a yellow Post-it note were Avery's name and cell phone number.

"This is why we contacted you," Burke said.

"Where did you find it?" Harrison asked.

"On the floor, at the foot of the bed. Like someone had dropped it."

"And who might that have been?" Avery said. "I thought your working theory was that Mark was alone."

"Well, Mark, of course."

"Only two problems with that theory, Detective," Avery said.

"And those are?"

She pointed to Burke's cell. "He wouldn't need to write down something he already knew."

"And the second?"

"That isn't Mark's handwriting."

Avery waited until they were back on the road before sharing her find with Harrison.

"Jesus, Ave. This is evidence. I shouldn't even be touching this. Where did you find it?"

"Stuck to the bottom of the nightstand drawer."

The small bluish sheet of paper, though larger and a different color than the one Burke had shown them, was another Post-it note. Handwritten on one side was a strange rudimentary drawing, on the other was a long string of gibberish. Capital letters interspersed with dots and dashes.

After studying the note for a moment, Harrison looked up at Avery. "This *is* Mark's handwriting, isn't it?"

Avery nodded.

Harrison signaled the Town Car driver. "Take us back to the motel."

"What are you doing, Harry?" Avery said as she snatched the paper back from him.

"We've got to return that, Ave. Your mom would be pi—"

Avery shot him a warning look before he could finish the thought.

"She'd be wild, okay? Jesus, you're messing around in a police investigation, Ave."

"What investigation? You heard Detective Burke. It's either suicide or accidental overdose. He's already written this off."

"He may very well be right, Ave."

"Really? Where is Mark's cell phone then?"

"I don't know."

"I called it. The voicemail is full."

"Maybe Burke was right. Maybe he left it at home."

"I know Mark, Harry. He is . . ." Avery swallowed hard. "Was a tech guy through and through. He barely let his phone out of his sight to shower. He did not drive over a hundred miles from his home and check into that seedy little motel without his phone."

The driver slowed and pulled to the side of the roadway. "Do you guys want to go back to the motel or not?"

"Not," Avery said. "Take us to the airport."

"Back to Hartford?" the driver said, making no attempt to hide his surprise.

"Be reasonable," Harrison said. "Why don't we head into downtown Boston? A couple of nice clean hotel rooms at the Marriott or the Hyatt. We can discuss this again in the morning. Everything will look different. You'll see."

Avery addressed the driver again. "Take us back to Hartford."

"You're the boss."

Avery raised the privacy glass.

Harrison tried again. "Look, Ave, as it is we won't get back to the island until three. At the earliest."

"We're not going back to the island," she said, crossing her arms in defiance. "Detective Burke may not care how Mark died. But I do. He was about to see his year-long dream of opening the inn realized, Harry. He wouldn't do anything to jeopardize that—I can't even figure out why he was down here this close to the big day. Burke was right about one thing though."

"What's that?"

"It's obvious that I no longer knew anything about Mark's day-to-day life. But I'm going to rectify that."

"I'm almost afraid to ask. Where are we going?"

"To the inn."

Harrison cocked his head to one side. "You don't mean—"

"We're going to Maine."

7

It was nearly three thirty in the morning by the time Avery and Harrison reached the Hawk's Nest Inn. A massive three-story structure, the shore-front inn reminded her of something she had once seen on a postcard. They mounted the wide front steps to a long, screened porch, then stepped inside. Avery found the front doors locked.

"Thought the whole point of a hotel was to be open all night," Harrison said. "You know, 'we'll keep the light on,' or something."

"They haven't even opened yet, Harry."

Avery peered in through the etched glass of the doors at the dimly lit interior of a richly appointed lobby with white columns and plush furniture. At the far end of the space stood a massive antique registration desk that reminded her of one of her favorite romcoms.

"It sure looks inviting," Avery said.

"Not from the porch, it doesn't," Harrison grumbled.

"We'll just have to make do," Avery said.

Harrison dropped their bags onto a wicker loveseat then collapsed onto a nearby matching chair.

"You're not suggesting we sleep outside?" Harrison said.

"Why not?" She strolled over to a hanging daybed and patted its plush cushions. "We've got nice comfy furniture and screens to keep out the bugs."

"Great," Harrison said, sounding less than enthusiastic.

"Besides, someone will open the doors for us in the morning."

"You hope."

Avery settled on the daybed then kicked off her shoes. She checked her cell phone for new text messages. She located one from Carter that did, in fact, make her smile. The message accompanied a photo taken during their morning dive. So much had happened since . . . well, yesterday at this point. She typed a short response, "Mission accomplished."

A rustling noise came from the woods directly behind her. Avery turned to look but darkness made it impossible to see more than a few feet off the porch.

"What is it?" Harrison said.

"Thought I heard something outside in the bushes."

Harrison raised an eyebrow. "Let me get this right, you believe Mark was murdered, but you want to sleep outside on the porch of his new venture? Tell me again how that makes any sense."

Avery yawned. "It's probably just a bear, Harry," she said, giving him a mischievous grin. "Or a cat."

"Uh-huh."

"Do you really think someone would be lurking out there on the off chance that we, who have never even been to Maine, might decide to sleep on Mark's porch?"

Harrison didn't offer a response, instead he sniffed the air then rose from his chair. He activated the flashlight app on his phone and swept the beam around the inside of the porch.

"What are you looking for?" Avery said.

"This," Harrison replied.

Standing in the far corner of the porch was a tall wicker basket containing a dozen or so croquet mallets. Harrison walked over and selected one.

"Know any bears, or cats, that smoke?" Harrison said. With that, he disappeared down the steps and into the night.

"Wait up," Avery whispered as she slipped back into her shoes. She grabbed a second mallet, then chased after him.

It took a moment before she located him crouched in the bushes thirty feet from the porch. He was using his phone to take photos of something lying on the ground.

"What is it?"

"Cigarette butts," he said, pointing to a trampled patch of grass. "Three of them. And this one is still burning."

"Someone really is watching this place?" Avery's voice went up an octave as goosebumps rose on her arms. "What the heck was Mark into that caused all this?"

"Good question," Harrison said.

"Okay, maybe I was wrong, Harry," Avery said as they started back toward the porch.

"About the smoking bear?"

"No. I mean maybe we would be safer in a hotel."

"Undoubtedly. But there isn't anything around for thirty miles, Ave. Hotel or otherwise."

Avery sighed audibly, "And I sent our driver away."

"Worry not, princess," Harrison said as he held the screen door open for her. "You get some shut-eye."

"What about you?"

"I'll take first watch."

———

Avery awoke to birdsong, the sweet scent of Japanese honeysuckle, and the faint sound of someone nearby speaking in hushed tones. For a moment she had completely forgotten the events of the previous twenty-four hours. But as she stretched her arms above her head the memories came racing back. The phone call from the Boston detective. Mark dying in a shabby motel room. Even the hidden note. Her eyes flew open as she swung into a sitting position.

"Morning, sunshine," Harrison said as he handed her a large mug of coffee.

"Thanks. Um, how exactly did you get inside?"

"Julia let me in," he said as he stepped to one side.

Standing behind Harrison on the lobby threshold was an attractive young woman wearing a smart chiffon summer suit.

"This is Julia Bergin," Harrison said. "She's the manager of the inn."

Julia managed a thin smile, but Avery could see that she had been crying.

Avery stood and offered her hand as she approached Julia.

"Pleased to meet you, Julia. I'm so sorry it couldn't be under better circumstances."

"Thank you. And I'm sorry you both had to sleep on the porch. I hope it wasn't too uncomfortable."

Harrison spoke up before Avery could respond. "We slept like babies, didn't we, Avery?"

"We sure did." Avery agreed, though she couldn't help but notice that he had neglected to mention their uninvited nocturnal visitor.

As she sipped hot coffee from the ceramic mug, her eyes studied Julia. No one could miss the striking similarities they shared. From the thick dark hair to their wide blue eyes and lithe, fit figures. They were even about the same height. Mark's tastes had always been specific, from bourbon to antiques to women. It stung Avery a little to think he had replaced her with someone who better fit into the life he was attempting to build here.

"Would you like a tour of the inn?" Julia said.

"Very much," Avery said.

Julia turned the antique, sculptured brass handle and opened the door. "Welcome to the Hawk's Nest. Or at least what was going to be the Hawk's Nest."

Her facial expression telegraphed the realization that Julia had no idea what would happen now with Mark gone. Avery couldn't help but warm to her a little. Julia really was thinking of Mark first.

Julia continued, "I'm afraid we—I mean I—don't have the entire staff here yet. There was to have been round-the-clock personnel by the end of the week."

Avery and Harrison followed Julia into the hotel lobby. The space was simultaneously large and cozy. The air was thick with honeysuckle from the vines braided through every single flower arrangement. Avery turned in a slow circle as she took it all in.

"It's gorgeous," she murmured.

"You're more than welcome to stay," Julia said. "I'll have a couple of the guest rooms made up for you."

"Please don't go to any trouble for us," Harrison said.

"It's no trouble."

"Thank you," Avery said.

Avery could see Mark's stamp on every detail, from the cozy-meets-elegant mix of ornate oak trim outlining rag-rolled white walls with the barest hint of blue mixed in, to the huge picture windows taking full advantage of the coastal view. Each window was trimmed with stained glass that Mark probably salvaged from either this property or one nearby. Over-stuffed chairs and sofas with distressed white wood accents beckoned with artfully placed books and blankets. A marble and brass chess set rested in the center of a bistro table with blue upholstered chairs next to a window with a view of the woods. *Not a television in sight*, Avery thought. All of the windowless interior walls were lined with built-in cabinets and book-shelves. Each stuffed with old books or dotted artfully with small sculptures and the crystal clocks Mark had collected for years.

Closing her eyes for a moment, Avery felt her friend's presence in every atom of this place. When she opened them again, she saw Julia standing behind the antique registration counter. Painted to match the walls, the counter was trimmed with ornate mahogany molding. Rounding out the restoration was a polished granite slab upon which stacks of colorful sight-seeing brochures were carefully arranged.

"It's beautiful," Avery said.

"Thank you," Julia said, her face falling. "But I'm afraid it's all for naught."

"I don't understand," Harrison said. "You must have advance bookings."

Julia tapped a couple of keys on her MacBook. "Yes, the online bookings for next week are full. Now I'll have to contact every guest and explain that their reservations have been canceled."

"Why?" Avery said. "The hotel is fully staffed, right?"

"It is," Julia said, shaking her head. "But I'll have to let them go too."

"It's up to you, of course," Avery said. "But I'd go forward with the grand opening."

"But the estate," Julia said. "I don't know how any of that works."

"I imagine it will take Mark's attorneys a long while before they've worked out his estate," Avery said. "The inn was his dream. Open it, Julia. With everything he wanted for it."

Julia's eyes filled with tears as she nodded. "You're right. Carrying on is what he would have wanted me to do."

"If you're up for it, we'd love to see the rest of the property," Avery said as she looked at Harrison for his support.

"We sure would," Harrison said, feigning excitement.

8

The tour encompassed all twenty suites, a free-standing cottage, and a converted carriage house. Each space was as elegant and cozy as the lobby, furnished with gorgeous antiques. Some of them Avery recognized from Mark's private collection, while others appeared to have been newly acquired.

"He had such an eye for choosing just the right pieces," Avery said. "He could've had his own TV show."

Julia smiled at the compliment. "Funny you would say that. Mark often joked that a television show about his antiquing adventures was his fall-back plan if the inn failed."

"Was he," Avery paused and pulled in a deep breath. "Did he seem all right to you recently?"

"He pulled a muscle in his back showing the landscapers how he wanted something done in the flowerbeds last week, and he's been burning serious three a.m. oil in the office, but he was fine." Julia smiled. "Would you like to see the stables?"

"You have horses, too?" Harrison said.

Julia nodded. "Mark loved them. He rode every day. He wanted our more equestrian-minded guests to be able to enjoy the woods trails."

"How many do you have?" Avery asked as they approached an immaculate stone outbuilding.

"We have four quarter horses in all: a chestnut and three reds. Spree, the chestnut, was Mark's favorite."

When they had finished touring the grounds, Julia led them through the rear entrance along the inn's main first-floor hallway. She paused for a moment outside a closed door.

"What's in there?" Avery asked.

"This is—was—Mark's office."

For the first time since awakening on the porch, Avery realized that their trip wasn't only about finding answers. Like Julia, Avery was also mourning the loss of a dear friend.

"Would you like to see it?" Julia said.

"May we?" Harrison said.

"Of course."

Julia gripped the doorknob for a beat before turning it and pushing the door open.

Avery hesitated before entering the room. As much as the inn exuded Mark's tastes and passion, she knew his office would be even more personal, more overwhelming. Her eyes were immediately drawn to the antique desk at the center of the room. It was the same desk Mark had used at Hawkins Tech—an eighteenth-century solid mahogany piece with hand-carved accents passed down to him from his grandfather.

"I remember this desk," Avery said as she ran her fingers across its top.

"It was in his home office for almost a year," Julia said. "Until he purchased a new one and had this one delivered to the inn. The moving guys complained about how heavy it was for days."

"I'll bet," Harrison said with a chuckle.

Avery couldn't help wondering how Julia knew so much about what was in Mark's home. How long had Mark and Julia known each other? He had never mentioned Julia beyond her being his new assistant. Or had Avery only chosen to believe that was all Julia was to him? She let the entire exchange go, deciding it was none of her business.

Avery made a show of wandering around the room while Julia watched from the doorway.

After several moments Julia announced, "I suppose it's time to let our staff know about Mark. I'll be in the lobby if you need me."

"Thank you, Julia," Harrison said.

"Take all the time you need." With that, Julia closed the door behind her.

Door closed, Avery went straight for the desk, sliding drawers open one after the other and feeling along the underside of each as she had done in the motel.

Harrison turned toward the large bookshelf, removing random tomes and rifling through the pages. "What exactly are we looking for?"

"Anything that makes sense out of what we already found," Avery said.

"What you already found, you mean," Harrison said. "I wasn't the one pilfering evidence from a crime scene."

"Thought it was an overdose."

Harrison didn't respond.

"And Mark's phone," Avery said, changing the subject. "It had his whole life in it, and he always used a silver case. If you find a phone, bring it to me."

Avery began with the right-hand drawers, if for no other reason than because Mark had been right-handed. She reasoned if Mark had hidden another clue, it would be there. Starting at the top, she slid each of the drawers open. Carefully, she removed them from their wooden tracks, allowing her to check the individual compartments. The desk was deep, and Avery had to kneel on the floor to reach all the way to the back of each drawer's track.

Harrison sighed loudly. Avery knew it was for her benefit.

"What?" Avery said.

"I found the safe," Harrison said as he stood beside an open cabinet door. "And it's locked up tight."

"Key?" Avery said.

"No. Spin dial."

"Okay. Then we just need to find the combination."

"This is going to take forever, Ave. And we don't even know what we're looking for. Or if there's anything to find."

"Trust me. We'll know it when we find it."

Having searched and replaced each of the right-hand drawers with no phone to show for it, Avery switched to the left side of the desk. This time she started with the bottommost drawer and worked her way up. She was down to the last drawer in the desk, and was beginning to think Harrison might be right, when her fingers brushed against something metallic at the back of the top drawer's compartment. The object felt round and cool to the touch, protruding slightly above the surface of the wood. Avery tried prying it out with her fingernails, but it wouldn't budge.

"Think I found something, Harry."

"The combination to the safe?"

"Probably not."

Using the flashlight on her cell phone, Avery sat on the floor then slid backward under the desk for a closer look. The object was gold colored, about the size of a silver dollar, with a carved symbol at its center.

"Well?" Harrison said. "What is it?"

"I'm not sure. Hand me your pocketknife."

"Great, now we're going to damage a priceless antique desk," Harrison said as he handed her the knife.

With as much care as she could manage, Avery slowly pried the golden disk free from the desk, catching it before it hit the floor. After a quick examination, she focused her attention and the light into the remaining recess. The edges were smooth and appeared tailor-made for the medallion. No more than an eighth of an inch deep, at the center of the cavity was an intricate carving she couldn't quite make out. She activated the camera on her phone then snapped several pictures of the opening. After handing the knife back to Harrison, she scooted out from beneath the desk.

"What is it?" Harrison said.

"I don't know," Avery said before passing it to him. "Looks a bit like a coin."

Harrison slowly turned it over before returning it to Avery. "Not like any coin I've ever seen."

Avery placed the disk on the desk and then turned on a banker's lamp, allowing for a closer examination. The edges were smooth but uneven.

"It's really old, whatever it is," Avery said.

"Why do I feel like Nancy Drew and the Hardy Boys are about to pop out of the closet?" Harrison grumbled. "We need to get out of here, Ave."

"Just a minute."

Avery pulled out her phone again and opened the photo app. She flicked back to the pictures she had taken under the desk. One of the shots was out of focus and the other was upside down. After rotating the second image she could clearly see a cross and lion symbol. The exact same symbol Mark had hidden inside the nightstand in the Boston motel room.

9

Though the sun's rays had yet to appear above the horizon, a scattering of stratocumulus clouds were already warming to a pinkish glow. Both the wind and the ocean were calm, and Carter spotted only a few distant vessels. Alone on his boat, he steered toward his previously mapped coordinates of the undocumented wreck. This would be a great dive.

Solo diving is a foolish risk for the inexperienced or uncertified diver—much can go wrong underwater, not the least of which is drowning. Carter wasn't new to taking chances. It was simply who he was. Growing up, he had been that one kid who nobody wanted to call out on a dare. Nothing motivated him more than somebody telling him he couldn't do something.

The line between adventure seeking and stupidity can be a fine one, but Carter was properly certified to dive alone and had completed hundreds of successful solo dives—the butterflies he felt weren't nerves, but excitement at the prospect of a new find. He eased back on the throttle as he neared the coordinates, then retrieved his phone and played back the drone footage.

The *Wilhelmina* had been "the ghost wreck" in this part of the Caribbean since sinking under mysterious circumstances in 1997. All shipwreck stories come with a certain amount of mystique, but the *Wilhelmina* had become legendary among divers, mostly due to the reclusive nature of its owner, Philip Rothstein. According to news reports, Rothstein had made billions in the tech game before anyone even knew what a dot-com was. And he was said to have been the shadowy driving force behind many successful political careers. It was widely held that Rothstein had secreted valuables aboard his yacht, thinking that if he moved the boat around international waters, the assets—even if discovered—would be tax-exempt. Carter wasn't an accountant, but even he couldn't see the IRS being dumb enough to allow such a wide loophole. He had no idea if any of the stories about Rothstein were true or nothing more than urban legends fabricated by treasure hunters, but the lack of any sort of locator on such a lavish yacht had piqued his interest just the same.

Carter had researched and tracked Rothstein's yacht for more than a year before stumbling upon it quite by accident a week prior while putting his new underwater drone through its paces. He had done a double take upon seeing the partial name stenciled across the stern. The wreck was about sixty nautical miles from where it reportedly sank, raising several possibilities in Carter's head about why that might be. All of them suspicious.

In addition to being the first person to locate the *Wilhelmina*, Carter realized that he might finally be in a position to recover, or at least video-tape, his first actual treasure find. The possibilities of what it might mean to his social media reach and related sponsorships were the fodder of dreams.

As the video replayed on his phone, Carter felt the goosebumps rising again, particularly as the camera passed over the dimly lit stern. It was exhilarating to think he had discovered the wreck before anyone else. Keeping his discovery a secret was paramount to allowing the video debut to have maximum impact.

He confirmed his bearings one final time. He was directly over the location he had pinned on his GPS over a month ago. Carter rechecked the app he used to track the moon and tide depths. The current conditions were nearly identical to the day he had made the discovery. He killed the engine and dropped anchor. Showtime.

As he donned his equipment, Carter couldn't help grinning. He watched as the sun finally broke above the horizon, its bright golden hue dancing across the waves. The day was perfect. It was just him and his GoPro—the way it all started—for luck. He rechecked the tank gauges, then calibrated the dive computer on his watch to the approximate depth of the wreck and the time he would have, giving himself an extra ten-minute window for any contingencies. After rinsing his face mask and activating the video camera, Carter rolled backward off the starboard gunwale into the warm water of the Caribbean.

It took him less than ten minutes to reach the wreck. He could see the hull had sustained heavy damage to its port side, something akin to an explosion. Again, he couldn't help but wonder if Rothstein had scuttled his own vessel—or paid someone else to do it—then lied about where it went down to keep it from being located. Half of the boat's windshield was missing, and tiny fish darted in and out of the opening. Carter decided it was as good an entry point as any. He wished now that he had brought along a diving buddy, maybe even Avery, if only to obtain dramatic footage of him entering the wreck from another viewpoint. He knew how much his followers loved a bit of drama. He took his time filming the bridge before unclipping his guide line reel and tying off to a sturdy handrail on the stairs, then swimming down to explore the lower deck, keeping the line taut and avoiding traps as he went. Especially on a solo dive, the safety measure was important to ensure he would find his way out of the wreck if visibility became an issue in the water. Unlike some of the wrecks he had filmed, aside from a coating of silt, the *Wilhelmina* looked almost new. There was a vast difference between the longevity of the rust-vulnerable iron hulls of old and those manufactured from fiberglass.

After a cursory look at the main cabin, Carter headed to the yacht's aft section. If there was one thing he had learned while researching shipwrecks, it was that captains always kept their valuables close. The master bedroom was huge, with a larger footprint than any of the boats Carter had owned. He took his time videotaping and exploring the entire room, paying extra attention to the teak wall panels, pausing his exploration of the walls when he heard a muffled thumping sound. He swam back to the bedroom door and poked his head out, returning to examine the cavernous closet when he didn't see anything. Noise is odd underwater, and this wasn't the first time his ears had played tricks on him during a dive. He also knew he was extra antsy because he was alone.

Shaking his head, he poked and prodded carefully behind decaying woodwork in the closet. Pay dirt came in the form of a half-rotted panel behind a mirror mounted on the rear wall—the water had taken just enough of the wood for Carter to see the hidey-hole behind it. He flipped his camera down for a selfie of him giving a thumbs up, whipping his head and the light around when he saw a shadow cross the screen behind him.

Nothing there. All these years under the water, and here he was jumping because of a fish.

Turning the camera back to the wall, he removed the panel, revealing a built-in safe. *Now we're talking*, he thought, examining the lock. Great: the mechanism was a battery-operated biometric scanner, likely keyed to Rothstein's fingerprint. Having access to neither electricity nor Rothstein's finger, Carter's options were limited. He removed the knife from his dive belt and attempted to pry the powder-coated steel door open. It wouldn't budge. The only thing he succeeded in disturbing was a thick cloud of silt and rust.

His watch buzzed with the first warning timer he'd set, letting him know he had ten minutes of safety remaining at this depth.

He scoured the safe door for a weak spot and tried another angle with his knife, so absorbed in the task that he didn't notice the water shifting around his body in a way that meant something was swimming nearby until it was too late.

A flash of light from Carter's left meant danger was close—too close. He turned in time to see a trio of divers closing in on him. How did anyone else even know he was here when no one else was supposed to know where this ship was?

Sheathing his knife on the hip they couldn't see, Carter raised his hands in surrender—they had him boxed into the back of the closet, and he didn't like the three-to-one odds even a little bit. The divers ignored the gesture and attacked, the burliest one grabbing his right arm and yanking before landing a slow-motion punch to the side of his head. Carter had never fought underwater, but he quickly realized that it was nothing like Hollywood movies. He struggled with the burly diver while a second flanked him on the right and the third tried to kick his midsection. Carter threw an elbow into the side of the second diver's head, knocking his face mask askew and providing Carter with a good look at the man's face: he had blue eyes and dark brows, and a bump in the center of the bridge of his nose. Blinded by the saltwater and pressure, the man retreated to fix his mask. Carter liked his odds much better against two than three and turned his attention to his assailants.

The water didn't allow for much momentum behind a punch or a kick, and Carter wasn't strong enough to overpower three men in a wrestling match, which meant if he wanted any chance of escaping this encounter alive, he needed to get out of the confines of the bedroom before the second diver returned to the fray. Yanking the knife from its sheath, Carter turned for a better angle and jabbed his weapon at the burly attacker.

While Burly recoiled from the blade and Carter got his arm back, the third diver succeeded in puncturing Carter's air hose, releasing a cascade of bubbles. Carter panicked, realizing he was still sixty feet underwater and unable to make the switch to his pony tank while he was under attack. He swung his knife wildly, slashing the air hose vandal's forearm and giving himself just enough space to escape by swimming between them. Using one hand to try to stem the stream of bubbles pouring from his air hose, Carter kicked hard with his legs, following the guide line back the way he came.

He exited the wreck, then pushed hard for the surface, ascending rapidly. Carter's mind reverted to his training, and he exhaled slowly and steadily until his lungs were empty. He hoped that the trick would help him avoid an embolism, assuming he didn't drown before reaching the surface. While blowing past a safety stop wasn't the best idea, it was his only choice given the circumstances.

Carter's torso exploded from the waves, and he sucked in huge gulps of air. The black dots that had formed in his vision began to dissipate along with some of the panic he'd felt below the surface. Who were those men, and why were they trying to kill him? How long before they surfaced? Carter made out the low purr of an engine idling nearby and figured it belonged to his attackers' boat. Before he could locate the source of the noise, the water swirled as another diver surfaced behind him and he felt a sharp blow to the back of his head. Everything faded to black.

10

After learning that they were without means of transport, Julia lent Avery and Harrison the keys to one of Mark's vehicles to use around town. The car, a silver-blue anniversary edition Corvette, was the least inconspicuous thing either of them could imagine driving. It should have taken less than ten minutes to make the trip from the inn to Mark's sprawling Victorian home, but needing to combat the effects of sleep deprivation, they detoured to a Dunkin drive-through for coffee.

"You look good behind that wheel, Harry," Avery said as they pulled into the driveway of Mark's home.

"Really? Because I feel like a geriatric version of Magnum PI. This thing sticks out like a sore thumb, Ave. Not exactly a sleuthing mode of transport."

Avery finished her coffee and crumpled the cup. "That will never stop being a morning treat," she said.

Harrison smiled as he parked the car. They walked up the front steps, Avery pulling in a deep breath as she studied the stained-glass panels in the door.

"You can't be sure that Mark even knew that coin thingy was under there," Harrison said as Avery used the spare key she'd found at the inn to unlock the deadbolt. The key had been right where she knew Mark would hide it, inside the colonial secretary in his office.

"I'm not sure if Mark found it there or put it there, but he knew it was there," she said. "Why else would he draw that same symbol on the note he left me in the motel?"

"Note he left *you*?" Harrison said as he scratched his head. "Help me follow that leap, Ave."

"Mark knew I would go to Boston, Harry, because he knows—knew me. You tell me all the time how impetuous I am." Avery also knew, in her bones, that Mark knew she'd loved him as much more than a boss and a friend, but she wasn't saying that out loud. Especially not to Harrison.

"Yeah, but—"

"But nothing. Mark left my phone number so the police would call me, and he put the note in the nightstand hoping I'd find it."

"What about the other note, the one with your name and address? You said it yourself; it wasn't Mark's handwriting."

Avery couldn't explain that. But she knew there had to be a reason. Something she couldn't see yet.

"Maybe it's Julia's handwriting and Mark asked her to write the note," Avery said.

"Sure. We can ask her when we get back to the inn: 'Hey Julia, did Mark ask you to write down Avery's name and number for him so he could leave it in a sketchy Boston motel room to bait the detective into calling Avery?' " Harrison sighed. "All my spidey senses are telling me that even if you're right about that, it's the move of a guy who went there knowing he might die there."

Avery blinked back tears. "No."

"You heard Julia say his back was hurt and that he'd been in the office long hours," Harrison said gently. "Maybe the pain and the pressure of the lawsuit and the inn opening was too much for Mark. That's the most logical option."

"Screw logic." Avery cut her eyes sideways in time to see Harrison's jaw loosen slightly. "Yes, I said that. I don't care what anyone thinks or how obvious the answer seems to Burke or you or Sherlock Holmes himself. There's something I didn't know. Something maybe nobody knows. There has to be. And I'm not giving up until I find it." Avery pushed the door open and stepped inside.

A wall-mounted alarm panel began beeping a countdown almost immediately.

Harrison shook his head. "At least we won't have to sleep on a porch when they arrest us for burglary. I hear tell they have nice comfortable bunks at the county lockup."

Avery turned to the panel and casually typed in a code, instantly disabling the alarm.

"How could you possibly know the alarm code?" Harrison said.

"Easy. It was Mark's lucky number, his grandfather's birthday."

Harrison shook his head then walked a half dozen steps into the house before pausing at the doorway to the conservatory. "Hold up, Ave," he whispered.

"What now?" she said as she watched his hand drop instinctively to his hip. A year ago, it was where his police sidearm would have been holstered. *Old habits really do die hard*, she thought.

Harrison muttered something under his breath then looked around, locating a wooden baseball bat in the front hall coat closet.

"I'll never be able to look at sporting equipment the same way, Harry."

He choked up on the bat then entered the conservatory. After a moment, he waved her into the room.

"Take a look at this," he said, still whispering.

Avery looked down at the shards of glass on the floor. One of the windowpanes on an exterior set of French doors that led to a wraparound porch was broken.

"If someone broke in, how was the alarm still armed when we arrived, Harry?"

Harrison shrugged. "Perhaps you're not the only one who knew Mark's lucky number."

Harrison moved into the dining room with Avery right behind him. While he searched for bad guys, Avery scanned every detail of the rooms. Dark wood, stained glass, and heavy antique furniture seemed to be the theme. It was the kind of home no one would expect a tech guru to own.

But then again, Mark had always enjoyed throwing people for a loop. He had certainly thrown her for one.

Harrison was thorough, checking every nook and cranny in the house, even the attic. Avery remained quiet as she walked behind him, though she questioned if he might be too paranoid for his own good. She wondered how many times her mother and Harrison had cleared buildings together while working as detectives.

They searched the basement last. The space was stuffed to its considerable capacity with antiques in various states of disrepair. Included in the menagerie were headboards, bookcases, dining room tables, a Hepplewhite china cabinet, two wardrobes, and a large pile of reclaimed hardwood.

"Jesus, there's a lot of stuff in this house," Harrison said, finally relaxing his grip on the Louisville slugger.

"Mark never could walk away from a good deal," Avery said. "He always said if you're an antique aficionado New England is the place to be."

Finally satisfied that there was no one else in the house, Harrison followed Avery back to the second floor.

"Where are we going, Ave?"

"Mark's bedroom. If he left his phone anywhere it has to be here, and that's the best I have for a starting place."

Avery recognized the king-sized cherry four-poster bed from Mark's previous apartment in the city, but the tables, chaise, and massive wardrobe were new. Avery learned a few things about antiques from Mark during the years they had worked together, and she was immediately drawn to the wardrobe's beautiful burl laminate. Gliding her fingertips over the flawless finish, she could imagine his delight at the find, especially given his propensity for hoarding designer clothes and the lack of any significant closet space in the old house.

Avery had been looking for signs that Julia had spent nights here with Mark, a spare toothbrush, lingerie, anything, but she'd found nothing. Perhaps their relationship was truly professional.

"Mind telling me what we're looking for up here?" Harrison said as he began searching his half of the room.

"Answers."

Carefully, Avery opened the wardrobe doors, revealing a silvered and slightly warped but intact mirror on the backside of each. Aside from a small-for-Mark stack of Armani button-downs, the wardrobe was filled with nothing but paper. File folders, many in disarray, with errant pages and photos tossed about haphazardly. She was pleased to find nothing feminine hanging inside.

"What a mess," Harrison said.

"Mark was way too OCD to leave things this untidy," Avery said. "Even behind heavy doors."

"Maybe someone else has already been through it," Harrison said.

Avery picked up two photos by the edges and studied them. The first featured a large willow tree with wide, low branches showing its considerable age, surrounded by other trees. Moss hung in heavy curtains all around. Avery turned the photograph over. *Watercress, 1947*. The notation meant nothing to her. The next picture was a computer printout from an underwater camera of what looked to be the half-rotten hull and deck of a wooden Chris Craft. Written beneath the image in Mark's handwriting is *Swift Run, Boston*. Avery set the photos aside then looked through several of the file folders. She could tell pages had been removed as the flow of information was broken. Grabbing a large handful of the folders, she carried them to the table and sat down on the chaise.

Harrison looked up from his search of the night table drawers. "You got something?"

"Not sure." Avery handed him the two photographs. "These mean anything to you, Harry?"

Harrison studied them for a moment before handing them back. "Nope. Should they?"

"The Boston one might be relevant."

"Kind of a stretch, isn't it?"

"Mark wasn't a pack rat, Harry. These things meant something to him. You find anything?"

"Nothing that makes any sense. Just a bunch of random historical photos and what looks like old farm records. Mark was a history buff, right? Maybe he was writing a book."

"I doubt that very much."

"Why not? He could have been researching background information on the Hawk's Nest. People who stay at places like that love that sh— that stuff."

"We're staying there."

"And you love history as much as Mark did. See? Exactly my point."

Avery returned to the wardrobe and removed additional folders. She opened one from the middle of the stack. The first thing she found appeared to be what Harrison had just described as pages from an old farm ledger. The remaining pages in the folder appeared to be photocopies taken from a book.

"Why would someone break in here and steal a bunch of worthless local lore?" Avery said.

"You don't know for sure that even happened, Ave."

"Really? Who was marching around the house with a baseball bat acting like Dirty Harry? You sure looked like you were searching for a burglar."

Avery removed an oversized canvas bag from the trunk at the foot of the bed to load up the files anyway. She was grabbing the last few folders from the wardrobe when her eyes were drawn to something carved into the back lower right corner of the dark wooden cabinet. Pulling out her phone, she shined the flashlight on it: the lion and the cross.

She snapped a photo of the carving, then flicked back through her recent photos to the coin, comparing the two images. Avery had always been good at puzzles. She was the kind of person who did the NYT Sunday crossword in ink and raced against herself in sudoku. She had also been the chess champion of the Manhattan retirement home where she'd volunteered as a teenager, repeatedly outwitting some of the finest financial minds of the 1960s and 70s. Sometimes the pieces just took a moment to click.

"Mark was on a treasure hunt," Avery said, spinning back to Harrison. "That coin, the antiques, the photos, this symbol. He was searching for something someone didn't want him to find. Or they wanted to find it first. And now he's dead."

"You're just speculating, Ave. We don't know anything like that. You sure this isn't just a way to keep your mind off the app sale troubles?"

Avery shook her head. "It isn't."

"Ignoring the problem won't make it go away. Have you heard anything from the attorneys this week?"

Avery bit her lip, a flicker of worry crossing her face. "They called yesterday when I was on the boat with Carter, and I didn't want to answer. Then I forgot about everything when Burke called about Mark. I should have called back."

"When did you speak to them last?" Harrison asked. "What are Daimler Technologies leaning toward? Do we even know if they have evidence that Maggie lied to them?"

"I don't want to talk about it, Harry."

Harrison softened his tone a bit. "Maybe Mark knew something you don't. And not to start another argument, but losing a fortune can drive a man to drugs. It has driven many to suicide. You need to think about protecting yourself here. Your money is—"

"I should've known better, okay?" Avery snapped. "I mean, how ridiculous was this whole thing to begin with? Maggie is pretty and charming, but if she has half a brain in her head, I'll eat my shoes. Why did we trust that she legitimately got these people to pay billions for what was essentially a high-tech and extremely overpriced vanity vehicle? Because we wanted to. We won the lottery. They signed the papers, the check cleared, we rode off into the sunset. If the money goes as easily as it came, I'll deal. Trust me, I know how to live on a budget. I don't give a damn about anything right now except for Mark being dead. I want to know why. I don't have time to think about myself, and I certainly don't have time to think twice about Maggie friggin' Watters."

With that, Avery stormed off toward Mark's study.

Harrison might need more proof, but she certainly did not. She could feel it in her bones, with the kind of certainty that brought with it peace layered with excitement and a bit of fear. Whatever Mark was into had nothing to do with Maggie's lies and the jeopardy she'd brought to their deal. The deal Avery thought was long since closed and final only a month ago.

She entered the study and sat down, checking the desktop and the floor around the desk for Mark's phone to no avail. Was Harrison right? Was

Mark's treasure hunt just a distraction for her to focus on while the lawyers charging her a thousand bucks an hour did their jobs?

She pulled up the lion and cross photos on her phone again. The image looked like something from a children's book, or a Nicolas Cage movie. Distraction? Maybe. But no matter what, Avery was all in.

11

Carter struggled to open his eyes, squinting against the bright sunlight. In addition to the pain in his chest, he had a raging headache. He was seated on the deck of a boat and a quick glance around convinced him it wasn't his. No, this boat was older and in worse condition than *The Deuce*. Attempting to move his arms, he quickly discovered they were restrained behind his back.

"Well, that answers that question," a gruff male voice said from somewhere behind him.

"What question was that?" Carter said.

"Whether or not we killed you."

"Nope, still here," Carter said, trying to project just the right amount of confidence in his voice. Since he wasn't in fact dead, they obviously wanted something from him.

"Told you he was stupid," another male voice said.

Three men circled around and stood in front of him. Now stripped of their diving gear, he could clearly see their faces. None of them looked familiar, but one man had a large dressing on his forearm. The tallest of the three, a bearded man, leaned back against the port gunwale and folded his arms across his broad chest. In his reflective sunglasses, Carter saw *The Deuce* bobbing gently behind his own head, just a few feet away.

"I don't suppose you'd be interested in telling me who you are and what the hell you're doing here," the bearded guy said.

Carter opened his mouth, but before he could speak, the bearded man held up one hand. "Before you say something stupid, just know my friends here would like nothing more than to toss you overboard."

Carter glanced at the other men; both were grinning.

"In that case, my name is Carter."

"And what are you doing out here, Mr. Carter?"

"My job."

"Your job?"

"Yeah, I've been hunting for the *Wilhelmina*."

"Why?"

Carter calculated the odds that any of these men followed him on Instagram and produced a big fat zero.

"I'm a shipwreck hunter."

Two of his captors laughed at the comment. The third, who had yet to speak, drew his large diving knife and began to clean under his fingernails.

"I'm serious. I hunt wrecks, filming everything, then post the videos to social media."

"And how long have you been searching for the *Wilhelmina*, Mr. Carter?"

Unsure how to answer to avoid walking the plank, Carter opted for the truth. "About a year."

"Yeah? Well, we been searching for her a lot longer than you," Bandage Man growled. "And we mean to take that treasure."

"Treasure?" Carter said, trying to look as innocent as possible. "I figured those stories were just rumor."

Bearded Guy smiled for the first time. "Sure, you did. How is it that you ended up finding the *Wilhelmina* before anyone else? We're nowhere near where she supposedly went down."

Carter tried to shrug. "Luck?"

"Why don't we just end this guy and be done with it?" Bandage Man said.

"Look, I really don't care about any treasure," Carter said, his voice cracking. "That isn't how I make my money."

"Yeah?" Bearded Guy said. "'Cause it's how we make ours."

"I'll give you full credit for the discovery," Carter said. "Make you famous on my site as a bonus."

He nervously looked around at the three men. None of them spoke for the longest time. His eyes fixated on Mr. Diving Knife, who had finished with his nails and now held the knife in a threatening manner.

Carter continued, hoping to sweeten the pot, "You'll be entitled to the twenty percent finder's fee under international law, assuming there's anything down there. I don't want a dime."

The bearded man reached up and scratched his chin, as if considering his options. Finally, he nodded to Mr. Diving Knife, who moved toward Carter.

"Wait, wait," Carter said.

"Too late," Diving Knife said from directly behind him.

Carter closed his eyes tightly in anticipation of what would come next, but instead of a sharp pain in his back or across his throat, he felt the rope binding being sawed off.

"You're not gonna kill me?" Carter said.

All three men laughed.

"Of course not," Bearded Guy said. "You're Carter Mosley, aren't you? That thrill junkie from Instagram?"

Carter nodded. Was social media about to actually save his life? Being internet famous had brought some surprises, but that would definitely be the best one yet.

"How about a beer?" Bandage Guy asked as he helped Carter to his feet.

"Sorry about the little mix-up," Bearded Guy said as he passed a can of beer to Carter. "We didn't know who you were, and we couldn't risk having whatever treasure is on the *Wilhelmina* stolen out from under us. Not after all this time. You understand, right?"

Carter nodded. He understood all right, and that "little mix-up" was still throbbing at the back of his head. But he knew better than to verbalize his actual feelings with these men, especially with Knife Guy still flashing those shark-like teeth of his.

"No hard feelings?" Bearded Guy said as he extended his hand.

"None at all," Carter said as he gripped the offering.

After taking a long drink from the can—to settle his nerves—Carter engaged them in conversation, hoping to find out more about them.

"How long have you guys been at this?"

Bearded Guy answered first. "Rick and I have been working together going on six years. Ain't that right, Ricky?"

Bandage Guy answered, "Yup. Sounds about right, Vince."

"We didn't bring Nico in until about a year ago. He's like our security specialist."

Nico, aka Knife Guy, nodded at Carter and grinned his shark-like grin again.

"We've located four valuable shipwreck caches so far," Ricky said.

"And you got the twenty percent?" Carter asked.

"Only on one," Ricky said.

"We never claimed the other three," Vince added. "That twenty percent finder's fee is nothing but a money grab by the government. Any idea how much time and risk go into treasure hunting? Speaking of which, we've got a wreck to search, boys."

Carter finished his beer and picked up his Go-Pro and mask from the deck where someone had dropped them while he was unconscious, then climbed aboard *The Deuce*. "You guys sure I can't interest you in a shoutout on social media?"

"Thanks anyway," Vince said as he and Nico untethered the two boats. "But I think we'll take a hard pass. We do our best work off camera."

Vince returned Carter's diving knife and wished him well.

Carter fired up *The Deuce* and quickly put distance between himself and the pirates. He looked back at the three men who were quickly preparing for their next dive. He shook his head as he glanced at their stern. Stenciled above the dive platform was the name *Rogue*.

12

Avery began her search of the study, trying to remember everything her mother had taught her.

"A good search requires you to be methodical and thorough, Avery. Top to bottom, left to right, whatever method you choose be sure to finish one area before moving on to the next. Try and think like the person who hid whatever you're looking for. Where would you hide something you didn't want found?"

Mark enjoyed games, and he adored puzzles—strategy was a hobby for him, his brain always needing something to solve. A treasure hunt would definitely take that to new levels, and Avery wondered, looking around and thinking about Mark helping the landscapers and inviting her to visit him, if he'd been as bored here as she was in Key West. Maybe he'd gone looking for the wrong kind of adventure, though she still didn't want to believe he'd looked in a pill bottle.

Avery's mother, Valerie, and Harrison hadn't become the most successful homicide investigators in NYPD history by accident. Avery often wondered what Valerie would have made of her own success. Would her mom be happy for her? She'd never come right out and said it, but Avery was certain Valerie wanted to see her daughter follow in her famous law-enforcing footsteps.

Mark's study was oddly shaped, two long walls and two short ones, but absent even a single ninety-degree corner. In fact, the room was closer to a rhombus than a rectangle. Avery wondered if the room had been constructed that way originally, or if someone had altered the layout in later years to hide something like water damage. Or a secret compartment. If Mark had purposely parted with his phone, he would've put it where no one but Avery might find it. So what did she know that no one else knew?

Mark enjoyed practical jokes and hide-and-seek. He'd been known to embed code in app coding that caused funny glitches, setting a clock—and a prize—for Avery and two colleagues to see who could find and fix the code first. The year before her app sold, Avery won a trip to Hawaii on one, and she'd outpaced her coworkers three-to-one on wins over her tenure with Hawkins Tech.

She began her search by examining the seams where the walls met one another before moving to the floor and ceiling junctions. Typical for homes of the period, the walls in Mark's house were constructed of horsehair plaster backed by wooden laths. Unlike gypsum or sheetrock walls, plaster walls were incredibly strong, but brittle and prone to cracking. In other words, it would be much harder to conceal something within them. Tapping here and pulling there, she looked for loose baseboards or moldings. After twenty minutes of that, she gave up on the walls, focusing instead on the room's furnishings.

The furniture consisted of a floor-to-ceiling built-in bookcase, a beautifully grained secretary made from quarter-sawn white oak, three wingbacks, a black Boston rocker, a cherry sideboard, which seemed out of place in the study, and a beautiful antique desk.

Avery approached the bookcase first. At the center of the shelving hung a detailed pen and ink drawing of a grove of trees flanked by two birds: a cardinal and a raven. Avery shared Mark's interest in art, and though she found the piece to be lovely, she knew it wasn't to his taste. She checked the corners of the drawing for an artist's signature but couldn't find one. Thinking it might mean something later, Avery snapped several pictures of the piece with her phone. She searched through the book titles, removing random tomes and fanning through the pages for anything that might be hidden within, but nothing jumped out at her.

After she'd finished with the bookcase, Avery focused on the antique secretary located near the short windowless wall. The secretary was constructed with several long roll out shelves. Each of the shelves held a small stack of large, yellowed maps. She flipped through them until she located several detailed maps of the area. One was a boundary map of the Hawk's Nest property. Another map was of the land upon which Mark's home sat. The last was a map of the town dated 1764. The papers were brittle and torn in places with missing corners, and Avery handled them with care. None of the maps appeared to have been marked beyond their original faded printing. The second shelf held several rolled nautical maps marked in ink with small stars. The map locations were unlabeled, but Avery immediately recognized the familiar shape of the coastlines. One was a map of the Maine coast, two depicted the mid-Atlantic seaboard, and the last was a map of the Florida coastline. Her pulse quickened when she realized that the inked star off the Florida coast was remarkably close to her home in the Keys. The fact that Mark hadn't bothered to label the marked locations on any of the maps only added to Avery's suspicion that Mark knew something he didn't want anyone else to find.

Avery moved to the desk next, pausing to run her hand over the worn leather top. She recognized the style as Queen Anne. There were three drawers across the top and three drawers of assorted sizes within each pedestal. The acquisition had to be the reason Mark had moved his grandfather's desk to the inn, she thought.

Carefully, she removed each of the drawers, stacking them on the rug beside the desk. Aside from pads of paper and various office supplies, there was nothing of interest contained in any of the drawers. As she had when she'd examined the desk at the inn, Avery crawled underneath looking for embedded coins or hidden notes. There were no coins this time, but she did notice something odd regarding the inside dimensions of the left pedestal. She crawled out and double checked the drawers. The bottommost drawer, the largest, of the left-hand pedestal was shorter than all the other drawers by about six inches. Which could only mean that its opening was also shorter.

Avery removed the lamp and several notebooks from the top of the desk, then carefully rolled the desk onto its back. She could see by the way the desktop and pedestals were connected that it had been made to allow for disassembly.

She dropped to her knees and illuminated the rear of the left pedestal with the flashlight on her phone. The walnut laminate was cracked and separated in two places. Her eyes scanned the den for something she could use to pry the laminate away from the pedestal casing, stopping on an antique letter opener. Using the opener, she slowly peeled back the laminate until the entire piece fell to the rug. Someone had reattached the walnut with double-sided carpet tape. Avery didn't know all that much about eighteenth-century furniture construction, but she was pretty sure the tape was of a more recent vintage. Her eyes moved back to the exposed wood. A narrow seam ran around the entire remaining panel. Again, she availed herself of the letter opener and pried the board out of the pedestal, revealing a hidden cubby behind the bottom drawer opening.

Her excitement quickly dissipated as she realized the compartment was empty. Had Mark found it before her? Was he the person responsible for the carpet tape? Or had the previous owner hidden something?

A knock on the door frame startled her.

"I wondered if you were avoiding me," Harrison said as he entered the room carrying the oversized canvas bag that contained everything they were taking.

"Only partially," Avery said.

"Um, I guess I didn't know I was supposed to disassemble everything, Ave. What are you doing?"

"Looking for clues."

"Find any?"

"Just an empty hiding place." *Which may have once held a clue*, she thought. "How about you, Harry?" Avery asked as she stood up and brushed the dust from her hands. "Find anything?"

"No cell phones, but I got a couple things here," Harrison said as he handed her a blue file folder. "The first is this."

Avery opened the folder and saw that it contained a multi-page document. Her eyes welled with tears as she read the top of the first sheet. *Last Will and Testament of M. Hawkins.*

"He left it all to you, Ave," Harrison said.

"Left all of what to me?"

"This house, his share of the company sale, everything but the inn. That goes to Julia Bergin."

She flipped to the signature page. It was dated three months ago. She closed the folder and wiped her eyes before looking up at Harrison. "You don't think Mark knew that—"

"I don't know, Ave. It's better not to torture yourself thinking about stuff like that. Mark's will might not have anything to do with what happened to him. You said it yourself; he was Type A about everything. Maybe he was just putting his finances in order because his new business was getting off the ground."

Avery looked around the room at her inheritance. Maybe Harry was right. It was something Mark would have done. But it still didn't eliminate the possibility of suicide. Maybe he had been planning his own demise for months. She didn't want to believe it, nor was she willing to admit it, but the possibility hung there like the odor of something rotten.

"You find anything less emotionally charged?" Avery said.

"Think I figured out how the burglar got in and out," Harrison said as he held up a small sliver of glass. "Found this embedded in the hardwood floor of the entryway."

"I don't get it," Avery said.

"The intruder, or intruders, tracked this from the broken pane in the solarium. Probably in the sole of a shoe. I found scratches about the length of a step apart on the floor between the two areas."

"Meaning?"

"It may explain how they turned off the alarm."

"Then they did know the code. And they reset it before they left."

"Likely. Also, I found these." He held up a sandwich baggie containing two cigarette butts. "On the lawn outside the solarium. Same brand as last night's mystery guest at the inn."

"That can't be a coincidence."

"Hardly. How about you? Anything worthwhile?"

"Maybe," Avery said. She brought him up to speed, showing him the marked maps.

"Treasure maps? Come on, Ave."

"Why not? Mark was onto something, Harry. Here, give me a hand putting this desk back together."

Avery replaced the false panel, and the laminate, then righted the desk. Harrison helped her return the drawers to their proper locations. The last thing she did was replace the lamp and notebooks in their previous spots atop the desk, noticing the corner of a piece of paper sticking out from under the blotter as she did so. She pulled out printed copies of a flight confirmation and hotel itinerary. "He was coming to Florida," she said, scanning the type. "Next month, with a stop in Hilton Head, South Carolina. These dates show that he planned to be gone for a month." And he'd said nothing to Avery about a trip to Florida, which she knew bothered her more than it should've, so she didn't mention that part. Instead, she waved the papers at Harrison and said, "Would a man contemplating suicide book a monthlong vacation?"

"Not normally," Harrison said carefully.

Avery nodded, tucking the papers into her bag.

As she turned away from the desk, the floor beneath the Persian area rug made a hollow thunking sound under her foot. The noise caused her to stop. Avery knelt and rolled the rug back revealing the hardwood floor underneath. Normally, unless a repair had been done, hardwood floors are constructed using interlocking and staggered boards, nailed together along the subfloor joists. But this floor had a discolored panel approximately two-foot square hidden beneath the rug.

"Repair?" Harrison said.

"Or hiding place," Avery said. She ran her fingers along the seam trying to find a release mechanism.

"We could try prying it?" Harrison said.

"I thought you were the one worried about getting arrested for burglary?" Avery said.

"Feels like that ship has already sailed."

Avery used both hands, pressing hard in the center of the panel, and she heard a *click* as the wood depressed slightly. She lifted her hands and the panel moved up on one side about a half inch above the floor.

"Son of a b—" Harrison said.

"Gun," Avery said, finishing his thought before it went sideways. The panel, mounted on a brass piano hinge, opened out like a cupboard door, revealing a hollow between the floor joists.

Harrison placed his hands on his knees and bent forward. "What is it?" he said.

Avery reached into the space and removed two items. The first was a small leather-bound book embossed with a lion and cross on the cover. The second, constructed out of tarnished metal, looked like some kind of child's toy. It had two rings engraved with numbers and letters that lined up when turned on an adjoining post.

"Looks like some kind of enigma device," Avery said.

"A what?"

"A decoder, Harry."

"Why didn't you just say that?"

Avery wondered if the items might have come from the hidden compartment inside the desk. She set the decoder aside and picked up the book.

"I'm thinking about getting a lion and cross tattoo, Ave," Harrison said. "What do you think?"

She ignored him and carefully opened the musty book. It was a diary of sorts, dating back to the 1860s. Written in ink, the handwriting was intricate but cramped. The author's name was missing, the only clue was the initials J.S. Avery skimmed several pages, trying to get a feel for the contents.

"What is it?"

"Someone's diary. Looks like the account of a farmer who settled in this area shortly after Maine became the twenty-third state in the union."

"You think that's what whoever was here was looking for?" Harrison asked.

"Hard to s—"

They froze as a loud noise came from the kitchen.

Harrison started toward the study door. "Stay behind me, Ave."

Avery pushed past him. "Not happening. I'm better at hand to hand than you, Harry."

"And if they're armed?"

"As you keep reminding me, you don't have a gun."

They crept silently down the hall, through the dining room, toward a swinging kitchen door. Avery pushed the door open slightly but couldn't even see half of the kitchen. She felt two taps on her shoulder from Harrison, signaling that he was ready for her to make entry. As she moved into the room, Harrison right on her heels, a metallic crash sent them both into a defensive crouch.

Rocking back and forth on the floor near the center island was a large copper pot, knocked free from the rack above the island. Sitting atop the island was a fat orange tabby cleaning one of its front paws. The cat paused for a moment to assess the intruders then returned to its bath.

"Jesus," Harrison said.

"Afraid of a cat, Harry?"

"Hardly. I'm just not cut out for this burglar stuff."

The cat purred loudly as Avery scratched the top of its head while examining the purple collar. Engraved on it was the cat's name and Mark's phone number.

"Hello, Clara," Avery said. She scanned the room until she found Clara's food and water bowls tucked under a low counter in one corner of the kitchen.

Avery located Clara's food in one of the upper cupboards.

"So, Mark was a cat guy, huh?" Harrison said as he refilled the water bowl in the sink.

"No," Avery said. "He wasn't big on pets of any kind." As Avery scooped the canned mixture into a bowl she couldn't help wondering if Clara belonged to Julia.

"What now?" Harrison said as they returned to the study to retrieve the canvas bag.

"I need to get on a computer and spend some time researching these things to figure out what it all means," Avery said as she added the enigma device and journal to their collection.

"Then we're finally getting out of here?"

"Yes, Harry, we're leaving."

"Good."

Avery and Harrison were halfway to the front door when they heard approaching sirens.

"Dammit," Harrison said. "I knew it."

They both peered out through the sidelights of the entryway, eyes fixed on the roadway. Several seconds later a fire truck, ambulance, and police cruiser raced past without slowing.

Avery turned toward Harrison. "Are you thinking what I'm thinking?"

"They're headed toward the inn."

13

Samael finished his last set of incline push-ups then grabbed a towel to wipe the sweat from his face. He maintained a strict workout regimen, something he had done for years even before his time working in the intelligence community. A fit mind and a fit body were the two most important steps toward ensuring success.

He slung the white cotton towel over his neck then cracked open a fresh bottled water from the glass front refrigerator. As he paced the room's hardwood parquet flooring, his eyes glided over the gilded crown molding. Though he had personally overseen the purchase of the estate, he still found American tastes erred on the side of gaudy.

A man dressed in a tailored charcoal suit entered the room without knocking. Despite the tailoring, the bulge of a sidearm hidden beneath the coat was impossible to miss.

"I'm sorry, sir," the man said. "I didn't mean to interrupt your workout."

"It's okay, Lucius. I assume you have news for me."

"It's about Avery Turner and her bodyguard," Lucius said.

"What about them?"

"They arrived in Maine just as you predicted. They went directly to the inn and spoke with Julia Bergin."

"Are they still at the inn?" Samael said.

"No. They broke into the Hawkins home and departed with a heavy canvas bag. I have no idea what they may have taken."

Samael stretched his neck from side to side. "Thank you, Lucius. Keep me posted."

Avery bolted from the Corvette, leaving Harrison to park the car. She hurried past the cluster of emergency vehicles blocking the front steps of the inn.

A young, uniformed police officer, sporting a military style flattop, stepped in front of her before she could mount the stairs. His name tag read: *Gibbons*.

"Hold it right there, ma'am," Gibbons said, raising his hand like a traffic cop.

"You don't understand. I'm a friend of the owner. What happened?"

"I can't let you enter an active crime scene."

"What crime? We were just here."

As she uttered the words two emergency medical technicians, bookending a gurney, exited the inn. Julia was strapped onto the gurney, and she was bleeding from one side of her head.

Despite Gibbons's objections, Avery pushed past him, rushing to intercept the EMTs.

"Oh my God, Julia," Avery said. "What happened? Who did this to you?"

Julia was too weak to reply.

"She's in and out of consciousness, ma'am," one of the EMTs said as they moved toward the waiting ambulance. "We're taking her to Eastern Maine Medical Center."

"Will she be okay?"

"At a minimum she's suffered a concussion."

"What's the other possibility?"

"She may have a fractured skull."

Avery watched in shock as they carefully loaded Julia into the back. Before they could close the doors Julia reached out to the attending technician and mumbled something.

"What did she say?" Avery said.

The EMT turned to Avery. "Said she didn't see who hit her, but she heard voices coming from Mark's office. Said you'd know where that was."

Avery watched helplessly as they closed and latched the doors.

Harrison ran up behind her, still carrying the canvas bag containing all the things they had taken from Mark's house. "What the hell happened, Ave?"

Before she could respond, the ambulance pulled away from the inn, heading down the drive with its lights flashing and siren blaring.

"I understand you were just here before the incident," a voice boomed from behind them.

Avery and Harrison turned around and came face to face with another police officer. This one was every bit as physically imposing as Harrison. He wore a neatly trimmed graying mustache and four gold stars on either side of his uniform collar.

It took several moments and a look at Harrison's retired detective ID and badge before Sheriff Lionel Greene began to discount them as suspects in the attack on Julia.

"You and Mark Hawkins worked together, Ms. Turner?" Greene said.

"We were very close."

"My deputy said he overheard the victim relay a message to you through one of the ambulance techs. Something about Mark's office. What was that about?"

"Sheriff, Julia had just finished giving us a tour of the place less than two hours ago," Avery said. "One of the rooms she showed us was Mark's office. Julia said she heard voices coming from the office right before she was attacked."

Sheriff Greene keyed the radio microphone clipped to the epaulet on his uniform jacket and relayed the information to someone. After he had finished, Greene's attention shifted back to Avery and Harrison.

"I gotta say, the people in this town have grown rather fond of Mark

Hawkins. I count myself among them. This being Maine, folks are usually a bit suspicious of outsiders showing up and making changes. But Mark is loved by everyone. Hell, he funded the library expansion, a new roof for the middle school, and doubled the sheriff's department's equipment budget. He's a regular philanthropic godsend."

Avery smiled. "That sounds like Mark."

"Don't suppose either of you know when he's due back from his trip?"

"You know about his trip?" Harrison said.

"I bumped into him coming out of the bank a few days ago. Said he was headed down to Boston. Something about a rare find."

Avery swallowed hard before disclosing that Mark was dead.

Greene looked stricken. "Dead? I had no idea. How?"

Harrison jumped in before Avery could reply. "It was an accident. A tragic one."

After exchanging a knowing glance with Harrison, Avery followed up with, "Very tragic." They both knew Sheriff Greene would be able to check with the Boston police for details without too much effort. Avery hoped that he wouldn't, at least not until after they had departed.

Greene appeared to be searching for the right words as he turned to face Avery. "Young lady, you said that Mark died under tragic circumstances."

Avery nodded.

"And now you're here, all the way from Florida no less, when someone breaks in and assaults Mark's assistant. How is it that you two just happened to be up here in the middle of—whatever this is?"

Avery opened her mouth to speak, but Greene stopped her.

"I hope that you're not sticking your nose in where it doesn't belong. Surely *Retired Detective* Harrison told you what kind of hot water you'd be in if you were to interfere in a police investigation."

Avery couldn't help but catch the emphasis Greene attached to 'retired detective.' A quick glance at Harrison confirmed that he had too.

"I would never," Avery said, doing her best to project an innocence she didn't remotely feel.

"Uh-huh," Greene said looking back and forth between them. "What's in the bag?" he asked Harrison.

"Just a few necessities we picked up."

"Riiight. Well, since you've already had the tour, you might as well follow me inside. Maybe one of you can tell us if anything is missing."

14

Sheriff Greene handed both Avery and Harrison a pair of slip-on Tyvek booties and blue latex gloves.

The three of them entered the main lobby then stopped near the reception counter. Greene pointed out the telephone handset lying on the rug beside a large bloodstain.

"This is where the victim was found," Greene said. "We think she was struck with that granite paperweight." He pointed to a softball sized polished stone lying up against the base of the counter.

"Improvised weapon," Harrison said, thinking aloud.

"Very good, Detective," Greene said.

"I don't understand," Avery said.

"Means that the perp didn't bring a weapon with them," Harrison said.

"Probably expected the place to be empty," Greene said.

Gibbons, the deputy Avery had previously brushed past when they first arrived, walked up to Greene. His annoyance with Avery was still etched upon his face.

"What is it, deputy?" Greene said.

"Sir, we found fresh prints in the mud out behind the inn. Our evidence tech is photographing them now."

Greene turned to Avery and Harrison. "Other than you two and the victim, was there anyone else here this morning?"

"Not that we saw," Avery said.

Greene nodded and readdressed Gibbons. "Thanks, Lou. I'll be out to take a gander shortly."

After the deputy departed, Greene turned back to them. "Any idea if they kept a cash box or safe on the premises?"

"I'm not sure," Avery said.

"There is a safe," Harrison said. "In Mark's office."

Greene held out a hand, "Lead the way."

Avery shot Harrison a glare before following him to the office.

"It's behind a wall cabinet," Harrison said.

They stopped after entering the room. The cabinet door that Harrison had closed when they left was standing open, as was the door to the empty safe.

"Come with me," Greene said.

Avery and Harrison followed the sheriff to the rear of the inn where two deputies were working. The one holding the camera was dressed in brown coveralls with the word Evidence across the back in reflective lettering.

"What have you got, Vern?" Greene asked.

"Got several prints in the mud. The tread looks like a work style boot. Should be able to cast them for comparison."

"Can we follow them?"

"We tried. Lost the trail in the grass as soon as they entered the pasture."

"K9?"

"Off at training all week," the uniformed deputy said.

Greene eyed Avery's sandals and Harrison's Nikes. "Don't suppose either of you are traveling with work boots?"

"Nope," Avery said. "And Julia was wearing heels when we saw her."

Harrison spoke up. "It rained just before dawn, Sheriff. Whoever these prints belong to must have made them after striking Julia, on their way out."

"With whatever was in Mark's safe," Avery added.

"What do you think, Sheriff?" the evidence technician said.

"It's those damn opiates," Greene said.

Harrison nodded.

"I'm sorry," Avery said, raising her eyebrows. Given what the police in Boston had said about Mark's death, which they had not shared, she wondered how Greene made the leap. "You think Mark was involved in illegal drugs?"

"Not at all," Greene said. "But it has become our biggest problem locally: the area loggers were an early test market for opioid painkillers. OxyContin was marketed to local docs as a 'nonaddictive' way to help with the aches and pains that go with injuries loggers get." Greene snorted. "Non-addictive, my big toe. Stuff spread through this town like a virus. Wasn't long before the woods were full of addicts—and the crime that comes with addiction. Burglary, robbery, petty theft—addicts will steal anything they think they can sell."

"So you think this was a coincidence?" Avery asked.

"Gotta fund that addiction." Greene shrugged. "Folks around here knew Mark's story. They knew he had a great deal of money. I already told you how much he's helped us. Anyway, it's a small town. Word gets around that he's away and his new business is about to open. Probably didn't expect Ms. Bergin to be here."

"How did they get the safe open without help?" Avery said.

"Maybe they got it out of her," the evidence tech said. "No telling exactly what happened until we talk with Ms. Bergin."

The deputy chimed in, "We'll make the rounds, rustle up the usual suspects, see what we can turn up. These boot prints give us something to match up, assuming we can locate them. None of these guys are very smart."

"Likely just addicts looking to score some cash, Miss Turner," Greene said as he laid his hand gently on Avery's shoulder. "I'm so sorry about your friend. Mark's death is the entire town's loss."

Avery looked to Harrison for help, but he simply nodded in agreement.

"You folks staying here?" Greene said.

"Our bags are in two of the rooms upstairs," Harrison said.

"I can assign a deputy to keep an eye on the place if that would put your mind at ease. Though, it's not likely they'll be back."

"Thank you, Sheriff, but I'm not sure how much longer we'll be staying," Avery said.

"Okay. Well, let us know if there's anything we can do for you."

Greene handed his business card to Avery, then departed, leaving his deputies to finish.

Avery followed Harrison back inside the inn.

"You don't really believe that drug stuff Greene was selling, do you, Harry?"

"It does feel a little too convenient, given all that has happened."

"But."

"But Greene doesn't have half of the information we do, does he?"

"Because we didn't share it."

"Exactly," Harrison said as he started up the stairs to the second floor.

"Where are you going?"

"I'll meet you in the office. Just have to grab something from my bag."

Avery entered Mark's office and stood staring at the empty safe. She wondered if the person who assaulted Julia really knew how to crack a safe. It felt like something two different people had done. One impulsive, one not. She examined the dial on the safe. Did it take expertise to open one of these? Or could any idiot learn how by watching instructional videos online?

Harrison entered the room carrying a small plastic box.

"What's that?" Avery said.

"It's my fingerprint kit."

"From your time on the job?"

Harrison grinned. "Nope. Amazon. Twenty-nine bucks."

Avery watched as he set the kit on a side table and popped it open. "What are you planning to dust for prints?"

"The safe, and everything around it."

"Won't the deputies have done that?"

"Do you see any fingerprint powder?" Harrison said, pointing to the safe. "Besides, they just left, and they couldn't have been here an hour at the outside. Not sure we'll be able to count on them to solve this."

Avery watched as Harrison painstakingly dusted the cabinet and safe door. Several black smudges appeared but only two even resembled fingerprints.

"Now you lift the prints with tape and stick them on notecards, right?" Avery said.

"That's old school," Harrison said as he returned the powder and brush to the kit and pulled another device from his pocket. This one was about the size of a cell phone.

"What's that?"

"That is a fingerprint scanner."

"Let me guess, Amazon?"

"Hardly. You don't want to know where this came from."

Avery watched in amazement as Harrison slowly scanned each of the prints, even the partials.

"Isn't it more likely than not that those prints will belong to Mark?" Avery said.

"Maybe. Maybe not. Nothing ventured, nothing gained."

Harrison held the device steady as a purple laser light slowly moved across the prints.

"There," Harrison said as he finished.

"Now what?"

"We wait until we hear back."

"Did you email them somewhere?"

Harrison returned the device to his pocket. "Something like that."

Avery moved to the secretary behind Mark's desk and opened a file drawer.

"What are you looking for now?" Harrison said.

"Answers."

"Thought you got those already. You know, the coin, and that enigma thingy, the trip he was planning."

Avery ignored him and began looking through file folders. She knew Mark had a habit of mixing business papers with personal ones.

"Harry, you think Greene really believes all that drug stuff?"

Harrison shrugged. "Who knows. He mentioned drugs, yet he has no idea how Mark died. He might be on to something. Probably knows this town better than we do."

Avery paused as she located a file labeled with Maggie's name. She removed the folder from the drawer and began scanning through the pages. The first few were emailed correspondence from Maggie to Hugo Wagner, the head of the German tech company that purchased Avery's app. Avery had never seen any of these emails. A quick check of the routing list showed why: neither she nor Mark were copied on any of them. After reading them, she understood: the revenue projections listed were two hundred percent greater than the numbers Mark's accountants had compiled for them.

"Whatcha got, Ave?" Harrison said.

"Nothing important," Avery said, quickly stuffing the file into her bag. Harrison would say that was just more proof Mark committed suicide. Avery knew better, and despite Harrison's best expert efforts, she was more convinced by the hour that Mark's death was no accident—and no suicide, either. Maybe Mark was hunting treasure and then planning a trip to Key West because it provided both adventure and excitement for him, and a safety net for them both if Daimler won this lawsuit. Mark was quirky and hard to read at times, but he was fair. Avery couldn't see him letting her lose everything while he hunted down a new source of wealth. Maybe he was even interested in exploring what they might be together, if he really wasn't involved with Julia.

Avery swallowed hard, trying not to think about the fact that Wagner might have a case if Maggie misled him. Her app taught nobodies with too much disposable cash how to pay their way to the front of the VIP line at A-list night spots by using maps, statistical analysis of crowd histories, and effective tip amounts—who would think that program would generate the kind of money projected in these messages?

Someone who'd pay twelve billion for the technology, maybe. But if a court sided with them and reversed the sale. . . . Nope. She couldn't even allow that possibility to creep into her thoughts. Not today. Today she had more important things to worry about than Maggie's lack of a moral compass, or Wagner's gullibility. She was going to find out what Mark was into that got him killed. And who was responsible.

Avery turned and marched out of the office. "Come on, Harry. Let's grab our bags."

"Where are we going now?"

"Antiquing."

15

"We have to strike while the iron is flaming here, C," Josh Shapiro said through Carter's phone.

Carter held the phone to his ear with one hand while holding an ice pack against the back of his throbbing head with the other. He was only half listening to the pleas of his agent, who was in full sales mode, as he stared out at the crystal blue water. Carter's thoughts were a swirling mess, mostly consumed by how many hours had to pass before he could take more Advil, Avery Turner, and how close he'd been to dying at the hands of real-life pirates just hours ago. A distant and slightly annoying fourth was Shapiro's habit of calling him "C," a nickname he couldn't recall approving.

"In case you need reminding, the masses have short attention spans and fickle loyalties," Shapiro continued. "TV doesn't come calling for internet sensations every day, even when they're as photogenic as you. Like it or not, my aquatic friend, you're the flavor of the month. We need to meet with the execs this week, C. Why are you balking?"

"Why?" Carter said. "I'll tell you why. Because none of this was supposed to happen to me. The house, the money, the growing pile of women's underwear showing up for the past several months in my daily mail. None of it. I'm a beach bum, Josh. I dive for the thrill of the chase. This is all getting too crazy."

The ocean life had been in Carter's blood for generations. His whole family had survived on brawn, not brains. After high school, which he barely finished, he spent the next decade only working when he had to. He lived for the next adrenaline rush. Sky diving, scuba, surfing, anything that provided the thrills he craved. And life had been more fun when it had only been about those thrills.

"Look, I know I've got bigger things to think about now. I get it, Josh. But I like setting my own schedule every day. If we move on this TV gig, I won't be able to."

"Why does your schedule matter so much?" Shapiro said. "You do realize this television deal could set you up for life, right? Do you have any idea how much they pay some of those reality show people? Then there's licensing, bigger sponsors, a book deal, maybe even a real acting gig. Sky's the limit."

"I'm doing pretty well, for the moment," Carter said. And he was. Owing to a combination of inheriting his mother's frugality, and a bit of sound investing on his part, he was well set already.

"Moments pass, C. Trust me. I've seen it. You've got something original going here, but this is the digital age. You know as well as I, if you don't move on this, there will be a dozen Carter wannabees out there in six months. Younger. Hotter. More ripped, more daring, you name it. And each one of them will be only too happy to steal a chunk of your sponsorship money. You gotta grab opportunity by the horns."

Carter paused to consider why a television opportunity would have horns. This conjured up the image of a large bull with the word "Opportunity" branded on its side. *Great*, he thought. *Now I'll be thinking about bulls all day.*

"You don't have any idea what wealth is, my young friend," Shapiro said.

Carter shook his head. Why was everyone so focused on money? His mind drifted back to the text message his brother Brady had sent while Carter was trying to talk his way out of being killed aboard the treasure hunter's boat.

I got 2 words for you, brochacho: Guacamole Stix
And 2 more: Green Gold #KeyFest #NewMenu

The money from a television deal would help his brother's restaurant survive whatever the heck a "guacamole stick" might be, anyway.

Carter knew how efficient agents like Shapiro were at making money for their clients. He also knew that whatever the deal, Shapiro would pocket fifteen percent. Did he really have Carter's best interest at heart, or was Shapiro counting on making himself rich? Was Shapiro looking out for him at all?

"There's more to life than money," Carter said.

"True story. But wealth sure makes the rest of it a whole lot easier to navigate."

And Carter might've been shark food right that moment if those guys, Vince and Burly and Shark Teeth, hadn't recognized him from Instagram. Maybe a bigger TV audience would give him a road out of bigger trouble— and Carter had never had a problem finding trouble.

He stood up from the deck chair and wandered inside through the open slider door. Jousting with Shapiro was making his headache worse. His agent continued talking but Carter pushed the noise to the background. He tossed the half-melted ice pack and his Ray-Bans atop the counter, then switched the cell to his other ear. His eyes locked on a framed black and white photograph hanging on the wall adjacent to the bar. Sitting astride their bikes in the foreground were much younger versions of himself and Brady. Seated directly behind them on the steps of their trailer was their mom, holding a Virginia Slims between two fingers. Key West didn't have train tracks, but if it had, the Mosleys clearly would have lived on the wrong side of them.

Avery seemed to be doing okay with her wealth, but then maybe she had come from money. He didn't really know that much about her. Maybe Shapiro was right. He should take the money and run. Carter leaned in close to the photo and took a long look at his nine-year-old self. What could that kid possibly ever know about stocks and mutual funds? Hell, he still considered a slice of convenience store pizza a treat.

And Carter knew he was a lousy actor, no matter what Shapiro said. Real actors can hide their feelings on camera. Carter couldn't. Whenever he wasn't feeling up to the day's shoot, it showed—the resulting video sucked.

"So, what do you think?" Shapiro said.

Carter hadn't heard a word his agent had said during the last several minutes. He considered telling him that, or that their connection had broken up, but he knew it would only encourage Shapiro to keep going.

"Give me another day to think on it, okay?"

"You're not just blowing me off, right? You're really gonna consider it?"

"I promise. Call me tomorrow."

"Okay. I'll hold you to that. I'm typing you into my calendar for 4:30."

"Perfect. Thanks, Josh."

Carter ended the call and flopped down on the camel-colored leather sofa. Maybe he was a better actor than he thought, since Shapiro bought his put-off. The truth was, Carter was already thinking of reasons why he wouldn't be available for tomorrow's conversation. He knew he had to decide something here, but he didn't think it needed to be today.

He reached for his laptop then opened the Instagram app to see how the newly posted video was doing. Three million views in five hours, and twenty thousand new followers—a ten percent performance increase over last month's video featuring his exploration of the *Tigershark*. Not too shabby. Carter did some quick mental math regarding the amount of money today's video had earned so far. It was more than his mother had made in a year—but he couldn't help wondering how a television contract would stack up against it.

The direct messaging tag increased by five as he perused the feed. After clicking the like button on a few things, he typed out a short comment on a follower's video of a dolphin pod. Even after years in the water, the playful mammals still made him smile.

He clicked over to the DMs. The first three were gushing comments about his latest dive video. Carter replied to each with a simple, "thank you." He never knew what else to say, but it felt rude to ignore people. The fourth direct message was a photo, clearly taken from a bit of a distance. Curiosity got the better of him, and he clicked on the image then zoomed in. His heart rate increased as he recognized himself and Avery on the deck of *The Deuce*. The shot was taken as they prepared for yesterday's dive. He backed out of the image then checked the sender's profile. Scorpio1234. No followers, no photos, aside from a single profile photo of a sunset over water. And the only account Scorpio1234 followed was Carter's. Were it not for the photo of him and Avery, Carter would have chalked it up to a bot or a fake account. Whoever this was had been following him in the real world, not just online. He flashed back to the memory of the other boater as he and Avery had surfaced from the wreck. He returned to the message screen. As he studied the photo, bouncing bubbles appeared below it. The bubbles meant that Scorpio1234 was online and typing another message. Carter stared at his screen, not even hazarding a blink.

She's in over her head, Mosley. If you try to help her, she will drown. I'll make sure of it.

Carter felt the throbbing in his head worsen as his blood pressure rose. Whoever this clown was, the threat was clearly meant for Avery. Carter had already run into his share of social media nutcases, but this was something else entirely. It just became personal.

He snapped a screenshot of the message and another of the enlarged photograph, then closed the app without replying. He could have responded with something trite like "who is this?" or the ever popular "GFY" but what would be the point? Engaging a crazy would only add fuel to whatever fire they carried.

He retrieved his cell and opened a text to Avery, but he couldn't think of what to say. Besides, it appeared from their last meeting that she already had enough on her plate. Calls from the police, now indirect threats from an anonymous Insta user. Just who was Avery Turner? First Shapiro, now Avery. Both seemed intent upon complicating his mostly uncomplicated life.

Just checking in, Avery. No need to respond.

Carter hit send.

16

Rocky Point looked exactly as Avery had pictured. Like most coastal towns in the Pine Tree State, the tiny hamlet overflowed with old-fashioned New England charm from the church steeples to the brick sidewalks and old-fashioned cast iron streetlights. Likely redesigned by town planners as a tourist destination, Rocky Point had managed to maintain the feel of a turn-of-the-century village even as its main street buildings and homes were repurposed into a shopper's paradise. There were gift boutiques, coffee shops, restaurants, art galleries, and several antique dealers. Avery could see why Mark fell so hard for its character.

After making an initial pass to size things up, Harrison parked the Corvette in a two-hour space at the far end of the street.

"What's the plan?" Harrison asked, grunting as he hoisted his bulky frame up and out of the sports car's cramped cockpit.

"How do you mean?" Avery said.

"Are we playing the tourist role or what? An unlikely couple hunting antiques?"

"What would I be in the scenario? Eye candy for a midlife crisis?"

"Hey," Harrison said, pretending to be wounded.

Avery laughed for the first time since learning of Mark's death.

"I'm not sure we could pull that off, Harry. Especially since they've probably seen us tooling around in Mark's car already. No, I'm thinking we play it straight up as soon as we find Mark's local connection."

"You know most of these places just sell knock offs, right? Tourist traps. Leave a wooden rocker in the back yard for a couple of seasons and it suddenly becomes a weathered but highly valued antique."

Avery knew Harrison had a point. The antique business was as vulnerable to unscrupulous dealers as any. But she also knew that most towns had at least one real expert, and the locals all knew who it was. It took them the better part of a half hour browsing the shops, and the cost of two large coffees and two blueberry scones to get the name of the dealer they were after.

David Adams, the proprietor of Coastal Fine Antiques, was the expert they had been seeking. Slight of build, with wavy salt and pepper hair, Adams wore bifocals and spoke with a slight hint of a British accent, adding an air of authority to every word. He certainly looked the part to Avery. She couldn't help wondering what Harrison was thinking.

"Of course I know Mark Hawkins," Adams said as his face lit up. "He is one of my most knowledgeable customers."

"Was," Harrison grumbled.

Avery shot him a look of disapproval before explaining to Adams that Mark had died.

"I am sorry to hear that, Ms. Turner. Were you close?"

"Yes, we were," Avery said, thinking about Mark's will and Detective Burke and a bottle of Percocet in a seedy motel room and wondering how much of that she had imagined.

Shaking the thought off and explaining the reason for their visit, Avery showed Adams photographs of the antiques in question, but intentionally held back any reference to the desk. "We were hoping you might be able to tell us something about the provenance of these pieces—particularly this engraving in the wardrobe."

"I am familiar with the wardrobe and the secretary." Adams pulled out and opened a folder with Mark's name on the tab. "Mark purchased both pieces though me. The wardrobe dates to 1798, imported from France by a plantation owner in South Carolina, but I'm afraid I know nothing about any markings inside it. The secretary was manufactured in Michigan in

1908 by the Tubbs Company, solid oak with narrow drawers used to store papers in print shops. I found it at an estate sale in Boston."

As Avery felt disappointment wash over her, Adams's face brightened and he held up a finger.

"Hang on a minute," Adams said. "I may have something that could help you."

Avery and Harrison watched as the dealer rifled through some papers on a wall-mounted shelf behind the counter.

"Here it is," Adams said as he held up a business card. He passed the card to Avery.

The name on the front of the card read Owen Masters. Below the name were the words fine cabinetry, and below that was a telephone number. Avery immediately recognized the Florida area code.

"Mark recently inquired about a restoration expert," Adams explained. "Mark would only work with the best. Masters is the best restoration and modification artist on the east coast."

"May I keep this?" Avery said.

"I'm afraid it's the only contact record I have, but I can write down his information for you."

"Thank you."

Adams carefully recorded the information on a Post-it note, then handed it to Avery.

Avery examined the note looking for similarities between Adams's writing style and the writing on the note recovered from Mark's hotel room. If Mark was the victim of foul play, every one of his contacts might be a suspect. The handwriting was too close to call. She couldn't be sure.

"Did Mark say why he was looking for a restoration expert?" Avery asked.

"He didn't, but I am savvy enough to know I wasn't the only source of Mr. Hawkins's antiques."

"What about the cross and lion?" Harrison said. "Show him the medallion, Ave."

Avery removed the coin from her pocket.

Adams pulled on a cloth glove before taking the coin and studying it under a magnifying lamp.

"Have you ever seen one of these?" Avery asked.

"I haven't."

"How about the symbol?" Harrison said.

"I'm not familiar with this particular symbol, however the lion and Latin cross are both part of the Spanish coat of arms. Spain is the likely origin. Where did you say you located this?"

"We didn't," Harrison said, earning another glare from Avery.

After a moment, Adams returned the coin to Avery. "Ms. Turner, I'm afraid I only deal in antique furniture and housewares, not stamps or coins."

"I don't suppose you'd know a reputable numismatist in the area," Avery said.

Adams squinted one eye as he considered it. "None that I can think of."

"Do you mind if we look around?" Avery said.

"By all means," Adams said. "Take your time, I need to return a telephone call anyway. Do let me know if you have any questions."

"Thanks."

Avery and Harrison wandered around the spacious showroom floor as far from Adams's office as possible.

"What are we doing, Ave?" Harrison said.

"Sizing Adams up."

"Why?"

"Because I think he knows more than he told us. For starters, he knows what a numismatist is."

"Great. He's got one on me then. What is it?"

"It's a coin collector, Harry. Not a word most people would recognize."

"Including me."

"And I think there's a reason he knows."

"Yeah, he does the crossword in the *New York Times*. Probably one of those geeky words every puzzle-head knows."

"My apologies for leaving you," Adams said as he rejoined them on the floor.

"This is beautiful," Avery said, faking interest in an expensive-looking sideboard.

"You have superb taste, Ms. Turner. That is a Hepplewhite. As you can see, it is in excellent condition for a piece of this age."

"Yowza." Harrison said as he took a quick glance at the price tag before dropping it like it was on fire.

"Hepplewhites command top dollar, Mr. Harrison."

"What makes it a Hepplewhite?" Harrison said.

"It is named for George Hepplewhite, a celebrated cabinet maker and designer from the UK. He died in the late 1700s. As you can plainly see, his craftsmanship was second to none. These pieces are some of the most highly sought after in the business."

"It is nice, I guess," Harrison said, causing Adams to scowl at his lack of appreciation.

Avery jumped in again. "I don't suppose you can tell us what the last piece Mark purchased from you was."

"Don't even have to look it up. It was a Queen Anne desk. Early seventeenth century. Gorgeous walnut with a leather top. You know most collectors I know are into a specific style or period, but not Mark Hawkins. He is —my apologies, was—all about the story behind the piece. Mark cared more about who owned it or where it had come from than its appearance. It made him a highly unusual collector in this business."

"Mark was always interested in the people part of history," Avery said. "I wonder how many tidbits he uncovered about that old inn."

"Oh, I can shed some light on that," Adams offered. "Mark and I delved into that extensively. The Hawk's Nest, originally known as the Smith House, was built by a confederate officer, rumored to have been a union sympathizer for the northern forces. It was alleged at the time that Smith might have been a spy who passed vital information to the Union army."

"Smith was his name?" Avery said.

"Let me guess," Harrison said. "John?"

"Indeed, it was," Adams said. "John Smith is the very name listed in the Rocky Point town records."

"Really?" Avery immediately thought about the initials J.S. marked on the ledger she'd found hidden beneath the floor in Mark's den, now in the tote bag locked safely in the trunk of the Corvette.

"Though, I always wondered if John Smith might have been an alias on account of the spy story," Adams said.

"I don't remember ever hearing about this chapter of the Civil War," Harrison said.

"Because it was never proven, Mr. Harrison. Had the confederacy won the war, Smith, or whoever he was, would have been tried and hung for treason. Personally, I've always thought it made perfect sense for someone like that to live in the middle of the Maine woods."

"The desk you said Mark bought last—can you remember if there were any unusual markings on the piece?" Avery asked.

"Honestly, I didn't look that closely because Mr. Hawkins located the desk himself. Another dealer down the coast was involved, but Mark asked me to act as his representative in the deal. I remember Mark was so excited to get it into his house that he had me arrange to pick it up for a Sunday delivery. Come to think of it, that shop also dabbles in rare coins. The owner might be able to help you. Her name is Williams. Louise Williams."

"Is it nearby?" Harrison asked.

"Newburyport, Massachusetts." Adams checked his watch. "And they close at 7:00."

Adams wrote down the business name and address before they departed.

"Are we really going to drive all the way to Massachusetts, Ave?" Harrison asked after they were back in Mark's Corvette.

"Of course not," Avery said. "We'd never make it in time."

"Good. A hot shower and about twelve hours of sleep in a big fluffy hotel bed would be perfect."

"We're flying to Massachusetts, Harry."

"How?"

"I texted Marco as we were leaving the shop. He's waiting for us at the Bangor International Airport all fueled and ready."

"Of course he is," Harrison said with a roll of his eyes.

Avery caught him checking the rear-view mirror again.

"What is it?" Avery said as she looked in the passenger side mirror. "The Nissan?"

"No. Black pickup, two back. Fell in right behind us not long after we left the antique shop."

"Coincidence?"

"Not likely. I saw the same truck parked down the street earlier when we were buying coffee and scones."

Avery turned and peered through the rear window. "I can see at least two people inside."

Harrison checked the fuel gauge then the road ahead. "I don't know exactly what we've gotten into, Ave, but we've got someone's attention. How far to the airport?"

Avery looked at the GPS on her phone. "Um, thirty miles, give or take. What are you thinking?"

"I'm thinking we lose these knuckleheads. You game?"

"Thought you were worried about getting in trouble with the local police."

"Let's just say after committing a burglary, and interfering with not one but two police investigations, I am rethinking my options."

Avery gave him a smirk. "Let 'er rip, Harry."

Harrison buried the throttle on the throaty-sounding Corvette, squawking the tires. The rapid acceleration of the high-performance car propelled them back into the leather bucket seats as they quickly passed the SUV directly in front of them.

"Man, oh, man," Harrison said. "I gotta get me one of these."

"Any idea what the penalty is for criminal speed?" Avery asked.

Harrison turned toward her, raising and lowering his eyebrows Groucho-style. "They gotta catch me first."

It didn't take long before the black pickup—and the rest of the traffic—were merely dots in the rearview.

It took them just over a half hour to reach Bangor International Airport's private departure terminal. Ten minutes later they were taxiing down the runway in Avery's Gulfstream. Harrison, who'd been awake all night keeping watch over Avery, was splayed out and snoring in a recliner long before they reached cruising altitude.

Avery powered up her laptop and ordered a rental car to be waiting for

them in New Hampshire at Portsmouth International Airport at Pease.
Next, she began scouring the internet for more answers.

Avery and Harrison arrived at the Newburyport antique shop at 6:35, an
antique bell mounted above the door announcing their entry. A smartly
dressed, white-haired woman was haggling with the lone customer over a
gilded Cheval mirror. Surprisingly perky for a man who had so little rest,
Harrison immediately fell into character as he pretended to browse the
showroom floor.

Avery stayed close to the action, admiring the mirror. She couldn't help
thinking how nice it would look on the wall in the sitting room at Hawk's
Nest. The man was attempting to talk the woman down twenty dollars
below the mirror's $250 asking price. As Avery listened to the conversation
drone on, she realized there was only one way to end the negotiations.

"I'll give you two-sixty," Avery said, causing the customer's mouth to
drop open in disbelief. "That's ten over asking."

The man's face reddened, and he sputtered for a moment before
offering two-seventy.

Avery bowed her head and stepped back.

"Sold, for two-seventy," the woman said.

While the man paid for the mirror, he continued to give Avery the stink
eye. As a consolation prize, Avery volunteered Harrison to carry the mirror
to the man's vehicle.

Following the men's departure, the woman eyed Avery through thick
bifocals, her green eyes sharp. "While I appreciate your help with my sale,
you aren't here shopping for a mirror, are you?"

"Guilty as charged," Avery said. "I'm looking for the owner of this shop,
Louise Williams."

"You found her. What can I do for you, Mrs. . . . ?"

"Ms. Turner. I'm looking for information on a piece you recently sold."
Avery pulled up one of the cell phone photos of the desk from Mark's home
office and turned the screen toward her. "I'm wondering if you might know
its history."

The bell chimed again as Harrison returned to the shop.

Williams's brow furrowed as she looked up from the phone. She looked back and forth between Avery and Harrison before saying anything. It was obvious that she was sizing them up.

"That desk came from an estate sale in Martha's Vineyard. It was beautifully cared for and needed little work. The buyer found it online, I only acted as the middle woman on the sale. The purchase was handled by another dealer up the coast in Maine. His client paid well over market value."

Avery considered this for a moment. Mark was a tech guy, and a tough negotiator. Why wouldn't he have emailed Mrs. Williams and brokered his own deal? The obvious answer was that Mark had been looking to remain anonymous. But still, Adams would have known. Would Mark have put that much trust in a dealer he had known for less than a year? Nothing about this made sense.

"Excuse me a moment while I lock up," Williams said as she made her way to the front door and locked it. She flipped the sign in the window from open to closed then returned to the counter.

"Can you tell us anything about the desk itself?" Avery asked. "Like how old it was?"

"The dealer said the family had records that dated the piece back before the revolution."

"Was there anything unusual about it?"

Williams shook her head. "I only saw it for a few minutes after it came in that Friday. As I said, it appeared to be in very good condition. We wrapped it for shipping. The other dealer had it picked up the very next morning."

"Was it original, or had it been restored?"

"There are some incredible restoration artists out there, Ms. Turner, but I couldn't see where any work had been done. But like I said, I only saw it briefly."

"Can you tell us anything more about the estate sale on Martha's Vineyard?"

Williams paused a moment before rifling through a stack of papers behind the counter. "Here it is. The family name is Madison."

Avery caught a glance at the page, noticing a familiar name, E. Corbacho, scribbled on a sticky note attached to the paper. "I don't suppose you acquired any other pieces from the estate sale?"

"Just one. An old vanity from the 1890s. Had some damage to the top. It isn't here now."

"Were there any other inquiries about specific pieces from that estate sale?" Avery asked, trying to remember where she'd seen the name Corbacho.

The woman's eyes narrowed. "Why are you asking all these questions?"

Avery exchanged a quick glance with Harrison.

"Did you folks purchase the desk?" Williams asked.

"No, the desk belongs—belonged to a friend of mine," Avery said. "I don't suppose you know anything about a lion and cross symbol?" Avery said.

Williams didn't respond to the question, but tipped her head to one side and gave Avery a look she couldn't quite read.

"If there's anything at all you could tell us about that symbol, it might help," Avery pressed. "Does it mean anything to you?"

With surprising agility for a woman of advanced age, Williams pulled a pump shotgun from beneath the counter, chambered a round, then leveled it at Avery's chest.

17

For the second time in less than twelve hours, Avery watched as Harrison instinctively reached for the gun on his hip—a gun that wasn't there. Avery slowly raised her hands—attempting to calm the woman—even as her brain raced to figure out what they might have said, or done, that set her off. Avery decided that coming clean was their best option for escaping in one piece.

"The man who purchased the desk was a close friend of mine and he's dead," Avery said. "His name was Mark."

Williams's hard expression softened slightly. She kept the gun trained on Avery but eased her finger away from the trigger. "How did he die?"

"I think someone may have killed him."

"Who would want to kill your friend?"

Harrison spoke up, "Judging by the weapon you're holding, I think we might be on the right trail."

"I had nothing to do with your friend's death," Williams said, her eyes flitting between Avery and Harrison.

Harrison took a step toward the counter, "Might be easier to believe if you weren't threatening us with a shotgun."

Williams swung the barrel of the gun until it was pointed directly at Harrison. "Not another step."

"We only came here looking for answers," Avery said. "We thought you might be able to help us."

Williams kept the gun pointed at Harrison, but her eyes returned to Avery.

"I don't know your friend Mark, and I don't know you. Let's see some ID, from both of you."

Avery reached for her wallet and removed her driver's license.

"Set it on the counter," Williams said. After Avery complied, the woman looked to Harrison. "Now you. Take out your ID and hand it to Ms. Turner. Slowly."

Harrison retrieved his ID then handed it to Avery. Avery set Harrison's license on the counter beside hers, then raised her hands again.

Williams moved forward slightly as she read their identifications.

"Key West?" Williams said. "You're a long way from home."

Avery nodded. "I'm just trying to figure out what happened to my friend."

Williams nodded in Harrison's direction. "And you need hired muscle for that?"

"While I appreciate the backhanded compliment, I am not hired muscle. Yes, I work for Avery now, but I was once her mother's partner on the job."

"What job?"

"NYPD, fifth precinct. Her mother and I were homicide detectives."

She glanced back at the IDs. "All I see is a Florida driver's license. If you were a detective, where's your badge?"

"May I?" Harrison said as he lowered his hands again.

"Careful."

Harrison flipped open the ID case, revealing his retired NYPD gold shield. "Satisfied?"

"You armed now?" Williams said.

"If I were, we wouldn't be having this conversation," Harrison growled.

"He's telling the truth, Louise," Avery said. "He isn't carrying."

"Lift your jacket and turn around."

Harrison did as she asked.

"Satisfied?"

"Now your pant legs. I know some of you carry those ankle holsters."

Again, Harrison complied.

Williams took one last look at Avery, then lowered the barrel of the gun but maintained her grip on it. "You probably think that I'm over-reacting."

"A bit," Avery said. "Did we do something to spook you?"

"Ever since I got involved with the sale of that desk, things have been weird. I've been followed. Even had a strange man come in here asking questions."

"Were you threatened?"

"Not in so many words. It wasn't what he said, it was the menacing way he said it. I don't feel safe anymore. You say your friend died?"

"Mark. The police are calling it an overdose."

"But you think he was murdered."

Avery nodded. "Mark didn't use drugs."

"What brought you here? I assume you found something."

"May I?" Avery said, gesturing to the cell phone in her pocket.

"Go ahead."

Avery pulled up a photo of the coin she had removed from Mark's desk at the inn.

"We found this hidden inside a desk that belonged to Mark's grandfather."

The old woman's eyes lit up with recognition as she eyed the coin. A moment later she returned the gun to its place under the counter.

"You make sure the safety's on?" Harrison said.

"It isn't loaded," Williams said.

Harrison exhaled an audible sigh of relief.

Williams looked at them a moment before speaking. "Your friend's last name was Hawkins, wasn't it?"

"Yes," Avery said. "But how—I thought you didn't know the buyer's name?"

"Adams told me who it was. And Mark wasn't his real given name, was it?"

Avery glanced at Harrison, then shook her head. "No, it wasn't. But how do you know that?"

"Would someone mind telling me what the hell is going on here?" Harrison said.

Williams came around from behind the counter and headed toward the rear of the store. "Come on. I want to show you something."

They followed her into a cramped office at the rear of the showroom.

"Did Mark ever visit you in Florida?" Williams asked.

"No. He was busy restoring an inn in Maine. He was so excited about sharing his new project with me. I was supposed to see it next week, but—well, you know."

"Did he say it like that? His new project? Not the inn."

"As a matter of fact, he did. I'd assumed he meant the inn."

"Ms. Turner, I think your friend may have been working on another project entirely."

Williams plopped down at an antique roll top desk that was piled high with books and invoices. Avery and Harrison watched as she turned on a lamp and began rifling through one of the stacks.

"Here it is," she said before turning and handing Avery an old, yellowed newspaper clipping.

Harrison cleared off a wooden chair for Avery to sit on, then stood beside her.

The article, dated 1973, was cut from the Charleston newspaper. As Avery read, her jaw dropped open. The subject of the story was a man named Marion Hawkins, a naval captain and decorated hero of WWII, who became a treasure hunter after the war. Hawkins was leading an expedition in search of lost treasure when his vessel went down in a storm off the Carolina coast, killing everyone on board. Hawkins was rumored to have been searching for General Brent Oswald's gold, a fabled fortune of the Confederacy that disappeared during the war—if it ever existed—and had spawned dozens of stories and theories about its loss and location. It was clear from the black and white photograph that Mark was the perfect likeness of his grandfather.

Harrison read along with Avery over her shoulder. "Marion?" he said. "Tell me that wasn't Mark's real given name."

Avery nodded. "He had it legally changed years ago."

"I can see why," Harrison said.

"Did Mark ever talk about his grandfather?" Williams asked.

"Idolized him. He knew all about his grandfather's navy exploits."

"But he never mentioned the treasure hunting?"

"No, he didn't," Avery said. "Not to me." She couldn't help but wonder what else Mark hadn't shared with her. In two days, so much of what she had been certain of was in question, Avery realized she really didn't know Mark as well as she had thought.

"You honestly believe someone murdered Mark Hawkins?"

Avery looked at Harrison. "Harry?"

Harrison squirmed uncomfortably before answering. "Given what we know about Mark, yeah, his death does seem suspicious."

Avery passed the newspaper clipping back to Williams. "Do you think there's a connection between this treasure and Mark's death?"

Williams removed an ancient hardcover book from the musty pile stacked on the floor beside her desk. She flipped through the pages until she found what she was looking for, then handed it to Avery.

"Take a look at the drawing," Williams said.

Avery's eyes widened with recognition. The page featured an artist's rendering of a coin identical to the one Avery had pried out of Mark's desk. The desk previously owned by Captain Marion Hawkins.

"The picture of a coin you showed me was believed to have been part of General Oswald's missing treasure," Williams said.

"Proving what exactly?" Harrison asked.

"That the treasure existed. It is widely believed that those coins were minted specifically to keep track of the treasure. An unknown number of them were said to have been included inside each of the missing trunks, along with other valuables. Stories about this treasure, and what it might have meant for the war, have been retold for more than a hundred and sixty years."

"How many trunks were there?" Avery said.

"If the stories are true, as many as a dozen. Did you really find one of these coins?"

Avery pulled the coin from her pants pocket and handed it to the woman. She watched as the woman carefully examined the coin, holding it under the desk lamp and turning it over.

"Do you have any idea how many people are actively searching for this treasure?"

"How many?" Avery said.

"I know of at least a half dozen outfits hunting for it. And I'm sure I don't know about all of them."

"The more the merrier," Avery said with more bravado than she felt. What chance did she and Harrison have of finding something quasi-professional treasure outfits were struggling to locate?

"I don't understand how people find this such an interesting pastime," Harrison said.

"Because there's a great deal of money to be made, *if* you know what you're doing."

Recalling a comment Carter had made about treasure hunters being more dangerous than sharks, Avery made a mental note to learn everything she could about the missing treasure. And if Marion Hawkins believed that the treasure had sunk in the ocean, it might be time to see if Carter would have any interest in joining the hunt. He was, after all, the only diver she knew and trusted. Then again—Mark was dead, and she and Carter were getting to be friends, but they weren't anywhere near "die for the same cause" kind of friends. Maybe calling him wasn't such a bright idea.

"Why would Mark Hawkins care about any of this?" Harrison said. "He already had billions."

But he might have worried he was on the verge of losing them. Avery didn't say that out loud.

"It might not have been about money at all, Harry," Avery said, telling herself it could be true. "Mark may have simply wanted to finish what his grandfather started. I mean, the man was Mark's hero, and he gave his life trying to find that treasure."

The room was silent for a long moment as the irony of Avery's words hung in the air. Mark had never mentioned this bit of Hawkins family lore, but surely he knew how the grandfather he idolized had died, especially if it was in the paper. Again, Avery wondered what else Mark had never told her.

Finally, Williams spoke up. "It may have been about the money too."

"How much could a few coins like that be worth?" Harrison scoffed.

"There were a lot more than just a few," Williams said. "If the stories are true, the treasure could be worth as much as seventy-five to a hundred billion by today's standards."

Harrison whistled. "That's a lot of motive."

"People have been known to kill for a lot less," Williams said.

"And the standard finder's fee is twenty percent?" Avery said.

"Assuming the finder reports it," Williams said. "A black-market sale to a private collector could garner as much as fifty percent, if it didn't get you killed first. Treasure hunters are a cutthroat lot."

"Maybe the treasure has already been found," Avery said. "How would you know?"

"Trust me. I would know." Williams looked directly into Avery's eyes. "You need to be incredibly careful about what you're getting yourself into, young lady. There are people who will stop at nothing to find this treasure."

"And just how is it that you happen to know so much about this missing treasure?" Harrison said as he snatched the coin back from the woman and returned it to Avery.

Williams grinned. "I'll show you."

18

Samael was mentally wrestling with the call he had just received from one of his people on the ground. The crew had lost their targets—the targets being Avery Turner and the ex-cop, Harrison.

Despite the direction Samael's life had taken following his military service and his time in the intelligence community, some habits were so deeply ingrained in his nature that he was powerless to stop them. Things like clasping his hands behind his back while awaiting his superior, his use of the word sir, and maintaining an impeccable appearance. Details mattered.

During the call Samael had maintained an even and low-key tone in his responses, a skill he had mastered over the course of many years. Projecting an outward calmness to mask the maelstrom within was an effective way of keeping his enemies off balance, making retribution far easier. Samael had told the man that he was most distressed by the failure. There were several things he wanted to say, things like: How could you lose two people driving a bright blue sports car in a thinly populated state completely unfamiliar to the target? The man who had failed him had been lulled into thinking that Samael was merely disappointed. But the truth was that this man, and the man assisting him, would never fail anyone again. Samael would personally see to it.

Samael unlocked his cell and hit the speed dial. It was time for an update from his southern connection.

His contractor answered the call without fanfare. "I wondered when I would hear from you."

"What have you learned about Carter Mosley?" Samael asked.

"He is nothing more than an adrenaline junkie. Teaches scuba diving, sky diving, and pretends to be a treasure hunter."

"Pretends?"

"Yes, sir. He's a social media influencer. Through blind luck and good looks, Mosley has amassed a formidable following by posting his dive videos to Instagram."

"And advertisers pay top dollar for access to those followers." That explained Mosley's money. "What is the subject of Mosley's dive videos?"

"He dives shipwrecks."

"But you just said he isn't a treasure hunter."

"He isn't. He talks about sunken treasure in his diving videos, but it's a gimmick. Mosley hasn't reported a single find of his own. His videos are documentaries of wrecks that others have previously located. He cashes in on other people's finds via his online popularity."

"How exactly did Mr. Mosley connect up with Ms. Turner?" Samael said.

"They live near each other in the Florida Keys. Their relationship appears to be nothing more than two nouveau riche Gen Zers, with too much time and money, who have started spending time together."

"But they are diving together, correct?"

"They are. Mosley has been instructing her."

"You're confident that they're just diving for recreation? No other purpose?"

"I am," the contractor said.

Samael didn't share the man's confidence. Avery's newfound interest in scuba diving was troubling. The timing was suspicious given her connection to Mark Hawkins.

"I want you to keep a close eye on Mosley," Samael said. "Where he goes and what he does while he's there."

"Alright."

"And let's send him a warning."

"What kind of warning?"

"I'll leave that to you. But I want the message to be clear enough that Mosley won't be inclined to indulge any treasure hunting fantasies Ms. Turner might approach him about."

"I'll take care of it."

19

Using an electronic fingerprint reader, Louise Williams accessed a hidden compartment at the bottom of her office safe. She removed several trays of expensive-looking antique jewelry, revealing a gold coin that looked exactly like the one Avery had pried out of the desk belonging to Mark's grandfather. Avery gasped as she leaned forward for a closer look.

"You asked me how I know so much about the lost treasure," Williams said. "My father was a historian who specialized in maritime history. I suppose, like many others, my father became obsessed with the stories of this treasure and what it might have meant to history had it not been lost."

"You must have a greater connection to this than just that your father was into it," Harrison said, waving a hand at the drawer holding the coin.

"My father, Benedict Williams was on Marion Hawkins's boat when it went down. Like Hawkins, Benny gave his life trying to recover the treasure."

Avery extended her hand, her eyes on the coin. "May I?"

Williams handed the coin to Avery.

Avery felt a sense of awe as she held another coin from the lost treasure in her hand. For the second time that day.

"Truth be told," Williams continued, "my father's pursuit was the primary reason I got into the antiques business. Guess I imagined other clues might surface, eventually."

Avery studied the coin, comparing it to Mark's. It didn't take long for her to discover that there was one major difference. "Your coin was minted with a different Roman numeral," Avery said. "Mark's coin has a II but yours has an XI on it."

"I wonder why the different numbers?" Harrison mused.

"I'm not positive," Williams said, "but I believe it might add validity to the story that there were a dozen trunks in all."

"How so?" Avery said.

Williams pointed to Mark's coin. "To date only five of these have been recovered, yours being the fifth. Except for the one my father possessed, each of the others bore the Roman numeral two, like the one you found."

"Meaning?" Harrison said.

"Meaning they all came from the same trunk. My father's had to have come from a different trunk."

"Trunk number eleven," Avery said.

"Precisely," Williams said. "I told you that the coins were placed in each of the trunks as a way of keeping track of them. My father was convinced that the coins were intentionally minted with twelve different numbers."

Harrison looked at the books that were stacked next to Williams. "Are those all about this so-called lost treasure?"

"They are," Williams said.

"On the off chance that we don't have time to read them, and given the fact that people seem willing to kill anyone who attempts to insert themselves in this hunt, maybe you could give us a recap of exactly what we're dealing with?"

"The original treasure was said to have been smuggled out of Spain in the late 1770s, during the early part of the Revolutionary War. If you recall your history, throughout the war Benjamin Franklin and John Adams spent a great deal of time in France."

Avery jumped in, "Weren't they over there trying to convince Louis to join us in the fight against England?"

"Louis didn't need much convincing. And what Franklin and Adams really needed was money."

Harrison nodded. "That's true. The continental army was flat broke."

Avery couldn't help but smile as Harrison's inner history buff peeked out.

Williams waved a dismissive hand. "The founding fathers knew the soldiers fighting for freedom would fight whether they were broke and starving or not. They were sick and tired of British oppression and lack of representation from King George."

"Then why waste the efforts of two of America's most brilliant negotiators, a whole ocean away?" Avery asked.

"Building a nation takes money—a lot of it. They knew that even if they won, they didn't have the resources it would take to get our American experiment off the ground. This treasure was their way of ensuring the success of the country they were trying to build."

Harrison nodded as Williams spoke but raised a skeptical brow. "And after all this time nobody has located it?" He asked. "How do you know if any of these stories are even real?"

"Some of it has been found," Avery said, as she held up Mark's coin and pointed to the one in Williams's hand.

"Alas, these few coins do not a treasure make," Williams said. "But they do tend to support its existence."

"How did your father come by his coin?" Avery asked.

"My father won it in a card game in Richmond during prohibition. The man he took it from told him he found it working in a mine."

"And the rest of it?" Harrison said. "How does one simply lose a treasure that valuable?"

"Who said it was lost?" Williams said as she returned the coin to the hidden compartment and the trays of jewels to the safe before securing it.

"I don't understand," Avery said.

"I believe the treasure may have been hidden, intentionally, and then moved again during the Civil War."

"Where?" Avery said.

"Some speculate that the general's gold—whether they mean Washington or Oswald—is underwater, in a ship that sank, either during the revolution or in the waning days of the civil war, depending on who you ask, off the Atlantic coast or in the Florida Keys." Williams sighed before continuing. "The legend has endured for centuries, growing with each generation. I have seen lives wasted searching, yet, apart from a few gold coins, nothing has been recovered."

"So, do you believe that?" Avery said.

"No," Williams said. "I have a different theory."

Harrison leaned forward. "And that is?"

"It's gone. Pissed away. Maybe even gambled away. Men are greedy by nature, even men who have greatness in them. The founding fathers, regardless of what history has turned them into, were mortal men." Williams looked directly at Harrison. "You were a policeman. What happens to a fortune that only a few people know about?"

"You mean like proceeds from a robbery? The coconspirators usually start infighting and picking away at it until it's gone."

"My point exactly."

"But what about the war effort?" Avery held out her hands in a *look around you* gesture. "Or the construction of our democracy? America did happen, after all."

"Alexander Hamilton taught the US early on how to leverage debt. Once that happened, foreign treasure was no longer vital to the survival of the union. I believe a chunk of it wound up in Virginia, perhaps even helped fund the confederacy, but anyone who thinks there's enough of it left now to amount to anything is a fool."

"Then why was Mark killed?" Avery asked with conviction she wouldn't have had about her friend's fate before this little old lady pulled a gun on them.

"I said they were fools. I never said they weren't dangerous. Some people refuse to accept failure." Williams glanced at the antique clock on the wall. "I need to go home now." She stood and led them back to the front of the store.

As Avery and Harrison stepped out onto the sidewalk, Williams apologized for brandishing the shotgun.

"My advice to both of you is to go home. Forget that you ever saw any gold coins or symbols. Trust me, nothing good will come of pursuing this further."

"But—" Avery began.

"Good night," Williams said as she shut the door and locked it.

"Well, that was fun," Harrison grumbled.

"She kicked us out awfully abruptly," Avery said, her mind racing as she scanned the area for any signs they were being followed. She knew Harrison was doing the same as they walked back to the rental car.

"So, it's back to the Hawk's Nest then?" Harrison asked as they climbed inside the SUV.

"Do you believe a word of what that woman said, Harry?"

Harrison shrugged. "Don't know. Some of it I guess."

"And the treasure? Do you believe it's just gone?"

Harrison sighed deeply. "No, I guess I don't. If it ever really existed it must still be out there, or else we wouldn't have people following us and little old ladies pointing shotguns at us. She told us what she had to in order to find out how much we already know, and to make us believe her."

"That's what I think too."

"You're not gonna let this go, are you?" Harrison said as he started the car.

"Nope."

"Where to then?"

"Tonight, we find a comfy hotel in Boston."

"With hot showers and big comfortable beds?"

"Yes, Harry. We both need a good night's sleep."

"Amen to that. And tomorrow?"

"Tomorrow we're off to Martha's Vineyard to hunt for treasure."

"Why there?"

"I want to pay a visit to the home that Mark's new desk came from. Whoever killed Mark was after that treasure. And I'm going to make sure they never collect a single piece of it."

Avery watched Harrison's reaction to her assertion that Mark had been murdered. His face was easy for her to read—he didn't exactly believe it, but she could tell he was more open to the possibility than he'd been the day before. And she knew him well enough to know he probably thought letting her think there was a killer on their trail would make her more cautious.

She wasn't sure she agreed, though.

Harrison sighed. "And how exactly are you planning to keep them from it?"

"You and I are going to find it first."

"I was afraid you might say that. You know you inherited every bit of your mother's stubborn streak, right?"

Avery smiled as she punched the hotel address into the dashboard GPS. "I'll take that as a compliment."

20

Static crackled in Carter's headphones as the pilot radioed that they were at ten thousand feet and nearing the jump site. He stood and turned toward a handful of students. A quick check of their faces revealed a combination of excitement and nervousness, exactly what he had come to expect after a week of tandem jumps in preparation for their first solo skydive.

"Everybody ready?" he said, giving a thumbs up and shouting to be heard above the engine noise coming through the open door on the starboard side of the fuselage.

Five enthusiastic thumbs rose in answer to his question. Only one student was slow to respond. Arthur. The freckle-faced boy had blanched white and looked like he was about to lose his lunch. Carter could have guessed it would be Art, the closest thing this class had to a know-it-all. He had seen that false bravado many times before. Students projecting gravitas that vanished as soon as they realized they would no longer be tethered to an instructor.

Carter signaled the students to move toward the open door where a second instructor, who went by the nickname Kiwi, was awaiting them. As each student passed, Carter checked their straps and chute packs for the third time, confirming that their gear was snug and free from obstructions. Safety and redundancy were practiced by the staff and hammered into the minds of the students during the week-long class. Though the thrill of solo skydiving was second to none, and the goal for each diver, there was an inherent danger that came with jumping out of a perfectly good airplane.

The light on the bulkhead that separated the cockpit from the cabin changed from standby yellow to jump green.

"It's go time," Carter shouted.

Two at a time, the students sat on the floor in the open doorway, legs wrapped tightly under the belly of the plane, arms crossed over their chests, hands grasping the pack straps, just as they'd been taught. Carter and Kiwi simultaneously tapped the students on the shoulders and watched them lean forward and fall free from the plane. He couldn't help but be reminded of the similarities between the two distinct kinds of diving. Whether it was entering the sky, or the ocean, the execution was the same. As was the feeling of absolute freedom.

Without hesitation the next two students quickly moved into position and followed their classmates into the sky. Finally, the last two dropped onto their butts and prepared to dive. The student next to Art leaned out and dropped free of the plane as instructed, but Art froze. Carter nodded to the other instructor to go, signaling that he would stay with Art. After Kiwi dove out the door, Carter took a seat next to the scared student.

"You don't have to do this, Art. It's entirely up to you."

Carter could see the wheels turning as the boy watched his classmates. One by one, the bright chutes blossomed far below under a cloudless sky.

"I'm gonna do it!" Art shouted.

"You sure?" Carter said. Before he could utter another word Art leaned forward and fell from the plane.

Carter hesitated a beat, then followed the boy.

At first, everything seemed okay. Carter drew to within several hundred feet of the boy, waiting for him to deploy his chute. But nothing happened. Carter flipped over until he was facedown like a diver. His speed increased as he moved lower and closer to Art.

The boy frantically clawed at his ripcord, his eyes as wide as dinner plates.

Carter changed positions again. This time he rolled onto his belly and raised his legs up behind him, quickly closing the distance. He grabbed onto the front of Art's pack straps and faced him. He did his best to keep his voice flat as he yelled over the wind.

"You're safe, okay? No matter what, I got you."

The student continued to fail and kick, his struggling ripping the straps from Carter's grip. The boy was free falling on his back now, forgetting everything he had been taught as panic set in.

"Dammit," Carter shouted as he dove again.

They were much too close to the ground for Carter's liking, having long since passed the other students, drifting safely high above them. This time Carter went directly for Art's rip cord. He grabbed and pulled but the cord didn't budge. Carter wrapped one arm around the struggling boy and yanked on the cord with all his might. The nylon cord snapped off in his hand. Before the boy could drift away again Carter moved around to face him.

"Hang on, Art. I gotcha."

The panicked teen latched onto Carter's neck, choking off his air supply. Carter glanced at the rapidly approaching ground. No time for other options, Carter slid an arm under the boy's shoulder straps then deployed his own chute. The nylon expanded with a *whoosh*, immediately slowing their descent. Carter fought against the increased pressure of gravity as it threatened to pry the boy out of his grasp. With one hand, Carter attempted to steer them toward the ocean and as close to the sandy beach as possible. The water would mitigate their impact, saving both from severe injury, but Carter couldn't discount the possibility of drowning either.

He glanced at the boy in hopes that he might calm down and relax his hold on him, but it was obvious that Art was still too panicked for rational thought.

They splashed down harmlessly into the water. The waves had the desired effect as the boy released his death grip on Carter's neck. Art sputtered and coughed out salt water until he realized that the water was shallow enough to stand in. Carter unclipped his own pack, so it didn't drag him under, then helped the boy to shore. The two of them staggered up onto the sand just as the first of their group came running from a nearby meadow, the designated landing zone.

It only took a few moments for Art's cocky persona to return. As Carter helped him out of the harness, removing his drenched pack, the boy began to regale his classmates with a slightly modified version of his near-death experience. In Art's version he remained calm and cool as he assisted Carter in the rescue attempt. Carter shook his head, ignoring the yarn being spun, and moved a short distance away. His focus returned to Art's chute and ripcord. The pack had clearly been tampered with—the spring was missing, and the nylon cord had been cleanly sliced nearly completely through, while the remainder was stretched and frayed where it had broken when Carter pulled on it.

Kiwi ran up to Carter. "Dude, that was some crazy hero stuff. You saved that kid's life."

Carter cast an eye toward the nearby gathering of students where Art continued his fictional account. "Depends on who you ask."

"What's up with the chute?"

Carter held the pack up for him to see. "Someone cut the ripcord."

"Holy crap. Who'd want to do that?"

"I was going to ask you the same thing. Only the instructors pack these chutes, and I didn't pack this one."

"Let me see it."

Carter handed him the chute.

"I didn't pack this one either," Kiwi said, running a thumb over the clean-cut edge on the ripcord. "This would have been easy to miss checking the chutes. It's only cut part of the way through, so it would break off in his hand when he tried to pull it. But if you didn't pack this one, and I didn't pack this one, who did? You think somebody has it in for you?"

Carter was wondering the very same things. The instructors always took great care, packing everyone's chute as if they were packing their own. Yet it looked like somebody may have intentionally sabotaged his student's gear, nearly costing the boy his life.

"Or one of the other students has it in for Art."

"We should call the cops, Carter."

"And tell them what? That we run a seat-of-our-pants sky diving business and someone almost died today? We'll never sign up another student."

"Then what do you suggest?"

"Keep it under your hat for now. We can talk to the other instructors. Be extra vigilant. Triple check everything. If the kid's parents come knocking, it was just an equipment malfunction."

"No way, man. I'm not gonna be held responsible if something else happens. I say we go to the police with this."

More than being legally responsible, Carter did enjoy being able to sleep peacefully at night. He'd never forgive himself if they kept this quiet and someone got hurt. "Yeah, okay. You're right. You have a buddy at the PD, don't you?"

Kiwi nodded. "We go way back. He can poke around and keep it quiet. I'll hit him up on my way home."

Carter stood and slung the pack over his shoulder as the attention of the students turned to him.

"That was so awesome, Mr. Mosley!" said one student.

"Nice job," said another.

The back slaps and praise continued as the group moved toward the pick-up van.

As they walked, Carter replayed the sequence of events that led up to the jump. Was it possible that one of the other students did have issues with Art? Enough to kill for? Or had Carter himself been the target? The latter actually made more sense with a minute to consider it, because the identical chutes had been hanging in a row in the hangar, unlabeled, with no way for anyone to know who would get which one. But Carter was the lead instructor on this jump—even if he hadn't grabbed the sabotaged chute, he'd have been ruined by the kind of accident whoever cut that cord was trying to cause. Goodbye students, goodbye sponsors, definitely goodbye TV offers and agents.

Occasional brushes with death were par for the course when a person chased adrenaline the way Carter did—but this made the second day in a row that someone had nearly killed him. Attempted murder was not an everyday occurrence—not an any day occurrence, until yesterday, in fact— and Carter aimed to keep it that way. The treasure hunters the day before were serious about not letting anyone steal their finds, but they didn't strike him as the kind of guys who'd hunt him down and try sabotaging a rather random parachute. If they had wanted him dead, they could have fed him to the sharks yesterday. No, this was something else entirely. Crazy Internet troll? Someone Brady owed money to and didn't want to tell him about? No way to tell. Maybe he should talk with Kiwi's cop friend, too.

Avery Turner popped into Carter's head again just as his phone vibrated with an incoming text message from her.

U ever c anything like this on 1 of your dives?

A photo of a gold coin appeared on screen a moment later. Carter nearly dropped his phone. What was Avery into? He thought back to the Instagram message about not helping her. Was this about treasure? Was the cut cord another not-so-subtle warning? Carter flashed back to the strange boat he and Avery had seen after diving *Isabella's Dream*. Someone was following them.

Carter typed a reply.

No. Where r u?

Avery didn't immediately answer.

"You okay, my brother?" Kiwi said, clapping him on the back and startling him.

"Yeah, all good."

"Great. Let's get these kids back to the hangar."

As Carter walked around to the van's passenger door, he checked his cell one last time. Avery had gone silent.

21

It was late by the time Avery and Harrison arrived at the Boston Harbor Hotel, and unlike the dark and uninviting accommodations they had found at the Hawk's Nest, this hotel's front door was unlocked and its lights were burning brightly.

After handing over the rental to an enthusiastic young valet, Avery and Harrison dragged their bags and their exhausted bodies across the lobby to the registration desk where a dark-haired young woman greeted them.

"Welcome to the Harbor Hotel. May I help you?"

"Yes," Harrison said, speaking up before Avery could. "I need a long hot shower, minibar, and about twelve hours of uninterrupted sleep."

The woman grinned as Avery slid her ID and credit card across the counter.

"I reserved a two-bedroom suite under the name Turner," Avery said.

Several keystrokes later, they were tucked into an elevator on their way to the top floor.

Though she wouldn't admit it, Avery was every bit as exhausted as Harrison. The only thing keeping her going was the extra-large Dunkin' coffee she had purchased en route from Newburyport, and thoughts of tomorrow's trip to Martha's Vineyard.

"You excited about our trip to the island tomorrow?" Avery asked as they exited the elevator and walked down the hall toward their room.

"I'll be excited after I get some shut-eye. Have you ever been there?"

"Nope. You?"

"Yeah, your mother and I caught a case that took us out there about ten years ago."

"Is it nice?" Avery asked as she swiped the keycard across the electronic door lock.

Harrison grinned knowingly. "Nothing says money like Martha's Vineyard, Ave."

She pushed the door open then stepped inside and gave a whistle. "Except maybe this place, Harry."

"Definitely not the Holiday Inn," Harrison said as he dropped Avery's bags on the bed in the larger of the two bedrooms. "Shower time. I'll join you in the living room for a nightcap. Assuming I don't turn into a prune first."

A half hour later, after showering and changing into her PJs and a plush hotel robe, Avery was seated on a chaise in the living room near a large window overlooking Boston harbor. She had her computer in her lap reading up on Martha's Vineyard when Harrison walked in. He wore sweatpants and a badly faded New York Giants sweatshirt.

"No robe?" Avery said.

"I thought it might clash with my ensemble."

"How old is that thing, Harry?" she asked with a laugh.

"My lucky G-men shirt? Older than you."

"Let's hope it brings us some luck tomorrow."

"Now we're talking," Harrison said as he wandered over to the well-stocked bar cart. "This must be why they call this the presidential suite. Might I interest you in a night cap, m'lady?"

"Thank you, Harry. That would be grand."

The clinking of ice in glasses as Harrison prepared their drinks faded into the background as Avery's attention was drawn to Carter's last text message.

No. Where r u?

Avery typed a response. *2 bad. I was hoping you'd seen them scattered like confetti on the ocean floor. LOL H and I are in Boston 4 the night.*

Though it had been some time since Carter had sent the text, his reply was instantaneous.

U ok?

She paused for a moment before typing, trying to decide how much of their crazy twenty-four hours, if any, she should share. She didn't know Carter very well; besides, it was far too much information to share by text message.

All good. I'll fill you in when I get home. I seem to remember you promising another shipwreck.

K. B safe.

U 2

"Here you go," Harrison said as he handed her a glass of amber liquid.

"What is it?"

"Nectar of the gods, Ave."

Avery sipped as Harrison carried his drink across the room and plopped down on the plush couch.

"Who are you texting?"

"Carter."

"He ever seen one of those coins?"

"Said he hasn't."

"Assuming that this isn't just a wild goose chase, what makes you think we can find this treasure, Ave? I mean it has eluded real treasure hunters for more than what, a hundred and fifty years?"

"Because we have something they didn't." She leaned over and rummaged through the canvas bag they had taken from Mark's home, then held up the diary in one hand and the enigma device in the other.

Harrison nodded as his eyelids began to droop.

Several minutes later, Avery said, "If Williams is so sure the treasure is a myth and a waste of time, why is her one coin locked down tighter than a storm cellar in a tornado?"

Harrison responded with a deep snore, dropping the empty Baccarat glass to the plush carpet without so much as a *thud*.

Avery envied his ability to fall asleep so quickly, but she was much too wired for sleep now. She opened a spreadsheet on her laptop and set up columns for everything to do with the treasure hunt.

There were only three names mentioned in the diary: Annabelle, James, and Clara. As she added them to the spreadsheet, she wondered if the name Mark had bestowed on his cat was more than a coincidence.

Avery examined the enigma wheel. Its cutouts were lined up in different patterns with faint etchings around the outside of the base. She couldn't begin to make heads or tails of it, beyond the fact that it had to be some type of code breaker. She typed a few observations about the wheel into the spreadsheet before moving on.

She turned her attention to the stacks of ledger-style pages taken from Mark's wardrobe. Each of the sheets had faint wavy lines bordering their edges and spots across the middle. Closer inspection revealed that what she was seeing might be water damage. The ink at the top of the pages had nearly faded away, but on one page it appeared to read Bonnet Rouge, 1778. Avery knew the literal French interpretation was red hat. She opened a new search window on her computer, then queried the year along with the French name and translation. The first three pages returned nothing but links to the websites of fashion designers and various online companies. At the top of the fourth page, she hit pay dirt. It was an entry taken from a book on the revolutionary war.

Avery read as far as the book's sample chapter would take her. The *Bonnet Rouge* was a French ship built by a French company under contract with a private investor whose name she was unable to ascertain. She wondered if some of the details had been lost to time or if the owner simply wanted to remain anonymous. She opened another search window, then typed in words specific to the account she had just read. This search generated several hits from various nautical history links. One of the most promising links was to a French maritime museum. According to the museum page, the *Bonnet Rouge* had another odd quality, beyond the anonymous investor. The ship had been constructed with an underwater hold that was three times as large as the hull was above the water line. According to the entry, it was the first of its kind for a wooden ship of that era whose design would limit it to deep water routes only.

Some speculated that the *Bonnet Rouge* may have been used to transport munitions, soldiers, or even treasure. The sunken hold made the ship look more like a traditional fishing vessel, far less likely to draw the attention of pirates or enemy governments.

She looked again at the sheets she had removed from Mark's house and wondered if they might have been payments to sailors serving aboard the *Bonnet Rouge*?

The one other thing Avery couldn't seem to find, aside from the owner, was what became of the *Bonnet Rouge*. She tabbed open another search, this time focusing specifically on where the ship sailed to and from, but again there was little information.

She was startled by a particularly loud snort from Harrison whose head was now lying back across the top of the couch.

"Go to bed, Harry," she said. "You'll have a stiff neck sleeping like that."

Eyes nearly closed, Harrison hoisted himself up off the couch and shuffled toward his room.

"G'night," he grumbled as he closed the door.

"Night, Harry."

Avery was aware that she also desperately needed some sleep, but her mind was racing. She needed answers to at least some of her questions, or any attempt at sleeping would be futile.

The next thing on her list was the post it from the motel with its jumble of letters and numbers. Avery Googled various combinations of them, listed them backward and forward, but found nothing. Aware of Mark's love of puzzles, she wondered if he might have left her some kind of code. Something that, if found, wouldn't be understood by anyone but her. Counting the characters, she found there were nine. For the next several minutes she scribbled different arrangements of them until she arrived at three vertical rows set up in similar fashion to a sudoku puzzle. In that configuration they looked more like coordinates.

Avery opened one of the map apps on her laptop and entered the information. The corresponding location appeared on the screen in the middle of the Atlantic, thirty miles off the coast of South Carolina.

"Nice going, Ave," she said to the empty room. "There isn't any land there. What did they do, hide the treasure on the bottom of the ocean?"

Given the timeline of the treasure stories, and the lack of technology, Avery deemed this highly unlikely.

She sighed loudly, then made a note in the spreadsheet and continued through the bag.

In the middle of what she had come to think of as Mark's clues was the file folder containing Maggie's emails. Avery could feel her blood pressure rising as she opened the folder.

She took her time, reading each email multiple times. Slowly a pattern began to emerge. Each of the emails were dated four days prior to when the first offer had come in from Daimler Technologies, not from Maggie's Hawkins Tech email address but a Gmail account that Avery had never seen. Maggie's name was on the bottom of each one. Avery recognized the lines of code prefacing and following each message. It meant that they had been sent and encrypted in confidential mode and set to self-destruct after a week. Retrieving the emails would have required hacking into Google's servers within a specific period. Avery knew that the list of people working for Hawkins Tech who could have pulled that off was incredibly short. Avery herself, obviously. And Mark Hawkins was more than capable. *Had been* more than capable. She felt the sharp sting of loss again, along with the accompanying anger that Mark's life was over.

Was this about the lost treasure or the multi-billion-dollar sale of her app? She supposed it didn't matter. Either way, money had to be the motive.

Avery knew in her bones that Mark had to have been in on it. The membership growth, advertising, and profitability results promised in these messages far exceeded projections from Hawkins's own internal analysts. Avery knew that the information contained in these pages was seriously damning stuff. Avery's attorneys hadn't said a word about the existence of written evidence supporting Daimler Technologies' assertions. And Maggie had categorically denied any sort of misrepresentation, calling the lawsuit "buyer's remorse" from her first frantic call to them before their lawyers even knew what was going on. Harrison had watched the video call Avery had with Maggie. Afterward, he had likened Maggie to a cat on an electrified boat deck—with wide, wild eyes and a delivery to her speech that screamed of desperation. Maggie swore she would take care of everything. After Avery had hung up, she'd immediately called a very highly recommended and ungodly expensive attorney. Valerie Turner's only daughter wasn't about to gamble with her share of billions on the lacking intellect of a sales bimbo like Maggie.

But holding copies of the emails in her hands somehow made everything more real. Had she been an unknowing party to an elaborate fraud? Avery had always been dumbfounded that an app test-marketed in New York and LA as a thousand-dollar download had ever sold a single copy. The app promised that its users would be given odds that a certain tip amount could get them past the door at the city's hottest nightclubs where they might mingle with society's elite. The whole exercise had been a low-key joke to her—the offshoot of a probability and maps project that she had purposely taken on. Things had taken an absurd turn when Mark told her he needed something he could sell to someone besides engineering nerds who could write their own software.

But the internet is a wonderfully weird and occasionally magical place: a Wall Street nobody who was tired of being left out of the high life bought it and got himself into the rooftop lounge at PHD Downtown, where he went viral singing karaoke with a K-pop star on TikTok. When the guy posted about how he wound up in the club, the app made almost half a million dollars off downloads in a day. Avery added a feature that allowed users to input the tip amounts they paid the door staff successfully and wrote the code to increase the posted values by twenty percent to account for liars, Mark added more servers to handle the heavy load from the location-intensive app, and hundreds more videos circled social media showing regular college kids whose parents had too much disposable income and a range of Silicon Valley IT nerds partying with the likes of Lady Gaga and Justin Bieber in exclusive clubs. Suddenly, Avery's engineering-joke project had become profitable enough for Mark to roll it out in Chicago and London. When he went to test the market in Berlin, home to Berghain Panorama Bar, the most exclusive nightclub in the world, the staggering buyout offer from Hugo Wagner, Daimler's CEO, had come out of nowhere.

Or so Avery thought. As she read the emails again, she understood why Mark had given Maggie a cut of the sale for her negotiating services. And why her questions about the amount, at the time the offer was made, were shrugged off. Mark had said the club scene in Europe today was like the club scene in New York in the 1970s, and the Germans were confident in their purchase offer.

But why would Mark still possess hard copies of damning emails? And what else had he managed to hide convincingly from her? There was more truth in Detective Burke's comment about her not knowing Mark any more than she wanted to admit.

Avery had never trusted Maggie. Maggie with her big hair, fake lashes, silicone boobs and tottering stilettos. Maggie was . . . well, perfect for a job selling tech to computer geeks. Avery was surprised that Maggie had covered her tracks as well as anyone without extensive computer knowledge could. Since most people aren't even aware that Gmail offers the Inspector Gadget style self-destruct setting, Avery bet that Daimler's board members and CEO were shocked when they could no longer access the messages. They likely hadn't even searched for them until after a few months of what would have been disappointing data by these standards, when they began contemplating a lawsuit.

The twelve-billion-dollar question: Did Maggie—or anyone else—know Mark had these? Were these emails the reason he was dead? Could these have driven him to take his own life? Or be another reason someone may have wanted him dead? Only an hour ago, Avery had been so sure Mark was killed because of a treasure hunt. What if she was wrong?

Avery couldn't quiet her mother's voice in her head. *The easiest solution is usually the right one, Ave.*

Except the police weren't treating Mark's death as suspicious. And Maggie had taken a half billion dollar cut of the sale as a commission. If Mark had found evidence suggesting she lied to the German board of directors, his unfailing moral compass—one of the things Avery had always admired about him—would have forced him to set things right.

Yet he hadn't even mentioned them to Avery. Were they even valid? Or had someone planted them to be found in Mark's possession? Maybe the break-ins at Mark's home and at the Hawk's Nest weren't to take something, but to leave something behind. To plant fake evidence to derail the sale.

So many unanswered questions. Avery was beginning to think the world was even more cutthroat than she ever dared to imagine.

Harrison's loud snores in the next room pulled Avery back to the present. She needed to get some sleep too. Tomorrow would likely be another long day. With any luck they would find some answers on Martha's Vineyard.

She left the lights burning as she walked across the room and double-checked the locks on the door to their suite. She stared at the door for a moment, then dragged a heavy table in front of it for good measure.

The old woman at the antique shop had been a heck of a salesperson. Avery had believed her when they first walked out of the store. But was Louise Williams everything she seemed? Harrison hadn't thought so—and he was famous in law enforcement circles for his ability to spot a liar. But if she truly didn't believe the treasure existed any longer, why secret the coin away? And why did she have all those reference books so close by? At the first mention of the symbol, Williams had pulled a gun, albeit an unloaded one—though they had never actually checked the chamber.

It's time for Harrison to resume carrying a gun, Avery thought as she entered her own room and locked the door behind her.

22

Harrison awoke grumpy with a crick in his neck. Avery had at least managed to sate his hunger by ordering room service breakfast and coffee while he showered.

After departing from the hotel, it took them nearly an hour and forty-five minutes to make the seventy-three-mile trek from Rowes Wharf to Falmouth Harbor on Cape Cod. Avery had wanted to be on the nine o'clock ferry to Martha's Vineyard, but the snarled Boston traffic and the standstill on Bourne Bridge had put an abrupt end to those hopeful plans.

The *Island Queen* ferry shuttled passengers between the Falmouth Terminal and Oak Bluffs on Martha's Vineyard. The next transport to the island was slated for a 10:30 departure. Harrison dropped Avery at the terminal then parked the rental in the nearby commuter lot.

Having left most of their belongings at the hotel, they were traveling ultra-light. As the weather was overcast and breezy, Avery was glad she'd thought to dress appropriately in long sleeves and slacks, with a nylon windbreaker. Harrison wore jeans, a windbreaker of his own, and a base-ball cap. The *Island Queen* began loading passengers promptly at ten after the hour.

"At least this thing won't be crowded," Harrison said with a hint of sarcasm as they surveyed a crowd of about fifty.

"And you'll be able to grab another coffee," Avery teased.

"Just tell me we won't have to walk once we get there."

"Of course not. I've already rented us another vehicle."

"Another Vette like Mark's?"

"You'll see."

The ride over was uneventful, though several times Avery could have sworn she caught a dark-haired man watching them. Unsure, she didn't mention it to Harrison. After docking and disembarking, they walked up Oak Bluffs Avenue toward Ride On, the rental company.

The signs hanging in front of Ride On, a white two-story structure that appeared to have been repurposed, identified it as the rental place Avery had found online.

Harrison stopped walking in the middle of the road, mouth agape. "All I see are bike rentals, Ave. And that building across the street says something about flying horses. I'm not going to be a party to either."

Avery laughed aloud. "Relax, Harry. I booked us a four-wheeled vehicle."

He fixed her with a look that said he didn't quite believe her.

"Honestly."

After completing the paperwork, the bespectacled man behind the counter handed Avery the keys to the rental. "You're lucky you booked ahead," the man said. "This is our last vehicle. If you'd waited, you would have had to rent bikes."

Avery gave Harrison a wink.

Their rental, a pewter-colored late model Jeep Wrangler, was parked out front in between two motor scooters. Upon eyeing the scooters Avery laughed again. Harrison failed to see the humor.

"Look, Harry," Avery said, pointing to an adjoining building. "It's the Strand Theater. How cool is that? We'll have to come back when we'll have more time to enjoy it."

Harrison concentrated on driving while Avery punched in the estate address that Williams, the old antique dealer, had provided them.

"According to the GPS, we've gotta drive about four miles to the town of Tisdale."

Martha's Vineyard was vastly different from anything Avery had conjured up in her mind. The roads were paved, winding, and in far better shape than those on the mainland of Massachusetts. Twenty minutes later, Harrison pulled up and stopped at a formidable-looking set of iron gates guarding the driveway of the sprawling estate.

Avery let out a low whistle. "Is that a turret?" she asked, pointing to a copper-roofed spire protruding from a thick canopy of evergreens.

Before Harrison could utter a response, a large man dressed in a plain gray suit appeared on the other side of the gate. The man's biceps looked as thick as Avery's waist. She immediately noticed the telltale bulge of a handgun beneath his suit coat.

"I think he's armed, Harry."

"Yeah, I caught that."

"I don't think I've ever seen as many guns as I have in the past two days," Avery said. "Maybe you should start carrying again."

Harrison pointed toward his ankle. "I am."

He lowered the window and flashed the man a phony smile.

The no-nonsense guard didn't return the gesture, instead he took a long drag from a cigarette. "What business do you have here?" he asked, speaking in halting English with a thick, eastern European-sounding accent.

Harrison attempted to explain that they were trying to trace some antiques back to their origin. "There was a nice lady at an antique store who said she bought them here. We just—"

The guard raised his hand, cutting Harrison off in mid-sentence. "Mr. Corbacho is busy. No visitors."

Upon hearing the name, Avery remembered seeing it the night before at the antique shop. She leaned forward and flashed a smile of her own. "Can you please tell Mr. Corbacho that Avery Turner is here to see him?"

The guard hesitated a moment before repeating his earlier statement. "No visitors."

"Just tell him," Avery said.

The guard backed up a few paces, not taking his eyes off the car, as if Harrison might be foolish enough to try to slam through the wrought iron barrier in a Jeep. His hand moved toward the portable radio mic clipped to his lapel.

Harrison whispered out of the side of his mouth. "What are you doing, Ave?"

"Trust me, Harry," she whispered back.

They waited while the guard spoke into the radio in a language neither one of them understood. As he spoke, his attention shifted directly to Avery. He smirked around his cigarette. Still smiling, Avery held his gaze.

The reply came through the radio in the same foreign dialect. After acknowledging, the guard stepped back, and the gate swung open.

"Go ahead," the guard said, still leering at Avery as they passed.

"If this thing goes sideways, Harry," Avery said.

"Yeah?"

"You have my permission to shoot that guy."

Harrison drove up the long concrete drive toward the coastal side of the compound. At the center of the property, surrounded by hundred-year-old evergreens, stood a massive Tudor-style home with a kale-colored metal roof. The building's main structure, as large as Avery's high school, had a façade that was a mixture of weathered cedar shingles, brick and stucco. Sprouting from the center were two brick-fronted wings.

"Mind telling me how you did that?" Harrison asked.

"What?"

"Got them to open the gate?"

"I just reasoned it out, Harry. If Mark was murdered, it only makes sense that the killer, or killers, knew he was looking for the treasure."

"And?"

"You said it yourself. Someone has been following our every move. And neither of us believed everything that Louise Williams at the antique shop told us. She sold that desk for someone, and whoever that was must have known about Mark's search before his death. And, by extension, they would have known Williams."

"You think she told someone we were coming?" Harrison said.

"Wouldn't you?"

"What about Corbacho? How would he know you?"

"It was a bluff. I saw the name on the paperwork Williams showed us. Figured that had to be who she was dealing with on this end."

Harrison pulled up close to the main door to the house and parked, pulling out his phone and poking at the screen. "Your mom always said you were scary smart, Ave."

A handsome man dressed in a charcoal suit appeared at the entry doors and began to descend the wide stone steps. Avery paused as she reached for the door handle.

"Let's just hope I'm not too smart for my own good, Harry. You should let some of your old colleagues know where we are."

Harrison tapped one finger on the side of his phone. "Already did."

23

Avery and Harrison exited the Jeep as another of the estate's private security guards approached, this one dressed in the exact same gray suit the gate guard had been wearing. He held out his hand to them.

"I need both of your cell phones," he said, exhibiting the same Eastern European accent as the gate guard had.

Avery closed her hand over the cell in her pocket and shook her head, causing Harrison to pull back.

The guard persisted. "No phones in the house."

The man in the dark suit interceded. "It's okay, Marak," he said. "My apologies for making such a request, Ms. Turner. Mr. Corbacho has many priceless works of art inside and cannot risk flash photos. I'm sure you understand."

"I've worked in the technology business too long to ever turn my phone over to anyone. But if your goal is to keep it out of the house, that's easily accomplished. We'll just leave them out here."

"As you wish."

Avery leaned back inside the Jeep and opened the glove compartment.

Harrison passed his phone through the car to Avery along with the rental keys. Avery locked both of their mobiles in the glovebox then locked the Jeep and pocketed the keys.

Evidently satisfied that they represented no threat to his employer's art collection, the man in the charcoal suit led them up the granite steps to the main entry doors. After keying an entry code into an electronic wall panel, he opened the front door to the home then waved them inside. Harrison paused to study the threshold for half a second before following Avery.

The foyer was easily twice the size of the apartment where Avery grew up. She marveled at the gilt-inlaid floor mosaic depicting angels in an epic battle with demons and humans.

The walls of the main hallway were paneled and trimmed in rich dark hardwood, each filled with lavish oil paintings, each undoubtedly a masterpiece worth a fortune all by itself. China vases and bronze busts stood sentry atop marble pedestals along the hallway running to their left. The man motioned for them to follow him that way. Avery passed at least two pieces she recognized from an art history class slideshow at Princeton—the one she hadn't slept through.

Harrison leaned in close and whispered to Avery as they walked. "Why am I beginning to feel like the fly being led right to the spider?"

Thirty yards farther down the hall, the man opened a set of carved wooden doors. The room beyond, larger than the home's foyer, was lined with bookshelves and more priceless art. A massive desk stood at the center of the imposing space, and the man seated behind it rose to greet them from his throne-like leather chair.

"Come in, Ms. Turner," he said.

The doors closed behind them. The man who had led them to the room stood to one side, his hands clasped behind his back as if he were at parade rest. Avery and Harrison exchanged glances, then approached the desk.

Avery studied the man's face as they neared him. He had an olive complexion and a close-cropped beard that was just beginning to gray on either side of the chin. He wasn't what she would have described as tall, but he struck an imposing figure nonetheless in his three-piece Armani suit, tailored to show off the fit physique beneath. It was as if the man in front of them had been constructed from the most attractive features of actors Andy Garcia and Christian Bale.

Avery couldn't help but think she had seen him before, but it wasn't until he spoke again that she placed him.

"What a pleasant surprise. So nice of you to come all this way," the man said as he came around to the front of the desk and offered his hand to Avery.

"You're Mark's friend," she said, eliciting a smile from him. "An investor from the early days of Hawkins Tech."

"Emilio Corbacho." He gave a slight nod. "I'm deeply honored that you remembered me."

Corbacho's attention shifted to Harrison. "I don't believe I have had the pleasure of making your acquaintance."

"This is Harrison," Avery said.

"Pleased to meet you, Mr. Harrison," Corbacho said with a firm handshake.

"Likewise," Harrison said.

"Like knights into battle," Corbacho said.

"Excuse me?" Harrison said.

"The offering of the sword hand is an ancient custom to show there is no danger."

Corbacho spoke with a barely detectable Spanish accent, but there was a lyrical quality to his speech that exposed his bilingual roots. He gestured to the pair of leather guest chairs facing his desk. "Please, make yourselves comfortable."

As Avery and Harrison sat, Corbacho waved a hand to the man standing by the door, dismissing him from the room.

"My apologies if my need for high-level security unnerved either of you," Corbacho said. "My global business pursuits have earned me more than a few enemies."

"Understandable," Avery said, thinking about the gun strapped to Harrison's ankle that Corbacho's security guys had missed.

"Mark Hawkins was bowled over by your intelligence, Ms. Turner. He spoke often about how lucky he was to work with you."

"And I with him," Avery said, noting that he referred to Mark in the past tense.

"To what do I owe the pleasure of your visit?" Corbacho asked as he placed both hands atop the desk and interlaced his fingers.

"I came here to ask the owner about the desk Mark purchased from this estate, but now that I'm here, I'm wondering why you would use an antique dealer as a go-between to sell a desk to an old friend?"

"I did not. I purchased this estate sight unseen—at Mark's suggestion, actually. He attended a benefit gala here last year and when I mentioned wanting a place in New England, he told me it would suit me perfectly. He was right."

"As usual," Avery said.

Corbacho nodded. "As usual," he echoed. "The contract stipulated that the estate was sold fully furnished and decorated. It wasn't until after closing on the property that I learned some of the furniture was gone."

"Gone?" Harrison said.

"Yes. Sold by the greedy, underhanded son of the previous property owner. I didn't realize that it was Mark who acquired the desk until just hours before I learned of his death."

Avery let that sink in for a beat. Mark came to this house as a guest of the previous owner, suggested his friend purchase it sight unseen, and then contacted the previous owner and bought some of the furniture? He'd been ruthless in business, but that was a level up.

"How did you learn of Mark's death?" she asked.

"The tragic death of a wealthy man makes headlines, Ms. Turner." Corbacho held up a copy of the *Boston Herald*.

The headline read: *Billionaire Tech Guru Found Dead in Boston Motel.*

"I tried to call him just last night. I was worried about him, but I never anticipated," he tapped the newspaper, "anything close to this. I can't begin to tell you how saddened I am to learn of his passing. I will miss him. I haven't known many people in my life who could hold their own in a conversation or a game of chess with me, and Mark could do both."

"He was brilliant," Avery said, sadness clinging to the words.

"A brilliance that deserves to be celebrated," Corbacho said, thumping on hand on his desk blotter. "A toast. Would either of you care to join me for a drink?"

24

Utilizing an unseen remote, Corbacho opened a motorized wet bar ensconced behind one of the massive built-in bookcases. Avery watched in fascination as the bar and its contents slid smoothly into view.

"Ms. Turner?" Corbacho said as he approached the bar.

"I'll have Jack Daniels neat, if you have it," Avery said, attempting to suppress her emotions about Mark's death.

"I have a weakness for your Bourbon," Corbacho said, holding up a rounded bottle with a pewter jockeyed horse atop the cork.

"Is that . . ." Harrison's eyes popped wide. "Blanton's Black Label?"

Corbacho grinned. "Yes, sir."

"That's a very serious bottle."

"I'm a very serious man," Corbacho said. "Mark could always make me laugh. Another of many things I will miss about him. Would you like a glass, Mr. Harrison?"

Harrison looked tempted but shook his head. "Soda water's fine before lunch."

Corbacho returned with a small silver tray on top of which sat three heavy crystal glasses. He placed the tray at the front of his desk before returning to his chair with his own amber colored drink.

"To Mark," Corbacho said, raising his glass. "May he rest in peace, and may his memory bring only joy to those who loved him." The way he held Avery's gaze as he said the last words made her want to squirm in her seat. Exactly how much had Mark talked to this guy about her? She was dying to know but couldn't possibly ask.

Avery and Harrison raised their glasses. "To Mark," they said in unison.

Everyone sipped their drinks. Avery waited for Corbacho to speak. If there was one lesson she had learned while working for a decade in a male-dominated industry, it was that men like Corbacho would eventually fill the silence if you gave them enough of it. They loved to listen to the sound of their own voices.

Corbacho placed his glass precisely at the center of a stone coaster even though the liquid contained within wasn't chilled. Avery wondered if he was Type A about everything he set his hand to. She cast her eyes around the room, her gaze settling on a frayed, yellowed nautical map in a floating frame. It was similar to the ones she'd found in Mark's study.

"Are you a fan of history, Ms. Turner?" Corbacho asked, turning to the map.

"We both are," Harrison said.

"It's not my favorite hobby or anything, but I believe understanding history is the only way to make sure the worst of it isn't repeated," Avery said.

"Undoubtedly," Corbacho countered, waving one hand at the wall. "Feel free to take a closer look at the map if you wish."

Avery rose and approached the map, while the two men remained seated. Faded circles were marked near the coasts of France and Spain, and a dotted southwest route traced across the Atlantic, through the Caribbean, continuing up the east coast of the United States. If her estimate was correct, the map predated the civil war.

"My family has long held an interest in the stolen treasure of the *Bonnet Rouge*," Corbacho continued. "Are you familiar with it? The ship, I mean."

"Sounds familiar," Harrison said. "But I can't place it at the moment."

Avery, having just read about the ship less than twelve hours before, said nothing.

"The legend is fascinating, and a story Mark never tired of hearing. Perhaps I could tell it one more time in his honor? I know it backward and forward, because my great-great-great-grandfather helped to load that ship," Corbacho said. "He died, along with many others when the *Bonnet Rouge* sank. His brother, and later his son, searched for his remains—along with the remains of what they believed was a cargo supply ship destined for France. There wasn't much news released to the public at that time, and then only what the crown wanted people to know."

"Not so different from today," Avery said as she returned to her seat and gestured for him to go on.

Corbacho nodded his agreement. "Dark secrets still surround the *Bonnet Rouge* and her voyage. Both brother and son died without ever learning what became of their relative."

"That's terrible," Avery said.

"Many years later, the grandson located an old diary in the back of a dusty old sea chest. The chest was among the belongings of his grandmother, the sailor's wife, when she died in her nineties. In the diary, the sailor had written of heavy chests loaded deep in the belly of their ship, and a first mate who drunkenly claimed that the chests were loaded with gold being sent to France. It was said that King Charles was underhandedly aiding the French—and the Colonists—in their war with England. His goal was not only to reclaim Gibraltar from the British, but to take some of the southernmost colonies in America. Which of course could only happen if the colonial rebels were victorious in their bid for independence."

Harrison's brow furrowed. "If what you say is true, why is there no mention of this in any of the history books?"

"History is recorded by the victorious, Mr. Harrison. There is no mention of it because at the time, as an imperial power, Spain's involvement would have been seen by the British as exactly what it was, an act of aggression. By surreptitiously assisting France, and the colonials, in their attacks against a weakened and thinly stretched British Navy, at points with direct Spanish interest, Charles felt he was ensuring his legacy and the future of his empire."

Corbacho took another sip of his drink before continuing.

"King Charles was also hiding a fortune from a greedy Archbishop, and his own lazy heirs. Charles's plan was to send plain, unassuming trunks in wagons driven by trusted soldiers disguised as peasants over the Great

Pyrenees to France, where the coffers of coins and jewels would be transferred to a plain, unassuming French ship with a Spanish crew to avoid pirates—"

"The *Bonnet Rouge*," Avery murmured.

Corbacho smiled, flashing a row of perfectly bonded white teeth. "Yes. Everyone knew the French were broke and sinking every available penny into the fight against Britain. Very few pirates bothered with French ships. But the king wanted his own Spanish crew to ensure the mission was completed as ordered. The treasure was to arrive in the southern colonies and the promised amount—just enough to ensure a lengthy conflict—would be delivered to the American rebels."

"And the rest?" Avery said.

"The remainder would be hidden by Charles's men until such time as the king won control of that area. After that, the treasure would revert to Spain, its rightful owner."

"And how is it that you've come to know so much about this unrecorded piece of history?" Harrison said.

"Mr. Harrison, I have amassed a great deal of wealth and influence."

"You mean power?" Harrison said.

"My wealth has provided me with access to lost or hidden historic accounts that would have otherwise been inaccessible."

Avery watched Corbacho closely as he paused to take another drink. She could tell the man, drunk on his own power and knowledge, was enjoying every minute of this master class in history. She also knew there was much more to his storytelling than simply the pleasure of listening to himself talk. Corbacho was heading to a point. Avery smiled politely and took a sip from her own drink as she waited for him to make it.

"Charles wasn't the only diabolical mind in this scheme. Before the *Bonnet Rouge* left France, a small group of French soldiers, some of them already forming the basis of the resistance that would eventually lead to the overthrow of King Louis and spawn the French Revolution, smuggled out French and Egyptian antiquities along with gold coins and jewels stolen from the crown. They promised the Spanish captain a handsome payment to divert course through the Caribbean first to drop some of their cargo, before continuing onto the Americas. On the off chance that the enticement of money wasn't enough, they told him the additional cargo contained supplies for local victims of a hurricane that had devastated the islands and its sugar crop.

"Allies waiting in the islands could hide the treasure for the French rebels to reclaim later, when it would be needed to fund their uprising against King Louis. The captain, knowing he was already carrying the Spanish treasure, thought another stop provided him an opportunity to renegotiate with the French for a more lucrative payment. Ultimately, the ship was believed lost in a hurricane during its voyage from France to Haiti."

Corbacho leaned forward, placing his forearms on his desk, and fixed her with a grin. "While many fools have wasted their lives searching thousands of miles of ocean floor around Haiti for a ship that was only a hundred feet long, my ancestors understood that lost doesn't necessarily mean sunken. It is also used to refer to ships sent wildly off course that never arrived at the scheduled port. We focused on the route documented within the sailor's diary. Studying firsthand historical accounts is the surest way to piece together what happened."

Avery kept a neutral expression, realizing that both the diary and enigma device she found in Mark's study might have come from the desk Mark purchased from the estate. Not that she would say that without knowing Corbacho's motive for sharing this story.

Corbacho sighed before he spoke again. "The truth is that I hold myself partially responsible for Mark's death."

Avery sat up a little straighter. Was Corbacho about to confirm Mark had been searching for the treasure, as well?

"I should have realized he needed help the last time I spoke with him," Corbacho continued. "My resources are vast. I could have intervened. Possibly even stopped this from becoming our reality. I was too focused on my pursuit of the *Bonnet Rouge* and her secrets to notice the changes in Mark, and I will deeply regret that for the rest of my days." He touched his forehead, sternum, and shoulders in the sign of the cross.

"I don't understand," Avery said. Was it possible that Corbacho didn't know Mark had been looking for the treasure?

"Mark had been under a great deal of stress lately," Corbacho explained. "He was getting ready to open an inn in Maine and had recently learned that he was about to be sued by the company he sold his business to."

Apparently it was not only possible, but probable. Maybe no one who thought they were in Mark's inner circle truly knew him well—in a day and a half, Avery had figured out Mark was much better than she ever would've guessed at revealing only part of himself to those he kept close.

"Daimler Technologies," was all Avery said.

"Correct, Ms. Turner. I fear Mark may have been suffering from depression."

"You think Mark killed himself?" Avery's tone was sharper than she intended.

"My apologies if I have offended you," Corbacho said, holding his hands up. "That was not my intention. I only offer my insight into Mark's state of mind when we last spoke."

"And based on that, you believe his death could be a suicide?" Avery asked.

"The newspaper article indicated that he died from an overdose. Perhaps they were mistaken."

"We don't know for sure what happened," Harrison said. "Not yet anyway."

"Forgive my overstep." Corbacho bowed his head briefly. "Perhaps we can help each other."

"How do you figure?" Harrison said.

"This house was formerly owned by a family that can trace its roots back to the colonial shipyards they operated here. They built naval vessels for the colonial military as well as privateers. Mark, as I'm sure you know, was an expert in American antiques and an avid collector. I am sure he wanted the desk because it's one of a kind, a piece with deep history."

"Mark cared more about the story of a piece than the designer or the style," Avery muttered the thought Adams, the antique dealer in Maine, had shared.

"Exactly," Corbacho said. "In light of Mark's untimely death, I would very much like to have that desk here in this room, to remember my old friend by."

"We might be able to arrange that," Avery said. "What's the other side of the coin?"

Corbacho's brow furrowed. "I'm afraid I don't follow."

"You said we could help each other," Avery reminded him. "So far, all you've told me is about how I can help you."

Corbacho put his glass down and laughed. "Of course, of course. I am happy to help you in any way I can. I assume that Mark's legal troubles will also ensnare you." His eyebrows lifted to his thick hairline.

"They have," Avery said.

"Lawsuits are the playground fighting words of the business world, Ms. Turner," Corbacho said. "The first one is always a shock, but I've been through dozens, and am happy to share the influence and network of top sparring partners I've amassed. Business connections, attorneys, more information on any of Mark's antiques if you'll be helping with his estate sale. Ask and I will provide."

Avery glanced over at Harrison, then stood. Harrison followed her lead.

"That is a very generous offer, and I appreciate it, Mr. Corbacho. Thank you for seeing us, but I'm sure we've taken up enough of your time," she said. "Your hospitality is unmatched."

"I appreciate the two of you stopping by," Corbacho said as he rose from his chair. "I only wish it had been under more fortunate circumstances."

"I do as well."

"I know the desk would be a draw in an estate sale." Corbacho said. "I'd be happy to pay an additional twenty percent beyond whatever Mark paid for it to ensure its safe and timely return."

Avery considered telling him that Mark's things weren't hers to sell, but Mark's will indicated otherwise and she had no way to know whether or not Corbacho knew that.

"Allow me some time to discuss the proper procedure for making that happen with my attorney," Avery said.

"Of course."

"I wonder, might there be an easier way of contacting you again?"

"Certainly," Corbacho said as he removed a business card from the pocket of his suit coat and handed it to her. "My private number is on the back. And please keep me apprised of any memorial plans for Mark. I am here to assist however I can, and I'd very much like to attend."

As Corbacho walked them toward the door, Avery held up his card. "We have some things to take care of over the next few days, but I'll be sure to let you know what my attorney says as soon as I can."

Harrison stopped as he reached the door and turned to face Corbacho. "Thank you for the hospitality. I appreciate your offer to help Avery."

Corbacho smiled. "Anything for the young woman who meant so much to Mark."

25

Avery let out a deep breath as they drove through the iron gate.

"He was an interesting fellow," Harrison said.

"I think he and Mark met at Oxford, if I'm remembering correctly. I met him at a party maybe five years ago."

"Interesting that he's got a family connection to this treasure, too." Harrison mused.

"And that he volunteered that, but didn't seem to know it was something the two of them had in common when they were still friends all these years later," Avery said, wondering for the umpteenth time in forty-eight hours if she'd really known Mark very well at all. "Do you think he wants the desk for the same reason Mark did?"

"Probably. But I also think his offer to help you out with this lawsuit mess was more than your buddy Mark did, and if Mark cleaned the goods out of the desk already, it hurts nothing to let the guy have it."

"You think he was on the up and up?"

"Guys like him have always made me uncomfortable," Harrison said. "The money, the suits, the private security and servants. It's too much. But my lie detector bells didn't ring. He's rich-schmuck-business-guy slimy. Not coldblooded-murderer slimy."

"I thought so, too," Avery said, pleased with herself. "And he really might be able to help me with the Daimler thing."

She stared out the window. "I'm sorry that I pushed you into this, Harry."

"What are you talking about?"

"I'm still angry about Mark's death and it's kept me from thinking clearly. I just want answers."

Harrison reached over and gently took Avery by the hand. "First off, you haven't pushed me into anything. I'm here because I want to be, Ave. Secondly, I was going to say how proud Valerie would have been if she could have seen you back there."

Avery felt her throat tighten with emotion at the mention of her mother.

"You seemed every inch like you belonged in that place, and you didn't let that guy railroad you on the desk, either. You walked out of there in total control. I'm proud of you. And I'm with you for the long haul."

"You really think I'm on the right track?" Avery said.

"I certainly do. And to be honest, I'm kinda enjoying being back in the hunt."

"So, we keep going?"

"Gotta see it through to the end, right? Speaking of which, I got a hit back this morning on that fingerprint I lifted from the safe at the Hawk's Nest."

"And?"

"Some guy named Ronald Lee Babcock. Former military with a rap sheet that includes extortion, firearm possession by a prohibited person, and robbery."

"Why would he break into Mark's place?"

"Best guess? Ronnie's a bad guy for hire. Able to blend in where he needs to, crack a safe when the day's job calls for it."

"But then what we really need to know is who he's working for," Avery said.

"Maybe it's a group of shotgun-wielding antiquarians and Louise Williams is their ringleader."

"Or one of the groups hunting the treasure that Louise mentioned," Avery said.

"Who knows, Ave. What is obvious is that there are a lot of people searching for this gold. At the very least, Babcock's involvement blows up Sheriff Greene's theory about the attack on Julia Bergin being small town drug users. There's something bigger happening here."

Avery noticed Harrison avoided any mention of Mark's death, but she knew he had already made the connection, because so had she.

Samael disconnected the troubling phone call he had just received from one of his law enforcement connections. According to the paid informer, Babcock had been burned. He'd gotten sloppy and left a fingerprint behind. A fingerprint that Harrison had requested be checked. This was a big problem. A shame, as Ronnie had been a loyal soldier. But a link to Babcock meant a link to Samael. And both were unacceptable. Time to terminate his employment.

Samael's right-hand man Alexi appeared in the doorway to the study holding what appeared to be a small book.

"Is that what I hope it is?" Samael said.

"Indeed, it is," Alexi said.

"Where did you locate it?"

"Locked in the safe of her suite at the Boston Harbor Hotel. Evidently she isn't quite the worthy adversary you described."

Samael wasn't as quick to discount Avery Turner. While she may have underestimated his reach, she had been fearless enough to enter the hunt with nothing more than her washed-up bodyguard and a smile. Samael was sure there was more to her than met the eye.

"Will that be all?" Alexi said.

"Yes," Samael said as he waved the man away and returned to his desk. "Alexi—One more thing. Tell Ronnie I need to see him."

Avery and Harrison returned to Oak Bluffs to drop off the Jeep, Harrison returning the keys while Avery finished sending a few texts: two to check in with her attorneys, one to Carter, and one to Corbacho to thank him for his kindness again and make sure he had her number.

The warm sun and blue sky had begun to peek through the high clouds as they stepped into the considerable foot traffic on Oak Bluffs Avenue. Harrison suggested a bite to eat before their departure from the island on the three o'clock ferry. Lunch on Martha's Vineyard on a sunny afternoon sounded lovely—and normal. When Avery had complained about wanting more adventure, being on the business end of a shotgun and having thieves and hooligans lurking about wasn't what she meant. Looking around for the tenth time since they left Corbacho's, Avery and Harrison agreed that as far as either of them could tell, they hadn't been followed.

They selected an outside table under a brown and white umbrella on the tiny front patio of the Martha's Vineyard Chowder Company. After taking their drink orders, the young waiter left them to peruse the menu.

"I'm starving," Harrison announced.

"I didn't think I was that hungry," Avery said. "But now that I see the menu . . ."

"And smell the food," Harrison added.

"Outright famished," Avery finished.

Their waiter appeared and they each ordered a cup of clam chowder for starters. Avery chose the caprese salad and lobster dumplings, while Harrison indulged his cholesterol jones by ordering the hot lobster roll smothered in butter sauce with lemon, bacon, and herbs, extra fries.

"You really think that little old lady we met in Massachusetts is running some sort of crime ring?" Avery asked.

"I honestly have no idea what I think. I don't know what happened to Mark, I don't know who we should suspect and who we should dismiss, and I sure don't know what to make of all these stories of long-lost riches. It sounds like a movie script, not real life."

"Mom would say I don't know my rear end from a hole in the ground." Avery smiled.

"Val would not have said 'rear end' and you well know it."

They both laughed and it felt good, relieving some of the tension they had been lugging around since learning of Mark's death.

They ate while watching people stroll past. Avery knew that Harrison's focus was on making sure that no one was watching them.

"You know what I was thinking?" Avery said as she pushed away the plate containing the last few dumplings.

"Nope," Harrison said.

"I don't think the *Bonnet Rouge* could have reached its destination. At least not the one Corbacho was describing. His comment about it being lost but not sunken in the hurricane off Haiti was interesting, though."

"You mind?" Harrison said pointing at the dumplings.

"All yours."

"What makes you say that?"

"There were—are—a lot of people searching for the treasure this ship was carrying."

"Including Mark and Corbacho," Harrison said around a mouthful of dumpling.

"Right. But, to date, aside from a few coins, nobody has located the treasure."

"As far as we know."

"Okay. But that antique dealer, Williams, said that the entire world would know if it had been discovered."

"Your point?" Harrison said.

"I think something may have happened to it before it reached its final destination. And the something may be that the hurricane blew the ship off course, and it sank somewhere else entirely."

"You think the answer is in the diary?" Harrison lowered his voice and glanced around.

"What if Mark had it figured out already? What if the sticky notes he left at the motel were some kind of coordinates?"

"Pointing where?"

Avery explained her theory and what she had found the previous night regarding South Carolina. "The newspaper article did say Mark's grandfather died off the South Carolina Coast."

"But you said it yourself, Ave. Even if you're right about those being coordinates, and that's a big if, the area you found is in the middle of the ocean."

"It's not as big an *if* as you think. I took a close look at Corbacho's nautical map. There were marks all along the Carolina coastline. I think they might have been shipwrecks—Carter says there are dozens and dozens around the keys. The spot was thirty miles east of Hilton Head, and Mark had a trip to South Carolina booked before he died."

"That's a big coast," Harrison said. "Without more information, we'd be chasing a wild goose. If you ask me, this treasure hunting thing feels more like an expensive pastime for rich folks."

"Hey, in case you haven't noticed, I'm one of those rich folks now."

"Apologies, m'lady. What makes you think we'd have any more luck than the others who have tried unsuccessfully to locate this treasure? Neither of us knows the first thing about finding some two-hundred-year-old ship. If you'll pardon the pun, we are in over our heads when it comes to finding sunken treasure."

"You're absolutely right, Harry," Avery said as she pulled out her phone. "But I think I know why no one has found the *Bonnet Rouge* in more than two centuries. I read a tiny little fraction of a sentence last night that holds the key—I think."

Harrison raised his eyebrows. "I'm listening."

"The ship was unique for its day, with a massive hull underwater topped by something designed to look like a fishing vessel."

"What did Richie Rich back there say? 'A plain, unassuming' vessel? But with a huge cargo hold . . . perfect for carrying treasure." Harrison nodded. "And avoiding pirates."

"Precisely. But that also meant it ran deep water routes. That was the thing that stuck out to me. No one has found it because wherever it sank, it's too far down."

"And your month of scuba lessons means you're going looking for it?" Harrison put the last dumpling back on the plate and scowled. "No way."

"Carter has experience with deep water diving," Avery said. "So much that he wouldn't even tell me how far down he has actually gone. He would only say that he's certified to teach to 145 feet, which is deeper than a recreational diver can be certified to dive.

"And just how deep is the water you think Mark wanted to try off South Carolina?"

"A hundred and thirty-five feet by satellite estimate." Avery smiled.

Harrison shook his head in disapproval. "Tell me you're not dragging that Mosley guy into this."

Avery grinned. "His name's Carter, and I'm not dragging anyone. All I did was ask—and send Marco down to Florida to pick him up." She held up her phone, showing an incoming text from Carter. *On my way to the airport. C U soon.*

Harrison stared at her for a moment to see if she was serious. "That's what you were doing on your phone in the car?"

"We're meeting him on Hilton Head in time for dinner."

Before Harrison could protest, the Island Queen horn sounded, announcing its arrival at the wharf.

Avery downed the last of her sangria then stood up. "Come on, Harry. We've got a ferry to catch."

Carter Mosley hadn't been able to focus on much of anything since Avery's name popped up on his phone with a crazy request for a deep dive off the coast of South Carolina and a mention of honest-to-God lost treasure. After spending hours the night before with the local police answering questions about the rigged parachute, the last thing he could have predicted was Avery dropping a treasure hunt in his lap. The prospect of searching for and locating a significant historical shipwreck instead of the more modern fiberglass yachts owned by despots and drug lords, or the tired leftovers of others, was an intoxicating prospect.

He was on his way to the airport to meet Avery's pilot, Marco, his van loaded with every piece of equipment he could imagine needing, when he realized he still needed to check-in with MaryAnn, his go-to researcher. He double-checked the dashboard clock. If he hurried, he'd have just enough time to make one quick stop at the museum.

Carter found MaryAnn in her office sitting in front of the computer. He knew she was either hot on the trail of another acquisition or chasing a donation for the museum. He tapped on the doorframe so as not to startle her then stuck his head inside.

"Hey, lady."

"Hey, yourself," MaryAnn said as she pulled her glasses off and sat back. "I thought you'd forgotten all about me."

"As if." Carter stepped into the office, guilt creeping over him like a prickly wool blanket. MaryAnn was nice. She was gorgeous, with a little of the sexy librarian thing around the edges. But she liked her books and her artifacts and her quiet life inside the museum. She admired Carter's exploits and exclaimed over his stories, but her world was so far removed from his he couldn't even picture her in scuba gear or a flight suit.

"I haven't seen you since the benefit gala. You know: the one you bugged out of early."

"I can explain that." He grinned.

"I'm listening," she said as she plucked out the pin holding her blonde hair up, letting it fall around her shoulders.

"I had an emergency, but you were busy being the belle of the ball with a group of wealthy donors. I didn't want to distract you."

"Too late, Carter. You distracted me a long time ago. What are you doing later?"

"Um, that's why I stopped by. I'm heading for the airport right now. I think I've got a good lead on a shipwreck off the Carolina coast, but it's really old, and likely really deep." Carter didn't mention where the lead came from. If he had any hope of getting MaryAnn's help, Avery Turner's name was better left out of the conversation.

"How deep?" She raised her eyebrows.

"Deep enough that you don't want me to answer that." He returned her stare.

"Let me guess, you think I might be able to help you." MaryAnn's lips tipped up in the barest hint of a smile.

"You did help me find the *Wilhelmina,* after all. And I'll be sure and plug the museum in my dive video. Both videos."

"And a donation link in the description?"

"Goes without saying."

"If you manage to locate this mystery ship. And live to post the video."

"I can make this dive." He flashed a grin, knowing his confidence was a large chunk of his charm. "And I don't know of anyone better to help me find the site."

"Flattery will get you everywhere. What is the name of it?"

"The *Bonnet Rouge*."

Carter knew MaryAnn was as smart as she was beautiful. If there was ever a tidbit, fact, or rumor, to be found about anything nautical between the Chesapeake Bay and Cuba, MaryAnn was the only person Carter would want to look for it.

"Well?" Carter said. "Can I count on your help?"

"Oh, all right. Only because I can't stand to hear you grovel."

As they shook on it, MaryAnn held his hand longer than necessary, looking him straight in the eye.

"Is there anything else I can do for you?" she cooed.

Carter grinned. "Sorry. I got a plane to catch."

26

It was nearly four by the time Avery and Harrison arrived back at Rowes Wharf on Cape Cod. They climbed into the rental, ready to make the return trip to the Harbor Hotel knowing that they faced Boston's unforgiving rush hour traffic. Avery went online and booked four rooms at a fancy resort on Hilton Head. She sent a text to Marco and Carter with the relevant information.

"God, I don't miss having to deal with this kind of traffic," Harrison said. "Give me the Florida Keys any day."

"Relax, Harry. We're not in any rush. You'll be back there soon enough."

"Okay, Ms. Jet Set. Speaking of which, how exactly are we getting to South Carolina?"

"Marco. After he drops off Carter, he's coming to Logan to pick us up."

"Why doesn't he just fly up with Carter?"

"Because Carter will need time to charter a boat and find some equipment. And I want him to reconnoiter the area before we get there."

"Reconnoiter? Jesus, Ave. You're starting to sound like a fugitive from an A-Team episode."

"Starting to feel a little like one, too."

It was after five by the time they reached the suite. Avery loaded up her bags then did a last-minute sweep of the room, making sure she'd left nothing behind.

Harrison poked his head in. "Ready when you are."

"All good here, Harry. Just gotta grab the diary."

She knelt and punched in the four-digit code to the room's safe. The electronic latch released, and she opened the door.

Empty.

"Oh my God. It's gone."

"What do you mean gone?"

They both stared into the tiny vault.

"Someone must have followed us here and broken in after we left," Avery said.

"These people aren't screwing around, Ave. We gotta be more careful."

"What people? Nobody knows we're here except us."

"One of the trucks that I spotted yesterday, I guess?"

"You said no one was behind us last night. Besides, how could they have gotten from Maine to here in a truck as fast as we got here in . . ." Avery paused, going to the bed and picking up her backpack. She unzipped it and flipped it over, emptying the contents onto the bed.

"You okay?" Harrison asked.

Avery sifted through the jumble of keys, makeup, clothes, and credit cards, then held up a double-thick turquoise nail file. "This isn't mine."

"How can you possibly remember—" Harrison began, snapping his mouth shut when Avery slid a fingernail into the side seam of the object and popped it open to reveal a small circuit board with a red blinking light.

"I'll be . . . hornswoggled." Harrison waggled his eyebrows to punctuate his word choice and nearly made her smile. "When could someone have dropped a tracker in your bag? It was on the plane, wasn't it?"

Avery shook her head. "Yesterday morning and all night the night before, it was on the porch at the Hawk's nest. Could've been our watcher in the woods, or the safecrackers, or anyone else who happened by there in the chaos after Julia was attacked."

"I don't like this, Avery." Harrison paced the length of the suite. "Not even a little bit."

"Should we call the police?" she asked.

"And tell them what? If someone was smart enough to break into our room and safe, they wouldn't allow themselves to be caught on a hotel security video. If we report this, I can guarantee one of two things will happen. Either the burglar's face will be covered, or the cameras will have malfunctioned."

Avery sighed. "Someone is following us."

"And while Massachusetts does have stalking laws, if they're like the ones in New York, they're no real good until a threat is made. I can dust that thing for prints myself."

She closed it up and tossed it onto the bed. "If there's one on there that isn't mine, I'll eat my shoes."

"Me too. But I'll do it if it will make you feel better. Trust me, Ave, the Boston police aren't going to give a hoot about some old diary stolen from a hotel room. Not when they have real crime to focus on. Remember how Greene reacted to the cracked safe at the Hawk's Nest Inn? And he works in a tiny town."

Avery considered their interactions with the Boston detective and the Maine sheriff. Neither of them had seemed interested in pursuing things any further. And they couldn't share what they were really doing, not without being labeled conspiracy theorists. They'd be in a padded cell before the day was over, and whoever was behind all of this would be another step ahead of them. Another step closer to locating the treasure.

"Maybe you're right, Harry. But if Mark thought the diary was important, I can't just let it go. I'm calling the front desk."

"What about the code thingy?" Harrison said. "Did they get that too?"

"No. I kept it separate from everything else."

"Good. Where is it?"

Avery got up and crossed the living room. She got down on her knees and reached up under the couch where Harrison had fallen asleep the previous night. She pulled out the enigma and held it up for him to see.

"Mom always told me to keep my valuables separate."

"She didn't mean under the couch."

Sea water sprayed over the windshield as waves slammed against the hull of the fiberglass boat. Samael sat alone in the stern checking his phone while Babcock and one other man sat at the helm. They had been traveling out to sea for the last twenty minutes, maintaining a pace of about thirty knots, and were now far away from the shore and any other boats.

Samael signaled for the pilot to stop the boat as they had reached their destination. Neither one of the men knew what they were doing out here, but both had been in Samael's employ long enough to know better than to ask too many questions. They were told only what they needed to know to get the job done.

Samael remained seated as he instructed Babcock to keep an eye out for the boat with which they were supposed to rendezvous.

"You got it," Babcock said as he grabbed a pair of Bosch binoculars from inside the door that led to the lower deck.

"Nothing yet, Samael," Babcock said.

"Keep an eye peeled," Samael said as he pocketed the phone and stood. He approached Babcock from behind.

"Who are we meeting anyway?" Babcock said.

It was an unusual breach in protocol and Samael attributed it to Babcock having been his go-to man for so long. Babcock no doubt confused his importance to the organization and Samael directly with friendship, or at least something akin to it. While Samael had grown fond of the man, he couldn't abide sloppiness. And it was only a matter of time before Babcock's fingerprint was traced back to him.

Samael removed the garrote from the inside pocket of his suit jacket and allowed it to hang loose before gripping it at both ends. The boat captain glanced down at Samael's hands then back to his face. Samael nodded toward the hold and the captain nodded his understanding.

"I'm gonna grab something to drink," the man said. "You guys want anything?"

"I'm good," Babcock said.

"I'll take a bottled water," Samael said.

"Be right back," the pilot said.

"See anything?" Samael asked from right behind Babcock.

"Not—"

Samael moved with lightning quickness as Babcock lowered the binoculars. Before Babcock could utter another word, the piano wire was cinched tight around his neck. As the reality of his situation hit, he dropped the binoculars and began clawing at his throat, trying to get a hand under the ever-tightening wire. Samael drove his knee into Babcock's lower back and pulled on both wooden handles of the homemade garrote. Babcock let out an audible gagging sound as his struggles intensified. Samael held firmly, feeling the wire sinking deeper into his former subordinate's neck.

Babcock's head was beet red, and his eyes bulged as his blood pressure spiked. His attempts to struggle free were no match for Samael's upper body strength. Deprived of oxygen, Babcock quickly tired. His legs collapsed from under him, and his body drooped toward the deck as the captain returned with Samael's water.

Samael turned his head toward the captain without missing a beat, his voice almost pleasant. "Thank you. Just set it over there until I'm finished."

"Y-yes, sir."

It took thirty seconds before Babcock's struggles ended and his lifeless body collapsed to the deck. Samael knelt over him, continuing to hold tightly until he was sure it was over. After a long moment, Samael removed a glove and checked Babcock's wrist for a pulse. Confident that Babcock was dead, he unwound the garrote then walked over to where the captain had left his water and took a long drink.

After checking out of the hotel with no answers regarding the safe break in, Avery paused next to the Boston PD patrol car in the fire lane outside, dropping the tagged nail file into the cracked back window. It bounced onto the floor and under the seat like it knew what she wanted.

Harrison nodded. "Solid choice. That should throw off whoever stuck it there for a while, at minimum."

They glanced around and made a beeline for the rental car. Avery sent a quick text to Marco, who confirmed that he had landed and refueled and was now awaiting them at Logan.

"Is this the part where you say I told you so?" Avery said.

"Nope, I'm not gonna do that," Harrison said.

"I'm not sure who cared less: the hotel manager or the beat cop they sent over."

"It's just that Boston is a big city, Ave. The police have bigger fish to fry than some dusty old diary taken from a hotel safe."

"At least the manager was contrite about the cameras on our floor being offline," Avery said, waving a card. "Three free nights in the presidential suite isn't the diary, but it's not nothing."

False bravado aside, Avery couldn't shake the feeling that losing the diary had put them two steps back.

"Assuming you're right about the location of the wreck," Harrison said, in an obvious attempt to change the subject.

"*Bonnet Rouge.*"

"That's what I said. Assuming you're right about Mark having discovered its location, won't whoever took the diary be able to figure it out now?"

"But they don't have the enigma, Harry." Avery was trying to reassure herself as much as Harrison. "And they haven't got the note Mark left at the motel. I don't think they can figure it out without that. I'm far more worried about who took the diary in the first place. You don't think it was Mark's friend Corbacho?"

"He did want that desk," Harrison said. "But he was with us, and so was most of his staff. Shotgun Sarah from the antique store who warned us off the trail knew we had access to Mark's home, though. And she might very well have known more about the desk than she let on to us."

"But we didn't decide to come here until after we left there," Avery said.

"But we did get Corbacho's address from her. She could have sent someone after us if she suspected Mark cracked the secret of the old desk. For all we know she's in cahoots with the elusive Mr. Babcock." Harrison checked the traffic behind them. The rental jerked to one side as he made an unscheduled lane change.

Avery grabbed hold of the dash. "What are you doing, Harry?"

"Hang on, Ave," Harrison said as he stood on the brakes then made a quick U turn against a red traffic signal, narrowly avoiding a line of oncoming cars.

"I figured if someone wants us dead anyway, I could just oblige them. No?" Harrison said.

"Um, I'd rather stay alive long enough to beat them to the treasure if you don't mind."

"Relax. I'm just making sure we aren't being followed. There's nothing harder to tail than a crazy ex-cop who likes to make unexpected U-turns."

"Did it work?" Avery asked as she glanced into her side mirror.

"I didn't see anyone dumb enough to follow, if that's what you mean."

"Good. Would you do me a favor the next time you decide to pull a crazy Ivan?"

"What's that?"

"Warn me."

27

Marco touched down at the airport on Hilton Head Island just after seven o'clock. The black Expedition Avery had rented online was ready and waiting for them. The short drive to Bluffton, South Carolina, was everything Avery had pictured in her mind. Spanish moss hung from century-old Oaks, while palm trees backlit by the fiery setting sun dotted the lush landscape.

She had booked a four-bedroom cottage at Montage Palmetto Bluff, a high end Lowcountry resort overlooking the May River. The Lawson Cottage was a single-story residence over four thousand square feet in size. Avery imagined the open concept center hall would provide a nice meeting spot for them to plan their hunt, while the individual bedrooms scattered to the four corners would allow them some privacy. She wasn't overly optimistic about the prospect of Harrison and Carter getting along—Harrison was old school, methodical and by-the-book. Carter was Mr. Impetuous, a walking, talking fly-life-by-the-seat-of-his-swim-trunks professional beach bum/adrenaline junkie. Oil, meet water.

Harrison guided them along the winding, tree-lined street while Avery monitored their progress by GPS.

"This is it, Harry," Avery said. "Turn left."

The property was even more spectacular than it had appeared online, with a peaked center roof, recessed double door entryway, white clapboard siding with brick-colored shutters, and hidden accent lights highlighting both the architecture and landscaping.

"This is your idea of a cottage?" Harrison asked, garnering a smirk from Marco as they pulled into the winding drive.

"Well, it was the only four-bedroom unit available, Harry," Avery said. "I can still rebook if you'd prefer to share a room with Carter."

Marco laughed out loud until Harrison's reflected glare in the rear-view mirror stopped him in his tracks.

"Speaking of," Harrison said. "Where is Mr. Wonderful?"

"He's meeting us at the restaurant," Avery said. "We can't dawdle. They close at ten. Let's just dump our things and go."

"Sounds good to me," Harrison said as he grabbed several bags from the SUV's cargo hold. "I'm starving."

"You really didn't have to include me, Ms. Turner," Marco said. "I'm perfectly fine staying near the airport."

"Nonsense, Marco. I've already asked too much of you on this trip. You'll stay with us. And golf to your heart's content."

"Yeah, Marco," Harrison said. "Take a walk on the wild side."

"And you'll dine with us this evening," Avery added.

"Thank you, Ms. Turner."

"Oh, and Harry, The River House is business casual. Maybe throw on a jacket over one of your polos."

"They're going to overcharge for tiny, pretty food," he grumbled. "Why is it that they get to tell me what to wear?"

Avery raised one eyebrow.

"I know. Fancy people, fancy food, fancy clothes. I didn't say I wouldn't do it."

"The steak and seafood is supposed to be excellent." Avery smiled. "You'll forget all about the jacket with the first bite."

Avery and Harrison found Carter waiting for them at the far side of the restaurant, seated at a table overlooking the river. He stood to greet them. Avery grabbed his offered hand with both of hers. "Thank you so much for coming."

"Nobody ever has to ask me on an adventure twice." Carter grinned, shaking hands with Harrison and Marco. "I can make that dive. No problem."

The four of them quickly perused the menu while making small talk as the waiter took their drink orders.

"I think we're ready to order," Avery said as their drinks were placed before them.

They began with lobster bisque. Moving on to the main course, Avery opted for the Szechuan pepper duck breast with gooseberry sauce and baby cauliflower, while Harrison ordered the eighteen-ounce dry aged ribeye with whipped potatoes. Carter and Marco each had the Maine lobster tail, jumbo asparagus and pomme frites with truffle aioli.

Aside from small talk and the occasional rumble of ecstasy garnered by the exquisite culinary flavors, the table was largely quiet as they ate.

"I can't eat another bite," Harrison said as he slid the nearly empty plate away and sat back with his glass of beer.

"I don't think I've ever enjoyed such a fabulous meal," Marco said when he had finished.

"Well, you've earned it, Marco," Avery said. "And I'm sorry about how much waiting around you've had to do on our account this week."

"You are much too kind. It is my pleasure to be your pilot," Marco said.

"And the new keeper of the code breaker," Harrison added as he looked at Avery. "A jet always trumps a couch, right?"

Avery had watched Marco lock the enigma in the fireproof safe in the cockpit of her Gulfstream earlier as she told him a story about sentimental value, claiming she'd be heartbroken if anything happened to it and she was rattled after the hotel break-in. She trusted Marco with her life—literally, he flew her plane—but was beginning to think knowing the truth about that gizmo or the journal could be dangerous to his.

"It's safe where it is." Marco pushed his chair back and stood. "If you will excuse me, I'm going to call it a night. Need my rest for tomorrow's golf."

"Hit 'em straight, my friend," Harrison said, raising a glass.

"Good night, Marco," Avery and Carter said in unison.

"Buenos noches," Marco said as he departed.

"I like him," Carter said, turning back to Avery. "Want to tell me more about this device he's supposed to be guarding?"

She glanced around the dining room, making sure no one was listening to their conversation, then pulled up a photo on her phone. "Listen at your own risk. I'm not really sure what it does exactly."

"It's an enigma," Harrison said, giving Avery a smug grin.

"It certainly is, Harry," Avery said before her attention returned to Carter. "It's a code maker, or breaker, but I don't yet know how it ties in with the *Bonnet Rouge*. There's no question that Mark believed it was linked to the search somehow."

"Bring me up to speed," Carter said, still studying the photo.

For the next half hour, Avery recounted everything that had happened, pausing only when the waiter swung by to pour their coffee.

"And the guy on Martha's Vineyard turned out to be a friend of your friend Mark's, but you didn't know that before you went out there?" Carter asked. "Wild."

"Corbacho was actually quite charming," Avery said. "I know that he and Mark go way back, and I wonder if that doesn't have something to do with both of their families being tied to the search for this treasure. I also know that without the seed money from Corbacho, Hawkins Tech never would have gotten off the ground."

"Are you going to give him the desk?"

"I suppose?" Avery shrugged. "I haven't decided yet, though it seems easy enough, and according to him the previous owner of the house wasn't supposed to sell it to Mark in the first place. But I can deal with that later."

"Did you tell the police about the break-in to your hotel room?" Carter asked.

"I did," Avery said as she shot a glance at Harrison.

"I didn't think it was a good idea," Harrison said.

"Harry tried to tell me that the last thing the police would care about was a worthless old diary stolen from a hotel room."

"And?"

"He was right. They didn't care."

"I'm sorry you lost it," Carter said. "What was that you said about a tracker in your bag?"

"Whoever planted it is tracking a BPD squad car now." Avery grinned.

"And you have no ideas?"

"Oh we have several—someone in the woods near the inn the other night, whoever broke into Mark's safe and attacked his manager, or maybe even some sort of septuagenarian gang of rogue antique dealers." Avery smiled at Carter's widened eyes. "While I like the safecrackers as suspects because . . . well, safes were cracked in both places. . . . All we have to go on is a fingerprint from some guy named Babcock that Harry found in Mark's study, and so far Harry's friends at the NYPD have been unsuccessful tracking him down."

"That's . . . pretty deep," Carter said.

"Speaking of deep, tell us your thoughts about tomorrow," Avery said, changing the subject.

Carter finished off his beer before answering. "I secured us a dive boat right here at the resort marina. We're booked for a 7:30 charter."

"In the morning?" Harrison said, nearly choking on his own beverage.

"Harry is such an early bird," Avery teased before turning back to Carter. "So, tomorrow at 7:30? Did I choose a good launch point?"

"Yeah, I checked out the marina a bit before you guys arrived. Everything we'll need is nearby. This should be a good base of operations for what we're planning."

"What exactly are we planning?" Harrison said.

"We're gonna check out the coordinates that Avery came up with," Carter said.

"She did tell you how badly other people want this thing we're after, right?" Harrison said. "I mean, if there's something out there, this could be dangerous."

Carter exchanged a glance with Avery. "You really think someone killed your friend Mark over this lost treasure?"

Avery exchanged a look with Harrison before answering. "I can't prove it," Avery said. "But yes, I still do."

"Danger is my middle name," Carter said, folding his arms across his chest. "And it won't be the first time I've done something crazy. Count me in."

28

Avery awoke before sunrise. Her emotions ran the gamut, but a heady mixture of excitement and uncertainty led the charge. She was nervous about the distinct possibility she might be wrong about the coordinates. That the coded message left by Mark had an entirely different meaning, making today's dive nothing but a wild goose chase—and a waste of time they didn't have to squander. With coffee in hand, she found Carter outside checking their gear at the rear of his rented van.

"You're starting to act like a real shipwreck hunter," Carter said.

"How do you mean?" Avery said.

"Look at you. You've got the pre-hunt jitters. Worried that you're chasing ghosts instead of anything tangible. That is the definition of a treasure hunter, Avery."

"I thought you didn't hunt treasure, Carter. Isn't that what you told me? Something about a fool's errand."

Carter grinned. "What can I say? I am occasionally a fool."

"What's that thing you're messing with?" Avery said.

"It's a portable oceanic sonar device. Helps me pinpoint objects under water before I dive."

"You really think we'll find something?"

"Of course."

"How can you be so sure?"

"When was the last time you were wrong, Avery Turner?"

Now it was her turn to smile. "Touché."

Harrison, with a bad case of bed head, ambled up to where they were talking. Dressed in sandals, cargo shorts, and an untucked, loud orange and blue Hawaiian shirt, he was nursing a large, insulated mug of coffee. He looked anything but excited.

"Morning, Harry," Avery said. "See you found the Keurig."

"Morning," Carter said, closing the rear doors and pointing them to the passenger seats before he slid behind the wheel.

"We're still on for today, huh?" Harrison asked as he looked up at the sky before folding his long frame into a second-row seat in the van.

"Of course." Avery closed her door. "Why wouldn't we be?"

"I just figured with the fog and everything, maybe we shouldn't go miles out into the ocean."

"It's supposed to burn off by midmorning," Carter said, turning onto the short street that led to the marina.

"Besides, it isn't foggy underwater," Avery teased.

Harrison grunted something unintelligible and fell quiet.

"Any interest in learning to dive?" Carter asked Harrison. "I could teach you."

"Absolutely none," Harrison said, with the same look he'd give Carter for offering to drop him into a pit of vipers.

"Why not, Harry?" Avery said.

"It starts with eels and ends with sharks. Didn't you see *Jaws*?"

Carter and Avery both laughed.

"A good right hook will scare off just about anything underwater, though eels can be pretty territorial." Carter parked right in front of the marina and began unloading equipment.

"Yeah?" Harrison said, climbing out of the van and extending a hand to help Avery. "Then I guess Avery will be all set."

"You don't have to come with us if you aren't comfortable, Harry," Avery said, hopping down without touching his fingers.

Carter's head swiveled like he had ball bearings in his neck. "Us?"

"On the dive. Me and you."

"Me in the water, you on the boat," Carter said slowly, pointing to the double tank rack and equipment for one at his feet.

"Not a chance." Avery folded her arms across her chest and set her jaw.

Harrison leaned against the dock railing with a look on his face that said he'd give his left leg for some popcorn.

"A hundred and thirty-five feet is deep for a diver with your limited experience." Carter shook his head. "I know it doesn't sound like very far when you're thinking about distance from say, here to there," he pointed to the dock. "But stand it up, and it's a long way, Avery. I'm all for thrill seeking, but there's foolish and then there's . . ." he trailed off, still shaking his head.

"Stupid?" Avery asked, her voice sharp.

"I didn't say that."

"You stopped just short. I'm new, but I'm a fast learner, Carter. You don't get to be a billionaire at twenty-eight without unusual intellect."

"I might beg to differ with that on several levels," Carter began before pausing. "I know you're smart. And you really have learned fast. But I can't risk letting you get hurt."

"You said yourself you're certified to teach to a hundred forty-five feet," Avery said. "So call this lesson number one. I mean, it has to be safer than deep diving by yourself, right? What was the first thing you told me? Rule number one?"

"Never dive alone." Carter muttered to his shoes, leaning his forehead on one upturned hand for five deep breaths. He had notched dozens of solo dives, but only a couple of them this deep. And though Avery was coming up on being eligible for her deepwater certification, she hadn't completed the required training dives for it yet. This would be skipping ahead, but she was right about her intelligence—he'd never known anyone as smart as Avery.

When he finally looked up, he held Avery's gaze for what felt like a week. "You have to swear on everything you've ever believed in that you will do exactly what I tell you," he said. "I've already figured out you don't like taking direction, but this is an absolute for me. If you can't promise to follow every direction without question—without thinking—you stay at the surface."

Avery held up two fingers. "Scouts' honor."

"You were nev—" Harrison began, stopping short when her foot shot back into his shin.

"This is serious," Carter said. "I know I like to have fun, but it's possible I've never been more serious about anything in my life." He looked at Harrison, then back at Avery. "You could die."

"Then so could you, and I dragged you out here," she said breezily. "I'll do everything you say. On my mother's grave."

Harrison nodded at that one and Carter sighed. "I don't like this. But I'll go get you some equipment."

They watched him jog to the rental station. "Your mother always said you were like a dog with a bone when you wanted something," Harrison said.

"And you always said I got it from her," Avery retorted. "You don't think this is a mistake, do you Harry?"

"No. I'm pretty stubborn when I want to be, too. I trust you. You just worry about what's underwater, Ave. I'll keep an eye out for predators of the topside variety." Harrison patted the bulge on his right hip.

"You really think someone could find us here?" Avery said.

"They found that diary in the hotel safe, didn't they?"

"I checked all our stuff for more weird objects last night," Avery said. "I didn't find anything." She nodded down the dock, where Carter was heading their way lugging a second set of heavy gear.

He stopped in front of her and put her gear down before he returned the sonar device to its case, then checked his watch. "We should head down to the boat. It's a long ride out to the dive site and back."

Harrison and Carter hefted the dive bags and tanks, while Avery carried the sonar unit and a couple of canvas totes containing their provisions for the day-long trip: bananas, yogurt bars, bottled water, and motion sickness pills for Harrison.

Their charter was a beautiful thirty-six-foot Seahawk. All chrome and fiberglass, the spotless boat featured a flying bridge, with a cobalt-colored

Bimini top, a dive platform and twin Honda outboard engines. Avery laughed at Carter when she saw the name on the stern. *Fool's Gold.*

"Thought it was appropriate," Carter said.

"Morning, folks," the captain called as they approached.

"Good morning," Avery said.

"Great day for a dive," the captain said as he assisted each of them with their gear.

"If you say so," Harrison grumbled.

Their captain introduced himself as Nathan "Nat" Pelletier and told them he was a retired navy lieutenant with over two thousand dives logged over the course of his life.

Avery knew Harrison would warm up to Nat eventually. Both were cut from the same cloth. Two burly middle-aged men, each with a treasure trove of war stories to keep them occupied as the day wore on.

"So, you folks planning to dive one of the popular wrecks?" Nat said. "You know we've got a number of them."

Carter spoke up, "Actually, we've got another site in mind."

"Oh?"

"About thirty miles out."

"We'll be working off our own set of coordinates," Avery said.

"Treasure hunters?" Nat said with a glint in his eyes.

Avery exchanged a look with Carter before answering. "Something like that," she said.

After a quick tour of the boat and a mandatory safety speech, Harrison donned a life vest while Avery and Carter untied the boat from the dock cleats. Nat fired up the engines then steered them toward open water.

As Avery suspected, Harrison climbed up to the flying bridge and sat down beside Nat. Avery leaned against the port side gunwale, sipping her coffee as she watched Carter begin his inspection of their equipment. After a moment, her attention shifted toward the shore, watching as the resort faded into the fog.

"You honestly think we'll find anything?" Avery asked, trying hard to temper her expectations with logic.

"That's what makes this stuff fun, Avery. The unknown."

"I suppose."

"If everything you've told me is true, then you must be onto something, right? Someone thinks you are, or they wouldn't be trying so hard to stop you."

And it certainly looked like someone was trying to thwart their progress. But who? Harrison had joked about shotgun wielding antique dealers, but Avery had to admit Louise Williams and David Adams did seem to be part of a network of sorts. Well versed in history and valuable antiques, they would be hard pressed not to know what Mark was up to. And Williams had a personal connection to the general's gold, losing her father to the pursuit. Even had one of the coins secreted away. Was the surprisingly spry elderly woman more than she seemed?

Beyond who was throwing obstacles at them like banana peels in a high-stakes game of Mario Kart, Mark's death had occupied Avery's thoughts all morning. Was Corbacho right? Was Mark suffering from some deep depression over the pending lawsuit? The Mark Hawkins she had known would never have killed himself. Or was that just something she wanted—no needed—to believe? She didn't know. And she hated the uncertainty.

The fog dissipated quickly as the sun warmed the air. Avery scanned the horizon, half expecting to see another boat following, but there was nothing but ocean in their wake. She dumped the rest of her coffee over the side, then assisted Carter with the gear.

Twenty minutes later Nat throttled back on the engines.

"What's up?" Carter said.

"Got a weather warning," Nat said.

Avery looked around at nothing but clear skies and bright sunshine.

"What kind of weather?" Carter said.

"Might be some large waves incoming."

Avery looked at the water. It was choppy but nothing that appeared ominous to her.

"We'll keep going for now," Nat continued. "But we gotta be careful."

"Okay," Carter said. "I'll lash down our equipment and keep an eye peeled just in case."

Nat nodded and throttled the boat up again.

"Tell me this doesn't mean we're not going to be able to dive today," Avery said. "I don't think I can wait any more."

Carter grinned. "Look at you. You've got it bad, don't you?"

"I just want to know what's down there."

"We'll have to see what happens. Nat has been at this a long time, Avery. A lot longer than me. If he says we can dive, then we will. It's entirely his call."

Avery tried hard not to pout as they secured the dive equipment. She glanced up at Harrison. He looked calm, but she noticed that he was holding tightly to the Bimini frame. *He might just need those motion pills*, she thought.

Avery watched as Carter worked on the sonar device he had shown her earlier. He was busy attaching it to a long aluminum pole.

"We must be getting close," Avery said after a while.

Before Carter could answer, his dive watch began beeping. "We're here."

Avery signaled for Nat to stop the boat. He powered down the engines then shut them off entirely. The silence was a pleasant change from the noisy engines. The only sounds were Carter working and the occasional slap of a wave against the hull.

Avery could feel the excitement building, it was almost too much. She began to understand why people became addicted to adrenaline.

"So, this is your dive area, huh?" Nat said as he and Harrison descended the ladder to the deck.

"This is it," Avery said.

"I've never brought anyone to dive here before. Maybe you'll be in luck."

"Don't we need to drop anchor or something?" Harrison said.

"Don't need one," Nat said. "This baby's equipped with an electronic anchor."

"How's that?" Harrison said.

"It uses electric jets to keep us from drifting. Like what the cruise ships use to parallel park those monsters."

"This is quite the boat you own," Avery said.

Nat laughed. "I wish it were mine. Military pension doesn't go that far, I'm afraid. Nope, I just work for the owner."

While they continued to make small talk, Carter powered up the small digital screen connected to the sonar then began lowering the device over the side and into the water.

"Nat, could I get you to make a few short, slow passes back and forth over this spot?" Carter said.

"Sure thing," Nat said as he started back up the ladder. "Come on, Harry. I'll let you take a turn at the wheel."

"Harry?" Avery said. No one called him that but Avery—and her mom.

"What?" Harrison said. "Nat's a pretty cool guy."

Avery monitored the screen while Carter maneuvered the probe to the bow of the boat.

"What you're looking at is a long angle, Avery," Carter said. "I can't very well use a pole long enough to reach the bottom, so we're looking for anything that looks man made."

"Like a sunken ship?" Avery said, giving him a wry smile.

"Yeah, like that."

The water here was clearer than Avery would have imagined, but nothing like it was in the Keys. She could just make out various reefs and larger fish passing beneath the boat. They had been at it for the better part of an hour and Avery was beginning to think she had led them on a wild goose chase after all when she spotted something on screen.

"Carter," she yelled.

"You got something?" Nat called down.

"I think so," Avery said.

"Hang on," Carter said. "Let me take a look."

"I can't see it now," Avery said as he approached still holding the sonar pole.

"No worries. We recorded everything so I can play it back."

Carter carefully set the device off to one side of the deck as Marty and Harrison climbed down for a look.

The four of them huddled around the small screen as Carter replayed the last few minutes of video footage.

"There, right there," Avery said excitedly.

"You're right," Carter said, freezing the image on what appeared to be a reef and the outline of a debris field. "There is something there, just off the port side of the bow." He turned toward her. "Something old and half decayed."

"Can we get to it?" Avery said.

"Like I said, the sonar projects out and down. That's a little farther than I want to swim. We'll have to get closer."

Avery looked anxiously at Nat.

He gave her a wink. "Let's see if we can't put you right over it."

It took several seconds for Avery to regain her bearings after splashing overboard with Carter. Despite the clarity of the sonar-generated image, the ocean here was much less translucent than what she had become accustomed to off the Florida coast. Here, filtered light barely illuminated the underwater world. Carter had tried to talk her out of accompanying him, but Avery would have none of it.

"This is deeper than anything you've done yet," Carter had said as he helped her with her double-racked air tanks. "We have no more than seven minutes on the bottom, and you'll need to remember everything I taught you about ascending and follow my cues. Okay?"

"I got it, Carter," she'd said. "A lot more can go wrong on a dive like this. But you don't have to worry. I'll stay right with you. I won't do anything stupid. I promise."

Now that she was undersea, it was obvious that Carter had been right. This dive was completely different from anything they had done in Florida. There, Avery had been diving for pleasure: exploring the ocean floor, practicing her newly certified skills, and discovering underwater creatures in their natural habitat. The only shipwreck she had seen was one that had previously been discovered and likely explored thousands of times by other divers, with traffic heavy enough to keep most of the more dangerous sea life away. This wreck, assuming she was right about it being the *Bonnet Rouge*, had never been located by anyone. This was Mark's discovery as much as Carter's and hers. She was doing this for her old friend, because no matter how complicated he was or how frustrated and sad she felt thinking of him, she had loved Mark.

Carter broke her reverie by tapping on her headlamp. He pressed against the controls, incrementally increasing its brightness until she gave him an okay sign. He returned the gesture then pointed down, the water so deep the sunlight disappeared far above the floor. Avery nodded.

Carter had explained that consumption of air underwater was three times what they would use on the surface. The less they used now, the safer they'd be on the bottom and coming back up. She did her best to try to relax, but it was difficult as her excitement grew with every meter.

As they neared the ocean floor, the wreck, or what was left of it, began to take shape.

29

Much of the hull had disintegrated into the ocean floor, looking nothing like what Avery had imagined. In fact, it was so crumbled she completely understood why nobody had ever located it. Were it not for Carter's sonar picking up a manmade shape from above the surface so they knew what to look for and where, they might have swum right past it.

The remains looked more like a debris field than a shipwreck. Encased in algae and barnacles, the wreck was more vegetation and wildlife than ship, another thing that helped it stay hidden. Avery was mesmerized by the vibrant colors illuminated by the beams of their headlamps. A swirling mixture of ultramarine, Prussian, and cerulean arose from the blue green sand into conical shapes, reminding her of dried paint on an artist's palette. Particulates floated by like snow, while small, dull-colored fish playfully darted about. She was in awe of this strange new world.

As Carter signaled that he was about to begin filming, Avery backed off slightly to allow him a clear shot. She used the opportunity to check her gauges. All good. Carter caught her checking and nodded. He signaled for her to stay close.

As Carter quickly filmed overalls then closeups of the area, Avery used her diving knife to pry away some of the growth. If this were, in fact, the *Bonnet Rouge,* with so much decay there would be little chance of confirming it. She didn't know what she had expected after the passage of a hundred and sixty years, but even a portion of the ship would have been nice.

Unlike the freighter she and Carter had explored off the keys, if there was anything left of this ship's hull, it was buried beneath tons of sand and debris. He had previously explained how currents, tides, and tropical storms could reshape the bottom into something unrecognizable from one year to the next. Avery realized how lucky they were to find anything. The wreck of this ship, whatever it was, may well have been completely buried, even as recently as last year.

Carter put the camera away and showed her how to stir up sand and search through it. He pointed out nearby drifts of pale-colored sand, once again reminding her of snow.

Avery drifted along just above the ocean bottom, letting her gloved hands skim across the sand near the wreck as Carter searched nearby. She paused to dig through several of the drifts, but the sand resettled as fast as she could remove it. Carter flashed a thumbs up, telling her that it was time to head back to the surface. She marveled at how long and short seven minutes could feel all at once. Taking one last plunge into a drift, Avery spotted a glimmer of something metal at the bottom of the hole she'd made before sand clouded the hole, obliterating the object from sight once again. She jabbed her arm in again elbow deep and felt her hand connect with something hard and circular. Carter appeared in front of her ordering her to the surface. She pulled her arm from the drift and held the item up for him to see. The sand floated away, revealing the remnants of a pocket watch.

Realizing she'd broken her promise to stay right beside him, Avery followed Carter's every command as they swam toward the surface. At his insistence, they stopped twice to decompress. Both times she studied the broken watch while waiting.

Ascending to the surface was much easier than diving had been and would have been quicker were it not for the decompression stops. Avery was anxious to share her find with Harrison and do some online research on the piece.

Carter pointed toward the surface one last time indicating that there would be no further stops. Several minutes later they broke through, surrounded by waves. It took Avery a moment to realize that something was amiss: their boat was gone. Removing her mouthpiece, she turned to find Carter pointing in the other direction. Her eyes followed and saw the *Fool's Gold* in the distance, its engines wide open as it raced away from them.

Avery knew there was only one way they could have been abandoned. Treading water she spun about, searching frantically in every direction.

"There," she yelled, pointing at a brightly colored object floating on the surface nearby. Harrison, face down in the water. "Harry!" Avery yelled, kicking her feet hard in that direction as Carter moved alongside her.

They swam toward Harrison's body as fast as they could.

30

"Harry," Avery yelled again as she and Carter attempted to roll Harrison onto his back. It took several tries before they succeeded. Harrison's sputtering as he reflexively coughed up saltwater was a welcome sound—since Avery was frantically trying to figure out how they might perform CPR in more than a hundred feet of ocean water—but he was still unconscious. His breathing was labored, and he was bleeding from a deep head wound.

"We gotta get help," Avery said.

"My watch," Carter said. "I can send a distress signal through the GPS."

"Do it."

Carter had water rescue training as a scuba instructor, and showed Avery how to help him stanch the bleeding and to keep Harrison afloat while protecting his airway. Avery scanned the horizon for the *Fool's Gold,* but both the boat and Nat were gone.

"We've got to do something, Carter," Avery said as another wave washed over them and Harrison sputtered out more water.

"We've done all we can until someone comes for us. All we can do is pray."

Being overly independent, it had been a long while since Avery had pleaded for divine intervention. But she was a pragmatist at heart, and if prayer were all she had left, prayer it would be.

Avery had no idea how long they had been treading water and awaiting help. Stress made it feel like hours had passed, but she knew it hadn't been that long. Her eyes were growing weary from constantly sweeping their surroundings for ominous things like dorsal fins. A small slick of Harrison's spilled blood floated atop the water, causing Avery to regret her comment to Carter about lacking a healthy fear of sharks. They took turns holding Harrison's head out of the water and keeping him afloat. Carter used his short breaks to recheck his watch.

"How can you know the distress signal even went through?" Avery asked as her legs began to cramp from exertion.

"Guess I can't," Carter said. "But it's all I have, Avery. You gotta keep the faith."

Avery couldn't help but wonder what had occurred on the boat while they were underwater. Had whoever the heck was chasing them gotten to Nat, the boat captain? Or had they been followed to the boat? Someone could have followed them from the resort, but how would they have located them in the first place? Her electronic tracker search last night had been almost too thorough. Did they know about Carter? If so, maybe whoever it was had somehow tracked him to the marina. Paid off the captain he hired, perhaps? But why hadn't Harrison noticed that something was off about the guy?

"Is he still breathing okay?" Avery asked.

"He's breathing fine, Avery."

"What about water temperature? Is it too cold? I mean we're wearing wet suits, it's not the same for him."

"The water isn't cold enough to hurt him. He's gonna be fine. We just gotta get him to shore."

"Why don't we try swimming?" she said, realizing how ludicrous it sounded even as she spoke the words.

"Because we're miles from shore. We need to stay put so they can find us."

"You want me to spell you?" Avery asked.

"It's okay. I got him. Hey, how about we play twenty questions?"

Avery scowled at him. "Really? You're gonna try and take my mind off what's happening here with a child's game?"

"Why not? I mean unless you have somewhere else to be."

Carter's comment got them both laughing, despite their obvious peril.

"Okay," Avery said. "You first."

"All right. What was the hardest moment of your tech career?"

"That's easy. Ceding control of the app I developed to Mark. I had all kinds of ideas on refinements that would have made the mapping feature more useful and profitable."

"More profitable? It made you rich."

"Yeah, but I wasn't done with it. You might've picked up on the fact that I have control issues."

Carter grinned. "I never would have guessed."

"My turn, wise guy. Favorite ice cream flavor?"

"Depends on the day, but today I'd have to go with rocky road."

"How fitting."

"Ask me something more difficult then," Carter said.

"What scares you?"

"Serious injury."

"You're kidding. With all the thrill-seeking stuff you do?"

"That's just it. My whole life has been about chasing the next rush. When I was sixteen I spent my entire summer working, not for something normal like a car, but so I could take skydiving lessons in the fall. I love skydiving, scuba diving, all that stuff. If I got injured permanently, I don't think I could cope. You know what I mean?"

"I guess that kinda makes sense."

"What about you?" Carter said. "What are you afraid of?"

"That!" Avery screamed as she pointed to the large gray dorsal fin slicing through the waves directly at them.

31

Avery screamed again, still pointing as images of the next day's headlines raced through her brain like some macabre slideshow: *Death on the High Seas, Shark Attack, South Carolina Shark Scores a Hat Trick*

"Avery," Carter said. "Don't panic."

"But—"

"I need you to take care of Harrison. He's bleeding, that's probably what this guy smells."

At the mention of Harrison's name, Avery quickly refocused. "Okay," she said as Carter transferred Harrison over to her.

"Keep as still as you can, okay?" Carter said as he swam away from them.

"I'll try."

She watched as Carter put himself between her and the shark. Carter drew his diving knife, as it was the only weapon he had available. Avery felt her breath quickening as the dorsal continued toward them, not deviating and not slowing. Was the flip comparison she'd made days ago in the Keys to battling the sharks of Wall Street about to come racing under the water to literally bite her in the ass? This wasn't a board room or a safe cubicle with a programming setup, it was life or death, and the monster swimming their way was obviously serious.

Harrison began to stir, struggling slightly in her grasp.

"My head," he mumbled.

"Stay still, Harry," Avery said. "I got you."

The sound of a large engine approaching from behind drew her attention. A boat. A big boat. She whispered a thank you at the wide sky.

"Carter," she said as loudly as she dared.

"I hear it, Avery. Just keep still a little longer. The calvary isn't here yet."

She watched as Carter re-sheathed the knife and began to struggle out of his X-Tek twin tank harness.

"Don't look at me, Avery," Carter said. "Watch the boat."

It took every bit of willpower she had to peel her eyes away from the fin and focus on the large red and white Coast Guard vessel closing in on their position.

"What's going on, Ave?" Harrison mumbled.

"Nothing to worry about," she lied. "Help's almost here, Harry. Just be still."

Avery's pulse was pounding in her ears, nearly drowning out the sound of the approaching boat. Against her better judgement she risked a glance back toward Carter in time to see the dorsal slip beneath the surface.

Oh, my God, she thought. *We're not gonna make it.*

Carter's head vanished beneath the waves. For the longest moment she couldn't see Carter or the shark. Avery had never been more terrified in her life. The Coast Guard boat was directly behind her now, its engines slowing, but she couldn't tear her eyes from the spot where Carter disappeared. Suddenly, Carter's torso sprang from the water just as the shark's snout appeared above the waves, flashing a mouth full of razor-sharp teeth. Every muscle in her body tensed as she awaited the hell that was sure to follow. She watched as Carter raised an air tank directly above his head then slammed it down on the shark's snout.

Avery screamed as something splashed into the water right next to her. Following the sound, her eyes were rewarded by the sight of a life ring bearing the U.S. Coast Guard insignia.

"Grab ahold," yelled a voice from the deck of the boat.

Avery grabbed onto the ring with one arm, tucking it in tightly against her torso, while maintaining a grip on Harrison with the other.

"Hang on tight and we'll pull you in," another voice said.

She looked back at Carter as she felt a tug on the rope. There was no sign of the shark. The next few moments were the longest of Avery's life.

The three of them were pulled from the water by the Coast Guard crew without further incident. They were given bottles of water, blankets, and some ill-fitting but dry Coast Guard t-shirts and gray sweatpants. Avery struggled to focus, the aftermath of shock. Despite her jumbled thoughts, she knew what was happening. She refused to leave Harrison's side as one of the crew members treated his head injury.

"Gonna take a few staples to close this," the first officer said to Harrison.

"I'll be fine," Harrison growled as he pushed the oxygen mask away from his face.

"He's hard-headed," Avery said before she could stop herself from blurting out the thought.

Harrison put one arm around her and pulled her close.

"I knew you'd be fine," she said, her words muffled by his shoulder.

The captain, whose name patch identified her as Stringer, stood close by. Avery listened as she grilled Carter on the series of events that led them to needing rescue.

"How exactly did y'all end up out here in the first place?" Stringer asked.

"We were diving from a chartered boat called the *Fool's Gold*. The captain, a guy named Nat Pelletier, abandoned us."

"After he conked me on the head and tossed me overboard," Harrison said.

Stringer turned to another crew member. "Put out an ALCOAST for that boat and its captain."

"Aye-aye, ma'am," the crewman said.

"Let's see if we can't locate the owner, too."

Continuing her inquiry, Stringer asked what they were diving for. Carter explained that he was searching for a sunken ship.

"You're Carter Mosley," one of the other crewmen said. "I thought I recognized you from Instagram."

Another crew member spoke up, "Hey man, I follow all your dives. Great videos, dude."

Avery furrowed a brow, wondering how in the world they'd happened upon two random sailors who followed Carter online. Small world—then again, she'd seen stranger things just today.

"What kind of shark was that?" another crew member asked.

"A bull shark," Carter said.

"You guys are seriously lucky."

The banter between the crew and Carter continued, but Avery let it fade into the background along with the drone of the engine. The terrifying image of the shark's jaws coming out of the water popped into her head again, making her shiver. Avery turned and watched the shoreline draw closer. She pulled the blanket tight around her shoulders then leaned into Harrison for warmth. She never thought she'd be so happy to see land again.

32

The local police awaited them at the Coast Guard station dock. The last thing Avery wanted to do was answer more questions, but the officers would not be dissuaded. The silver lining was that the patrol sergeant persuaded Harrison to take a ride to the hospital and hung around to talk to them there. Avery and Carter sat in the exam room watching the doctor patch up Harrison, while the uniformed officer asked more questions and the sergeant looked on.

"You say you hired this Pelletier guy to take you out diving?" The officer asked Avery.

"That was me," Carter said. "I made the arrangements late yesterday."

"Online or by phone?"

"In person. I walked down to the docks and talked to him."

"And that was Pelletier?"

"Yeah. Nat Pelletier. Said he piloted the boat for the owner."

"And what did you say the name of this boat was?"

"*Fool's Gold*," Avery said answering for him.

Avery caught the knowing glance between the officer and sergeant. Did they not believe them?

"Now that's interesting," the sergeant said. "According to the coast guard, there is no boat named *Fool's Gold* registered in the entire state. Might it have been some other state?"

"No," Carter said. "It said South Carolina right below the name on the stern."

Avery felt her stomach drop at the prospect that they'd been played.

"How is that possible?" Harrison said from his perch atop the exam table.

"We all saw the name on the boat," Avery said.

"You saw *a* name on *a* boat," the sergeant corrected. "Most of these fiberglass boats have stick-on identifiers, adhered overtop the gel coat. Wouldn't be too hard to swap out, I imagine."

"Damn, that stings," Harrison said to the doctor.

"Beats bleeding to death," the doctor replied, earning some points with Avery.

"The guy, whoever he was, knew all about diving and seemed genuine," Harrison said. "Hell, I conversed with him the entire time we were on board. He seemed like a nice guy. Well, up until the moment he bludgeoned me."

"He definitely had experience diving," Carter said. "He knew too many details that only experience will teach a person."

They spent the next half hour going over their statements with the police. Despite Avery's efforts to extract information from the officers, she managed to get little in return for what they shared.

After the doctor had finished stapling Harrison back together and provided him with his discharge orders, the officer and sergeant accompanied them back to their patrol cars.

"You know you really should let the doc give you a CAT scan," Avery said to Harrison.

Harrison gave her his "not today" look, effectively ending the conversation.

"Okay then, now what?" Avery asked, letting her frustration show.

"We wait," the officer said.

"For what?" Harrison said.

The sergeant stepped in. "We have your contact info. And we've put out a description of the boat, and this guy who calls himself Nat Pelletier. We'll interview some of the locals and see if they noticed anyone matching the description you gave. And of course, the coasties will be on the lookout. But without something more to go on, that's really all we can do for now."

Avery wanted to voice her displeasure, but she knew she'd regret anything she said.

"Come on," the sergeant said. "We'll give you a ride to your vehicle."

Avery rode in silence beside Carter in the back of the officer's cruiser. She had nearly reached her breaking point, having had about enough of being played. Who was behind this? Were there really that many bad guys roaming the countryside looking for long-lost gold in the middle of a Thursday?

The police officers dropped them back at the dock, along with their gear. Before leaving, the sergeant handed each of them a business card with his cell phone number on the back, reminding Avery that she and Carter had left their phones locked safely in Carter's rental. Small miracles.

"I'm really sorry this happened to you folks," the sergeant said. "Call me if you think of anything that could help us locate Pelletier."

"Thanks," Harrison said as he took the card.

Avery turned on her heel and marched toward the van.

Carter drove them directly to the rental cottage. Avery surmised that Marco was still golfing as the other rental vehicle was absent from the driveway. She helped Harrison inside leaving Carter to collect their gear. Once inside, despite his protestations, Avery marched Harrison to bed.

"The doctor told you to rest," Avery said. "If you're not gonna have the CAT scan, then you'll at least have to adhere to his orders, and that's an order."

"Aye-aye, Captain," Harrison said, issuing a careful salute so as not to touch the large bandage covering his repaired head.

"I'll be back to check on you every hour," Avery said.

"I'm sure you will."

Following a long, luxurious, hot shower, Avery changed into her own clothes. She chose her favorite jeans and an extra-long loose fitting tee shirt. It was comforting to wear something both familiar and dry. Before heading to the living area, she checked in on Harrison. He was snoring loudly.

Avery found Carter seated at the dining room table with his laptop and dive camera. "Thank you for saving us from the shark," she said.

"You're welcome. Think it helped me get on Harrison's good side?"

"Going to take more than one measly little rescue there." Avery laughed. "Good luck with that."

"He's a tough guy to impress."

"What are you working on?" she asked.

"I'm reviewing the underwater video I shot at the wreck. Hoping it might help us somehow, seeing as how I no longer have the sonar recording."

"Why not?"

"Our fake captain made off with it."

"But we still have the coordinates, and this," Avery said as she walked across the room to retrieve the pocket watch from her dive bag.

"I'd almost forgotten about that."

"I didn't," Avery said, slowly turning it over in her hand as she returned to the table.

"Do you have any idea how lucky you were to find that? People spend their entire lives searching for shipwrecks and lost treasure, usually finding nothing but trouble. That seemed almost easy for you."

"Mark did the hard work running this race," she said. "I'm just carrying his idea across the finish line." She laid the watch on the table. "Are you as hungry as I am?"

"Famished. You wanna go out?"

"Not really feeling it after the day we had. Besides, we must keep an eye on the world's worst patient."

"Let's order out for pizza. Someone must deliver around here."

"I'll call over to the resort's front desk. What do you like on it?"

"Whatever you order will be fine."

"Suck up."

33

Less than an hour later, two large, piping hot pepperoni pizzas arrived along with a 6-pack of soda. Carter cleared his things from the dining room table while Avery grabbed some plates from the kitchen cupboards.

"Were you really gonna eat without me?" Harrison asked as he shuffled down the hallway yawning.

"Actually, I was trying to decide whether or not to wake you," Avery said.

"The aroma of food did that."

"How're you feeling, Harry?" Avery said.

"Like I got pistol-whipped with my own gun. God, that smells good. I'm starving."

"That's gotta be a good sign, right?" Carter said.

"What's this?" Harrison asked as he picked up the watch.

"Something we found at the dive site today," Avery said.

"It looks older than I feel," Harrison said.

"That it does."

Harrison turned his attention to Carter. "By the by, I guess I should thank you for saving me from Jaws out there today."

"Don't mention it," Carter said.

"Though it was your fault I got attacked in the first place."

"How do you figure that, Harry?" Avery said.

"He hired the guy."

Harrison waited a tick before allowing his stoic expression to morph into a grin. "I'm just messing with you. You saved us, and for that I'm grateful. Now let's eat."

"Didn't you say this boat was revolutionary-era?" Harrison asked around a mouthful of pie as he pointed at the watch. "I didn't realize they carried pocket watches way back then."

"Only the very rich," Carter said.

"What are the chances that really belonged to someone aboard that *Bonnet* boat?" Harrison said.

"*Bonnet Rouge*," Avery said. "And I think I might be able to shed some light on that." She pulled out her phone and began scrolling through the images until she found one she'd taken at Louise Williams's shop. She held the phone out for them to see. "It took me a bit to figure out why I thought it looked familiar."

"Who is that?" Carter asked, peering at the image of a newspaper photo on her screen.

"That's Marion Hawkins," Avery said. "Mark's grandfather."

"Jeez, that does look like it could be the same watch," Harrison said, squinting at the photo.

Carter waved one hand and took Avery's phone, scrutinizing the photo as he compared the two watches. "I think you might be right," Carter said. "Do you have any idea how preposterous that sounds?"

"I'm often right," Avery feigned offense.

"I didn't mean—" Carter began, and Avery raised one hand.

"Just messing with you, Mosley. I know how ridiculous a coincidence that would be, but that doesn't make it impossible."

"It makes it unlikely," Carter said.

"And yet, here we are," Harrison said as he grabbed another slice.

"Let's say for argument's sake you're right, and it's not just a similar looking watch," Carter said. "How does this help us?"

"I don't know," Avery admitted. "Other than to indicate that he found the wreck decades before Mark found the diary, which means maybe it doesn't matter as much as I thought that it was stolen."

"So if we ride that wave, this Marion dude found the wreck of the *Bonnet Rouge* and lost his watch, and never came home." Carter paused, holding up one finger and thinking about Vince and company at the *Wilhelmina* two days that felt like a lifetime and a half ago.

"Maybe you're not so far out there after all," he said, relaying the story of what had happened on his last solo dive. "Maybe old Marion Hawkins fought his own pirates and wasn't as lucky as I was. And either the watch fell to the sand in the fight . . ."

"Or Hawkins dropped it on purpose to keep it safe," Avery finished, her eyes wide. "Either of which could be why it was so easy for me to find today."

"Y'all are assuming a lot here," Harrison said, looking at Avery. "And you know what your mother said about assuming."

"I bet I do, too." Carter grinned. "But as you said, here we are. So do we have any idea how Marion came by this watch? Or why he'd take a pocket watch deep sea diving?"

Avery shook her head. "No, and if Mark knew—" Emotion prevented her from completing the thought.

"Reason I ask is I have a go-to on historical finds," Carter said.

"Who?" Harrison said.

"Her name is MaryAnn Everly. She runs a museum in the keys."

"Would that be the same museum where we met?" Avery asked.

"The very same. Want me to contact her?"

"Why not? Here, take a few pictures and send them to her."

Carter snapped photos of the watch from several different angles, then ran off to make the call.

Avery carried the watch into the kitchen. After rummaging through various drawers and cupboards, she found what she was looking for, a plastic potato scrubber.

"What are you gonna do with that, Ave?" Harrison asked.

"I'm hoping to remove some of the gunk built up on the back of this thing," Avery said.

She ran the faucet in the kitchen sink until it warmed, then wet the bristles. Using light circular strokes, she began cleaning the back and edges of the watch.

"Why don't you just hold it under the running water?" Harrison said. "I mean it's been underwater for years, right?"

"Exactly—it's been under constantly shifting water, so if moving water were the answer to cleaning it, it wouldn't still be so icky." Avery didn't look up.

Slowly but surely, the build-up began to come off, revealing a beautifully crafted piece. Avery scrubbed until a familiar pattern emerged on the outside of the back plate. Molded into the center was the familiar lion and cross design. She continued cleaning until the entire watch was exposed and shining.

"There's something etched into the frame of the bezel," Avery said.

"What is it?" Harrison said.

"Can't tell. It's too small to see clearly. Might be symbols."

"What are the odds this place would have a magnifying glass lying around?" Harrison said.

"Zero," Avery said.

"Wait a minute." Harrison sprung up from his chair, then grabbed the end of the table for balance. "Whoa. Guess I'm not ready for marathons just yet."

"Sit down, Harry. I can get whatever you need."

"Yes, ma'am. They're on the nightstand in my room."

"What is?" Avery said.

"My readers."

"Perfect," Avery said, hurrying down the hallway.

She returned with Harrison's glasses and slid them on. "What do you think? Are they me?"

"Um, no," Harrison said. "Not unless you're going for the old librarian look."

Avery gave him a cold stare. "They're your glasses, Harry."

"Touché. Will they work?"

"I think so," Avery said. "Tough on the eyes though. Hang on and I'll grab you a pen and some paper."

She returned from the living room and handed Harrison a small note pad of white paper and a ballpoint pen. "Prepare to copy."

"Prepared," Harrison said.

"Okay, here goes," Avery said. "I can't tell where it starts but I see a three, the letter R, a four, the letter L, a six, and either an A or another R."

"Great. More puzzles," Harrison said. "Now my head hurts even worse."

34

The following morning, Harrison talked Marco into driving him back to the Gulfstream before breakfast.

"What's so important that it can't wait until after we eat?" Avery said.

"I need a weapon," Harry said. "In case you haven't noticed, people keep trying to kill us, and that jerk yesterday must have taken my sidearm before he tossed me overboard."

"Treasure hunting is a high-risk business," Carter said.

"Not helpful," Avery said.

"We have to start being more careful, Ave. Whoever is trailing us is playing for keeps. Your world is computers and numbers and logic. This isn't what you're built for."

"I'm plenty tough, Harry," Avery insisted. "Mom thought so, too. She let me ride the subway to parties all over New York from the time I was fourteen."

"Ave, there was an undercover on every one of those subways with you and an unmarked sitting on the street outside of every one of those parties. Your mom burned every favor any cop ever owed her on you."

Avery's mouth fell open and she snapped it shut. "Go get a gun," she said.

"Not to worry, Ms. Turner," Marco said. "I'll get him there and back, safe and sound."

"Besides," Harrison said. "I want to hear all about his golf game."

"That'll give me a chance to fill you in on what MaryAnn found out about that watch," Carter said to Avery.

"We'll save you a seat at the table," Avery said, suddenly more interested in the watch than Harrison's choice of weaponry.

Avery and Carter walked toward the resort's main building, a beautiful nineteenth-century colonial style structure with massive columns supporting an oversized portico. They were seated at a corner table overlooking the water by a pleasant maitre d'hotel. Deciding to wait until Harrison and Marco returned before they ordered entrées, they started with coffee and blueberry scones.

"MaryAnn got back to you already, huh?" Avery said.

"She is very prompt," Carter said.

"For all the boys, or just you?"

Carter buttered his scone. "I honestly couldn't tell you. What I do know is that MaryAnn believes the watch was crafted by a Spanish jeweler sometime between 1650 and 1768."

"That's quite a range," Avery said.

"There is some disagreement between historians about the dates. It may well be the same watch Queen Maria gave to her husband on their only holiday together in 1759 just before she died."

Avery nearly dropped her knife. "Seriously?"

"MaryAnn said it's entirely possible. And if it is the same watch, it was part of the Crown Jewels kept at the palace until 1778 when it disappeared. The watch was thought to have been lost by the king, as he often carried it with him."

"Was it a one-of-a-kind piece?" Avery asked.

"That's the rub. This jeweler handcrafted over forty of these, each one slightly different so he could tell them apart."

"Making them difficult to fake, I would imagine," Avery said.

Carter nodded. "Still, it's a pretty cool find."

Avery washed down a mouthful of blueberry scone with coffee before speaking. "The legend has the treasure leaving Spain in 1778. If the watch went missing at that time, wouldn't it be more likely that it was sent as part of the missing treasure rather than lost?"

"I guess," Carter said.

"Why would the king send away such an important piece of jewelry? I mean it must have had great sentimental value to him."

"Too painful to keep after the death of his wife? Or maybe he considered the piece unlucky."

"Possibly," Avery said, unconvinced.

"So have you figured out what that code on the bezel means?" Carter asked.

"Not yet. I did some research online last night but came up empty. It would help if I knew where it began. Three numbers and three letters engraved on a round bezel aren't exactly helpful without some reference to a starting point."

"Maybe it's a combination," Carter said absently.

Avery nearly choked on her coffee. "What?"

"A combination."

"With a letter A?"

"Didn't you say one of the letters was obscured? Maybe that's not an A but an R. Anyway, MaryAnn said combinations were commonly used on pieces like that."

Avery jumped up from her chair just as Harrison and Marco approached their table.

"Hey, where are you going?" Harrison said as she hurried past.

"Order whatever you want and charge it to the house, Harry," Avery said as she hurried past them.

"What about you?"

"I'm not hungry anymore."

———

Avery returned to the rental then hurried to the kitchen where she had secreted the watch. After the burglary to their Boston hotel room, the electronic safe was the last place she would be storing her valuables from now on.

The watch was right where she had hidden it, atop the counter in the foil bag of coffee grounds. She dusted it off over the sink then took it over to the table and sat down. She examined the bezel closely. It was impossible to tell if the letter in question was an A, or an R, but if Carter was right a combination made perfect sense. 3 R, 4, L, 6, R. But which order? There were a minimum of three order possibilities to the combination, if that's in fact what it was, or six if she led with a letter instead of a numeral. The only movable external piece of the watch was the dial protruding from the main casing. Avery pulled gently on the dial until she felt it click into place. Turning the dial had no effect on the watch's hands. She looked back at the bezel then got up and grabbed the pad and pen from yesterday. Avery wrote down the six possible combination orders, starting with 3R. She pushed the watch dial in then pulled it out again and began turning it in full revolutions carefully following the codes she had written.

The first three combinations yielded nothing. Avery was following the fourth combo, thinking that she was on a wild goose chase and that the letter in question really was an A, when seams appeared on opposite sides of the bezel. Using her fingernails, she pried at the seams until both halves of the bezel swung open on unseen hinges.

Avery could barely contain her excitement. With the bezel open the casing came apart easily, but instead of the clue she had expected to see, there were only tarnished cogs and gears.

As she tipped her hand to set the watch down, the light illuminated the interior differently, catching her attention. Upon closer examination, she noticed what looked like another sealed compartment.

Avery went to the butcher block and retrieved the smallest knife she could find. Using the tip of the blade she was able to pry open the compartment. The thin hollow was empty, concealing only the back of the watch's outer casing. Her disappointment quickly dissipated when she noticed the casing was engraved.

She laid the watch flat on the tabletop then sat down again for a closer look. Availing herself of the flashlight on her phone, she could plainly see that the engraved image was a map. There were mountains, a large house, a church, a river, a waterfall, evergreen trees, a cave, and something that may have been a large rock. In the center of the waterfall symbol was a letter X.

Avery pulled out her camera and snapped several photos of the entire map along with detailed closeups of each symbol. Her excitement faded as she realized that nothing on the map was labeled in any way. There was no obvious key, nor even a simple northern designation. She knew this could be an important clue in their hunt for Mark's treasure, but without labels or a key—or any idea who in the past three or four centuries had even carved it—it was useless. The engraved map might have depicted any one of a thousand places around the globe.

"Who makes a treasure map without a damn key?" Harrison said as he leaned over the table for a closer look.

Standing on the opposite side of Avery's chair, Carter weighed in. "Whoever made it already knew where the treasure was located, at least approximately. They wouldn't have needed a key—just the reminder. There's a school of thought in treasure lore that people often kept maps and keys separate, too."

"Like you and the enigma thingy." Harrison poked Avery.

"So if they hid the map for someone else, all they would need to pass on to that other person would be the key," Marco followed.

"So we've got a watch that doesn't tell time, and a map that doesn't lead to anything," Harrison said. "We were almost shark chow, and we're no better off than we were before we found this."

"Maybe not," Avery said. "Carter, take a shot of this and send it to Mary-Ann. See if she has any ideas."

"That's your plan?" Harrison said.

Avery got up from her chair. "Nope, that's my backup plan."

"Where are you going?" Carter said.

Avery grinned. "To work on my primary plan."

She raced upstairs to her laptop, opened her software design program, and began frantically typing in code. What she was attempting to do would take some time, and a certain amount of luck, but if she were right, she already had the skills necessary to decipher the location on the map.

Three hours later, Harrison knocked on the open door to Avery's room.

"Just wondering how you're making out and if you'd like to join the rest of us for lunch?"

Avery turned around in her chair and beamed a big smile.

"Does that mean yes on the lunch?" Harrison said.

"No, it means I figured it out."

"What? How?"

"Never mind that now. Get packed. Tell Marco we're headed to the airport."

"Now where are we going?"

"Virginia."

35

It took them the better part of three hours to check out of the resort, drive to the airport, return both rental vehicles, then load the jet with their diving equipment and belongings. The more Avery thought about the mapping solution she had arrived at, the more she became convinced that she was right about their destination. She was anxious to get in the air, but bowed to Harrison's demand that they take the time to pick up lunch before taking off. She realized that he was still recovering from a concussion and needed to keep his strength up.

They were wheels up just after three in the afternoon.

"Man, I could get used to traveling like this," Carter said as he looked out the window.

"Don't get too used to it," Harrison mumbled between bites of a large roast beef sub.

Avery shot Harrison a look and he responded with an unconvincing expression of innocence, made completely ludicrous by the piece of lettuce dangling from his lips.

"It has come in handy this week," Avery said.

Carter ran a hand across the leather seat. "This baby's much too nice to jump out of."

"Quite a compliment from the adrenaline king." Avery nodded a thank you.

"Any plane is too nice to jump out of," Harrison said before he took another giant bite of his sandwich.

At Avery's request, Marco had done some research of his own regarding the best place for them to land within proximity of Big Stone Gap, Virginia. The nearest private airstrip was in a town called Wise. Avery figured if they were still being chased, a private airport would draw far less attention, minimizing anyone's ability to follow them.

"Explain to me again how you figured out the location from that stick-figure map?" Carter said.

"It's hard to explain without boring you, but I wrote a program similar to what I did with the app I sold."

"The one that made you filthy rich?" Carter said, giving her a mischievous grin.

"Independently wealthy," Avery corrected. "Basically, it's a map-based algorithm that takes whatever information that's fed into it and converts it into a location probability score."

"Like gambling odds?" Harrison asked as he came up for air and wadded up the sandwich wrapper.

"Yeah, like that. I used the map we found and compared it to known images within existing map data systems. It uses online records of satellite and topography maps over a period of time, as well as general location comparisons."

"How did you decide on a time frame parameter?" Carter asked as he leaned forward. His intense expression earned him an eye roll from Harrison.

"I picked a period from 1778 to 1952. And I limited the search area to the southeastern U.S. since the *Bonnet Rouge* allegedly sailed for the south during the revolution. Also, I remembered that the coin that antique dealer from Newburyport showed us was said to have come from a mine in Virginia. There are three waterfalls off a trail in this area, all relatively near a Church built in the late 1740s—which is also close to the personal home of the owner of the Oswald Coal Company."

Harrison and Carter agreed that her idea was brilliant.

"Only if it works," Avery said. "There are dozens of variables I can't account for."

"So, how sure are you that this Rock City place is the right location?" Harrison said.

"Big Stone Gap," Avery said. "And I'm ninety-seven-point-six percent sure. Or, the computer is, anyway."

Carter whistled. "That's a pretty accurate guesstimate."

"We'll see," Avery said as she pulled up a photo of the original map again.

"Don't suppose you've figured out how someone keeps managing to follow us, have you?" Harrison said. "Seems like they are always one step ahead or directly on our heels, and given your resources, I don't get it. You haven't found any more things in our bags that aren't ours?"

Avery had been working on that very problem. "No trackers. But I have a different idea of how they might have found us in South Carolina. Our phones." She held hers up.

"Tracking software?" Carter asked.

"Could be," Avery said. "Possibly cloning the hard drives, too, though."

"But how?" Harrison said. "We haven't given our phones to anyone."

"No, but we have left them unattended," Avery said. "At least twice. Yesterday while diving with Captain Ahab, and before that on Martha's Vineyard."

"I've done the same," Carter said. "I'm not nearly as attached to mine as some people are."

"Since Mark's was missing from the motel room where he was found and we didn't find it in Maine, it makes sense to me that—assuming murder, which is even easier today—whoever dosed him with the laced dope stole his phone, which probably means they wanted something on it, and they know their way around the back doors on these things enough to expect they could get it."

"But we locked them in the glovebox both times, Ave," Harrison said. "Inside a locked vehicle. And the phones were passcode locked."

She cocked her head to the side. "Seriously, Harry? Did you think someone wouldn't be able to crack your 4444 passcode?"

Harrison frowned at Carter, who was laughing. "Hey, now he knows it."

Carter weighed in after getting himself under control, "What would cloning the phones get anyone?"

"A great deal," Avery said. "We've been calling and texting people for help, taking pictures of clues, and searching online sites for information. Cloning the phones would give them a digital map of sorts to all our movements."

"That's just great," Harry said.

"How would that help them to physically track us?" Carter said.

"The cloning wouldn't physically show our locations, but a tracking program surreptitiously installed on the phones would. They could listen in on our conversations with the right malware, and definitely read our texts. We've talked about places in the presence of our phones multiple times."

Harrison removed the cell from his pocket and looked at it with disdain. "Then they could be tracking us right now?"

"Not with airplane mode on," Avery said.

"How can we be sure before we turn it off?" Harrison asked.

"I'd need to scan the hard drives of all our phones, looking specifically for that kind of software installation."

"Can you do that?" Carter said. "I mean with what you have available?"

"Hey, Junior Mint," Harrison said. "When it comes to computers, Avery can do anything."

"No time like the present," Avery said, holding out her hand for Harrison's phone.

"Better hope you haven't been browsing any x-rated sites," Carter joked.

Avery turned her attention to Carter. "I'll be checking yours too," she said.

Harrison laughed until his head hurt.

"You know five women named Liz?" Avery asked as she scanned the contacts list on Carter's phone.

"Never a popcorn stand nearby when you need one," Harrison said as he looked on with amusement.

"Elizabeth is a common name," Carter said.

"And you have three Lenas," Avery continued.

Harrison raised his eyebrows at Carter.

"One of those is a cousin."

"And the other two?"

"Are not."

"Ask him how many MaryAnns," Harrison said.

"Oh, there's only one MaryAnn," Avery said with a grin. "Isn't that right, Carter?"

36

The sun had already descended behind the Cumberland Mountains by the time they touched down on the tarmac in Wise, Virginia. After a brief discussion, they all agreed that searching for lost treasure, over hazardous and unfamiliar terrain, while being tracked by murderous thugs, was a pursuit best conducted by the light of day, following a good night's sleep.

The airport manager was preparing to leave for the day when they dragged themselves inside the small terminal building.

"Car rentals?" the man said with a chuckle. "Sorry. Nothing like that out here. In case you hadn't noticed, this is a pretty remote area. Most folks looking for big city amenities land in Johnson City or Knoxville."

Harrison jumped in, "We're trying to avoid big cities because—"

"Because of the crowds," Avery interrupted, coming to his rescue.

"Well, if you hate crowds, you've come to the right place." The man, whose plastic name tag identified him as Johnny, turned to look directly at Carter. "Say, don't I know you?"

"I have one of those faces," Carter said, keeping his expression flat.

"Nah, I'm good with faces. It's the names that trouble me." Johnny said, snapping his fingers. "Wait—you're Carter Mosley. Man do we love watching your videos. My whole family follows you. Takes me back to those old Jacques Cousteau National Geographic TV specials. What was the name of that boat?"

"The Calypso," Carter said. "And thank you. I'm glad you all enjoy them."

Avery stared. First the sailors on the Coast Guard boat, and now this guy in the middle of Nowhere, Virginia? She hated social media, but that was too much coincidence to let slide.

"So, what brings you out this way? We're a long way from the ocean here."

"We're doing some research," Avery jumped in again before Carter could answer.

Johnny cocked his head to one side like a German shepherd. "Our library is only open on Thursdays and Saturdays, but my cousin Myra has a key."

"That's very kind of you to offer," Carter began.

"It is, thank you so much. But that still leaves us with a transportation problem," Avery said, attempting to get them back on topic. "And without a place to stay for the night."

"You seem like nice folks," Johnny said.

"We're the best," Harrison said with a grin.

"If you'd like I can call my sister-in-law. She owns a bed and breakfast in Norton. Strictly no frills, but it is clean, and she does like to cook."

"That's awfully nice of you." Avery smiled. "But we'll still need a vehicle so we can get out there."

"I think I can take care of that too."

Twenty minutes later, they gathered their belongings and stepped outside as a panel van that was probably older than Avery and Carter pulled to the curb. Stenciled on the side in bright letters were the words *Trail Magic*. The taxi, owned and operated by airport manager Johnny's other cousin, was used to transport hikers between the various trailheads and hostels in town.

Avery sat up front with their gregarious driver, a tanned middle-aged woman with a firm handshake who told them to call her Bev. "My momma thought Beverly sounded glamorous and important, but it's always been too fancy pants for me."

Given Bev's salt-of-the-earth appearance—her freckle-dusted face lacked so much as a smudge of makeup, her auburn hair was woven into a long, thick braid and she wore no-fuss jeans, a plaid shirt, and work boots —Avery agreed, instantly warming to Bev's friendly, no-nonsense demeanor.

"I hear tell that you folks aren't from around here," Bev said.

"Nope," Avery said. "Only here for a quick visit. Thought we might take in some of the sights while we're here, though."

"Well, if it's scenery you want, missy, we got plenty. One of the reasons the hikers and four-wheeler folks love it so much. We're right smack dab in between the Cumberland Plateau and the Blue Ridge Mountains, and we got a ton of trails. I tell people that Norton is a hiker's paradise."

"Bet they love this van," Harrison said as he shoved an empty can off to one side with his foot.

"Sorry for the mess back there, hon," Bev said as she looked in the rear view. "I just transported some hikers from Black Mountain to Duffield. Lord, they smell something awful after a few days on the trail."

"Smells like one might still be hiding back here," Harrison said.

Bev laughed loudly. "Your friend is hysterical," she said.

"That's Harry," Avery said, turning in her seat to stare him down. "A real laugh riot."

Avery turned back to Bev. "Black Mountain, that's over near Big Stone Gap, right?"

"That's right. The Gap, that's what the locals call it, used to be a big coal mining town. Now, like most of the towns 'round here, they're trying to rein-vent themselves as outdoor destinations. You know, hiking, biking, fishing, all that back to nature stuff."

"Are you originally from here, Bev?" Avery asked, detecting a slightly different accent than what she'd expected.

"Nope. From Georgia actually. Moved here after I dropped out of college. Had a few relatives scattered about, like my second Cousin Johnny, who you met at the airport. I thought to myself, Bevvie, get yourself to Virginia."

"You a hiker, yourself, Bev?" Carter said.

"Lawd, yes. Hiked every one of these trails at least a couple of hundred times. Knees started giving me trouble a few years ago, so I started up this hiker transport business. Makes me feel like I'm still a part of it, I guess."

"Maybe you could suggest some sights for us around The Gap," Avery said.

"Be happy to."

Bev dropped them off at the bed and breakfast with a promise to pick them up again in the morning. The home was a quaint two-story white hip roof colonial set back about fifty feet from the roadway. It featured two brick chimneys and a large covered front porch that wrapped around to the left side. A shingled porch roof was supported by a half dozen Greek revival style columns, giving the southern home an air of dignity. Avery and the others lugged their gear past the stone wall up the lighted walkway toward the front door.

"Come in, come in," a friendly voice greeted from inside as Avery knocked on the screen door.

They stepped inside and were instantly taken by the yeasty smell of fresh baked bread.

"Oh, man, does that smell good," Harrison said, practically drooling.

A large woman wearing an apron and a head scarf came down the hall to greet them.

"There you are," she said. "Welcome to my home. The name is Imogene Blakely."

"Avery Turner," Avery said as she started the introductions. "This is my assistant Mr. Harrison, and Carter Mosley."

"Lovely to meet you all," Imogene said. "Johnny told me all about you. Said you needed a place to lay your heads. I happen to be empty now, so you've got your choice of all the upstairs rooms. Communal bathroom's at the end of the hall."

"Thank you," Avery said.

"What smells so good?" Carter said.

"I figured you folks hadn't eaten yet. I've got some chicken and dumplings going in the kitchen."

"My new favorite phrase," Harrison said, earning a toothy smile from Imogene.

"Well now, Mr. Harrison—"

"Harry, please."

"Okay, Harry. Y'all drop your things upstairs and we'll eat as soon as you're ready."

"Yes, ma'am," Harrison said as he hurried toward the stairs.

After dinner, Avery, Harrison, and Carter settled in the downstairs gathering room in front of the fireplace, which their host had lit to ward off the unseasonable evening chill.

"I could get used to this," Harrison said rubbing his full and contented belly.

"Me too," Carter said. "Imogene is really nice."

"Are there women who aren't nice to you somewhere?" Harrison asked.

"Not according to his contacts list," Avery said, holding up their phones. "I've got good news and bad."

"Why does there always have to be bad news?" Harrison said.

"Let's start with the good," Carter said.

"Okay. The good news is tomorrow's weather is supposed to be great for our hike into the Black Mountain foothills."

"Excellent," Harrison said. "Nothing I like better than hiking in the bug infested woods of Virginia."

"And the bad?" Carter asked.

Avery returned their cell phones. "Tracking and cloning software was installed on both of your phones. Which might explain the phony Hilton Head dive captain, and why someone has been right in step with us the entire way."

"How could they have gotten to me in Florida?" Carter asked.

"I'm not so sure they did," Avery said. "But the fact that we know each other isn't exactly a secret."

"We all left our phones in the rental during the dive." Carter said slowly, thinking about the photos someone had DM'd him on Instagram. That guy hadn't been friendly, and definitely knew Avery and Carter were friends.

"Good thing too," Harrison said. "Or they'd be at the bottom of the Atlantic."

"You think whoever did this got them out, dumped this software in them, and then put them back?" Carter asked.

"Maybe?" Avery asked. "They could have paid off the rental company clerk for an extra key, even. I'm not sure that's likely, but it's not impossible."

"Is the tracking software on yours too?" Carter said.

"No," Avery said. "And I can't explain that."

"Maybe they figured you'd find it," Carter said. "Which means they had to know your background in IT."

"Can you remove it?" Harrison said, looking at his phone as if it might bite him.

"I don't want to," Avery said. "I reprogrammed it to ping your locations in random places. It will also delete every third word from monitored texts and divert a mic request to the Elvis playlist I installed for both of you."

"The king saves the day," Harrison said.

"Something like that." Avery smiled. "Whoever did this will think their software is malfunctioning, at least for a while."

"So, what's the problem?" Harrison said. "Your face says there's still a problem."

"The problem is, whether it's Louise Williams or Babcock or the midnight smoker from the Hawk's Nest, they already know we're here."

"But they don't know why," Carter said hopefully.

"No, but it won't take them long to figure out what we're up to."

"I'm not really equipped for hiking, Ave," Harrison said.

"Yeah, my sneakers probably aren't meant for wandering around mountains either," Carter said.

"We'll take care of that in the morning," Avery said. "I checked, there's an outfitter in town. We'll get you both fitted for boots and gear before we head into the hills."

"Just so I'm clear on this whole hiking into the foothills thing," Harrison said. "How high is Black Mountain?"

"A little over forty-two hundred," Avery said.

"Feet?" Harrison said.

"Relax, Harry. We're not making a summit. Nobody would have hidden the treasure that high."

"Thank God," Harrison said.

"No, what we're looking for is likely hidden around one of the three waterfalls near Big Stone Gap. Probably close to Elk Knob or Pine Spur."

"And how tall are those, dare I ask?"

"Less than three thousand feet."

"My feet hurt already. And you're sure this isn't just another wild goose chase?"

Avery shrugged as she studied her laptop. "We go where the clues lead us, Harry."

Carter chimed in, "Much like your homicide detective days, I would imagine."

"It's nothing like my detecting days, Junior. Not once did we have to purchase hiking boots to solve a murder."

Avery quickly covered her plan for the next day, showing them the route they would be taking on an online trail map.

"What time are we planning to head out?" Harrison asked.

"I'll have breakfast ready by six thirty," Imogene said from the hallway surprising all of them. "Can't have you climbing mountains on an empty stomach, Harry."

"You're too good to us," Harrison said.

"Thank you, Imogene," Avery said.

"Least I can do for you folks. Now if you don't need me for anything else, I'm gonna call it a night."

"Good night," they said in unison.

"Did you know she was standing there?" Harrison whispered.

"I wonder how much she heard?" Carter said.

"Think she's gonna snatch that gold right from under us, Junior?" Harrison said.

"She's hardly a threat," Avery said.

Harrison chuckled. "Last time I had that thought I almost took two barrels from a lady so old she might have been at the signing of the Declaration of Independence."

"It's gonna be a long day tomorrow, guys," Avery said. "Bev promised to pick us up by eight. We need to get some shut-eye."

Carter yawned loudly. "Between the dumplings and this fire, I'm half asleep already."

37

Avery supervised the purchases made by Carter and Harrison, noting with some amusement that for all his protesting, Harrison seemed pleased with his new gear. Which may have had something to do with the attractive middle-aged female salesperson waiting on them.

Avery was already sporting her well-worn trail shoes. She kept a pair on the plane, never knowing when the adventure bug would bite. In addition to boots, she bought each of them hydration bladders with accompanying packs, wicking pants and shirts, and a couple of pairs of mid-weight socks. Harrison picked out a wicking ball cap at the saleswoman's suggestion and a funky shaped hickory walking stick. Rounding out their purchases were the energy must-haves: power bars, and gorp—a mixture of seeds, dried fruit, and nuts.

It was nearly nine o'clock by the time they arrived at the trailhead. Bev had been gracious enough to wait while they shopped.

"Give me a jingle when you're ready to be picked up," Bev said. "Maybe give me a thirty-minute heads up in case I got another transport going."

"Thanks so much," Avery said.

"Yeah, thanks, Bev," Harrison said as he bounded out of the van with newfound vigor.

"Man, I can't believe how great these boots feel," Harrison said. "I'm ready to take on this mountain."

Avery exchanged a knowing glance with Carter, both suppressing a smile. While Harrison's workout regimen was grueling, it was mostly weights, heavy bag, and hand to hand combat training. He had resisted her attempts to add cardio to his routine at every turn. She wondered how long it would be before Harrison's newfound love of hiking ended.

They had each powered down their phones before departing from Imogene's bed and breakfast on the off chance that Avery had missed one of the tracker programs. Whoever had installed the spyware knew they were in western Virginia, and there weren't that many places to rent a room around here. No reason to give them the trail too.

The Roaring Branch trailhead was located off Route 23, aptly named Roaring Branch Road, about a mile outside of Big Stone Gap and directly across from the Powell River. The humidity was elevated, while the sun attempted to burn through the low-lying mist. Avery knew they'd need to refill the hydration bladders, so she'd packed a small filtration pump in her own pack.

Like the start of most trails, Roaring Branch's first hundred yards were deceiving. Moss covered stone steps constructed into the side of the gentle rise made it seem easy. But the stairway ended quickly, and the real hiking began. Loose rocks, deadfalls, and gnarled tree roots made the steep ascent difficult if not treacherous.

The mountainous flora was lush and damp, an assortment of rhododendrons, ferns, old growth hemlock and oak. To their immediate right, running parallel to the trail, was the confluence that fed the Powell River. The constant din of the running water was soothing and, for the most part, they hiked in silence.

"How're you holding up, Harry?" Avery asked after about twenty minutes of listening to his grunts and groans.

"Just ducky," he growled. "What happened to those nice stairs?"

Carter laughed.

It wasn't long before they came to the first water crossing.

"How are we supposed to get across that?" Harrison said, testing the depth with his newly acquired walking stick.

"We ford it," Carter said.

"Ford it?"

"Yeah, wade through it."

"In my new boots? You've got to be kidding."

"Come on, Harry," Avery said. "They're hiking boots. Gotta break 'em in sometime."

They had been climbing for about a half hour when they located the first of the three waterfalls that Bev had described: a beautiful cascade that transformed into gravity-defying mist wherever it landed on boulders. Miniature rainbows floated in the vapor like holograms where beams of sunlight passed through the canopy of trees. Avery was in her element, having spent many weekends hiking wilderness trails when she'd still worked for Mark. It was a terrific way to shake off the stress of IT work, as well as the claustrophobic concrete and pavement surrounding her city life.

"What specifically are we looking for?" Carter said as they stopped to catch their breath.

"I wish I knew," Avery said. "The map just showed a waterfall near here."

"There has to be more to it than that, Ave," Harrison said.

"Why don't we split up and climb either side of the waterfall?" Avery said. "If there is some kind of opening in the ground, we should be able to find it, right?"

Harrison spoke up, "I've got a better idea. Why don't you and Boy Wonder crawl all around the waterfall, and I'll keep watch for bad guys right here on the trail. How's that sound?"

Avery agreed to the plan, largely because she was worried about Harrison slipping and falling on his recently injured noggin.

They spent the next half hour inspecting either side of the waterfall for a cave or any kind of depression that could have been used to hide something as large as the general's gold. Most of the rock ledges were angled and slick with moisture. Several times Avery found herself pinwheeling to maintain her balance. And once she'd come face to face with a blue racer. She froze, not even daring to breathe, until the curious snake finally slithered away. For a moment she considered warning Harrison about the presence of reptiles, but then she thought better of it.

Being completely out of his element, he hardly needed anything else to worry about.

Coming up empty, they hiked a mile farther up the trail until they came to the next waterfall, the largest of the three.

"They are *all* still alive?" Even with a weak cell phone connection Samael could hear the anger dripping through his phone.

"It would appear so," Samael said calmly.

"How is it that Avery Turner and her band of misfits managed to thwart us again?"

"I don't know, sir. The Coast Guard stumbled onto our assassin before he could get away clean. He's in police custody as we speak."

"And if he talks?"

"He won't."

"And the payment?"

"Untraceable." Samael said. He had no use for tantrums: emotion was a useless trait, a waste of energy. "What do you want me to do about the *Bonnet Rouge*?"

"Where are they now?"

"They've packed up and flown to Virginia."

"Which can only mean they didn't find anything on their diving excursion."

Or they did and it pointed them in another direction. Samael kept the thought to himself.

"Forget the wreck and find Turner!"

"As you—"

The line went dead before Samael could complete the sentence.

Things were getting out of hand. As far as Samael was concerned, the rational approach was to simply let Turner locate the treasure then take it from her.

Samael wondered how long it would be before he, too, was deemed expendable. Having personally witnessed what became of those who had crossed this man—usually at the hands of Samael himself—he did not need a reminder. It was only money that made him powerful. Money and fear of the larger-than-life legend he'd carefully built around his name. But Samael knew the truth. He was the real power behind this greedy man. The only thing he lacked was money.

Perhaps their association had run its course.

Morning quickly blistered into afternoon. Now it was Avery's turn to be cranky. Hot, tired, and scratched up from crawling through undergrowth, she was becoming more discouraged with every step. Avery and Carter crossed back to the trail to meet up with Harrison, who was already enjoying a lunch break of water and power bars.

"These things taste like a mixture of cardboard and sawdust," Harrison said.

"Check the label, Harry," Avery teased. "I believe those are the main ingredients."

"What do you think?" Carter asked between bites.

"I think we're wasting our time," Avery said.

She'd been so sure of her computer program that she hadn't stopped to consider that it might lead them astray. Mark had taught her early on, no matter how brilliantly a software program was written it would only be as good as the information fed into it.

Harrison looked much the same as he had at the start of the hike, while she and Carter were as covered in scrapes and mud as if they'd just returned from battle. A battle they'd lost.

"Maybe we're just on the wrong trail," Harrison offered.

Avery could tell by his gentle tone that he was being sincere.

"Maybe," she said. "But I'm thinking that I've missed something along the way."

"You mean here on the trail?" Carter said.

"No. I mean we've gathered a lot of information from various sources. I may have misread or overlooked something. Let's head back and regroup."

"Now you're talking," Harrison said.

As they passed the initial waterfall, Avery pulled out her phone and powered it up to place a call to Bev.

"Know what I'm thinking about, Junior?" Harrison said as he brushed past Carter.

"No," Carter said.

"A shower, clean clothes, and sawdust-free food."

38

Bev's mud-splattered van was parked in a small turnoff near the trailhead. She was standing beside it, waiting for them as promised.

"Well, you certainly look like the kind of hikers I'm used to," Bev said. "Nothing like a little mud to set you right. Was it everything you hoped?"

"Not exactly," Avery said as she shed her pack.

A crease appeared between Bev's brows. "You didn't see the waterfalls?"

"Oh, we saw them alright," Harrison said.

"Up close and personal," Carter said.

Bev laughed as she helped them toss their gear into the rear of the van.

She drove them back to Imogene's bed and breakfast, dropping them off with a promise to return in time for dinner to transport them to a great Italian place she knew.

"Why don't you join us?" Avery said. "My treat."

"Well, I don't—"

"It's the least we can do," Harrison said.

"All right," Bev said. "I'll join you."

As promised, Bev drove them to dinner at a quaint family-owned establishment called The Southern Tortellini & Pizza. The two-story brick-fronted building was tucked away several blocks off the main drag next to a barbershop. Stepping into the lobby they were overcome by the aroma of garlic, basil, and oregano.

"Oh, my God," Harrison said. "I've died and gone to heaven."

"Careful you don't slip on your own drool, Harry," Avery teased.

They were seated in a small private room just off the main dining area. Bev introduced the server as another of her cousins.

"This here is Clayton," Bev said. "Clay these are my new friends from—"

"Florida," Avery said as she shook his hand and made the introductions.

"I'm more of a transplant," Harrison said.

Carter raised his hand, "Born and bred in the land of sunshine and surf."

"Carter teaches diving," Avery said.

"Scuba?" Clayton asked.

"And sky."

"Yeah, this guy's a jack of all trades," Harrison said as he rolled his eyes.

"Now you can add hiker to the list," Bev said.

"How long have you worked here?" Avery asked Clayton.

Clayton smiled and exchanged a glance with Bev. "Actually, I own this restaurant."

"And you wait tables?" Harrison said, clearly surprised.

"Can't find enough help. Anyway, I enjoy mingling with the customers. Can I interest you in something from the bar?"

"Why don't we split a bottle of wine," Avery suggested. "I mean, we are having Italian." Seeing that they agreed, Avery asked for their best red.

"Better make it two bottles," Harrison said.

"Very good," Clayton said. "And I'll bring you a basket of warm bread too."

"Now you're talking," Harrison said.

After Clayton departed to fetch their wine, Bev asked what brought them all to Wise.

"What? You don't believe it was for the great hiking?" Avery said.

"Not when your gear still has the price tags," Bev said, giving Harrison a wink.

A young man approached their table carrying a cloth covered breadbasket.

"Hello, Danny," Bev said.

"Aunt Bevvie," Danny said before looking at the others.

"Danny these are my friends."

"Hello, everyone," Danny said.

"Pleased to meet you, Danny," Avery said.

"I have Down's syndrome," Danny said matter-of-factly as he set the basket on the table. "Aunt Bevvie says it makes me special."

"It certainly does," Bev said as she reached out and pulled him in for a hug and kiss on the cheek. She whispered in his ear, "I think we might need another basket of bread."

"Be right back," Danny announced loudly.

"He's Clayton's youngest," Bev said as she watched him go.

"He's a sweet little guy," Harrison said.

"And a hard worker," Bev said.

Clayton returned with their wine and began to pour. After he had finished, Avery proposed a toast: "To friendship and new adventures."

"*Salute*," Carter said. Avery smiled at his proper use of Italian.

"You still haven't told me what brought you here," Bev said as she set her glass down.

"It's a long story," Avery said.

"You might not believe us if we told you," Harrison said as he slathered a healthy dollop of butter across a piece of warm bread.

"Try me," Bev said.

"Well, truthfully, we're here searching for lost treasure," Avery said.

"Is that a fact? And how do you suppose it might have come to our little corner of the world?"

"We don't really know how, or even if we're on the right trail for sure," Avery confessed, frowning at the idea that her new program hadn't worked like she thought it would.

"We must be getting some kind of close," Carter said. "Bad elements aren't putting trackers in your bags and on our phones for their own personal entertainment."

"You don't think we're entertaining, junior?" Harrison feigned offense.

"Don't forget the shark," Avery said. "We could legitimately have our own TV show this week." She kept her eyes on Carter as she spoke. He became very interested in his second slice of bread.

Bev laughed aloud. "You guys are too much."

"They're serious," Harrison said, pointing to the now-smaller wound dressing on his head. "We've been up and down the East Coast following leads, and someone has been so desperate to stop us that they tried to kill us day before yesterday."

Bev's eyes went wide, her mouth popping into an O. "Okay, I'll bite. This treasure," she said. "What exactly is it?"

"It's known as the general's gold," Avery said.

"And y'all think it's here? At Big Stone Gap? In a waterfall?" Bev's voice went up an octave with each question.

"We did," Avery said. "Now I'm not so sure."

"There's no gold in the waterfall," Danny announced confidently as he delivered the second basket of bread to the table. "The gold was in the old mine. Soldiers put it there."

The entire table turned to stare at him, Carter very nearly dropping his wineglass.

"What did you say, Danny?" Avery said.

Danny looked at Bev before answering.

"It's okay," Bev reassured. "You can tell them."

"The gold isn't in the waterfall. It's in the Brashton Mine."

"How do you know that, Danny?" Carter said.

"It's not a secret," Danny said. "Everybody knows. My grandpa told me."

"Thank you for the bread, Danny," Bev said. "Run along now and see to the other tables."

"Okay, Aunt Bevvie."

"Danny's grandfather worked the mines before they closed," Bev said as soon as Danny had trotted off. "That tall tale has floated around for years. No one ever found any treasure, but I suspect every town has its legends, now doesn't it? Keeps things interesting. Gives the old timers something to speculate about over a checkerboard, entertains the kids around a campfire —and occasionally brings interesting folks like yourselves around to our little slice of paradise."

"What exactly is this particular legend?" Harrison said.

"Something to do with gold to fund the Civil War. Supposedly it was smuggled here by the confederate army. Hidden in one of the really old mines. They used dynamite to blow up the tunnel to keep the treasure hidden. At least that's the version I heard."

Avery felt a chill as an image popped into her head. Louise Williams, the old woman from the antique shop, had told them about the origin of her coin. She said that her father had won the coin in a card game. The man he'd beaten said that the coin had been found in a coal mine. Could this be the same mine?

"You're serious?" Harrison said.

"I didn't say I believed it," Bev said. "Just telling you what I heard."

Avery sat back and sipped her wine, her mind replaying what Bev and Danny had just told them.

Bev caught Avery looking at her and gave her a smile.

Everyone they had met since coming here certainly seemed helpful and pleasant, but was it real? Or was there more to this place than met the eye? Something more sinister beneath the surface of this charming little hamlet. Something buried along with the treasure Mark gave his life searching for. Williams had seemed pleasant too—right up until she'd aimed a shotgun at them. How long before someone did that here?

39

Samael descended the steps of a sleek private jet onto the tarmac at the Wise airfield. Dressed in a smart charcoal suit and trench coat, carrying a leather portfolio, he looked every inch the businessman, as though he had been sent to negotiate a corporate buyout. He spotted the two men standing beside the Lincoln Town Car, awaiting him as instructed. He greeted them with a nod as he passed by and entered the building that sufficed for an airport terminal.

Inside he found a forty-something man behind the counter speaking into the phone. The man acknowledged him by holding up a finger, never missing a beat as he continued his conversation.

"That's right. I can connect you up with a local pilot. If you're looking for flying lessons, he's one of the best."

The man nodded as he listened to the person at the other end of the line. Samael had removed his overcoat and hung it over one arm while pretending to study the flyers that covered one entire wall. He thought about how near Avery Turner must be. And how close she might be to the treasure.

The man was finishing his call as Samael approached the counter and presented his most disarming smile. He would get the information he needed from this man. One way or another.

"Evening, friend," the man said as he hung up the phone. "What can I do for you?"

"Good evening," Samael said. "I'm here on business and I wonder if you might be able to direct me to a nice hotel."

"Sure thing. I assume you already have ground transportation."

"I do."

"My recommendation depends on how far you're willing to travel."

"As far as need be. Also, I wonder if you might have seen my friends. We were all due to arrive late yesterday, but I'm afraid I was delayed."

"We had quite a few arrivals yesterday. Can you describe your friends?"

"A young couple accompanied by a rather formidable-looking middle-aged fellow."

"Sure, I remember them. Carter Mosley, the scuba diving guy from Instagram, was one of them."

Samael's smile widened. "That's right, he is. I don't suppose you'd know where they went, would you?"

"The mines all closed about fifteen years ago," Bev said. "Right about the time they began strip mining. You noticed the railroad tracks near the trailhead?"

Avery, hanging on every word, nodded.

"Well, strip mining made getting the coal out much easier and safer. There was no need to go underground anymore, they just strip the coal right out of the side of the mountain and load it directly into rail cars."

"And no one has been inside the mines since?" Harrison said.

"There was one crazy entrepreneur who'd heard those buried gold stories. Bought up the commercial tunnels from the coal companies. He went at it for about six months. Tried several things to locate the so-called treasure."

Avery thought about Corbacho, who clearly had the money to do something like that and had family ties to the treasure and an interest in the lore. Had he been here years ago? Because, clearly, he hadn't found the treasure.

"Do you remember his name?" she asked.

Bev touched her chin. "Seems like it was a funny one. But danged if I can call it up after two whole glasses of wine."

"So what happened?" Carter said.

"Legal troubles, he said. We all suspect he plain ran out of money."

Oh. Corbacho definitely didn't have that problem.

"Did the guy ever find anything?" Avery said.

"Not so far as I know."

"Are the mines still accessible?" Avery said.

Bev paused a moment. Avery could tell she was considering whether to divulge something.

"Y'all ought to talk to Sonny Landon. He used to be the foreman for the company that ran the Brashton Mining operation. He's still the caretaker of sorts. Knows every inch of those mines. I could see if he'd be willing to meet you, assuming you're interested."

"We're interested," Carter said.

"Very interested," Avery said.

After dinner Bev drove them back to Imogene's B&B. Bev promised to be in touch the next day as soon as she spoke with Sonny. Avery was so excited about the possibility of a real lead, she wondered how she would ever sleep.

Avery's phone buzzed with an incoming text as Bev stopped the car outside Imogene's. She checked the screen. Emilio Corbacho: *It really was lovely to talk with you. At the risk of overstepping, I filled an attorney who has worked for me many times in on what I know of the situation with Daimler. His information is below, and he is expecting your call. Please know I'm happy to help, as I know Mark would want me to, and I hope to see you again.*

Avery typed back a quick *thank you* and bid Bev goodnight before she followed the guys inside.

In the kitchen they discovered a note propped up in front of a plate of cookies.

Help yourselves. There's tea on the counter. Imogene

"Hermits," Harrison announced has he pulled out a chair and sat down. "Don't mind if I do."

Carter joined him. "I haven't eaten these since I was a kid."

"When was that, yesterday?" Harrison said before taking a monster bite.

Avery walked over to the stove and turned on the kettle. "As I see it, there are two ways to attack the research on this."

"And those are?" Harrison said around a mouthful of cookie.

"I'll find out what I can through online sources. And Carter, I need you to reach out to your museum friend."

"MaryAnn Everly," Harrison said absently.

"Yes, Ms. Everly," Avery said. "Have her find out everything she can about the Brashton Mines."

"Okay," Carter said. "I can have her check into that crazy guy Bev mentioned, too. The one who ran out of money looking for the treasure."

Avery stopped what she was doing and glared at him. "I know what you're doing, Carter. You're trying to tell me that you think this is a waste of time. That I am no better than the last rich guy with a big ego who tried this. But there is a substantial difference."

"Which is?"

"That guy was doing it for the money."

Carter glanced from Avery to Harrison and back again. "Aren't we doing it for the money?"

"I don't need the money, Carter. I'm doing this for Mark. In fact, if we find the damn treasure, I may just donate my share of it to a museum."

Both men stared at her, wide-eyed. Neither dared speak.

"Now, I plan to see this through until the very end," Avery said. "Who's with me?"

Harrison and Carter both raised their hands.

"Good. I'm glad to hear it."

"One condition," Harrison said.

Avery's eyes narrowed. "What?"

"No more mountain climbing."

Avery laughed. "Deal."

40

All three of them were early for breakfast—the aromas of homemade spinach quiche and slab maple bacon wafted up the stairs and under their bedroom doors like a siren call. Just before eleven the previous night, Avery had received a text from Bev telling her that Sonny Landon was more than willing to meet with them. She added that he was excited about their visit. Between bites of deliciousness and steaming mugs of coffee, Carter relayed what he had learned from MaryAnn.

"Just so you know, this latest request cost me an expensive dinner and flowers," Carter said.

"Seems like a small price to pay," Avery said. "I'm happy to foot the bill, if you'd like."

"I got it, but thanks." Carter tipped his head to one side as he watched Avery sip her coffee.

"It is for the cause after all." Harrison said. "And I suspect you'll get something out of that expensive dinner besides a good steak, anyway."

Avery laughed.

"You guys don't know this woman," Carter said.

"Playing with fire, junior?" Harrison took a bite of his quiche.

"More like playing on the surface of the sun," Carter said. "But what's done is done, and MaryAnn must have been up until the wee hours researching this because the stuff she sent me came in around three."

Avery made a mental note about the benefits of using such a dedicated source as MaryAnn in the future.

"According to MaryAnn, there are several mentions of this treasure contained in obscure documents recovered since the Civil War. Some are vague references found in seized confederate dispatches. Others are stories found in letters and diaries about this General's Gold. It looks as though the treasure may have been stolen and re-hidden several times over. The last mention she could find involved its discovery in the South Carolina Lowcountry on the land of a plantation owner loyal to the confederacy. The trunks were removed from the plantation under the cover of darkness. The operation was overseen by a small group of trusted confederate soldiers. Using union soldiers captured during the Civil War as forced labor, they secretly transported the treasure by rail to the western mountains of Virginia. The plan was to hide the entire treasure in a coal mine located on property owned by a confederate general named Oswald, before sealing it off until the war had ended."

"What good would that have done?" Avery said. "The union soldiers would know where the treasure was hidden."

"Not if they were sealed inside with the treasure," Harrison said, sipping his coffee.

"My God," Avery said.

"The horrors of war, Ave," Harrison said.

Carter continued. "There are indications that the involved confederate officers planned to use the money to reconstruct the southern states after winning the war."

"And we all know how that turned out," Harrison said.

"Oswald . . ." Avery drummed her fingers on the table "Oswald. Why do I know that name?"

"That's the guy they said shot JFK, right?" Carter offered.

"No. I mean, yeah, but that's not the bell that's ringing." She glanced at Harrison, who shrugged. She sighed. It wasn't going to come to her if she kept trying to think of it right then.

"With any luck, this Sonny Landon guy will know more," Carter said.

Avery nodded, smiling a thank you.

"Sonny knows those mining tunnels like the back of his hand," Imogene said, popping her head out of the kitchen. "If he likes you, he'll tell you what you want to know."

"Will he like us?" Avery asked, wondering what kind of superhuman hearing Imogene had, since they'd been careful to keep their voices down after last night.

Imogene smiled. "I like you fine, but I like everybody. Sonny's a bit of an old cuss, shut up out there in the country coughing up part of his lungs by the day. But I don't see anything for him to dislike." She said the last words with her eyes on Harrison.

"Thank you, Imogene," Avery said, suppressing a smile.

"Sure thing. Y'all expecting anybody else?"

They exchanged a glance. "No. Why?"

"You're sure?" Imogene's brow furrowed. "Johnny said your other friend got in late last night. I haven't seen him yet, but there's a car I don't recognize just down the way across the street. I was going to take him some breakfast and apologize if he had to sleep in his vehicle."

Avery glanced at the time, keeping her face impassive. "Maybe Johnny misunderstood. Eat up, boys. Bev's due here within the next half hour."

Bev was right on time, but her hiker van was nowhere to be found. Instead, she was behind the wheel an of old International Scout. At Harrison's suggestion she parked on the street behind Imogene's, allowing them to sneak out the back way.

"Thanks for this," Avery said to Bev as they all piled inside her SUV. No one had dared so much as venturing near the front windows at Imogene's before they left. Harrison had gotten Imogene's description of the car: a black Lincoln Town Car, and for now, that was enough. Big Stone Gap was the sort of place where a car like that would stick out.

"Nonsense," Bev said. "Happy to help. Besides, it's not every day I get to go undercover."

"The people trying to beat us to the gold are dangerous, Bev, and we don't even really know how many of them there are for sure," Avery warned. "I'd completely understand if you didn't want to get further involved. And I told Imogene to be careful around strangers, but it might not hurt for you to tell her, as well."

"Dangerous?" Bev asked with a toothy grin. "They haven't met my family. Trust me, I got deeper roots and more firepower around here than you can imagine. Let them just try to mess with us."

"Okay then." Avery said. "Let's go talk to Mr. Landon."

Sonny Landon's home was tucked back in the foothills about ten minutes outside of town at the end of a badly rutted dirt drive that rose from a secondary road to an opening in the woods. Standing at the center of the clearing was a turn-of-the-century home in dire need of repair. The wood shingle siding was curled and discolored wherever haphazard improvements had been attempted. Several of the window openings featured weathered particle board in place of panes of glass. And a handful of asphalt shingles were missing from the roof.

A scattering of outbuildings stood to the right, all even more neglected than the house. Parked in front of what had once been a garage was a rust-riddled Ford F-150 with a silver-colored cap installed above the truck's bed.

Bev parked the Scout near the side entry door to the house just as a white-haired man dressed in faded overalls, work boots, and a plaid chamois shirt descended the steps to greet them.

"Hey, Sonny," Bev called as the group approached the man.

"Hey, yourself," Sonny's voice crackled with the kind of rasp that comes from years of breathing coal dust ten hours a day.

"Like you to meet some friends of mine," Bev said as she began the introductions.

"Thank you for agreeing to see us on such short notice," Avery said.

"The pleasure is all mine, young lady. Don't get many visitors nowadays. Won't you come in?"

They followed him up the stairs and into the kitchen. Avery was surprised to see the inside of the home was spotless, exactly the opposite of the exterior's appearance. While the furniture and decor were old and dated, everything was clean and appeared to be in good working order. The smell of freshly brewed coffee emanated from an old chrome coffee maker standing sentry atop the laminate counter.

Sonny turned to Harrison. "I hear tell that you're an ex-cop," Sonny said.

"Guilty as charged," Harrison said.

"Then you gotta be a coffee drinker."

"We all are," Avery said.

"Good. I hope you all like it strong. Go on, sit. Won't be a minute."

The three of them sat in mismatched wooden chairs at an old pedestal table covered with a red and white checkered vinyl tablecloth while Bev and Sonny prepared the coffee.

"Lived here long?" Avery asked, trying to get a conversation started.

"All my life," Sonny said. "Used to be my parents' house. Needs a little work to get her back in her prime."

"Don't we all," Harrison said.

Sonny let out a raspy laugh that ended in a coughing fit. Bev passed him a tissue from her pocket without comment and set about serving coffee.

After everyone had steaming mugs and creamer, Bev took a seat next to Sonny, across the table from the others.

"So, Bevvie says you want to know about the mines, huh?" Sonny said.

"We're hoping you might be able to help us find something we've been searching for," Avery said.

"And pray tell what might that be?"

"The general's gold," Avery said. "You ever hear of it?"

Sonny exchanged a knowing glance with Bev then took a sip of the hot black coffee.

"Might have," Sonny said. "Y'all think there might be gold in these here hills?"

"I don't know, Mr. Landon, and that is the God's honest truth," Avery said. "But we've followed a lot of clues that have led us here and Bev tells us we're not the first people to wind up here on this particular chase."

"I hear there's some shady characters trying to keep you from findin' what you're lookin' for," Sonny said.

"You got that right," Carter said.

"Bev said you've been looking after these mines a long time," Harrison said. "We figured if there was something to these stories, you'd know."

Sonny looked at Avery. "You the leader of this posse?"

Avery smiled. "I guess you could say that."

"Why don't you tell me how you got this far."

41

Avery laid out as much information as she was comfortable revealing, beginning with her working alongside Mark Hawkins. She covered Mark's death, the note he'd left for her to find, the coin, the pocket watch, and the diary. Harrison and Carter inserted the occasional fact or validation to what she was saying. The one thing Avery left out was the enigma device. Since as far as she knew no one outside her team was aware of its existence, she figured she was better off keeping that to herself.

Sonny listened intently without interrupting.

As Avery finished, Sonny drained the last of the coffee in his mug, then rose from the table. "Who wants a refill?"

Avery waited patiently as he topped off their mugs. Sonny wasn't reacting the way she had anticipated. She couldn't tell if she'd said something wrong, or if he didn't believe her. Or had he missed the point of her speech entirely?

Sonny finally resumed his seat. "You think someone may have killed your friend because he was getting too close to finding this treasure?" he said.

"I do," Avery said as she struggled to keep a lid on her emotions.

"Any idea who is trying to stop you?"

Avery sighed deeply before speaking. "We have several possibilities, from a mercenary gang led by a former soldier to an elderly antique shop owner with family ties to the treasure hunt."

"And those are only the ones we know about," Harrison added.

"How did Mr. Hawkins die?"

"Police think it was an overdose," Harrison said. "He'd been having back problems, took a Percocet laced with Fentanyl."

Sonny pursed his lips as he looked at Avery. "But you don't believe it was an accident?"

"I knew Mark," Avery said. "I realize I'm biased, but I never once saw him take anything stronger than an Advil. He would never have killed himself, accidentally or otherwise. Someone killed him or had him killed." Avery needed to believe it, because the possibility Mark committed suicide was simply too painful to think about.

Harrison patted her hand. "I'm honestly not sure what to make of Hawkins's death. On the one hand, I worked homicide for twenty years and as a cop I think it could go either way. If Avery is right, the person we're dealing with is clever enough to have gotten rid of Hawkins while avoiding police involvement. What I do know is that someone—or even several someones—has been pursuing us since the moment we got involved. Someone with a long reach and plentiful resources."

Sonny nodded, his attention returning to Avery. "You're hoping to avenge your friend by snatching the treasure out from under his killer's nose?"

"Yes, sir," Avery said.

Sonny's eyes narrowed as he spoke again. "You sure your motives have nothing to do with becoming wealthy yourself?"

"She's already wealthy," Carter said, earning a glare from Harrison.

"It's okay, Harry," Avery said as she put a hand on Harrison's forearm. "Carter's right. I don't need the money, Mr. Landon. And I don't want it. What I do want is to fulfill Mark's dream and beat the person who took his life at his own game."

Sonny took a moment to smooth the white hairs of his mustache. Avery could see the wheels turning inside his head.

"Assuming for a moment that this general's gold is real, what would you do with it if you found it?" Sonny said.

"From what we've learned, the treasure is real," Avery said. "And it has been the source of much death and destruction. I thought it might be time to do something good with it."

"Such as?" Bev said.

"I can't speak for everyone here, but for my share, maybe donate it to a museum," Avery said. "Sitting here this morning, I wonder if the finders' fee wouldn't be useful to the hospitals here that treat black lung disease."

Sonny quietly sipped his coffee as the room grew uncomfortably quiet. Avery wondered if they were about to be given the bum's rush when Sonny nodded.

"Show me this gold coin you found."

Avery slid her hand into the pocket of her jeans. Instead of showing him a cell phone image, she handed him the actual coin.

Sonny's eyes sparkled with recognition as he turned the heavy coin over in his hand, examining it. After several moments, he returned it to Avery.

"You folks ever seen the inside of a coal mine?" Sonny asked.

The three of them shook their heads in unison.

"Then we better get you equipped."

Samael was doing his best to maintain his composure despite the lack of progress. He had easily obtained the address of the bed and breakfast where Turner and the others were staying thanks to the overly cooperative, albeit naïve, airport employee, Johnny. But that had been more than sixteen hours ago. Surely they should have spotted Avery and the others by now. Something was amiss.

"Sorry, Mr. Samael," hired muscle number one said from the passenger seat of the rented town car.

Imbecile number two weighed in, "We've been sitting here all night and other than the old lady who owns the place, nobody else has come out."

Samael, who had parked his rented Audi behind their rented town car, climbed into the Lincoln's backseat, so as not to be more obvious than they already were. As he eyed the two buffoons in front of him, who he had begun to think of as Thing One and Thing Two, he allowed himself a particularly vivid momentary fantasy. A fantasy where he smoothly drew the SIG Sauer P228 from its holster and emptied every 9mm round he had into their thick skulls, depositing what little brain matter they both possessed all over the inside of the windshield.

Samael silently counted to ten before speaking. "Did it ever occur to either of you that they might have spotted you and gone out the back way?"

"Told you we should have covered the back," Thing One said.

Samael sighed deeply as he considered his options.

"And you're sure the owner has gone out?" Samael said.

"Yup," Thing Two said. "Drove off about twenty minutes ago. Had a bunch of those reusable canvas bags. Probably went shopping."

When all else failed, the direct scheme had always worked best. Samael decided he would approach the house as a potential lodger, the best dressed lodger the old bat had ever hosted.

"Wait here while I take a look inside," Samael said as he opened the door and stepped out. "You think you two can handle that?"

Avery accompanied Sonny in his pickup, while Bev followed with Carter and Harrison in the Scout. Splitting up allowed a very tickled Harrison to commandeer the passenger seat of the Scout, while Avery got a chance to chat up Sonny.

"Bev told us that nobody knows these mines like you," Avery said.

"She's right," Sonny said. "I've spent nearly my entire life here in one capacity or another."

"And now you're the caretaker."

"That I am."

"What does a caretaker do, exactly?"

"A little bit of everything. I give tours to tourists about three months out of the year. Rest of the time I keep an eye out for trespassers and maintain the equipment. None of the locals care about this stuff anymore, not since it stopped putting money in their pockets. Small towns are like that."

Sonny activated the truck's left blinker and slowed to allow an oncoming car to pass.

"Also, I maintain the structure that holds up the tourist shafts. Can't have them dying on me," he said with a wink. "Bad for repeat business."

Avery laughed. "I imagine it would be. So, that's where you're taking us?"

"No ma'am, it is not. Not unless you want your time wasted. Place I'm taking you isn't tied up in some foreclosure garbage or owned by someone with more money than sense. The place I'm taking you is all mine, if you'll forgive the bad pun. It was left to me by my daddy."

"And you think what we're looking for might be there?"

"Wouldn't be taking you there if I didn't."

42

Samael walked up to the front door of the bed and breakfast where he found a handwritten note taped to the window.

Back in a couple of hours. If you purchased an online reservation, feel free to toss your things in the proper room. Imogene.

Sometimes it was just too easy.

Samael opened the door then stepped inside. He paused at the threshold after closing the door behind him, listening to see if any of the occupants were present. He kept perfectly still for close to a minute. He heard the whir of a dishwasher cycling somewhere near the back of the first floor where he imagined the kitchen was located. The pronounced ticking of what sounded like a grandfather clock came from around the corner to his left. Aside from those sounds, Samael heard nothing else.

"Hello," he called out. "Anyone here?"

Hearing nothing, he walked from the entryway into the main living room. On the opposite side of the space stood what looked like an antique podium. Something a maitre d' might use when seating guests. Atop the podium was an open ledger. Samael flipped the page back, quickly finding what he was looking for. The name Avery Turner was scrawled across the bottom of the page, along with her Florida mailing address. Below her entry were the names of Harrison and Carter Mosley.

Samael carefully explored the first floor, making a mental note of every-thing he saw. Off the kitchen he found the rear mud room. Looking through the door glass he could see the path likely taken by Avery and her friends that led to a stone wall with a painted picket fence-type gate. The gate opened onto a paved street parallel to the one where his hired Mensa candidates were currently parked. He wondered if it had been Avery who figured out that they were being tracked, or if the overgrown ex-cop had spoiled his fun. Either way, it was obvious that they were now engaged in tradecraft, and clever enough to outsmart the tail he had put on them. Though he didn't imagine the latter would require much in the way of cleverness.

Finding nobody on the lower level, nor any clue as to where his quarry might be, Samael climbed the stairs to the second floor.

As they continued along the winding back roads up into the foothills, Avery asked Sonny about the pictograph map that had led them to the Roaring Branch Trail.

"Is there any mention of a watch or a map key in your local legends?" Avery asked, glancing in her side view mirror to make sure Bev's Scout was still behind them. "I was pretty sure the waterfalls here were the ones from the etching."

"Can't say I've heard of one," Sonny said. "You really got all that from an etching inside a watch?"

"Well, there was a lot more to it than that. I had to write a whole computer software program to home in on the location. And there were time period variables to consider. But I was lucky enough to know it had to be near the Atlantic Seaboard."

"You're talking way beyond my technical know-how, young lady. But since you made it this far, I figure you must know what you're talking about. And it just so happens that I don't think you were wrong."

"But we searched all three waterfalls along that trail. There's nothing there."

Sonny turned his head toward her and grinned. "Nothing above ground."

Samael wasn't at all surprised to find the doors to the occupied rooms closed and locked. Though he was a skilled lock-picker, a useful tool to have in his prior profession, the cheap deadbolt locks that had been installed on the turn of the century painted wood doors were nothing but child's play. The only thing of concern was the fourth door. He had found the owner's quarters located on the first floor in the rear ell of the building, so he knew it wasn't occupied by her. Assuming Avery, Carter, and the cop each had their own room, the fourth was one too many. He would need to be cautious during his search. It wouldn't do to have to kill a surprised guest. Collateral damage draws unnecessary attention from law enforcement.

The first room he entered had to belong to Harrison. Oversized men's clothes littered the floor next to the closet. Though muddy, the garments appeared new. And, upon closer inspection, the clothes were constructed of a wicking fabric. The kind of items one might wear on a hike. Samael searched drawers, the closet, even beneath the bed, carefully returning everything to its original position to avoid leaving any trace of his presence. Finding nothing of value, Samael retreated to the hallway and relocked the door.

Carter's room was next. Once again, he found brand new muddy outdoor wear on the floor. Whatever they had been up to, it was obvious they hadn't wasted any time after arriving in town.

The third room he entered wasn't a guest room at all, but a storage space full of extra furniture and cleaning supplies. Samael's earlier angst disappeared as he realized there were only three actual rooms occupied. He had wondered what the sleeping arrangements were between Avery and Carter, but the search of Carter's room confirmed that Mr. Instagram was alone.

After securing the storage room, Samael moved down to the far end of the hall and performed a quick check of the bathroom. Hanging from a

chrome shower head was an empty hydration bladder. More hiking para-
phernalia.

Samael returned to the last unchecked locked room. Avery Turner's
room. He had just popped the lock and was reaching for the decorative
glass doorknob when he heard the sound of someone opening and closing
the front door.

"Hello?" a voice called out.

"We're here," Sonny said as he pulled off the dirt road into a small grassy
turnout, leaving enough space for Bev to park beside his truck.

Avery looked around but saw nothing that resembled what she had
envisioned the opening to a mine would look like.

All five of them piled out of their respective vehicles, then followed
Sonny to the rear of his truck. He unlocked the cap and dropped the tail-
gate, revealing an abundance of mining gear: rubber boots, plastic hard
hats with headlamps, and a pile of bright yellow rain pants and jackets.

"Didn't know what sizes you might need," Sonny said.

"Why do you have all this stuff?" Harrison asked.

"What do you think the paying customers on my mine tours wear?"

Bev joined in, "Vacationing city folk don't much care for having their
shorts and sandals ruined by coal dust."

They each donned clothing that most closely matched their sizes.

"Good thing these come with suspenders," Carter said as he showed
how loose the rain pants were at the waist.

"Maybe if you didn't eat like a bird, Mr. Caesar salad with dressing on
the side," Bev said, garnering a belly laugh from Harrison.

After they were dressed, Sonny checked to make sure their headlamps
were working properly. He pointed to a case of bottled water on the floor of
the truck's payload bay. "Might want to pocket a couple of those as we're
going underground."

They followed him toward the wood line where a rusty wire cable
stretched across what might have been an old dirt track drive but was now
thick with tall grass and weeds. They skirted the cable to the right of a

thick evergreen and continued along the trail. A hundred yards in they came to an old, weathered barn that appeared to be an abandoned lumber mill.

"This old sawmill belongs to you?" Avery said.

"Does now. Was once my grandfather's. This is where they cut the timbers used to reinforce the mines."

"I don't understand," Carter said. "I thought you were taking us to a mine."

Sonny and Bev exchanged a look then chuckled at some private joke.

"Patience, young man," Sonny said as he dug out an old key ring from his pocket. He inserted the key into a rusted padlock that was holding a chain together across sliding barn doors. At first the key wouldn't budge.

Avery wondered how long it had been since anyone had used the barn.

At last, the key turned and, after a bit of finagling by Sonny, the lock slid open. He pulled the chain free and tossed it into the tall grass at the front of the barn. He eyed the rusty door runners overhead, then turned to Harrison and Carter.

"You two, give me a hand shoving these doors apart. They were always trouble, and with all that rust it won't have gotten better."

"I can move that, Mr. Landon, y'all stand aside," Carter said with a confident grin.

He stood in front of the left-hand door, put his shoulder into the center crack between them and his hands on the right-side handle, set his feet, and shoved to the right.

Nothing moved but a few flakes of rust that drifted onto the brim of his hard hat.

Avery swallowed a laugh, unsure if the red in Carter's cheeks was from exertion or embarrassment.

"Need a hand, junior?" Harrison stepped forward.

"I must have pushed in the wrong place," Carter muttered, stepping back and studying the doors.

"Must have," Sonny said, keeping his face serious but unable to hide the twinkle in his eye.

"Maybe the sweet spot is just up higher," Harrison said, not bothering to mask the slight condescension as he stepped in to help. "I am taller."

"Be my guest," Carter said. Avery could tell he wasn't mad, but he was tiring of Harry's ribbing. She poked Harrison.

"I'm not young enough to try it alone," Harrison said, his tone kinder. "Together on three?"

Avery smiled.

It took a bit of grunting and groaning by both men before either door budged, but eventually they were able to shove hard enough to create about a four-foot opening, revealing the inside of the dusty space.

Sonny entered ahead of them, pausing to take a deep breath. A potpourri of earth, oil, and lumber dominated the space.

"So many memories in that smell," he said.

Cobwebs hung from the beams and disused equipment scattered about the interior of the barn, while dust motes swirled above the dirt and sawdust at their feet.

"Wait here," Sonny said as walked to the far corner of the barn and opened a wall-mounted panel. He flipped numerous breakers, bringing several banks of overhead florescent lights flickering to life and lending color to the dingy space. He activated additional switches, and the sound of machinery hummed around them.

Carter leaned in close and whispered to Avery. "Are we sure the guy's operating with a full deck?"

Before Avery could respond, Sonny turned around and answered for her.

"All fifty-two cards, young man. And perfect hearing."

"Sorry," Carter said sheepishly.

"Must be something in the water," Avery said. "Imogene has better hearing than any CIA agent, I'm convinced."

"It's the mines," Sonny said. "You have to pay attention to the smallest sounds the Earth can make—hearing the very beginnings of a cave-in can mean the difference between life and death. Imogene's daddy worked the mines, she grew up in and out of the tunnels."

He moved to a stack of old timbers lying on the floor near the center of the barn.

"Gonna need a hand with these," he said.

Between the five of them they were able to move a dozen 8 x 8 beams aside in short order. Avery was surprised that the beams weren't heavier. She imagined the wood was so old and dry that the timbers were only a fraction of their original weight.

After they had finished moving the pile, Sonny grabbed an old push broom. The dust rose in clouds as he swept, making the interior of the barn look foggy. Avery and the others did their best to cover their mouths and noses, but Carter still sneezed.

When the dust finally settled, Sonny dropped to his knees, feeling around until he found what he was looking for. He pried a rusty metal ring from the dirt, then pulled upward, revealing the outer seams of a heavy wooden trap door.

"Could do with a little help," Sonny said as he strained to lift the door. Harrison and Carter both grabbed onto the sides and helped him slide the door out of its steel frame. They dragged it out of the way and dropped it onto the barn floor.

"What is that?" Avery said as she peered into the void.

"The entrance to my mine," Sonny said proudly as he stood upright and brushed the dirt from his knees.

"Your mine?" Carter said. "You own a mine?"

"Left to me by my grandfather."

"Didn't you say he ran a sawmill?" Harrison said.

"He did," Sonny said. "He also built the mill on top of the mine entrance to hide it from nosy parkers like that guy who went bankrupt searching for your treasure."

"The last guy never searched here?" Avery said.

"Nope," Sonny said. "No way for him to even know it existed."

"How did you manage to keep it a secret?" Harrison asked.

Bev spoke up, "Who do you think he hired to be his guide when he purchased the mines and conducted his searches?"

Sonny smiled. "Never let 'em see you coming. Now, who wants to look inside my mine?"

43

Avery followed Sonny through the opening in the floor, descending an iron ladder until she reached the mine floor. Strung from overhead support beams were several incandescent light bulbs, spaced every ten feet. Unlike the dry and dusty barn, the mine shaft was dank and cold, the temperature easily down fifteen degrees since they'd left the barn. She turned around and stared down a tunnel that disappeared into darkness. The passage was about five feet high and eight feet wide. Running along its middle was a set of narrow-gauge tracks.

"It's like another world down here," Avery said.

"You ain't seen nothing yet," Sonny said.

"I don't see any canaries," Harrison said as he stepped off the ladder.

Sonny laughed aloud. "We've got fresh air."

Avery could hear the distant mechanical sound again, closer now. "Where does the air come from?"

"Feel that movement?" Sonny said as he held up his hand in the direction of the tunnel.

They all nodded.

"There's a number of air shafts drilled into the mountain which draw air from the surface at regular intervals," Sonny said.

"Wouldn't all those shafts make the mine less stable?" Harrison said, the concern in his voice clear.

"Nothing stable about a coal mine," Sonny said with a wink. "They just let us breathe a little better."

"How far does this thing go?" Carter asked.

Sonny turned around to look at Avery.

"Remember when you asked me about the map you found? The one that took you to the Roaring Branch Trail?"

"Yeah," Avery said. "I was certain that the information on the map led us to one of the Roaring Branch waterfalls."

"Technically, you were right." Sonny pointed into the darkness. "This mine is over a mile long. At the far end it intersects with three others. One of those shafts leads to a point directly underneath the Roaring Branch Trail."

"Then the map was right after all," Carter said.

"Only it wasn't three dimensional," Avery said. "It didn't account for the z-axis."

"The what?" Harrison said.

"The depth, Harry."

"You mean we hiked that stupid trail for nothing?" Harrison grumbled.

"Yes and no," Sonny said.

"You channeling The Riddler, Sonny?" Harrison asked.

"You wouldn't be here if Bev hadn't told me you were determined enough to make that hike," Sonny said.

"What's that crackling sound?" Carter asked.

"That's the mountain talking to us," Sonny said. "Like I said before."

"Come again?" Harrison said.

"This mountain is made entirely of coal. This shaft runs downhill from here, deeper into the earth. The farther down you dig, the more coal weight there is above you. That downward pressure makes that Rice Krispies snapping sound."

"Guess what else that sound is?" Harrison shook his head, his lamp beam swinging an arc in the darkness. "That's the sound of me climbing back up that ladder. Lost treasure or not, I'm not going underground that's 'talking,' no matter what anyone thinks it's saying." Harrison lifted his jacket and patted the holster of his Glock 9mm. "If you need me, I'll be topside watching for that Lincoln Imogene mentioned."

"I'll join you," Bev said.

Avery looked at Carter. He cast a glance down the mine then gave her a nod.

"I'm in," he said.

Avery turned to Sonny. "How do we get down there?"

"Well, the easiest way is—"

"Wait a minute, Ave," Harrison said. "How do you know that there's even anything down there? If there was something to find, don't you think Sonny here would have recovered it already? You're chasing ghosts. Risking your neck, and Carter's, for a tale of lost treasure."

Avery looked at Sonny again. "There's a reason you brought us down here, Mr. Landon. What is it?"

Sonny looked at Bev before he answered.

"When I was still a young man, I went down to that tunnel, the one that runs directly under the waterfall. Nobody ever used it, as far back as I can remember. My daddy told me about a collapse, said it was too dangerous, so they closed it off with a wooden barricade and 'Keep Out' signs. Except I knew it wasn't true."

"How?" Avery asked.

Sonny waved a hand. "I've always had a way of listening to the mountain. I also read every book on geology Ms. Whitworth at the library could beg, borrow, or steal from all over the state. That section wasn't volatile enough to have caved in anytime since it was dug out, from what I could tell. Which meant there was something daddy didn't want me to see."

"What did you do?" Carter asked.

"I did what any self-respecting young man would do, I bypassed that barricade and went down in there myself."

"And?" Harrison said, with one foot still on the bottom rung of the ladder.

"There was a partial cave in, and it was recent. Made no sense, mind you, but it sealed off the tunnel pretty good. But I crawled over it and kept going. Eventually I found another cave in. A much older one."

"How could you tell?" Avery said.

"Because I found bones among the rubble. Human bones and scraps of clothing that looked like they might have been part of a soldier's uniform."

Avery felt a shiver as she thought back to what Harrison had theorized about the captured union soldiers. Prisoners forced by a confederate general to move the gold by dark of night into the mines. The idea that the men might intentionally have been sealed inside with the treasure all these years was both terrifying and thrilling at the same time, because it meant they might be close to discovering the treasure.

"You're not really gonna risk your lives to go look at a few brass buttons and some old bones, are you, Ave?" Harrison said.

"What makes you think there is treasure hidden down there, Mr. Landon?" Avery said, ignoring Harrison.

"This," Sonny said as he pulled two gold coins from his jacket pocket. "I found them in the rubble right before I got to the bones, and the bones were my cue to skedaddle. Wasn't nothing worth enough money to make me disturb anybody's final resting place."

The coins were identical to the one Avery had found in Mark's study. Identical to the one the old antique dealer had locked up in her safe. Even had the same number designation as the one Avery had found, which, if the story about the coins being numbered to match each of the twelve sea chests was true, meant that each of the coins found thus far had come from the same chest.

"Why are we disturbing their resting place today, then?" Carter asked.

Sonny coughed. "I'm a much older man now, one who's had a decent life and made peace with the fact that I'll meet my maker soon enough if I'm making a mistake." He pointed to Avery. "When she said she wasn't looking to get rich here, I knew. It's time. If y'all find the gold, we can unpack the cave-in and give those men the Christian burial they should've had many years ago."

Avery handed the coins back to Sonny. "Show us how to get down there."

Samael sat at the kitchen table watching as Imogene Blakely prepared his coffee. His artificial charm and expensive clothing had completely fooled the woman. He felt a bit like the Grinch after being caught pilfering everything in the house.

"We rarely get any famous guests in town," she said. "Let alone here at the B & B. How long have you been Mr. Mosley's agent, Sam?"

"You know, I can't even remember myself," Samael said. "Some days it doesn't seem real."

She crossed the room and set the hot mug and creamer on the table in front of him.

"I can't thank you enough for your hospitality, Imogene. You must have been surprised to come in and find me skulking around your home. Carter and I got our wires crossed."

"Are you here to research another treasure hunt video?" she asked as she sat down at the end of the table to his right with her own coffee.

Samael leaned forward and lowered his voice in a conspiratorial tone. "You know I'm really not supposed to say, but it is entirely within the realm of possibility."

"I knew it."

"I hope Carter didn't let the cat out of the bag."

"Oh, no. I may have overheard something, but I wouldn't want to get Mr. Mosley into any trouble."

"My lips are sealed. What did you hear?"

"Only that they were discussing the old Brashton Mine and a lost treasure that belonged to some general or other."

Samael flashed his most disarming smile as he lifted the mug to his lips. "Tell me more."

44

Avery gripped the sides of the mine cart tightly as they descended into darkness. Her breakfast had nearly made a reappearance three times already. She wasn't sure whether it was the excitement of what might lie ahead or the jerking and bumping of their conveyance as its wheels crawled along the uneven metal track. With only their headlamps to illuminate the way, the long tunnel quickly devoured the light the farther into the mine they traveled.

Sonny sat at the rear of the transport while Avery and Carter sat beside each other at the front. The only good thing about the mechanical clanking and whining of the winch was that it drowned out the crackling noises from up above. Avery was trying not to think about the ever-shifting mountain of coal.

"Relax," Carter said. "It hasn't collapsed yet."

"Not helpful, mind reader," Avery said.

"You dove more than sixty meters day before yesterday without batting an eye—you're not white knuckling that rail because you're scared of this kiddie roller coaster ride," Carter said.

Sonny whistled to himself as they descended, but Avery couldn't decide if that was comforting or deeply disturbing.

After what seemed an eternity, Sonny brought the cart to a screeching halt.

"Welcome to the end of the line," Sonny said, his voice echoing off the walls. "Everybody out."

Avery didn't care for his ominous phrasing. It was a little too close to what she was already feeling.

They all climbed out of the car and walked forward into another antechamber similar in size to the one beneath the barn. Their headlamps swept the far wall like spotlights at an opening night gala. Avery could see the entrance to the three tunnels Sonny had previously described. Each of the passages appeared narrower and lower than the main tunnel. And none of them were equipped with rails. Which meant they would be walking, hunched over, as they continued.

"You can see what's left of the barricade I told you about," Sonny said as he pointed to the crudely constructed wooden gate blocking the entrance to the tunnel on the far left.

Nailed to the wood were hand painted signs that read "caution" and "danger," each with a crudely rendered image of a skull and crossbones.

"Here," Sonny said. "Give me a hand prying this thing apart."

The gate was so old that many of the boards splintered as they tugged on them, their rusty nails squealing in protest. When they finished, the entrance to the tunnel looked like a gaping mouth full of rotted teeth.

"This last part's a little uncomfortable," Sonny said. "You folks will have to be careful not to hit your heads as you go."

"You're not coming with us?" Avery asked.

"Bit cramped in there for three people," Sonny said. "I figured you'd both want to see it for yourselves."

Avery and Carter exchanged an uneasy look. Once again she was reminded of the shotgun toting antiquarian and the phony dive boat captain. Was Sonny leading them into a trap? Or was she just being overly cautious?

"Oh, almost forgot," Sonny said as he retreated to the cart to retrieve something. "Here, you'll need these." He handed each of them a wooden handled spade.

"What's this for?" Carter asked.

"Figure you'll want to dig around a bit. See what you can see."

"Thanks," Avery said.

Avery and Carter stood at the entrance for a moment looking at each other. Carter waved one arm and grinned. "Ladies first."

Avery and Carter moved quickly along the narrow passageway. The beams of their headlamps bobbed up and down, accentuating the craggy surface of the walls and elongating their shadows. The floor of the tunnel was littered with debris that had previously fallen from the ceiling, requiring them to take great care with each step. The rock walls affected every sound, a reverberating mix of sharp echoes and the crunch of footsteps. Overriding all of it was the constant foreboding crackle of a mountain of coal shifting overhead.

Avery estimated that they were two hundred yards from where they had left Sonny when they came across the first cave-in. Lumps of black rock filled the space almost to the ceiling.

Avery crouched, directing her lamp into the narrow opening of blackness between the top of the pile and the roof of the mine.

"And here we have the actual end of the line," Carter said.

Avery whipped her head around. "Excuse me?"

"We can't get through that, Avery. It's a solid wall of coal God knows how thick, and we have a couple of gardening tools."

"Sonny said he crawled over it as a kid." Avery looked for a foothold on the front of the pile. "I might be able to get over it."

"Be reasonable. There's like a foot and a half between this pile of rocks and the top of the mine. And that's just what we can see. It's too risky. And I never say that. I am Mr. Risk."

"Listen to me, Mr. Risk. You have no idea what it took for me to get this far. This place scares the heck out of me. There is no way I could ever make myself come down here again."

"So your solution is to climb into something I don't even think is a good idea? Have you met me?"

"What I've done is, I've chased this thing all over the eastern seaboard.

I've been followed, robbed, and nearly fed to a shark. There's at least one guy actively trying to kill us. Probably killed Mark, too. I have no idea who I can trust. I haven't been home in like—what day is this?"

"Tuesday. I think."

"See, I thought it was Friday. That's how far into this I've dug myself. I am going to try and reach the other side. I have to know what's over there. For Mark's sake. Are you going to help me or not?"

Carter stared for a moment in silence. Avery wondered if she had pushed too hard. Finally, he brushed past her and jammed his spade into the pile, removing a shovel full of coal and depositing it on the tunnel floor.

"We can't dig it out," she said. "We'll starve to death before we get two more steps."

"You need footholds if you're going to climb this wall." He moved up about a foot and removed another shovelful diagonal from the first.

"You're pretty smart, Mr. Risk," she said, joining him.

The debris was hard and cold, and Avery could see the steam of her breath in the beam of her headlamp. She heard her own labored breathing over the crackling sound of the mountain, louder now that it was barely a couple of inches from her head. The icy fingers of panic squeezed her insides as she inhaled the odor of diesel and sulfur and felt the gritty soot of the anthracite against her face.

Why didn't I listen to Carter?

Because you would never know if the treasure was here, Ave.

Yeah, but what if I get stuck down here forever?

"Stop it, Avery," she said, shoving her inner voice away. "Focus."

She inched forward, face down.

With each movement, her back and buttocks scraped against the roof of the mine shaft, adding to her fear of getting stuck. It was only through sheer willpower and superhuman stubbornness that she was able to keep moving.

Seconds became minutes as inches added up to feet, Avery's heart pounding in her ears overtaking her lungs and the mountain for loudest sound in the void.

The obstacle ended up being about thirty feet long. It only took Avery about ten minutes to traverse the top of the pile, but it was the longest ten minutes of her life.

Loose coal slid from beneath her torso as she crawled out on the far side of the cave-in and struggled to regain her feet. The mine ahead was clear again, and as black as night as far as she could see. The claustrophobia was fading, but only slightly.

"Are you through?" Carter yelled from the far end.

"I made it," Avery called back.

"What's it look like?"

"Like where you are, but darker."

Despite the chilly air inside the mine Avery was perspiring. She removed her helmet and wiped her brow, blackening her face with more coal dust in the process.

"I'm gonna see where this thing leads," Avery said before continuing.

"Be careful," Carter said.

Avery walked on, for how long she couldn't have said. Neither time nor distance seemed to mean anything this far beneath the earth. Eventually she reached another obstruction. This time there was no space above the slide. Just an impenetrable pile of coal and rock filling the tunnel all the way to the ceiling.

Sonny's story of entombed soldiers' remains made the hair on her neck prickle as it stood up. She could easily imagine a skeletal hand reaching out from under the pile and grasping her by the ankle.

"Not cool," she said aloud. "Keep it together, Ave." It sounded like something her mother would have said. "Remember why you're down here."

She began to dig around the edges of the pile, carefully removing a spade full of stones at a time. Each time she shoveled out a space, loose coal slid down from above, negating her progress. It was akin to using a bucket to drain a lake.

After several minutes of shoveling, something flashed near the bottom of the pile. Just a glint of reflected light, but it was enough to draw her attention. She dropped to her knees and swept debris out of the way using her gloved hands. There it was. Exactly as Sonny had described. Moldy cloth with brass-colored buttons wrapped around . . . an arm bone. The material was deteriorated and coated in black dust, making it impossible to determine its original color, but it was clearly some type of uniform. She tore one of the buttons free from the fabric and held it up to the light. The button came from a Union soldier's uniform, she was sure of it. Something terrible had happened here: a horrific mass murder that never made it into any history book.

Something poking out of the rubble beside her knee caught Avery's attention. She pulled the item free. It was a small, hand-stitched satchel made from a heavier canvas-type fabric than the uniform remnants, in remarkable shape considering how long it must have been down there. Inside, she found a leather-bound journal and half a dozen of the gold coins. Water-stained and mildewed around its edges, the pages of the journal were in rough shape. Avery returned everything to the satchel, then stuffed it into her hip pocket.

She moved to continue her digging just as the beam of her headlamp began to flicker.

"Don't even think about it," she said, her breath quickening. She removed the plastic helmet and tapped the lens with her finger. "Please, don't do this to me."

The light extinguished, leaving her with nothing but the image of the filament burned into her retinas, in pitch darkness, with no sense of direction.

45

Avery spent the next several moments crawling around the floor of the mine, reaching out blindly for the shaft wall but finding nothing. How was that even possible in a space this tiny? Every ounce of her willpower went into avoiding a full-on panic attack, but the fingers of dread had returned, tightening around her chest, making breathing difficult. The image of the dead soldier's arm popped into her head again, along with the sound of something moving. Avery froze and listened. The sound was impossible to pinpoint in all the crackling and echoes, but it was growing louder. And closer. She was about to scream when a faint light bobbed into view.

"Avery," Carter yelled.

"Down here," she croaked, her shoulders sagging with relief.

The beam of Carter's light drew nearer until he was standing in front of her.

"You okay?" Carter asked.

"My stupid headlamp died," she said, the desire to protect her skull from falling rock the only thing keeping her from throwing the helmet at the wall. "What are you doing here? I thought you were too afraid to crawl over the cave-in."

"I couldn't very well leave you down here on your own, could I?" Carter helped her to her feet then handed her a small flashlight. "No self-respecting adrenaline junkie gets beat out at risk taking by a newbie."

"Thanks," she said.

"Is that what I think it is?" Carter said, focusing his lamp on the bones.

"Exactly as Sonny described it."

"Jesus, Avery."

She pulled a bottle of water from the pocket of her jacket and drank half of it. Her hands were still shaking from her brief game of blind man's bluff.

"You okay?" Carter said.

She recapped the bottle. "Not really. Let's just get this over with."

The two of them took turns moving coal from the pile and scattering it across the floor of the tunnel behind them. They made quick progress by rolling several large stones out of the way by hand, revealing more bits of fabric and more bones. After toiling for about twenty minutes, Avery plunged the tip of her spade into the pile and struck something hard and metallic.

They looked at each other.

"Was that what I think it was?" Carter said.

"Only one way to find out," Avery said.

They both dropped to their knees and began digging into the pile with their hands. Slowly they exposed one end of what looked like a wooden sea chest wrapped in rusty chains. The steel reinforcement bands of the chest were corroded and falling apart, but the chains held firm.

"Step back," Carter said.

Avery moved back a few paces and watched as Carter drove the pointed end of the spade into the rotted wood. The chest fell apart, spilling its contents onto the floor of the mine.

"That. Doesn't. Look. Like. Gold." Carter accentuated each word as if it were its own sentence.

Avery couldn't speak. She couldn't even blink. The mess on the floor was like a train wreck she couldn't look away from and wanted to instantly forget, all at the same time. She crouched and reached for a handful of the trunk's rusted contents.

"It's just pieces of iron," Avery said.

"This one's a railroad spike," Carter said as he pulled one free. "What the hell?"

Avery's mind raced as she dug out more of the chest's contents. Scrap metal. Nothing but trash. Had the entire thing been a fool's errand?

"People died here, Avery." Carter gestured to a bone, skeletal white gleaming through the coal dust even in the weak light. "For this?"

Avery couldn't believe what she was looking at. Every clue had led them closer to this point. And there was at least one chained and locked chest brought here, just like the legend said. But aside from a few scattered gold coins, there was nothing of value in it. That had to be intentional.

"I think I know what happened," Avery said at last. "The clues we've been following were meant to misdirect us. To misdirect anyone trying to locate the treasure, rather."

"Well, it worked," Carter said as he broke into a fit of hysterical laughter. "We're about as far from anything valuable as we could be. This whole goose chase was a fairy tale, minus the golden eggs."

"You're not hearing me, Carter. The coins that were left down here were meant to convince anyone who got this far that there was treasure down here. Treasure that needed protecting."

"Like Sonny's old man tried to do."

"And his grandfather too. Someone went to a great deal of trouble to keep anyone from finding the secret of this mineshaft. To make sure the treasure stayed safe."

"After this, what makes you so sure there is any treasure to find?" Carter said.

"The coins," Avery said holding up what she had found. "These coins are real."

"So now what do we do? I mean besides getting the hell out of here."

"We backtrack. If the clues we found fooled us, they fooled everyone else, too. We need to retrace our steps and figure out what we missed."

46

Avery and Carter rode in silence as Sonny slowly guided their transport back toward the mine entrance. Exhausted on all fronts and filthy with coal dust, they resembled chimney sweeps from merry old England at the end of a long day.

No longer concerned with the bumpy cart or the ambient crackling—being trapped in utter darkness with the bones of murdered soldiers will do that to a person—Avery's mind raced back through the chain of clues they had followed, all the way to the beginning. The same clues that had brought them to a literal dead end. She considered that for a couple hundred feet of track. The coal mine, the danger, the hidden entrance, the cave-ins. This was a purposeful, planned dead end: that tunnel wasn't the final destination, it was a red herring.

But why?

And what did Sonny, who was whistling again, know about it?

Treasure hunting was giving Avery trust issues—a week ago, she'd have found Sonny and Bev and the whole town delightful, and now she couldn't tell if they were really as friendly as they seemed, or if they were part of some kind of plot Avery hadn't quite figured out yet.

What if whoever ordered the union solders down into miles of darkness with those trunks knew the gold was gone? What if the legend wasn't a fairy tale—but a heist story?

There had to be a key or a clue somewhere that she had missed. Something that pointed in an entirely different direction. But where was it?

What did Avery have that no one else hunting the treasure had? Besides the watch that had led them here, that list was the things Mark had spent who knows how long looking for: the coordinates, the enigma, and for a hot minute, that journal.

The journal someone had stolen from her hotel in Boston.

The journal that came from the desk Mark bought from the estate on Martha's Vineyard. The desk Louise Williams and her 12-gauge spent half a day alone with before it shipped to Maine from her shop. The desk Mark's old friend Corbacho had offered to buy back from her so he'd have a memory of Mark in his home—even offering her more than whatever Mark had paid for it. Corbacho, who'd been so kind when she'd shown up unannounced, so sweet and slightly flirty in his messages . . . and who had a family interest in the treasure he'd even told her about.

Could he have . . .

No.

Surely Corbacho didn't buy a massive, furnished New England estate because he wanted an old desk. Right?

Right. Corbacho was Mark's friend, and Avery had searched the antique thoroughly, only managing to locate one hidden compartment—and it had been empty.

The watch? It had been in the ruins of the boat Marion Hawkins died trying to find. Marion and Louise Williams's father.

Louise had a coin. A shotgun. And a lot of jewels in that fingerprint-sealed safe. She'd told them the story about gold chased by generations through two wars, and two generals . . .

Oswald.

The Civil War general she mentioned was Oswald.

Avery glanced back at Sonny before she turned to Carter, leaning close to whisper so low that surely even Sonny's super miner ears wouldn't pick up her words. "We need MaryAnn again."

"Do you have any idea how many favors I owe her already?" he hissed back.

"Suck it up, buttercup. I remembered why I knew the name Oswald, besides JFK. That's the family who used to own all these mines. Whoever planted the phony treasure here must have known where the real gold went. Seems like the general who owned this land is a good place to start looking."

"Remember what I said about treasure hunters, Avery. You're starting to get that same look. The one hardcore gamblers get when they've maxed out five credit cards at the casino ATM, while trying to figure out how to bet their actual home on the next hand because they just know they're due for a big jackpot."

Avery pursed her lips. "Just ask your friend, please," she whispered.

Sonny brought the cart safely to a stop at the top of the rails. He switched off the motor then chocked the wheels.

"Well?" Harrison said as Avery climbed the ladder to the barn. "Did you find anything?"

"We sure did," Carter said. "Fool's gold."

"I don't understand," Harrison said.

"There's nothing down there but trunks of scrap iron," Avery said.

"And old ghosts," Sonny said. "I guess most local legends turn out to be more fiction than fact." He looked at Bev. "Not that we need to ruin it for the young'uns."

"Of course not," Bev said. "You folks ready to head back?"

"I am," Avery said, wondering how many nightmares would come from the minutes she had spent alone in the dark with Sonny's old ghosts.

"Me too," Carter said. "I've had more than enough excitement for one day."

"Thank you for allowing us to impose on you, Sonny," Avery said.

"Nonsense. It was my pleasure. Been a while since I was down there. Kinda felt like a youngster again."

After peeling off the borrowed gear and saying their goodbyes, Avery, Harrison, and Carter climbed into Bev's Scout. Avery only wanted three things: a shower, a loaded pizza, and another chance to look at the journal that was stolen from her. She wasn't even sure why, but she couldn't shake the feeling there was something in it that would make this whole thing make sense.

"Anything from Imogene?" Avery asked as she buckled herself into the passenger seat of Bev's scout.

"Some guy let himself in this morning after she left to go grocery shopping. Claimed to be your agent," she glanced at Carter in the rearview, who shook his head so quickly a blink would have obscured it.

"That's an awfully weird thing for someone to say," he said.

"Awfully weird," Avery echoed, fixing him with a gaze over her shoulder before Bev started talking again.

"Imogene thinks he was poking through your rooms. She tried to figure out what he really wanted—besides to know where y'all went—but she texted a while ago to say she didn't have any luck and he up and left."

"Speaking of Imogene and unannounced visitors—I don't suppose the two guys in the Lincoln are friends of yours, are they?" Harrison said to Bev.

"No friends of mine," Bev said as she checked the rear-view mirror.

"Nor yours?" Avery asked Carter, craning her neck to look through the SUV's back window.

"Never seen them before," Carter said. "But how the hell did they find us way up here?"

"These guys are crafty," Avery said. "And the more important question is, can Bev lose them?"

Bev looked over at Avery and grinned. "Hang on, city girl."

She downshifted and jammed the accelerator to the floor, forcing them all back in their seats. The Town Car fell behind, but the Scout's power plant was no match for the much larger V8 under the hood of the luxury car. It took only seconds before the Lincoln was back on Bev's bumper.

"You wanna play, huh?" Bev said to the rearview. "Okay, let's play."

She stepped down hard, locking the brakes and skidding to a stop at the next curve. Bev cut the wheel hard, driving off the pavement onto an unmarked woods path.

"Where are we?" Avery asked as she grabbed ahold of the ceiling strap.

"This is an ATV trail," Bev said.

As they bounced over the uneven terrain, branches crashed against the windshield and scraped along the side of the SUV. Avery glanced into her side mirror. The Town Car was still behind them, bucking like a bronco over the humps and struggling to keep up.

"I hope that's not a rental," Harrison said as he looked back at their pursuers.

"Why not?" Carter said.

"'Cause it's getting beat all to hell."

"It's about to get a whole lot worse." Bev laughed.

"What do you mean?" Avery said.

Bev answered by way of stopping in the middle of the track and quickly shifting into four-wheel low. "This is gonna be steep."

The Scout continued forward and, as it rounded a bend, the ground disappeared in front of them.

"Grab onto something," Bev said. "The next mile is about a ten percent downgrade."

"What exactly does that mean?" Harrison hollered from the back.

"Means we're gonna make fast work of our descent," Avery said.

"Think of it as a rollercoaster ride," Carter said.

"Oh, great," Harrison said. "I hate rollercoasters."

Bev accelerated and the SUV lurched forward, nose down along the steep incline.

Avery kept a close eye on the Lincoln as it bounced and fishtailed over the rough trail. One thing was obvious, whoever was behind the wheel was deadly serious about catching them.

Avery glanced back through the windshield and saw flowing water quickly approaching. "Is that what I think it is?"

"Yessiree," Bev said. "A river."

"Can we get across that?" Carter asked, concern taking his voice up half an octave.

"Guess we'll find out," Bev said.

The Scout never slowed as it hit the water. Spray exploded over the hood, washing over the windshield and roof like an ocean wave. Harrison hollered something unintelligible.

"She needed a good cleaning anyway," Bev said, eyeing Harrison in the rear view.

The SUV powered up and over the opposite embankment. Bev brought it to a sudden stop as the ground leveled out.

"You can open your eyes now, handsome," Bev said to Harrison.

Avery rolled her window down and leaned out to get a better look. The Town Car was hung up on a large rock in the middle of the river. The current had turned the Lincoln sideways.

"Did we lose 'em?" Harrison said.

"Oh, yeah," Carter said. "And they look pissed."

Avery watched as the passenger fought his way out of the car and tumbled into the water. He stood up and glared at her, then reached inside his suit coat.

"I haven't seen that guy before." Avery slid back inside the Scout. "But he isn't too happy with us at all."

"How can you tell?" Harrison said.

As if in answer to his question, the rear windshield exploded inward.

"That might be a clue," Carter said.

Bev mashed the gas pedal to the floor, leaving their pursuers safely behind.

47

As soon as Avery was able to reestablish cellular service, she called Marco and requested that he come pick them up.

"How soon would you like me there, Ms. Turner?" Marco said.

"How about an hour ago?" Harrison yelled from the back seat.

Avery grinned. "You heard?"

"On my way."

There was little conversation between them as Bev drove back to Imogene's B & B.

"I'm so sorry about involving you in this," Avery said.

"Are you kidding?" Bev laughed. "This is the most fun I've had in ages."

"We've got to get packed," Harrison said.

"How long before our friends catch up with us again?" Carter said.

"Well, they don't have cell service up there," Bev said.

"Or a car," Avery said.

"But they have guns," Harrison said. "I think we should skedaddle out of here and get to the airport as soon as possible."

Bev agreed to return in about thirty minutes to transport them to the airport, allowing them time to clean up, grab their stuff, and say goodbye to Imogene. "It would take those clowns twice that long to walk back down from the river," she assured them.

Avery headed directly to her room, grabbed her shower bag and a change of clothes, then hurried to the bathroom at the end of the hall.

She scrubbed the dirt and grime from her skin using the hottest water she could stand, trying to wash away the memory of the dead soldiers trapped inside the mine. What a horrible way to die.

Avery toweled off and quickly dressed. She exited the bathroom surrounded by a cloud of steam, passing Carter in the hall.

"Did you leave me any hot water?" Carter asked with a wink.

"There's plenty of cold," Avery said as she opened the door to her room.

She closed the door and tossed her soiled clothes on the floor. It wasn't until she opened the closet door and caught a reflection in the mirror that she realized she wasn't alone.

She spun around and saw a man standing in the far corner of the room beside the bed. Dressed in a suit and tie, he was grinning and pointing a gun at her.

"Ms. Turner," the man said with a nod. "A pleasure to finally meet you."

"Who are you?" Avery snapped. "And how did you get in here?"

"I am Samael. I believe you are already acquainted with my employer, Emilio Corbacho."

Harrison didn't need a shower, as he wisely hadn't taken part in the mining expedition. After tossing his belongings into a bag, he returned to the first floor to keep an eye out for their friends from the Lincoln.

The house was quiet after spending the day with the mountain crackling and Bev talking, and for only the second time in his life, silence made Harrison uneasy. The first time that had happened, he'd been working a case—and it had turned out there was a murderer in the next room. Harrison hurried through Imogene's first floor, calling her name. He wanted to ask her about the guy who'd been looking for Carter, anyway.

When she didn't answer on the third try, Harrison quickened his stride toward the kitchen. Stepping through the swinging door, he heard a thump.

"Imogene?"

Thump. It was coming from the pantry.

Crossing the room in three long strides, Harrison nearly yanked the door off the hinges.

In the floor, he found Imogene—bound, gagged, and sporting a nasty goose egg on her forehead. But she was breathing and seemed unharmed save for the bump on her head.

Harrison pulled his gun and raced toward the stairs.

Samael pointed toward the pile of dirty clothing on the floor. "Doing a bit of mining I see. Searching for lost treasure, were you, Ms. Turner?"

"Why are you following us?" Avery asked as her eyes scanned the room for anything she might use to disarm the intruder.

"Why haven't you returned Mr. Corbacho's property?" Samael retorted as he glided around the bed toward her.

Surely this guy was bluffing—Corbacho was kind and helpful, and he had been Mark's friend.

"Why did you kill Mark Hawkins?" Avery blurted her educated guess, her eyes on the pistol in the man's hand.

"Mr. Hawkins's death was most unfortunate. It's always tragic to watch a loved one succumb to drug addiction. Allow me to offer my heartfelt condolences on your loss."

"You know what you can do with your condolences," Avery said as she stepped to her left and waited for Samael to come within striking distance. "And Mark never used illegal drugs in his life."

Samael ignored her comment and moved toward the door. As he reached for the deadbolt, he said, "I'd hate for us to be—"

The door burst open as Harrison entered the room, knocking Samael off balance and into a nightstand. With Samael's attention shifted to Harrison, Avery stepped forward and delivered a round house kick to the side of Samael's head. The blow sent him sprawling headfirst into one of the hardwood bedposts.

Samael landed on the rug and his gun skittered across the floor.

"Thanks, Harry," Avery said as she retrieved the weapon then pointed it at the dazed man.

"Don't mention it."

Carter came running into the room wrapped in a towel. "What's going on?"

"You know this guy, junior?" Harrison asked.

"Am I supposed to?"

"I think we'd all be better off knowing who he is and why he's here." Harrison opened his backpack as Avery held the gun steady. "She's a good shot, mister. I wouldn't so much as sneeze if I were you."

48

Using several zip ties from his bag, Harrison bound Samael's wrists to the bed's footboard, then proceeded to frisk him thoroughly. He checked every conceivable hiding place, tossing everything he found on the bed: a cell phone, a spare magazine for the gun, a large folding knife, a leather billfold containing credit cards and cash, two sets of keys, and a passport. The last item Harrison found was a length of piano wire with wooden handles at either end.

"What's this for?" Harrison said, holding up the wire.

Samael shrugged. "I like cheese."

"A hundred bucks says forensics would find blood on that," Harrison said to Avery, who didn't answer, but held the gun steady even though the intruder was tied up. He had scared her, just standing there quietly with this gun pointed at her until she noticed him, and Val Turner's daughter wasn't a fan of being afraid.

"A betting man, Mr. Harrison?" Samael asked.

"Not in a long time," Harrison said. "It's a figure of speech. Who are you?"

"I am chief of special projects for Corbacho Oil."

"He's lying," Avery said. "Emilio Corbacho was Mark's friend."

"Emilio Corbacho is no one's friend but his own. We have that in common," Samael said.

"This passport says you're Samael Lovato, from Barcelona." Harrison tossed it onto the bed and glanced at Avery. "If you know Corbacho so well, what kind of bourbon does he favor?"

"Blanton's Black Label. I'm not even sure he likes the stuff, he just wants things that are rare—like this treasure he's wasted half a lifetime searching for." Samael looked around. "Seeing no trunks, I take it your expedition today was fruitless?"

"What property?" Avery asked.

"I beg your pardon?" Samael asked.

"You said return Mr. Corbacho's property," Avery said. "What property?"

"The antique desk. Hawkins came to own it under questionable circumstances."

"The diary isn't in it." She watched his face carefully as she spoke.

"The diary is on Mr. Corbacho's night table, where it's been since my men procured it from your hotel suite in Boston," Samael said. "It has proven worthless. He wants the desk."

Before she could reply, Carter returned to the room fully clothed and jerked his head toward the window. "Bev is out front. What should we do with him?"

"Oh my Lord, Imogene," Harrison smacked a palm against his forehead. "He knocked her out and tied her up, she's in the pantry."

Carter jumped back toward the door. "How did you forget that?"

"A little busy here," Harrison growled.

"The old lady is fine. I didn't hit her hard."

Avery waved the gun in the general direction of the piano wire and the knife on the bed. "I'm bizarrely thankful you didn't do worse. Thank you."

"Messy collateral damage causes unnecessary complications with local law enforcement," Samael said in the same flat tone. "Especially in places like this where anyone could be the sheriff's favorite cousin."

"Your call, Ave," Harrison said.

"I say we call the police," Avery said.

"That's going to take time," Harrison said. "Are you okay with that?"

"It won't," Avery said. "Everyone here does actually seem to be family. Imogene can ID him as her attacker, and they don't need to know we even saw him."

"Did Imogene tie him up after he knocked her out, then?" Carter asked.

"No, Bev did when she came looking for her cousin."

Carter pointed. "That's pretty good."

"Thanks."

Avery tried to hand Harrison the gun and he raised both hands. "Do you know how many people that thing has killed?"

"No?"

"Me, either, but I'm betting the answer isn't zero. Leave it in the closet."

"You're jeopardizing the people in this town you've grown fond of," Samael said. "I won't be deterred from my mission."

Avery glanced at Harrison.

"Now he's bluffing," Harrison said, pulling out his phone to call 911. When he'd reported the situation anonymously, he waved Avery and Carter into the hall and locked the door with Avery's key. "Mosely, go get Bev and you two help Imogene, she's in the pantry."

"What are we doing?" Avery asked as Carter headed for the stairs.

"Loading the Scout, we probably have three minutes to clear out of here before the sheriff arrives and we're stuck for a week while they investigate."

Bev shoved the keys to the Scout into Harrison's hands before he even finished asking. "Take it and go, I got plenty of rides to get it back. Leave the keys under the front driver's tire and don't get yourselves killed wherever you're headed." She turned to Carter. "There's a pistol in the glovebox. You best take it with you, just in case."

Avery apologized to Imogene again and the older woman waved her off a third time. "You did nothing wrong, Missy. I'm a tough old broad, and we've got things under control here." She pointed to the street, where the faint sirens were getting louder fast. "Y'all get on, now. My old heating ducts carry sound like Dolly carries a tune, and that slick piece of work had one thing right—I am the sheriff's favorite cousin. He's going to be plenty mad when he gets here."

Buckled into the passenger seat while Harrison drove, Avery queried Google maps to see which airport was closest to them. She needed to divert Marco. She believed Samael was a liar, but just in case he wasn't—a man as smart and resourceful as Emilio Corbacho would likely have someone waiting to pick up the trail if his lead henchman lost them. Leaving the area from a different airport than the one they'd arrived at would at least make them a little harder to find.

The closest airport she could locate was the Tri-Cities Regional Airport in Tennessee. She typed and sent a short text message to Marco.

Have you landed yet?

After a moment came Marco's reply, *20 minutes out.*

Change of plans. We'll meet you in Blountville, TN @ the Tri-Cities Regional Airport.

Y?

Long story. C U in an hour.

Roger.

Harrison hit the drive-thru at a fast-food burger joint because everyone was starving. Carter was texting with Bev and offered periodic updates: the sheriff arrested Samael for assault without incident, which surprised Avery, and Imogene was watching Wheel of Fortune with an ice pack on her head.

They ate en route to the airport. Avery handed her remaining fries to Harrison, then opened her backpack and removed the journal she'd taken from the mine. They needed something to point them in the right direction and this was the only new lead.

The leather-bound journal was brittle and water-stained, but it held together as she carefully read each entry. The author, a private in the Union Army named Joshua Butler, had clearly used a fountain pen or quill pen of some sort as the script was delicate and flowery, reminding her of the Declaration of Independence.

The journal entries were dated 1863 and encompassed the period surrounding Butler's captivity as a prisoner of war at Camp Sumter in Georgia. As near as Avery could make out, Butler had been a regular army union soldier captured during battle. Butler described the conditions at the camp as deplorable, citing overcrowding, insufficient food and water, and extreme heat. Most of the thirty or so pages in the journal pertained to his time at Sumter, but the last several were different. Butler described that he and approximately thirty other men were removed from the camp under the cover of darkness and transported to a plantation near the shores of South Carolina, where they loaded valuable cargo aboard a train that carried them alongside the trunks to Virginia. According to Butler, their captors told them that this was an important mission that, if successful, would bring an end to the war. They were promised clemency if they succeeded, and possibly freedom. Avery shivered as she thought back to what she had seen in Sonny's mine and the fate that awaited Butler and the others. She had seen firsthand what had become of them.

Butler and the others had no way of knowing that they were being set up and would ultimately be killed as a diversion to keep anyone from finding the real treasure. Entombed for eternity along with crates full of nothing but scrap metal, deep underground in a Virginia coal mine. What a horrific ending to their story, Avery thought.

"Anything helpful in there?" Carter asked, pulling Avery from her reverie.

"Did you reach out to MaryAnn yet, about the Oswald family?"

"Um, not yet. Been a little busy."

"You're right. I'm sorry. I'm just trying to figure out what to do next." Reading the diary, she wondered if the gold had ever left the plantation at all.

"You're gonna owe me big time for this."

"Correction," Avery said with a smirk. "You're going to owe MaryAnn big time."

49

Samael found the Audi parked right where he'd left it, two blocks from Imogene Blakely's bed and breakfast. He unlocked the vehicle with a key Barney Fife back there hadn't found because he didn't check Samael's shoe —his time in the intelligence world had taught him that preparation was the key to a successful escape, so he was always prepared.

He removed a second SIG Sauer P228 from a locked case hidden under the spare tire inside the trunk. Once inside the car, he retrieved a clone of his phone from the glove compartment since he hadn't been able to retrieve his from the country sheriff before he climbed out the window at the three-room police station. He plugged the device in and powered it on. The battery was only partially charged, but the display showed several missed calls from a familiar number. Ignoring them, he opened the GPS tracker and activated the search mode on the app, manually entering the device password from memory. He had slipped the tracker into Avery Turner's backpack while she was in the shower. He knew she'd find it soon enough, but hopefully not before it could give him a lead on where she and her band of lucky misfits were headed.

It took several moments for the GPS to connect, but once it did the signal was strong. They were on Route 72 heading toward Dungannon. He placed the phone on the console, angling it to allow him to monitor the tracker. As he reached for the ignition, his phone chimed with another incoming call. It was Thing One.

"Talk to me," Samael said.

"Been trying to reach you, boss."

"I was—tied up. You have good news for me?"

"The information you got from the B & B owner panned out. We found Avery and the others."

Samael's head hurt, but not enough to keep him from wanting to toy with these imbeciles a little longer. "Excellent. Where are they now?"

"We had an accident trying to follow them off road. We lost them. What do you want us to do?"

"Are you mobile now?"

"Yeah. We got another car."

Samael wished he still possessed the garrote. "Meet me at the airport."

Even without the tracker, Samael knew there was no way Turner and the others would be dumb enough to attempt to depart from the same airport they had arrived at. But it didn't matter. He needed to get to his plane, and he needed to sever his link to Thing One and Thing Two. Shooting them at the airport would be messy. Besides, he had already drawn enough attention toward himself for one day. He needed a new plan.

Samael started the car and pulled back onto the roadway in the direction of the airfield. He slowed to allow an older woman walking a dog to cross the street. The grateful woman waved, and Samael gave her a warm smile in return. But his smile had nothing to do with her. He smiled because he had figured out how to rid himself of his baggage.

———

They left Bev's vehicle just as she asked them to, and Carter texted her a pin and a photo of the location. She thanked them for the adventure and warned them again to be careful.

Carter assured her they would before pocketing his phone, tucking her revolver into his backpack, and lugging everyone's bags onto the plane.

Marco's only question was where they wanted to go. Avery looked at the union soldier's journal in her hand, which pointed them to a South

Carolina plantation she knew nothing about, then shifted her gaze to the window with Samael's insistence that he worked for Corbacho and Corbacho wanted Mark's desk ringing in her ears.

She was still lost in thought when Carter started talking.

"Oh man. Guys." He waved his phone. "Bev says Samael gave the deputy on duty the slip on a bathroom break. Apparently, their lone cell doesn't have a toilet, so they take prisoners to the restroom in the hall."

"This has gotten out of hand, Harry," Avery said. "These people, whoever they're working for or with, are deadly serious. The sooner we locate the treasure, the sooner we'll be out of harm's way. Marco, can you complete the preflight checks and file the flight plan last? A few extra minutes might help me decide on a destination, but I don't want to wait too long if that Sam guy is on the loose."

Marco nodded before disappearing into the cockpit to start his preflight routine.

"I don't know if the right move is to go to South Carolina, where the trunks in the mine came from, or to back to Maine." Avery tapped her foot. "Whether that guy back at Imogene's works for Corbacho or not, Corbacho did tell us he wants Mark's desk."

"What makes you think the desk is still in Mark's house if these guys want it so badly?" Harrison asked.

"Because that man, Sam, asked about it just a couple of hours ago," Avery said. "Mark's place and the inn have both probably been crawling with cops off and on after the break in and attack on Julia."

Harrison sat back in his seat and shrugged. "We'll see."

Avery removed the enigma from one of the jet's many storage compartments and carried it back to her seat. She began to twist the wheels again, hoping for answers, but the device's purpose was like an unknown language. It meant nothing. She couldn't help but wonder if Mark had simply hidden it along with the diary not knowing if it was related to the general's gold at all. Maybe she had mistakenly made that leap after finding the two items together. She set the enigma aside and returned to her laptop, reexamining everything they had learned or uncovered to date. Carter took the seat beside her as she read.

"I just heard back from MaryAnn," he said. "She located some photos and a list of Oswald family holdings and addresses."

"Now we're talking," Avery said as she opened a new search bar. "Let's start with the addresses."

The first three meant nothing to Avery, and the fourth address included the land surrounding Sonny's mine. She was beginning to wonder if this might be a waste of a favor when Carter read off an address in Martha's Vineyard.

Avery asked Carter to repeat it, typing it into Google and nodding. "That's the estate Harry and I visited. The home Corbacho purchased, but it wasn't owned by anyone named Oswald."

"That's because they no longer owned it," Carter said. "Corbacho bought it from the guy who purchased it from the Oswald family. The original house was built by the Oswalds in 1797. MaryAnn attached a few photos."

"Let me see," Avery said.

"I forwarded them to your email."

"Why didn't you say so?" Avery asked as she closed out the search bar and opened her inbox. The first image depicted a handsome young man in uniform. The caption identified him as General Brent Oswald and the photo was dated 1860, just prior to the start of the Civil War.

Carter looked over Avery's shoulder as she studied the pictures. "According to MaryAnn, it was Brent Oswald's father who built the home on Martha's Vineyard and purchased the coal mine we just visited. Oswald's grandfather owned a plantation in South Carolina around the time of the Revolution."

"What became of Brent?" Avery said.

"He suffered a head injury during the war and returned home a different person. By all accounts he was disturbed and volatile. If PTSD had been a thing then he likely would have been given that diagnosis. MaryAnn found writings attributed to the general accusing his right-hand man of everything from stealing the family fortune to absconding with the coffers of the confederacy."

"The treasure?"

Carter shrugged. "Who knows? Google has nothing for that specific term."

Avery sighed as she scrolled through the other photos. The pieces fit, but beyond that there was nothing to point them toward what became of the treasure.

"There was one interesting side note," Carter said. "Oswald's closest friend was a regiment captain named Jonas Schilling. Schilling was a plantation owner who handled intelligence for the confederate army during the war."

Something clicked in Avery's mind upon hearing Schilling's name. She scrolled back to the first photo. It showed General Oswald standing beside a desk. Seated behind it was another man in uniform.

"Did MaryAnn happen to find any pictures of Schilling?"

"She didn't send any. Why?"

"Because the guy sitting beside Oswald in this picture is wearing captain's bars on his collar."

"Guess it could be Schilling," Carter said. "How is that relevant?"

"I don't know," Avery said. As she reduced the photo back to its original size, her eyes drifted away from the men to the rest of the image. "Oh my God," Avery said.

"What?"

"This is Mark's desk."

Schilling was seated behind the very desk that Mark snatched away from Corbacho.

Avery continued, "The one Harrison and I found in Maine. The one Corbacho spent millions on an old house to get his hands on, if you believe that Sam guy."

Neither of them had noticed Harrison standing behind them until he spoke up. "Maybe it wasn't the diary after all," Harrison said. "Or even that enigma thingy you haven't been able to make heads or tails of."

"What do you mean, Harry?" Avery said.

"We thought the diary or the device held the key to this whole thing, right?"

"As did whoever stole the diary," Avery said.

"I think we can operate on the assumption that your new friend Corbacho isn't a good guy," Carter said. "We lose nothing if we're wrong and gain some important insight if we're right."

"Yeah, well, what if we were all wrong about the diary itself?" Harrison said. "What if Mark wanted that desk for another reason?"

"Like?" Carter said.

"Like, in the before times, way back before you kids had the Internet—"

"You mean back when you walked ten miles to school," Avery teased.

"Yeah, uphill, in the snow," Harrison said as he reached over and mussed her hair. "Back then when families wanted to preserve something to be passed down through the generations like family trees, recipes, or secrets, they would hide the information in furniture. The thought being that large items of furniture would be much harder to lose than journals or letters, and that they would remain within the family."

"But we already searched that desk, Harry," Avery said. "The journal wasn't even inside the desk, remember? It was hidden under the floor."

"You searched *inside* the desk, but you didn't examine the desk itself."

"I don't get it," Carter said.

Avery shook her head. "You mean to say you think the answer might have been in Mark's study this whole time?"

"Could be that simple," Harrison said.

"Sharks, coal mines, and assassins with guns?" Avery said. "Being left for dead in the middle of the ocean? And what we are looking for might've been sitting in Mark's house this entire time?"

Harrison nodded. "Not bad for an old flatfoot, huh?"

Avery turned her attention to Carter and opened her mouth to speak.

"Yeah, yeah, I know," Carter said. "You want me to bribe MaryAnn, again, to find out everything she can about Captain Schilling and hidden maps in old furniture."

"It's like you read my mind." Avery smiled.

"Let us know when you and MaryAnn pick a date," Harrison teased. "I look dashing in a tux."

"Ha ha. Very funny."

"I'll let Marco know you've decided we're going back to Maine," Harrison said as he started toward the cockpit.

"Bangor International, please," Avery said. "What would I do without you, Harry?"

"Let's hope you never have to find out."

50

After speaking with Thing One, Samael phoned the pilot and told him to have the jet fueled and ready. Ten minutes later, Samael pulled onto the tarmac and parked near Corbacho's private jet. He paused a moment before exiting to examine his surroundings. Always a pragmatist, he sought to plan for every eventuality. Perhaps it was his past employment with an intelligence agency that made him suspicious, or maybe it was because he hadn't heard from Corbacho recently. The closer Avery Turner had gotten to the General's Gold, the more impatient and unhinged Emilio had become. Why wasn't he bugging Samael for an update now? Something was amiss.

The jet's running lights were ablaze, and the engines were running. The pilot was visible in the cockpit and the steps were down. All very inviting. Too inviting. As he scanned the area for threats, Samael removed the gun from the pocket of his overcoat and double-checked that it was fully loaded, including one in the chamber. He pocketed the SIG then stepped from the car and looked toward the plane. The pilot waved to him with his left hand, a signal that only the two of them knew. Samael returned the gesture. Something was wrong.

Samael closed the door of the Audi and slid the phone from his pocket. He punched up the speed dial for Corbacho, then leaned back against the side of the car and waited for his employer to pick up. Three rings, then five, then the voicemail kicked in. He disconnected the call and pocketed the phone. Unknowingly or not, like a poker addict holding a straight flush, Corbacho had just shown his hand by going silent. The old man had sent someone to terminate Samael. The why didn't really matter. Had he sussed out Samael's plan to double-cross him as soon as the treasure was located? Or was he just unhappy with the recent setbacks? Samael was ready. He slid his hand back inside the overcoat and gripped the gun, prepared for whatever came next.

Headlights washed over the side of the jet from behind the Audi as another vehicle approached, but Samael maintained his focus on the stairs leading to the aircraft. The only question remaining was had Thing One and Thing Two been assigned to terminate his employment, or was someone else waiting for him aboard the plane? Samael smiled and slid his finger inside the trigger guard as a familiar figure appeared in the doorway of the jet and lifted his hand in greeting. As the approaching vehicle neared, the figure descended the steps. Samael pushed himself away from the car and assumed a defensive stance. The time had come to make his case for a severance package.

It was midnight by the time Avery and the others arrived at Mark's private residence. Every light inside was lit and a car and a van were parked near the trees off the driveway.

"Looks like we've got company," Harrison said as he slowed, but then drove past the end of the driveway before stopping a little ways down.

"Not exactly how I was hoping this would go," Avery said.

"Why should this part be any easier?" Carter grumbled from the back seat.

"You think they figured out the desk thing too?" Harrison said.

"I think that creep back in Virginia said Corbacho wants the desk, and it's dark and there are no cops here, so it makes sense that there are thugs here no matter who sent them or why," Avery said.

Harrison pulled out his phone and poked at the screen, frowning.

"What now?" Avery asked.

"Well, my buddy back on the job says it appears the guy who left the fingerprint at the inn the other day, Babcock, was found washed up on a beach in—funny enough—Bloody Point, South Carolina. The sharks did a number on a lot of him, but he was a big dude. And their coroner says he was strangled with a piano wire." Harrison typed something back to his friend.

"Samael."

"Sounds like a case of a hired goon who failed one too many times." Harrison put his phone down and put the car in gear, pulling into a nearby driveway to turn around. "But that's no real help to us now, except another tick mark in the these-people-are-serious column. How do you want to do this, Ave?"

"We know they're here, but they don't know we are," Avery said. "So I guess we just go in and see what we see?"

"I'm in front," Harrison said with his don't-argue glare.

"You still have Bev's gun?" Avery asked Carter.

"Right here," Carter tapped his bag. "Never shot one before, but I've seen every *Die Hard* movie a dozen times, so I'm sure I can handle it."

"That'll be great if we happen to run into a fictional German terrorist," Harrison said as he pulled the rental off the road and killed the lights. "Give me the gun before you shoot yourself."

"You're already armed, Harry," Avery reminded him, taking the pistol from Carter herself.

"And if there's more than two armed men inside?" Harrison said.

"Then I guess I'll just have to stay behind you two," Carter said. "I hope you're as good at shooting as I am at fending off sharks."

There is nothing worse than a friendship betrayed. It was a lesson Samael had learned long ago. Greed is a powerful aphrodisiac, its price different for each individual. As Samael stood over the lifeless body of Alejandro, his friend and former associate, he wondered what Corbacho had offered in exchange for that betrayal.

It turned out that neither Thing One nor Thing Two were part of Corbacho's reception committee, which was lucky for Samael. It meant that he'd had back-up long enough to take care of Alejandro. After disarming him, they marched Alejandro at gunpoint into the woods at the edge of the airport perimeter. There had been some begging and pleading, which Samael had expected but never fully understood given the business they were in. The price for betrayal was always death. It shouldn't have been a surprise. In the end, Samael executed his friend with one round to the temple, before he turned on the other two.

Samael was thorough as he searched each of the men, removing their identification and phones. The cops would eventually figure out who they were, but it would take longer without ID. As for the murders, none could be traced back to him, as he had used Alejandro's gun to kill Thing One and Two. After executing Alejandro, Samael wiped the gun clean and placed it in his dead right hand. The cops might have their suspicions, but without a witness there was no way to prove anything beyond a murder suicide between hired guns. And, as they were all professional bad guys, how much effort would the cops really put in?

Samael grinned as he walked back toward the plane, recalling the look of surprise on Thing One and Two's faces when they realized they wouldn't be leaving the woods either. Joy was in the little things.

As he ascended the steps of the waiting jet, Samael considered a question posed by Berkeley in his *Principles of Human Knowledge* concerning trees in a park with nobody to perceive them. He turned and took one last look toward the woods then pulled the steps up and secured the door.

Finding the front door unlocked, Avery's team slipped into Mark's home with Harrison in the lead followed by Avery then Carter. Avery wasn't surprised to find the alarm panel had been disabled by hot-wiring of sorts, the wires sticking out of the wall in the foyer, taped together to give the monitoring company an uninterrupted "all clear" signal. Shouting came from somewhere deeper inside the first floor. Carter retrieved the wooden bat that Harrison had used as an improvised weapon during their first visit, holding it up proudly. Harrison rolled his eyes. As stealthily as possible in the creaky old house, they moved single file in the direction of Mark's study.

The room was brightly lit while the hallway remained dark, providing Avery and the others with some cover. The interior of the study was in total disarray, a far different condition than when she and Harrison had last seen it. Books, pulled from shelves, littered the floor along with desk drawers and their contents. Standing, backs to them, were two men, one of whom was holding a gun. On the far side of the room stood three more armed men. All the occupants were shouting and threatening each other with guns.

Avery held up her hand, signaling Harrison and Carter to wait. She realized that the chaos had provided them with an opportunity to figure out what was happening before they acted. Avery and Carter stacked up to the left side of the door while Harrison stood opposite them. It appeared to Avery that three men standing at the far side of the room were working together and that the two closest to them had walked in and taken the others by surprise.

"I asked you first," the bearded man wearing cargo pants large enough to hold half of Fort Knox said. "What are *you* doing here?"

"We have come to retrieve a piece of furniture that belongs to our boss," the man said calmly. Avery nodded, wondering how many hired goons on the east coast were currently employed by rival treasure hunters—and if she should have hired a few of her own.

"What furniture?" Cargo pants said.

"That desk," the unarmed man said. "And if you've damaged it in any way, you'll be sorry."

"I hardly think you're in a position to be making threats," Cargo Pants said.

Avery stayed in the shadows, interested to see if this particular problem might take care of itself since it didn't look like they were all working together and almost everyone in there had a gun.

"Your turn," the unarmed man said. "Why are you trespassing here?"

"We're searching for treasure," Cargo Pants said.

The diminutive man to the right of Cargo Pants, whose rifle was longer than he was tall, spoke up, "We've been at this for two years now, and we think it's hidden inside this house."

"That's right. Hawkins bought this house because the treasure is here somewhere." Cargo Pants nodded.

"Have you found it?" The unarmed man asked.

"Sure. Yesterday. We're hanging around to see how long it takes the cops to notice." Cargo Pants rolled his eyes.

"Maybe Hawkins found it already and sold it," the unarmed man offered.

"Nah, we're too well connected," Cargo Pants said. "We'd have heard about it if he had."

Harrison gave Avery a nod indicating his agreement.

"Well, you can do whatever you want to this house," the unarmed man said. "But we're taking the desk."

Avery turned to Harrison and shook her head. *No, they aren't.* She turned to find Carter had disappeared.

"Now what?" Harrison mouthed.

Avery shrugged. She had no idea why Carter had wandered off, but if she had learned anything in the brief time she'd known him, it was that he was a thrill seeker with a flair for the dramatic.

"What's so important about this damn desk anyway?" Cargo Pants asked as he tapped it with his boot.

"Don't do that," the unarmed man shouted. "It must not be damaged."

Before anyone could respond there was a deafening crash as something sailed through one of the study's French doors and landed on the floor. Using the distraction to their full advantage, Avery and Harrison leaned around the doorframe simultaneously pointing their guns at the room's occupants.

"Drop your weapons!" Harrison barked. "Now!"

The unarmed man turned toward Avery and Harrison with his hands up. For one tense moment, none of the room's other occupants complied. Avery could see the wheels turning inside their heads as they rushed to calculate their options.

"Last chance, or I start dropping you one at a time," Harrison said.

"I'm unarmed," the unarmed man mocked. "Will you be dropping me too?"

"Don't tempt me."

One at a time the other four men tossed their guns on the floor. As Avery and Harrison moved in, Carter stepped in through the broken French doors holding the Louisville slugger. Avery noticed Carter's smile falter as his eyes shifted to her left, but it was a split second too late. Before she could react to her blind spot, a previously unseen henchman grabbed her from behind. He put an arm around her neck and held a gun to her head.

"Drop it, missy," the man hissed as he dragged her farther into the corner away from Harrison and Carter.

Without pausing to think, Avery tossed her gun in Carter's direction. As he snatched the gun from the air, Cargo Pants and his two partners used the distraction to their advantage, sprinting out into the night and leaving their guns behind.

Harrison and Carter circled around from different directions keeping all three of Corbacho's men in their sights.

The man holding Avery was strong, and she could feel the front sight of the gun digging into her temple. She could tell from the awkward way he pulled her backward, slightly off balance, that he was a bit shorter than she.

"Let her go or I'll shoot," Harrison barked.

"You won't," the man said. "You might hit the girl."

Avery watched in disbelief as Carter turned his gun on one of the other men.

"Let her go or I'll shoot your friend," Carter said.

The man holding Avery laughed. "Go ahead. I never trusted him anyway."

With his gun still trained on the man holding Avery, Harrison shook his head. "You have no idea what you've gotten yourself into, friend."

"Is that supposed to scare me?"

Harrison gave Avery the slightest nod.

She bent slightly at the knees, pulling her assailant forward and creating a small gap between their heads. The shift in leverage was all she needed. As the man tried to pull her upright, she used his own force against him, throwing her head up as hard as she could, the back of her skull making direct contact with the center of his face. She heard as well as felt the sickening crunch of cartilage and bone as the man's nose shattered. Before he could recover, Avery twisted the wrist holding the gun away from her head, causing the man to cry out. The gun fired harmlessly into the ceiling, sending a shower of plaster down on them. Avery spun to her right and flipped the man over her left hip. He landed on the hardwood floor. The impact knocked the wind out of him. She twisted the gun from his grasp and placed one foot squarely in the center of his chest. Avery pointed his own gun at him while he lay on his back gasping for air.

"I did warn you," Harrison said.

After checking in with the pilot, Samael made himself comfortable in the cabin. He opened the GPS tracker on his phone and saw that Avery Turner was on the move, headed toward New England. He didn't know what was in the journal she'd taken from the mine, but whatever it was, it was leading her back to Maine. He'd bet his life on it. Which was exactly what he was about to do.

He knew Corbacho wasn't taking his calls, but there was one person Corbacho was waiting to hear from. Samael pocketed his cell and retrieved the one he had seized from Alejandro's corpse. He punched in the number for Corbacho's cell phone.

Corbacho answered on the second ring, "Is it done?"

"I guess that depends on your point of view," Samael said.

A long moment passed before Corbacho spoke again. "I don't suppose you'd be willing to negotiate?"

Samael smiled at the old man's predictability. Always the businessman. "I'm listening."

With all three men zip tied and seated on the floor, Avery began to question them.

"Who sent you? Corbacho?"

The man with the shattered nose tried to answer, but his face was swollen so badly that none of them could make out the words.

"Come again?" Harrison said, holding a hand to his ear. "We didn't quite catch that."

"He said we don't know anyone named Corbachio," the second goon said.

"It's Corbacho," Carter said.

"Yeah, well, we don't know him either."

Harrison rolled his eyes at Avery. "Aren't you glad these guys aren't on our side?"

"Look, I'm telling you, we don't know who you're talking about," the unarmed man and apparent leader said. "We're working for a guy named Sam."

I knew that creep was lying, Avery thought. They had been sent here by Samael. She looked at Harrison. His face didn't look as sure as she felt that these guys had just exonerated Mark's old friend.

"How much was Sam paying you to retrieve the desk?" Avery said.

"Free gland," the mushed-faced man said.

"Three grand," the other goon translated.

Avery paced the floor for a moment as she considered their options. The desk was still in play. Assuming it held the clues they were searching for, nothing had changed. These guys weren't pros, they were just trying to earn a buck.

She turned toward Samael's bagmen. "I'll give you four thousand to forget you were ever here. Deal?"

"Dweal," mush face said.

"Good with me," goon number two said, nodding like crazy.

She turned her attention to the leader. "Deal?"

"Four grand works. Cash."

51

At seven thirty the next morning, Avery, Carter, and Harrison sat around the desk amid the debris on chairs dragged in from the dining room.

"I'm not sure how long we can safely stay here, Ave," Harrison said as he reached into a pink pastry box for another Boston cream.

It had been a short night as they each took a turn standing guard while the other two slept or studied the nooks and crannies of the old desk. At daybreak Carter and Avery had driven to a local donut shop, returning with a Box O' Joe and an assortment of donuts—which the three of them were making quick work of—while Harrison remained behind to keep watch.

"He's right, Avery," Carter said.

"Of course, I'm right."

Carter continued, "We might not be able to scare off the next group."

"Or buy off," Harrison said, raising his Styrofoam cup of coffee in salute and giving Avery a wink.

Avery knew they were right, but she also felt that they were close to locating the treasure. They had to be. Samael wanted the antique desk, and he already had the diary, he'd admitted to stealing it even if he had lied about what he did with it afterward. No, she wasn't leaving until she found Mark's gold. Assuming there was anything left to find.

She washed down the last bite of her lemon-filled pastry, then stood and walked around the desk, careful to avoid the scattering of books and debris littering the floor. It seemed impossible to think that the clue they needed might be hidden in plain sight when they'd been over every millimeter of the thing several times now.

As she opened her mouth to speak, the front doorbell rang, startling all three of them.

"Who the hell could that be?" Carter said as he rose and pulled a gun from the waistband of his jeans.

"Easy there, Tex," Harrison said. "It might be a friendly."

"Yeah, I can't imagine Samael ringing the bell," Avery said as she headed toward the hallway.

She approached the front door with Carter and Harrison hot on her heels. As she entered the foyer, she could see the outline of a woman through the frosted glass.

She opened the door to find Maggie Watters, who had sold her app and apparently lied to the Germans in the process, standing there with her jaw hanging open as she met Avery's gaze.

"A-Avery," Maggie stammered. "What are you doing here?"

"I could ask you the same," Avery said, her anger welling up.

"I came to see Mark."

Avery's fury fizzled as quickly as it had risen. How could Maggie not know about Mark's death? Did she even know what a newspaper was?

"Mark is dead, Maggie," Avery said without fanfare.

"What?" Maggie said. Her eyes immediately welled with tears, making Avery feel horrible for being so blunt. "I don't understand. I spoke with him last week before I left for Paris. He was excited about his Inn and heading to Boston to look at an antique—he said the seller had asked to meet him at a place in a sketchy part of the city, but the piece was a key part of his collection."

Harrison and Carter wandered off to give them their privacy while Avery brought Maggie into the library and explained how Mark had been found dead in a Boston motel room. She gave Maggie just enough time to digest the news before going for the jugular.

"I'm surprised you dared to show up here after what you've done. I know all about the falsified financials you used to broker the buyout of Hawkins Tech and my app."

Maggie looked like someone had slapped her across the face. "How do you know about that?"

"Not even gonna deny it, huh?" Avery demanded.

"Of course, I deny it. I didn't mess with the numbers, Avery. I swear to you."

"Then how do you explain the documents I found?"

Maggie paused to take in their surroundings before answering. "What the hell happened in here?"

Avery followed her eyes around the room. "Long story. The police are on it, though."

Maggie removed a tissue from her purse and dabbed her eyes. "I came here to plead my case to Mark. I didn't commit fraud in any way. The financials I used to support the takeover were solid. If anything, I may have been a bit too conservative. The documents you found are bogus. Fakes created by the CFO of Daimler Technologies to try and save his job."

"I don't understand," Avery said. "Why would they do that?"

"Because they overextended themselves, thinking the return on their investment would happen overnight. They were working a back door deal that Mark didn't know about. The plan was to turn around as soon as this deal was complete and sell your program to a company in the UAE for a healthy profit. The Germans would keep Mark's company and everything that came with it, except for your app."

"I'm not following. How did they mess that up?"

"They didn't. The company in the UAE backed out of the deal as soon as Mark's deal went through. Daimler is cash poor and without an influx of capital soon, they'll be out of business entirely. They faked my emails hoping to back out of the takeover and sue all three of us."

"Can you prove any of this, Maggie?"

Maggie dug into her purse again and handed Avery a flash drive. "I backed everything up just in case. Everything has a time and date stamp."

"I hope you have more than one of these," Avery said.

"About twenty."

Avery wondered what the best way to go on the offensive against

Daimler Tech would be. Perhaps she would break her ironclad rule and finally take to social media to drop the bomb. Maybe Carter would be willing to share his audience and expertise. She'd have to tell him she'd figured out his secret first, though.

"Mark always said trust, but keep copies," Maggie said. "I came here to show him." Her voice cracked as she continued speaking. "But I guess I'm too late."

Avery leaned over and hugged Maggie until the sobbing passed.

As Avery walked her back to the door, Maggie looked around at the state of the home's interior again.

"You sure everything's okay here? I mean, it looks like a hurricane blew through."

"Like I said. The local police are on it," Avery lied. Anything to get her old colleague out the door.

They hugged once more in the doorway.

"Thank you for coming, Maggie. And for being more thorough and honest than I gave you credit for."

"That's nice of you to say. I think. Good luck, Avery."

When she was sure that Maggie had gone, Avery returned to the study and found Carter and Harrison busy at the desk.

"What are you doing?" Avery said.

"Carter got a call from MaryAnn while you were talking to Maggie," Harrison said. "Everything good with you two?"

"All good, Harry. And the rest can wait. Now tell me about MaryAnn."

"Turns out, Harrison was right," Carter said.

"Again," Harrison said sticking his chest out proudly.

"About what, specifically?" Avery said.

"About things hidden on the furniture, and not just inside," Carter said. "MaryAnn said that it wasn't uncommon for people to use fruit-based acids to mark notations and such on the wood. If the person doing it was highly skilled, they could easily hide the markings in the grain of the wood or mask them with stains and varnish."

"We're looking for homemade eighteenth-century invisible ink?" Avery asked.

"More or less," Harrison said. "What we need is a reagent solution that will react with those acids."

Avery looked at the desk for a moment. "So, what? You're planning to run down to the reagent store in a town that barely has a pharmacy?"

Harrison grinned. "Nope. I've got another idea."

"Care to share with the rest of the class, Harry?" Avery said.

"I'll be right back. You two keep an eye on that desk."

Avery and Carter cleared a space amid the clutter to allow for a thorough examination of the desk. They removed and stacked each of the drawers in the order that matched their original positions within the desk.

Avery examined every surface while Carter kept watch. Avery supposed if one of their adversaries did make an appearance, they still had the mini arsenal left behind by last night's unexpected guests.

"I don't think Harrison likes me much," Carter said.

"Sure he does," Avery said. "He just doesn't trust you yet. Don't take it personally. He was a cop, remember. Harry doesn't trust anybody."

"What did your friend want?" Carter said.

"She was looking to clear up some business issues with Mark."

"She didn't know he was dead?"

"She's been out of the country."

"Sorry you had to be the one to tell her."

"Thanks."

Now armed with the truth about the faked emails, Avery needed to figure out how best to unravel the damage Daimler Tech had done to Mark's reputation—and her own. There would be time to address that soon enough. She'd tell Carter the whole story then. Right now she needed to stay focused on finding the general's gold. She picked up one of the left-hand desk drawers and began studying each surface.

They both reacted to the sound of a car door closing.

"Tell me that's Harry," Avery said, tensing slightly.

Carter looked through what was left of the French doors.

"It is," Carter said.

Harrison came in brandishing a paper bag.

"What's all that?" Avery said.

"Everything we need," Harrison said. "Eye protection, latex gloves, and surgical masks."

"What's in the bottle?" Carter said.

"Ninhydrin," Harrison said. "The reagent I told you about."

"No way you bought that around here," Avery said.

"Nope. It's on loan from my new best friend in the county sheriff's crime lab."

"You're kidding," Carter said.

"You didn't tell him why you needed it, did you?" Avery said.

"Of course not. If I'd told them that I was hunting for lost Civil War treasure they would have taken me to get my head examined."

"Or given you your own reality show," Carter said. Avery glanced at him, but didn't say anything.

Using the flashlight from her phone, Avery crawled underneath the desk and searched the surface of each panel.

"I don't suppose MaryAnn mentioned where these secret drawings or notes might be marked on furniture pieces?" Avery asked.

"No. She said the location could vary greatly, assuming of course that there's anything to find."

"Sure." Avery sighed, looking at the little bottle of reagent Harrison had managed to score. "So we'll just shoot in the dark?

"Did you check the drawers?" Harrison said.

"Yeah," Avery said. "Nothing there that I could see."

Avery twisted herself this way and that searching for anything out of the ordinary. She was about to give up the search when she noticed something odd within the grain of one of the inside panels.

"I think I might have found something," Avery said as she crawled out from under the desk. "Help me flip this thing over."

After clearing more space on the floor, they flipped the desk onto its face, revealing the underside more clearly. Avery pointed out what she had found.

"It's pretty faint," Carter said. "I can't tell if there's actually something there or not."

"What do you think, Harry?" Avery said.

"Don't look at me. I've got a condition known formally as "old guy eyes." Besides, that's why I got this stuff," he said as he held up the bottle of Ninhydrin.

"Show me how to use it," Avery said.

After a quick tutorial, Avery donned the protective items that Harrison had purchased then began spraying the area she'd located with the chemical reagent. Harrison and Carter kept watch just outside the room.

"How long is it supposed to take, Harry?"

"Depends. Don't stand there breathing it though. That stuff is a killer."

Avery walked to the French doors, removed her mask, and breathed in the cool outside air. After a few minutes, she walked back to check. A purplish image had begun to reveal itself.

"Holy cryptography, Harry," Avery said. "It actually worked."

"Of course it worked," Harrison said as he and Carter approached. "All those years working homicide with your mom, I learned a thing or two."

"Well, what is it?" Carter said as he leaned in.

"Looks like a willow tree near a large house," Avery said.

"Mr. Cargo Pants did say he thought the treasure was here," Carter mused.

"Yeah, he struck me as a real genius, but the desk has only been here a couple of months," Harrison said.

"There's more," Avery said, watching the lines appear. "There are dots between the tree and the house and something off to the side that looks like waves, a jagged coastline, more dots, and maybe a hole in the ground."

"A hole in the ground?" Harrison said. "Like what, a quarry?"

"Or maybe a storm cellar," Carter offered.

Avery was amazed at the amount of detail that was still appearing. It was like watching a film developed in a dark room, only instead of photo paper this image was appearing on wood.

"Hand me my phone, would you?" Avery said to Carter. "I want to snap some pictures of this."

There was something familiar about the willow tree, but Avery couldn't quite remember what it was. Had she seen one recently? She snapped photos from several different angles, trying to minimize the glare from the flash.

"Come on, Ave," Harrison said. "This is all just supposition. We've got no idea what, if anything, that map has to do with the missing gold. The desk came from Martha's Vineyard either way, so there's a great chance whatever this shows isn't even around here. You want to sneak past the armed goons to search that Corbacho guy's property and find out the hard way that Sam wasn't lying to you back in Virginia?"

Avery stood upright and put her hands on her hips. "Maybe you're right." She sighed. "This whole thing is crazy. But I'm not ready to give up yet. I think we're close. Mark certainly thought so."

Carter said nothing but crossed his arms in defiance. He joined Avery in staring down Harrison.

Harrison looked back and forth between them then rolled his eyes. "Okay, okay, I'm just an insensitive jerk. Let's go look for a hole in the ground."

Avery grinned. "I don't think you're insensitive, Harry."

52

Armed with cell phone photos of the desk's hidden map, flashlights, and the rain slickers they found in Mark's utility room, Avery and Carter set out into the rain to try and follow the clues, while Harrison remained behind.

"You really think that map depicts this property?" Carter said.

"I don't know," Avery said. "It has the large house, the ocean, and the rocky coastline."

"So do a million other properties."

Avery nodded. "The willow tree is throwing me off, though. I know I've seen one just recently, but I can't recall where."

"Don't shoot the scuba instructor, but . . . could it have been on that Corbacho guy's place down on Martha's Vineyard?"

"I've been flipping back through every memory of his grounds as much as it causes me physical pain to admit Harry might be right about that," she said. "But no, I really don't think so."

"A photo or a painting?" Carter said.

Avery stopped walking and squealed. "You're a genius, Carter! It was the painting built into the center of a bookcase in Mark's office at the inn. I'd need to see it again, but I remember thinking it was a tree from the deep south because it was covered in moss."

"Maybe that's where the treasure is. Down south."

Avery couldn't allow herself to think about that. They had already come too far, risked too much. Ignoring the comment, she pressed on.

Daylight waning by the step, they trudged through miles of fields and woods.

"I don't get it," Avery said. "We haven't seen a single willow."

"Maybe there was one here and it got cut down," Carter said. "I mean, that desk is how old?"

"Then let's focus on more permanent things like the foundation, or a storm cellar."

After referencing the map photo again, they turned in the opposite direction. The beams of their flashlights bobbed along in the darkness as they followed the map to where the cellar should have been and beyond, all the way to the ocean cliffs.

Avery sighed as she gazed out over the water, listening to the waves crashing on the rocks below. The wind had picked up, making their trek even more uncomfortable. Avery looked at Carter. Rivulets of rainwater ran down his hooded face. He was a good sport. Sticking with her through all her craziness.

"How are you holding up?" she said. "You want to call it a night?"

"I'm okay. Once the rain gets past the slicker, you really can't get any wetter. I think I may have reached water stasis."

Avery laughed.

"Let's try looking for the cellar another way," Carter suggested.

"I'm listening."

They returned to the house, then performed another search of the property using an imaginary grid. They swept the grounds one quadrant at a time, until they nearly stumbled into an old granite foundation.

Avery rechecked the map. "This is nowhere near the hole shown on the map."

"Agreed. But we may as well check it."

Carter climbed down into the overgrown cellar, while Avery remained up top illuminating the way with her flashlight. She listened as he moved about far below.

"How is it?" she said.

"Dark," he hollered up.

"Anything shiny?"

"Not unless puddles count. This thing was built on top of a ledge, Avery. I don't see a place to hide anything."

They returned to the house to find Harrison sitting in a wingback beside a blazing fireplace, sipping Mark's Scotch. Curled up in his lap was Clara, Mark's cat.

"I thought you were keeping watch, Harry," Avery said.

"I am. But that doesn't mean Clara and I must be uncomfortable. Anyway, I've taken precautions."

"Such as?"

Harrison pointed around the room. "I repaired Boy Wonder's handiwork on the French doors with plywood and rewired the alarm panel. I was just waiting for you two to return so I could change the code and set it to stay."

"I knew there was a reason I kept you around," Avery said. "Now if you could only cook."

"Dinner's in the oven," Harrison said, raising and lowering his eyebrows mischievously.

Dinner turned out to be two large pepperoni pizzas Harrison was keeping warm in the oven until they returned. Avery scavenged through Mark's walk-in closet and bureau for some dry clothing for herself and Carter.

"What do you think?" Avery said as she modeled the pajama bottom and plaid chamois shirt combo.

"I think they might be a little big," Harrison chuckled.

"Well, at least they're warm," Avery said. "Let's eat."

After dinner, Avery booted up her laptop and began to scan the photos she'd taken of all the maps found in Mark's office into the computer. Next, she opened the map finder program she had written while they were on Hilton Head then uploaded each of the images into it.

She glanced over at Carter and Harrison. Lost in conversation, they were bonding over a bottle of Scotch. She smiled, happy that they had found at least one thing in common. Her attention returned to staring at the progress bar and silently cursing the agonizingly slow rural Internet connection. As she waited, Avery replayed in her head all the leads they had followed so far. It was frustrating to think how far astray they had gone, but she supposed that was precisely the point. If the treasure were easy to locate, it would have been found decades ago.

She thought back to the gruesome scene in the Virginia mine. Although what they had found was only someone's attempt to misdirect, it did appear that they had been on the correct track. And, so far as she knew, it was closer than anyone had gotten before, since the trunks were still buried in the collapsed coal. What she needed now were the clues that led to the real thing.

As she stretched her neck her eyes moved about the room, their location occurring to her in a different way. He could have opened an inn anywhere. Cargo Pants said Mark bought this house because of the treasure, and while the guy hadn't stricken Avery as the rocket scientist type, he sounded sure of himself. Of course Mark's house had to mean something. Why else would a tech magnate move to a place where the internet crawled slower than 1995 AOL dial-up? And why would he have changed his will to make sure it went to Avery in the event of his untimely passing? Julia could have shipped the desk to Florida if that was all there was to it. No, this was more than a coincidence. There had to be answers here. But where were they? She was still missing something.

53

The next morning, Avery awoke disoriented. She had fallen asleep on the floor of the study wrapped in a blanket. She found Carter and Harrison still in the living room, passed out on the couch and wingback, respectively. Deciding to let them sleep, Avery tiptoed to the kitchen to make coffee. Clara waited for her.

"I don't suppose you have any answers," Avery said as she reached down to scratch under her chin. The cat didn't so much as purr.

Thirty minutes later, two sleepy and slightly hung over men stumbled into the kitchen.

"Over served?" Avery teased.

"I don't want to talk about it," Carter said.

"Must have coffee," Harrison said as he plunked down at the table across from Avery, his hair sticking out in every conceivable direction. Carter fetched mugs of coffee for himself and Harrison, refilled Avery's, then joined them at the end of the table.

"I've been thinking," Avery began.

"Of course, you have," Harrison said.

"What about?" Carter said.

"The diary we found here."

"You mean the diary Sam stole from our hotel room safe?" Harrison said.

"Yeah," Avery said. "That diary, or at least what I read of it, seemed to be all about trying to run a profitable farming operation."

"From what you said, it didn't seem all that profitable," Carter said.

"That's right," Avery said. "It didn't. So, if we think the diary was written by the man who built this house, where did he suddenly acquire all his wealth? I mean, look at the size of this place."

"The lottery?" Harrison offered.

"Be serious, Harry," Avery said.

"Maybe he switched businesses after the war," Carter said.

"Yeah," Harrison said. "Something more profitable, like lumber. No shortage of trees around here."

"Or maybe he stole the treasure from Oswald and brought it here with him," Avery said.

"Maybe bluebirds will fly out of my nose and wash the dishes," Harrison grunted.

Avery scowled at him.

"I think what my drinking buddy there means is 'how do you figure?'"

"I went back through every single thing," Avery said. "And remember how MaryAnn told Carter that Oswald claimed the confederate coffers, or whatever he said, were stolen by his right-hand man?"

"Sure."

"I got to wondering why Mark, who hated winters in New York, would have bought property in Maine instead of opening an inn on an island somewhere," she swallowed hard at the thought of what might have been. "And why he'd have chosen this house in Maine, with its crackly, plodding internet access."

"Cargo Pants said the treasure was here." Harrison sat up a little straighter and squinted his bloodshot eyes.

"And that's how I figured." Avery nodded.

"For all we know the treasure could be in one of the fields Farmer John was supposedly planting," Carter said.

"Or under the inn," Harrison said absently, folding his arms on the table and resting his head on them.

Avery fixed Carter with a grin.

"What?" Carter said.

"Tell me she's not suggesting we dig up the inn," Harrison said, muffled.

Avery batted her lashes, still smiling at Carter.

"No," Carter said. "I'm not doing that again."

"Doing what?" Harrison asked without looking up.

"Calling MaryAnn," Carter said. "Do you know how many promises I've made already?"

Avery folded her hands under her chin and smiled wider. "Please, Carter?"

"All right," Carter said. "What do you want me to ask her this time?"

"Here's a list," Avery said as she tore off a sheet of paper from the notepad she'd been writing on.

Harrison held up his mug in salute to Carter. "Godspeed, young man."

The three of them showered and changed into clean clothes. After disabling the alarm, Harrison walked the perimeter looking for signs that anyone had been about. He found nothing, but it didn't put his mind at ease. They had stayed here far too long for his liking.

"I really think we should consider a different base of operations," Harrison said.

"Where would we go?" Carter said.

"And why?" Avery said. "This is my house now. Besides, the treasure is close. I can feel it."

"Yeah, and I can feel that Samael character and maybe Corbacho himself just around the corner," Harrison said. "If those bozos you bought off really were working for Samael, how long do you figure it will be before he shows up to take the desk?"

Before she could answer Carter's cell rang with an incoming call.

"It's MaryAnn," Carter said.

"Why don't you put it on speaker so we can all get properly introduced to her?" Harrison teased.

"That's a good idea, Harry," Avery said. "We should all hear what she has to say."

Begrudgingly, Carter obliged. After a round of brief and awkward introductions, MaryAnn shared her findings.

"I had to do a deep dive to find the information you wanted on Jonas Schilling, Carter," MaryAnn said. "As you already know from the photo I sent of him and General Oswald, Schilling was a captain in the regular confederate army. Schilling's family owned a plantation in South Carolina, and he was a well-respected member of the military. Schilling and Oswald were very close, and the general put him in charge of intelligence. But then something happened. About a year into the war, Schilling freed his family's remaining slaves. A highly unusual move for a ranking member of the confederate army. There were rumors about him being a union sympathizer. Even a spy."

"Same thing the antique dealer here in town said about John Smith," Avery murmured.

MaryAnn either didn't hear her or chose to ignore the comment, garnering a raised eyebrow and smirk from Harrison.

MaryAnn continued. "Schilling seems to have completely disappeared in the fall of 1863."

"Could he have been captured or killed in battle?" Carter said.

"It's unlikely," MaryAnn said. "There isn't a single record listing his name after September of 1863. Granted, the casualty lists weren't always complete, but someone as important as the intelligence commander of the confederate army would have been noted."

"Especially if he'd been killed or wounded by the union army," Harrison said.

"Exactly," MaryAnn said. "They would have wanted to crow about that."

Avery turned to Harrison and mouthed the words: *teacher's pet.*

Harrison stifled a laugh.

Avery moved closer to the phone to be sure she was heard. "MaryAnn, it might only be a coincidence, but the original owner of the home we're staying in was a man named John Smith. Same initials as Jonas Schilling. He moved here in 1863, and a local antiquities expert mentioned a rumor about Smith being a civil war spy. Any chance you could search for records about John Smith prior to his arrival in Maine near the end of 1863? Something tells me that you won't find any."

"Maine is deep in union territory. For pete's sake, General Joshua Chamberlain lived there. I would think Schilling/Smith would have been a hero," MaryAnn said. "Why would Schilling live under an assumed name in Maine?"

"Because he'd stolen a fortune in confederate gold," Avery said.

"I'll get back to you," MaryAnn said, abruptly ending the call.

"I think your girlfriend might be jealous," Harrison said to Carter.

54

"Boasting the fourth-longest oceanfront shoreline in the United States, Maine's rocky coast, with its many inlets, hidden coves, and islands has long been a favorite locale for weapons smugglers, pirates, and, in more recent times, drug mules," Harrison read from his phone screen.

Avery couldn't help wondering how much of that history had factored into John Smith's decision to purchase the oceanfront property.

The maps Avery had located appeared to show things in relation to their positions on the grounds, but over time buildings get razed and trees are felled. The granite cliffs abutting Smith's property, though hazardous to search, were far less likely to be altered by man or Mother Nature over the course of a century or two. With that idea in mind, Avery began studying the maps in a completely new way.

Perhaps the directions weren't to a hole in the ground, but a hole far under the ground, accessed from another position entirely. Like the mine in Virginia cut into the ground directly under the waterfall, where she had originally searched. Smith, or Schilling, or whoever he was, might have been thinking three-dimensionally.

Carter had suggested that the best way for them to examine the cliff face, without risking injury, was by use of his underwater drone.

"You brought a drone with you?" Harrison asked, not bothering to mask his disbelief.

"You didn't?" Carter grinned.

Avery returned the smile, her hopes creeping up again as a plan took shape.

Carter checked the maritime forecast and found that high tide was within the hour, perfect for what they'd need to do.

"All we need now is a boat," Carter said.

"I'll take care of that," Avery said. "Let's go!"

"Need I remind you what happened the last time?" Harrison said.

"This will be a shark-free adventure, Harry," Avery said. "I promise."

Needing water access that would allow them to get close enough to place the drone underwater, they packed up Carter's equipment then drove across town to the marina where Avery rented a Boston Whaler. Carter piloted the boat toward the cliffs while Avery tested the computer link to the drone. Harrison kept a lookout for trouble. It took them less than ten minutes to make the trip out to the cliffs.

"Assuming you're right," Harrison said, "and there really is a cave here, how do you know it'll be below the surface? I mean, these cliffs are steep. The cave could just as easily be above the water, right?"

"Not if Smith did what we think he did," Carter said.

"And that would be?" Harrison said.

"He would have had to use a boat to transfer the treasure, Harry," Avery said.

"Which means, if there is a cave here, it would have to be located between the low and high tide water marks," Carter said.

"Check out the gray matter on Mosley," Harrison said to Avery. She smiled when Carter blushed.

"It's close to high tide right now," Carter said. "So, this little baby is gonna give us a peek below the surface. If there's a cave here, she'll find it."

———

Harrison took the helm, allowing Carter to operate the drone. Sweeping back and forth along the cliffs, Harrison was careful to avoid getting too close to the shoreline and the jagged rocks protruding from below. Avery moved up to the bow, close to Carter, and studied the monitor for any large crevasses in the cliff face. For more than an hour they trolled back and forth along the front of Mark's property finding nothing. Despite the drone's high intensity lamps the visibility underwater was limited to only a few feet. Between wave movement, thick bands of kelp, and the varied depths of the rock outcroppings, Carter was extremely limited in how fast he could search without risking damage to the drone.

Avery was beginning to get the sinking feeling that she had led them on another wild goose chase when she saw it. A large, jagged opening in the cliff face surrounded by seaweed.

"Do you see it?" Avery said excitedly as she studied her own monitor.

"Indeed, I do," Carter said.

"You think it's large enough to hide what we're looking for inside?" Avery said.

"More than large enough," Carter said. "At least at the opening. I'm gonna try and get a look inside."

Avery watched in real time as the camera moved through the murky water, past the strands of kelp into the cave. The overall depth of the chamber was impossible to judge, but it was clear that it continued much farther into the side of the cliffs. The ceiling of the cave was irregular and rough, while the floor appeared smooth and much flatter. Not level exactly, more like layers of ledge.

"How far have you gone in?" Harrison said.

"About twenty-five feet, so far," Carter said. "Not sure I dare to go much farther though."

"Why?" Avery said. "Can't we keep looking?"

"The signal is beginning to break up. Too much bedrock. If I keep going, I'll lose the drone for sure."

Carter carefully navigated the drone out of the cave and back to the surface. Leaning over the gunwale, he retrieved it from the water.

Avery pinned their exact location on her GPS, allowing them to quickly locate the cave on their return.

"Let's head back, Harry," Carter said.

Avery smiled at his use of Harrison's nickname—one good bottle of Scotch and Harrison's tough guy veneer dissolved into friendship.

"So now what?" she asked, disappointed that they hadn't seen more.

"Now we have two choices. We either dive the cave tomorrow at high tide, or we wait until low tide and walk in."

"Walk in?" Harrison said. "Seriously? How do you propose we get close enough to do that?"

"We rent a RIB," Carter said.

"Okay, Mr. Mariner, I'll bite," Harrison said. "What's an RIB?"

"A rigid-hulled inflatable boat."

As they headed back to the marina, Carter explained his plan.

Back in Mark's kitchen, they sat around the table eating Thai takeout and replaying the cave video on Avery's laptop.

"So, the cave is big enough to walk inside?" Harrison said. "It doesn't look all that large on the monitor."

"It is, Harry," Carter said. "It opens to about ten feet high on the inside. Six or so feet wide."

"And the floor looks pretty smooth," Avery said. "Probably from decades of ocean water flooding in and out of it."

"That's another thing," Harrison said. "Assuming I have any intention of going in with you, and that's a big if, how does this whole underwater, not underwater, thing work? I'm not a huge fan of drowning. Especially inside a cave."

"It takes about six hours to move from low tide to high, and vice versa," Carter said. "If we time it so that the water is near low tide but still receding when we arrive, I figure we should have about two hours to poke around before the water gets too deep to safely remain in the cave."

"That doesn't sound like a lot of time to explore," Harrison said.

"And we still don't know how deep the cave is," Avery said.

"The drone only penetrated to about twenty-five feet before I had to call off the search, but you can tell from the video that the inside of the cave goes much deeper."

Harrison turned to Avery. "And you really think Smith, or Schilling, or whoever the hell he was, hid the gold in this cave?"

"If we've put the story together correctly, it makes sense," Avery said. "Schilling was Oswald's right hand and best friend. He was a high-ranking confederate intelligence officer, likely in charge of the secret mission to use the POWs to move the treasure to a mine on Oswald's family property."

Harrison nodded, his brow furrowing, and Avery talked faster. "But Schilling had his own secrets, namely that he was an abolitionist and a Union spy. So why would he want to let the confederacy keep this gold—or let Oswald have it, if he thought Oswald planned to steal it himself?"

"Greed is a powerful motivator," Harrison agreed.

"Exactly," Avery said. "So Schilling filled the chests with worthless iron scraps, sprinkled in a few coins, and blew up the tunnel, killing the transport crew in case anyone tried to look inside a chest—that way no one could tell the secret. He smuggled the treasure out of the south and went practically as far north as he could, changed his name to John Smith, bought some land, and built a farm. Schilling had owned a plantation before the war, remember?" She held Harrison's gaze. "The cave is the place around here least likely to change over decades or centuries, and the water and treacherous surroundings make it naturally secure. Which means if my theory is right, it's the most logical place for Schilling to have stashed the treasure, and the map inside the desk was a way to leave its location for future generations."

"But Oswald suspected Schilling had stolen the gold and wrote about that, so at some point after Schilling died, his family acquired Schilling's desk and it ended up on Martha's Vineyard," Carter added.

Harrison nodded slowly. "Where Mark bought it out from under Corbacho's nose. As theories go, this one is pretty solid, but people have searched for this thing for centuries, Ave. Don't get your hopes up."

Avery grinned. "My hopes have left the stratosphere, Harry. But we'll find out, one way or the other, in just a few hours."

55

As usual the accuracy of the local weather forecast left much to be desired. While the sky was indeed mostly clear, the winds were gusty, making the waves much higher than predicted. As Avery, Carter, and Harrison motored away from the marina in the rented RIB, water was already splashing over the bow.

"Tell me again how seaworthy this thing is," Harrison said.

"Relax, Harry," Avery said. "It's virtually unsinkable."

"They said the same thing about the Titanic, Avery," Carter shouted to be heard above the roar of the outboard.

"I was just starting to like you," Harrison shouted back.

Avery laughed; the banter helped relieve a bit of the anxiety she was feeling. Her stomach was in knots, and had been since she awoke around three a.m. She had lain in Mark's bed for a half hour thinking about all the things that could go amiss with today's hunt, before finally tiptoeing to the kitchen to start the coffeemaker. Following that, she checked to make sure that the alarm was still set to stay and that all the home's entry points were secure.

Satisfied that everything was still locked up tight, she'd returned to the kitchen to find Carter pouring a mug of coffee.

"Thought I might find you here," he said, handing her the mug.

"Excited?"

"More like anxious. You said it yourself. A lot can go wrong."

"That's true, but we've planned for almost every contingency. What did I tell you about scuba diving?"

"Do your checks but trust the process."

"Exactly."

Their conversation had been hours ago in a safe, well-lit kitchen, though. Now as Avery sat in the bow of the RIB, feeling the chilly spray of seawater, trusting the process was harder than it had sounded.

Avery hadn't verbalized it to Carter or Harrison, but she was worried. Worried because she was fresh out of clues. There were no more maps, no leads to check. Even Smith/Schillings's attempts at misdirection were used up. If they couldn't locate the treasure inside the cave today, they would be finished, and she knew it. She wondered if the others did too.

She glanced back at Carter. He removed one hand from the wheel and gave her a wave. She smiled and returned the gesture then looked at Harrison. He wasn't facing her direction, instead he was maintaining his grip on the hull while alternating between looking behind them for anyone following, and likely checking the waves for dorsal fins. She couldn't blame him for worrying about either threat, though the cold New England water eliminated all but the two-legged one. Avery went back to staring at the cliffs. If the guys were aware that this was their last chance to find the gold, they were doing an excellent job of hiding it.

The ocean looked even more foreboding as they neared the cave. Peaks of titanium atop gray waves hid the dangers below. Avery squinted her eyes, focusing on the rocks just above sea level, excited to get her first look at the cave above the waterline. It was one thing to watch the underwater drone footage, but a completely different experience to see a dark unexplored cave in real life. The opening in the rocks had been there for centuries. Perhaps Smith had been the first person to set foot inside. Maybe no one had visited since. She couldn't help wondering if Smith had ever been tempted to go back inside to make the occasional withdrawal.

"You ready, Avery?" Carter shouted, pulling her back to the present.

"Ready," she said as she grabbed the end of the rope and readied herself to make the leap from the craft to the ledge protruding to the left of the cave opening. She moved her feet apart trying to steady herself against the onslaught of waves striking the craft from the side.

"Be careful, Ave," Harrison said.

Carter put the nose of the RIB within a yard of the ledge. The bow bounced up and down and Avery waited to time her leap to shore with the bow rising. The gum rubber on the bottom of her water shoes held the ledge as she stuck the landing perfectly. She moved the bow rope to her teeth and grabbed onto protruding rocks with both hands as she shimmied toward the cave. She held onto the cave's outer edge with one hand while wrapping the rope around her other. One last maneuver would take her past the slippery seaweed lining the entrance and into the cave. As she prepared to jump her left foot slipped, causing her to lose her balance.

Avery knew she was going to fall awkwardly. This left her two choices: either shove herself backward into the choppy water and whatever rocks lie below, or risk injury by landing on the exposed stone ledge. In a split second, she chose option number one, plunging beneath the waves, the cold water taking her breath away. She steeled herself for the pain she associated with breaking an ankle—or worse—on the sharp rocks below the surface, but it never came.

Maintaining her hold on the rope, Avery kicked her legs and resurfaced. The boat had drifted away from the rocks. She knew that Carter was intentionally moving back so as not to pin her between the boat and the ledge. She released the rope as she felt the tide pulling her away from the cliffs. She turned away from the RIB back toward the cave and watched as the receding water poured from the cave's mouth like a waterfall. As she bobbed up and down in the frigid waves, she could hear both Carter and Harrison hollering to her. She knew they wanted to lift her back into the boat. But if she allowed them to pull her back in, they might try and abort.

"It's too dangerous, Ave," she could imagine Harrison saying.

Another twenty minutes and the cave would be well above the waves and much harder to access. It was now or never. If she could time her approach with a wave, she might be able to ride the swell directly into the cave.

Determined to make it, she kicked with her legs and pulled with her arms, swimming as hard as she could toward the mouth of the cave. Six feet. A deep breath. Four feet. Two feet. Her plan worked nearly to perfection as a swell pushed her up and over the entrance and into the darkened cave. Her left arm scraped the edge of the cave opening and she landed hard on her chest on the stone floor, momentarily stunned.

Avery's legs still protruded from the opening. She felt the water rushing past her as it exited the cave, threatening to pull her back into the ocean. She spread her arms wide, grabbing at the rock walls. Using every ounce of her remaining energy, Avery slid her legs up and under her, planting the balls of her feet on the cave floor. She rose like a sprinter in the starting blocks then crab walked forward until she was safely inside.

Allowing herself a moment to catch her breath, Avery answered Carter and Harrison's shouted concerns with a thumbs up. She began searching around the inside surface of the cave for something she could use to tie off the RIB. She located an oddly shaped, barnacle-encrusted rock protruding from the upper portion of the cave wall. It wasn't much, but it would serve their needs. Avery signaled for Harrison to toss her the rope.

Carter slowly inched the RIB forward while Harrison stood near the bow with the rope coiled and ready. It took two tries before Harrison hit the mark and Avery snatched the rope.

"Got it," Avery said before quickly lashing it around the improvised mooring.

Carter set the outboard motor to slow reverse, pulling the line taught.

"You sure you're okay, Ave?" Harrison said. "You're bleeding."

Avery checked her left arm. The sleeve of her top was torn but the skin beneath was only scraped. Nothing that would require stitches.

"I'm fine, Harry," she said. "Toss me some of that gear."

Though the boat was tethered to the cave, the waves were still wreaking havoc on it. Harrison and Carter looked like they were trying to balance atop a mechanical bull. As Avery had previously, Carter timed his throws to match the rising swells. She caught all three of the gear bags cleanly, tucking each behind nearby rocks to keep them from washing out of the cave.

"Okay," Avery said to Carter. "Your turn."

Carter turned to Harrison. "You good with this, Harry?"

"I got it. Just signal me when you're ready to be picked up."

The plan was to drop off Avery and Carter and their gear. Afterward, Harrison, who was armed, would take the RIB out far enough away from the cave to ensure that anyone who might spot him wouldn't know what Avery and Carter were up to.

Avery backed away from the entrance far enough to give Carter a place to land, but close enough to help steady him when he did.

"Here we go," Carter said as he balanced himself on the bow. "On three. One. Two. Three."

Carter leapt cleanly, landing just inside the cave on his feet. He locked hands with Avery and remained upright.

"Showoff," Avery said.

"You really okay?" Carter said, his face close enough that she could feel his warm breath on her water-frozen cheek.

"Stop fussing and untie Harry before he has a stroke out there."

Looking worried, Harrison gave them one last wave before throttling up the RIB's engine. Turning, he headed farther out into the cove. Avery and Carter collected their gear and donned their headlamps.

"You ready?" Carter said.

"Let's do this," Avery said unable to contain her excitement. "Let's go find the general's gold."

Samael followed Harrison's progress through high-powered binoculars as the ex-cop motored away from the cliffs in an inflatable Zodiac. Samael had been monitoring Turner and the others' progress for the last two days. Using remote game cameras and camouflage clothing, he'd seen them walking Mark Hawkins's property. Yesterday he'd watched as they rented a Boston Whaler from the local marina. He hadn't been able to follow to see where they went, but he knew exactly how long they had been gone. Today he'd been ready. Having spent the night on his own rented boat, he watched from a distance while they loaded the RIB and headed for the cliffs.

Only two things had surprised Samael. The first was that they had located a cave hidden within the cliff walls. Even now, looking back from his own vessel, the cave was difficult to spot. The irregular shape of the cliff face made the entrance look like any other deep depression. Or at least it did until he saw Turner and Mosley duck inside. The second thing that Samael hadn't expected to see was that he wasn't the only one following Avery Turner's progress. He swung the binoculars away from the Zodiac to the far side of the bay where Corbacho and two of his employees were pretending to fish.

He'd expected Corbacho to at least try harder to appear to honor the deal they'd made—for him to continue tailing Turner himself, no more hired help, and recover the treasure and for them to split the proceeds.

Samael grinned as he lowered the binoculars and adjusted the ball cap on his head. Whatever happened today, whether Turner located the treasure or not, one thing was certain. Corbacho and the others weren't leaving there alive. Not if Samael had anything to say about it.

56

Avery led the way into the dark cave. The memory of their coal mine exploration still fresh in her mind, she couldn't help but feel a tinge of apprehension. But Carter remained with her this time, and both of their lights were functioning properly. The tide had receded to the point that the floor of the cave was nearly water-free. The only exceptions were the low-lying areas of undulating ledge that acted as tidal pools trapping the seawater. The sound of water dripping from every surface served as a constant reminder that the cavern had been completely submerged only hours before and would soon be again.

"This is so cool," Avery said as they slowly moved forward. "I've never done anything like this."

"It's a first for me too," Carter said. "FYI, we've now gone farther than my drone did yesterday."

"Uncharted territory," Avery said.

"Just be careful, okay? We have no idea what secrets this place holds."

"You're not getting all Indiana Jones on me, are you, Carter?"

"Hardly," Carter laughed. "Just take it slow, okay?"

They carried two gear bags apiece, one slung over each shoulder. The bags contained an assortment of items Carter thought might come in handy. There were pry bars, extra lights, a pair of mini bolt cutters, and several pony air tanks—half liter Scuba tanks—in the event of trouble.

"How are we doing on time?" Avery said, checking her watch.

"So far so good. Less than twenty minutes until the tide shifts back."

The cave twisted to the left then dipped sharply before reappearing about twenty feet down the tunnel. The area in between was entirely underwater, and they had no way to gauge its depth.

"Hang on a minute," Carter said as he opened one of the gear bags and removed a thin, telescoping aluminum pole. Releasing several of the locking mechanisms, he extended the pole to its full length of six feet then used it to probe the bottom of the recess, determining that the water was only about three feet deep at its maximum.

"Better safe than sorry," Carter said. "Sometimes these things end up being deep underground reservoirs or even new tunnels."

"Thanks for the warning," Avery said.

They splashed through the depression and continued.

Corbacho had passed impatient before Avery Turner made it into the cave abutting Captain Schilling's property, and he was about to come out of his skin as Harrison steered the boat away from the cave. "How long until low tide?" he said to Alex, his new right hand.

"Nearly there, sir. What do you want to do about the cop?"

Corbacho liked that Alex called him sir. The gesture reminded him of Samael, though Alex was nowhere near as resourceful. Corbacho swung around and adjusted his binoculars until Harrison came into focus. The ex-cop was still bobbing around in the inflatable craft. It would have been easier to kill him now, but Corbacho was a man who liked to keep his options open for as long as possible. The out clause was a sound principle of business. Given the attachment between Avery and Harrison, the former detective might make a useful hostage if it came to that.

"It's time," Corbacho said. "Let's go grab the cop."

"Yes, sir," Alex said as he throttled up the engines.

"I assume he's armed," Filipe said. "What if he doesn't want to join us?"

"Then we convince him."

Avery and Carter passed three more depressions of varying lengths as they continued along the tunnel, but none of them were any deeper than the first. Rounding another bend, they came face to face with a solid wall of rock. The end of the cave.

Avery felt her heart sink. "It can't be, Carter," she said. "The treasure's got to be here."

"If it is, we missed it."

Avery let the bags slip from her shoulders, and the strap on the left raked across her injured flesh, making her wince. She smacked her open palm against the side of the cave in frustration. "Damn it."

Carter said nothing. Avery knew he was letting her vent. She wanted to break something. She was angry. Angry that they'd wasted so much time following false clues and maps meant to misdirect them. Angry that Mark had been killed, for nothing. The last time she'd felt this helpless was just after her mom died. She hated the feeling then, and she was hating it now.

Utterly defeated, she turned to Carter with her shoulders slumped forward and walked toward him. Carter wrapped his arms around her without saying anything. She laid her head against his chest and closed her eyes.

Harrison swam to the surface and sputtered out a mouthful of seawater. The cold was a bit of a shock, but he wasn't half as shocked as he'd been moments before when the large boat carrying the guys who'd been watching him for nearly a half hour intentionally ran down the RIB and he had been forced to dive out of it. He'd seen the boat, and the guys, but he hadn't expected the broad-daylight full assault. He turned to see the inflatable craft floating upside down in the waves. Its hull had ripped in two, and the outboard motor was torn from its mounts. The prop sticking out of the water resembled a child's windmill.

The large yacht that had nearly killed him swung around for another pass.

Emilio Corbacho and a man Harrison had never seen before leaned over the port side of the boat.

"Oh, dear," Corbacho said smugly. "I do hope you opted for the insurance on your rental boat, Mr. Harrison."

The second man laughed.

Harrison reached back for his gun, intending to put several holes in both men, but found only an empty holster. Another firearm lost at sea. Two in less than a week. He hadn't lost two guns in more than two decades on the job.

"Perhaps you'd like to come aboard," Corbacho said. "Seeing as how you no longer have any reliable transportation of your own."

Corbacho's goon tossed an orange rescue ring over the side toward Harrison. With much reluctance, Harrison swam over to it and grabbed on.

"Wouldn't want to see you drown," Corbacho said.

"That's funny," Harrison said. "'Cause I'd be fine watching you."

This time it was Corbacho's turn to laugh.

Suddenly aware that her clothes were soaked and clingy, Avery disentangled herself from Carter. "Thanks," she said simply.

"Anytime." He cleared his throat, turning back the way they'd come.

Avery dragged her foot along the edge of the floor where it met the wall of the cave.

"Why did you lie to me?" she asked, her voice soft.

"I am a lot of things, Avery, but a liar isn't among them." Carter sighed. "Is this about the Instagram thing people were talking about in Virginia?"

"Did you think I was stupid?" She leaned on the cave wall and folded her arms over her chest.

"You made a whole big thing about how you hate social media, how you won't ever open an account anywhere, you never look at it," he said. "I told you everything I do, Avery—I just left something out."

"You told me you filmed shipwrecks, Carter. You never said anything about having a gazillion followers. You're like some kind of social media rockstar."

"Hardly a rockstar, and I didn't tell you because it was cool that you didn't know. I wanted you to like me for who I am."

"I do." She smiled. "But it would have been nice to know women mail you their underwear. Just for general purposes, if you ever invited me over or something."

Carter's face turned red. "That's not endearing. It's weird. Just in case you ever find an address for Ryan Reynolds or something."

Avery laughed. In the smack middle of the worst failure in a life packed with accomplishments, Carter made her laugh.

She shook with it until her sides hurt before she caught her breath and patted his shoulder. "I needed that. Apparently, I suck at hunting treasure, and I'm not sure I've ever sucked at anything. Except beer pong—played once at a college party and I really wasn't any good."

"We might have missed something on the way in here, you know."

"How could that possibly be? The passage is barely wider than we are."

"Those low places we crossed through water," Carter said. "The standing water also hid whatever lay below."

"Yeah, but we walked across them," Avery said. "They felt solid underfoot."

"That doesn't mean there wasn't something underneath," Carter said.

They retraced their steps until they were back at the last of the four water-covered depressions they had previously crossed.

"So how do we do this?" Avery said.

Carter grinned. "I don't suppose you brought a sump pump, did you?"

"Jeez, this guy I know, who told me what we should bring, never mentioned a sump pump."

"I wouldn't listen to that guy again," Carter said.

"Don't worry," Avery said. "I won't."

Carter grabbed his goggles and a pry bar, along with one of the mini tanks from a gear bag. "Without a pump there's only one way I know of to check the bottom properly."

Avery's eyes followed Carter's headlamp as he swam beneath the surface along the second watery depression.

Carter sprang to the surface, pry bar in hand. "I found something!" he said after pulling the pony tank's mouthpiece from his lips.

"What?" Avery said. "The treasure?"

Carter shook his head. "Not that cool. But it is a false bottom. I'll need your help getting it up."

Avery squinted in her disapproval. "Really? Is that your idea of a come on?"

"If I was hitting on you, you wouldn't have to ask." Carter grinned. "Seriously—help. Grab your pry bar, mask, and air and give me a hand."

Unlike the trouble that Avery and Carter had experienced while trying to gain access to the cave from the small RIB, Corbacho's yacht, due to its size, was both more stable and came equipped with a long steel gangplank. Alex positioned the starboard side parallel to the cave opening. After setting the auto anchor controls, he slid the aluminum ramp over the side and into the mouth of the cave.

Corbacho's other man held a gun on Harrison.

"After you, Mr. Harrison," Corbacho said. "Time to see what your friends have been up to."

Harrison hesitated as his mind raced for a way out of the situation, but he couldn't come up with anything. His clothes were soaked, and his gun was lying at the bottom of the Atlantic Ocean. Not his best effort by far.

"Move," the goon said, shoving him forward.

Face masks off and air tanks discarded, Avery and Carter stood side by side in nearly three feet of water. They were exhausted from prying up and removing the large stones covering the hollowed-out recess under the cave floor, but the sore muscles and freezing water didn't matter even a tiny bit. Mouths agape, they stared down. The beams of their head lamps refracted in the water, illuminating the shimmer of gold, silver, and jewel encrusted heirlooms.

57

"My God," Carter said. "You found it."

Avery was speechless.

Carter replaced his face mask then dove down into the hole. A moment later he resurfaced with a large handful of the treasure and passed it to Avery. She needed both hands to hold it.

The sparkling colors threw rainbows onto the cave walls.

"I've never seen anything so beautiful," Avery said as she stared at the bounty.

"The tide is coming in, Avery. We better think about heading back if we don't want to get trapped in here."

"Yes, indeed," a voice said from behind them.

They turned to see Corbacho pointing a gun at them and blocking their way out. Behind him stood another man holding a gun on Harrison.

"I'm sorry, Ave," Harrison said.

"It isn't your fault, Harry," Avery said.

"I must tell you," Corbacho said as he stared at the treasure she held. "I'm impressed, Ms. Turner. I never considered you to be much more than a nuisance. I certainly didn't imagine that you'd locate my treasure for me."

"It isn't your treasure, Emilio," Avery hissed.

"Oh, that's right. You're still trying to avenge the late Mark Hawkins. It's always so tragic to see a young life taken by drugs."

"I know it was you," Avery said. "Mark would never have killed himself."

Corbacho grinned. "And I never imagined that he would dare cross me. It is truly amazing how far some will go for fortune." His attention turned to Carter. "And fame. Isn't that right, Mr. Mosley?"

"I don't mean to interrupt, Mr. Corbacho," the goon said. "But the water is really coming in now."

Avery looked down to see foot-high waves washing past their captors into the depression in which she and Carter stood. The incoming tide had already begun to obscure the lower portions of the cave floor. Harrison's feet were now underwater.

"Yes, I suppose you're right, Alex," Corbacho said. "We'll have to leave the recovery for another day. It's a shame you and your friends won't be able to witness it, Ms. Turner. I should have hired you instead of Samael."

The unmistakable boom of gunshots echoed through the cave, causing Avery and Carter to duck their heads in unison.

Instinctively, Corbacho turned to see what had happened. For a split second nobody moved, and then both of Corbacho's henchmen collapsed face first into the shallow water coating the cave floor. Behind Harrison stood Samael. Smiling.

"Did I hear you right, sir?" Samael asked. "Thinking of replacing me, again?"

Avery could see the confusion in Corbacho's face. No longer protected, he swung his gun back and forth between Samael, Harrison, and Carter.

Harrison moved to one side as Samael stepped forward, his gun trained on Corbacho.

"What kind of man makes a deal one day only to break it the next?" Samael asked.

"I'm sure we can come to some kind of understanding here," Corbacho said as he backed up a step.

The water level was rising quickly.

"There's more than enough here for both of us, you know," Corbacho said, momentarily losing his footing in the waist high water, his voice cracking with fear. "We can kill them and split the treasure tomorrow."

"You gave away your chance at that by coming here to double cross me. Again. You're alone, unguarded, and outmatched, Emilio. What makes you think I'd settle for half?" Samael said. "Or even let you live to see tomorrow?"

Avery, who was nearly underwater now, exchanged a quick glance with Carter. She gestured to the pony tank still strapped to her arm. Carter nodded his understanding. Corbacho and Samael were too focused on each other to notice the sound—Sonny Landon would have said Avery was listening to the cave.

No one blinked, all eyes on Corbacho and Samael, and theirs on each other.

And then it happened, a wall of water bearing down on them from the mouth of the cave, roaring like an approaching freight train.

Avery inserted her mouthpiece and quickly dove below the surface. She saw twin muzzle flashes, but the sound was muffled by the water.

Avery and Carter were tossed about as if caught in a whirlpool, the rushing tidal wave scuttling everything in its wake. Avery fought to maintain her position until her eyes caught sight of one of the gear bags. She swam toward it and grabbed a spare pony tank. She had to find Harrison— and quickly. Before she could move, Carter grabbed onto her arm. He signaled for her to swim for the cave entrance. The pressure of the flowing water was beginning to abate as the cave was nearly full.

Avery swam as fast as she could, with Carter right behind her, toward where she thought she had last seen Harrison. She nearly collided with Corbacho's lifeless body as it tumbled by on her right. Her headlamp illuminated him for just a moment, but it was long enough for her to see the gaping hole in his forehead and the shocked expression on his face. She pressed on, frantically searching for Harrison. She expected to see Samael's body next but did not. Instead, she saw Harrison's legs kicking for all they were worth. Having found a small air pocket in a recess at the top of the cave, he struggled to keep his head above water.

"Harry," Avery shouted as she surfaced beside him. "Here. Use this to breathe."

He was too winded to answer but complied.

Avery realized that they didn't have another mask. She would have to guide him out of the cave. "Close your eyes, Harry. Kick your legs and hold on tight."

Harrison squinted his eyes closed and nodded.

Avery bit down on her mouthpiece and swam for all she was worth. She struggled to recall how far into the cave they had been when they'd located the gold, but she couldn't be sure. She tried to focus on nothing but moving forward. Harrison was doing exactly what she had asked, and if anything, they were moving faster than she might have on her own.

She had no way of knowing how much air was left inside the half-liter tank. She had already depleted some while helping Carter uncover the hiding place within the cave floor. She knew she was breathing much too hard. The small air tanks were designed as a backup when Scuba diving, not for escaping underwater caves full of armed assassins.

"Emergency air," Carter had said. This certainly qualified.

Avery hadn't seen Carter since before she'd found Harrison. She hoped Carter was right behind them, but there was no way of knowing.

Rounding another bend in the cave, she saw it. A lighter shade of water that could only mean sky above. The entrance was merely another twenty or so feet away. She drew another breath but came up short. The tank was empty. Fighting the urge to panic, she spit out the mouthpiece and kept going. Half a breath would have to do. Almost there. Harrison was still holding on. Exhaustion set in quickly, though. Her arms and legs were slowing. Her oxygen-starved chest heaved, and black spots began to dance across her vision. *Oh no you don't,* she thought.

"Never give up, Avery," her mother's voice said. "No matter what life throws at you. Never quit."

Then they were out. She and Harrison broke through the surface.

Avery gulped in the biggest breath of air she had ever drawn. Fresh air. Gloriously cool, fresh air.

"We made it, Ave," Harrison said. "You did it."

"Carter?" Avery said as she whipped her head around. "Where's Carter?"

Before Harrison could answer, Carter popped up about ten feet away.

"Oh man," Carter said. "Now, that was a rush."

58

Corbacho's boat had maintained its position in front of the now-underwater cave, but with the rising tide the metal plank had fallen overboard.

"Come on," Carter said. "This thing has a diving platform and a ladder in back."

It took a minute or so for them to assist Harrison up onto the boat. Exhaustion had left him with zero leg strength. Luckily, his upper body was still as strong as a bull.

"Let's get out of here," Carter said as he climbed behind the wheel. He disengaged the auto anchor, then throttled up the engines. "Hang on."

"Thank you for saving me, Ave." Harrison said.

Avery wasn't sure who had really saved whom in the end. She was simply grateful to be alive. She plopped down across from Harrison, spent.

"Hey," Carter said. "Catch."

Avery reached up and snatched the gold coin out of the air. She held it close, examining the details. A smile spread across her face as she read the Latin numerals VI. The coin had come from an entirely different chest. The stories were true. She wondered if King Charles could have imagined how far astray his fortune would travel from its intended purpose. It begged the question of how different the history of two countries might have been had the treasure not been stolen.

Avery decided they would contact the police as soon as they got back to the marina. Sheriff Greene hadn't seemed like he trusted them all that much during their brief interaction at the Hawk's Nest. She wondered what he'd have to say about the four bodies back in the cave.

"Don't look now," Harrison shouted. "But we've got company."

Avery whipped her head around to see a smaller boat, a bow rider, in their wake and closing fast. There was no mistaking the man behind the wheel. It was Samael.

"Hang on," Carter said. "Let's see what this baby will do."

Carter turned to Starboard and buried the throttle, racing away from the marina and out to sea.

"Unless Samael lost his gun, we're gonna need a weapon," Avery said.

"Don't look at me," Harrison said. "I lost mine when Corbacho's goon ran this thing over the blow-up dinghy and tried to turn me into fish food."

Avery got up and staggered toward the forward cabin, grabbing for anything that would help her stay upright as the boat slammed over the waves. If there was a weapon aboard this boat, she would find it.

"He still gaining on us," Harrison called as he climbed the ladder to the bridge on shaky legs.

"I don't know how he's doing it in that little Bayliner," Carter yelled. "I've got this thing wide open and the waves are banging the hell out of us."

"He's using our wake against us," Harrison said. "Smoother water inside."

Avery scoured the cabin but found nothing. It looked like Corbacho and his men hadn't spent much time below deck. She wondered how long Corbacho had been following them. She held on tight as she ascended the steps to the main deck. Samael had closed the gap between them. He was now less than twenty yards off the stern and still closing.

"You find anything?" Carter hollered down from the flying bridge.

"No," Avery said. "There's nothing down there."

"Stay down there, Ave, and take cover," Harrison said. "If he's still got a gun we don't want to be bunched up and make it easy for him.

Before Avery could respond, a piece of trim directly above her head exploded, showering her with fiberglass debris.

"Get down," Harrison shouted.

Avery ducked down behind a row of seats just as two more rounds punched through the fiberglass bulkhead directly below where Harrison and Carter stood.

"He's coming around port side, Avery," Carter said as another bullet ricocheted off a chrome support post supporting the Bimini top.

"Faster," Harrison yelled.

"I can't," Carter said. "The sea's too rough. We're barely staying upright now."

Another bullet whizzed just over their heads.

"Look out, Harry," Avery yelled.

"My turn," Harrison said as he pushed Carter to one side. "I'm gonna run this bastard down, Carter. It's the only way. You two grab something sturdy and hang on tight."

Harrison cut the wheel to the left just as Samael began to overtake them on the port side. Samael mimicked the maneuver and backed off slightly.

"Oh, you don't like having someone run you over, huh?" Harrison yelled. He looked over at Carter who was hanging on for dear life. "His ex-boss enjoyed it, though."

Avery watched as Samael switched tactics, this time closing in on their starboard side. She rose to her feet but stayed low, crab-walking toward the rear of the boat. Samael grinned and took aim in her direction. She saw the muzzle flash just as she dropped down to the deck. The bullet connected with the outside of the hull directly in line with where she had been standing.

"Stay down, Avery," Carter yelled.

"If you think I'm gonna let you two have all the fun, you're crazy," she muttered to herself.

Avery low crawled the rest of the way to the aft seats then flipped up the cushions to search the storage beneath. There was nothing under the starboard seats except life vests. She switched sides, repeating the process. More vests but this time she found what she was looking for, a heavy metal anchor, buried underneath. She removed the anchor and its attached chain, set them on the deck, then went to work on the bolt that connected the other end of the chain to a coil of nylon mooring rope.

"He's coming up again, Ave," Harrison shouted.

Avery couldn't stop what she was doing to look. "Which side, Harry?" she yelled back.

"My left," Harrison said.

"What?" Avery shouted as the chain slipped out of her grasp.

"Starboard side, Avery," Carter said. "He's nearly on us."

She retrieved the chain and spun the nut until it dropped onto the deck. Pulling the bolt free, she released the rope. Avery wrapped the chain around one hand. Grasping the anchor with the other, she rose slightly to her knees.

"How close?" Avery yelled.

"He's about fifteen feet off the stern," Carter said.

"Let me know when he's right there," Avery said.

"Avery, stay down," Harrison yelled.

No sooner had the words left Harrison's mouth than a piece of teak trim exploded below his feet.

Avery knew Samael's focus would remain on the bridge and not on her.

"Where is he?" Avery shouted again.

"Ten feet off the starboard side, almost even with the stern," Carter yelled, his eyes popping wide when he figured out what she was up to. "Now, Avery, now!"

She rose to her feet, drawing her arm back as if she were about to throw a life ring. Samael was taking careful aim directly at the bridge. He was so focused on killing Harrison that he'd forgotten all about her. She swung the anchor high, tossing it over the starboard gunwale. The chain unraveled, sailing after the anchor like the tail of a deadly kite. Her aim and timing were perfect. Samael fired again. Avery saw the muzzle flash just as his head began to turn in her direction. She saw his eyes widen as he registered the threat. Samael raised his arm reflexively, but the anchor caught him squarely in the chest, and the chain followed.

Samael's body flew backward, bouncing off the top of the outboard before tumbling into the sea. The bow rider veered to the right and continued out to sea without a pilot.

"Oh my God, did you see that?" Avery said as she turned to check on Harrison and Carter.

Something was clearly wrong. Carter was down on one knee beside Harrison.

"He's hit, Ave," Harrison yelled as he throttled down the engine.

Avery raced up the ladder.

59

A crowd of at least thirty people stood at the far end of the wharf. The ambulance and three sheriff's department vehicles had been waiting for them as Harrison pulled up to the dock. Avery stood beside the gurney. She held Carter's hand in hers while the paramedics worked to stabilize the wound in his thigh.

"You were awesome back there," Carter said.

"If I'd been truly awesome, you wouldn't have gotten shot," she said.

"Looks like it's showtime," Carter said as he nodded toward the police vehicles.

Avery turned to see Harrison and another large-framed man walking toward them. The other man was Sheriff Greene, and he didn't look happy.

"How are we ever going to explain all this?" Avery said.

"I have no idea," Carter said.

"We've got to go now, miss," one of the paramedics said to Avery.

"Will he be okay?" Avery asked, squeezing Carter's hand a little tighter than necessary.

"He will be if you let him go," the other paramedic said with a smile. "We'll make sure of it."

"Okay." Avery dropped his hand. "I'll see you at the hospital."

She watched as they closed the doors to the ambulance then drove away.

Avery turned and came face to face with Sheriff Greene.

He considered Avery for a moment without speaking. She chanced a quick glance at Harrison, who only shrugged.

Her attention returned to Greene. "Sheriff," she said.

"Ms. Turner," Greene said. "Former Detective Harrison informs me that you may have left a few dead bodies in your wake," the sheriff said.

Avery nodded, wisely resisting the urge to smile at the ill-timed and unintentional pun. "Yes, sir. I'd say that was accurate. But none of us shot anyone, sir."

"Something about lost treasure, and ruthless international killers."

Avery looked at Harrison again, surprised that he'd been so forthcoming with the sheriff already.

"That's correct," Avery said.

"He also tells me that you just inherited Mark Hawkins's place."

"I did, sir."

"So these fellows were trespassing on your property, and they were armed, then."

"I suppose they were, yes."

The sheriff tilted his hat back on his head and leaned in close. "And is it your intention to keep the house, Ms. Turner? Maybe stay here occasionally. Add some excitement to our little town?"

"No, sir," Avery said. "I plan to sell it as soon as everything gets sorted here."

Greene moved back, rising to full height once again. "Young lady, that just might be the best news I've heard all week."

EPILOGUE

Avery looked up from her laptop as Harrison approached. He was dripping wet and waving his dive mask and snorkel at her. The turquoise water of the Caribbean stretched out all around them.

"That water is incredible, Ave," Harrison said. "I've never seen so many different colored fish."

"I've never seen you like this, Harry," Avery said.

"What can I say? This diving shi—stuff is really beginning to grow on me."

"What about the getting shot at stuff?" Carter said from behind Avery as he limped into view carrying a drink tray with two cocktails and a bottle of Corona.

"Hell, I had people shooting at me all the time when I was on the job," Harrison said.

Avery removed one of the glasses from the tray and shook her head. "No, you didn't. You took more fire last month than you did in the line. Carter, don't start believing Harry's war stories."

Harrison feigned a wounded expression. "I thought you loved my war stories."

"When I was ten," Avery said before taking a sip from the straw.

Carter laughed and held the tray out for Harrison.

"Which reminds me," Harrison said as he lifted the bottled beer off the tray. "How long are you gonna milk that little flesh wound in your thigh?"

Carter limped over to the beach chair next to Avery's and gingerly sat down with his drink.

Before he could respond, Avery came to his defense. "Sounds to me like Harry's jealous that you'll have a real war story to tell."

"Jealous?" Harrison scoffed. "Ha."

"Besides," Avery said. "Chicks dig scars."

"Really?" Carter said.

"Well, this chick does anyway," Avery said.

"Time for another swim," Harrison said, rolling his eyes. He set the bottle in the sand and slid the goggles back over his head.

They watched Harrison jog down the beach and into the water.

Carter gestured toward Avery's computer. "How's the app coming along?"

"I've nearly finished tweaking it," she said. "What about you? Did you get the trademark paperwork and the LLC registration back yet?"

"Should be here next week."

"Treasure Tech designs is a go," Avery said as she raised her glass and clinked it against Carter's.

Carter lay back in the chair and pulled the straw hat over his eyes. "Have you figured out all the features of the app yet?"

"Oh yeah. I've got map compilations, comparisons, ultrasound survey, speaker function, depth perception, water depth calculations, with gyroscope, and altimeter function. CO_2 dive calculations. You name it. If a smart phone chip can be pushed to handle a function, I've got it in there."

"Still thinking about selling it?"

"I'm not sure," Avery said. "Why do you ask?"

Carter lifted his hat and sat up in the chair facing Avery. "Well, I was thinking, some of Harrison's old military and police contacts could make use of that. Know where they're going before they head in."

"The government's never a bad customer to have," Avery said. "They pay reliably and quite well."

"Not that you need the money," Carter said. "Speaking of which, what's the latest on the Daimler lawsuit?"

"They've withdrawn it. Citing accounting errors on their end." Avery snapped her fingers. "That reminds me, I was supposed to call Maggie yesterday. Oh well, I'll reach out and set something up with her tomorrow."

"You're not at all worried about Daimler trying something else?" Carter said.

"Not anymore. And even if they did, the finder's fee for General Oswald's treasure will take care of that. It will be completely unlinked to the company sale, meaning it is untouchable. It also means Treasure Tech is fiscally sound for the foreseeable future, and there are a dozen hospitals in Virginia coal country that should be getting notice of substantial gifts earmarked for state-of-the-art pulmonary care equipment in the next few days."

She closed the laptop and turned to Carter. "What about you? Are you gonna take that diving for treasure TV deal?"

"Nope."

"Really?" Avery said. "Just like that?"

"That whole reality TV thing is nothing but a flash in the pan. I love diving, and the treasure hunting thing is beginning to grow on me, bullets and all—but reality television isn't for me."

"So, what are you gonna do?"

"I've given it a lot of thought and I think I've got a great idea."

"And? Don't be a tease. What is it?"

Carter pushed himself up awkwardly from the chair. "I found this really beautiful woman."

"You don't say. But beautiful women are a dime a dozen, Carter. What makes this one so special?"

"Well, she's fun to hang out with. She's really into hunting for lost treasure. She's super intelligent and very wealthy. She's even got her own private jet."

"I don't know, Carter," Avery said. "It sounds like this woman, whoever she is, might be way out of your league."

"Yeah, you're probably right," Carter said as he looked out over the water. "Too bad, though."

"What is?"

"I was going to ask her to join me on this really cool adventure."

"Adventure?" Avery asked as she fixed Carter with a mischievous grin. "Tell me more."

The Cardinal's Curse
The Turner and Mosley Files Book 2

Danger has a new destination.

An enigmatic invitation lures tech genius Avery Turner and thrill-seeker
Carter Mosley away from their recent groundbreaking discovery of the
General's Gold, offering them a chance to join an expedition on the cutting
edge of science. Drawn into the heart of Antarctica, they pursue a
legendary shipwreck that is fabled to house the long-lost crown jewels of
Norway. As they plunge into the quest, chilling tales of centuries-old curses
and an unsolved murder emerge, hinting at connections more profound
and perilous than they ever imagined.

With a stolen treasure worth millions at stake and the fate of the scientific
expedition in question, Carter must complete the most dangerous dive of
his life in the harshest conditions on the planet. As suspicious sabotage
cripples their equipment and unforeseen dangers intensify, the duo depend
on Avery's innovative technology and their unwavering trust in each other.
But amidst the ice, their gravest challenge might become determining
friend from foe.

ACKNOWLEDGMENTS

Working together to create these characters and get this book in your hands has been quite an adventure in itself. We've had great fun, become better friends, grown to love Avery, Carter, and Harrison (we hope you will, too), and are excited for many more adventures with them. We wish to express our gratitude to the following people for encouraging us to collaborate and for their invaluable assistance in successfully launching the Turner and Mosley Files: Andrew Watts, Randall Klein, Amber Hudock, Cate Streissguth, and the entire team at Severn River Publishing—thank you for getting excited about LynDee's new idea and helping team us up; our agents, John Talbot and Paula Munier, thanks for looking out for our best interests and parsing several contracts for this series; Reed Farrel Coleman and Brian Shea, thank you for offering us insight and encouragement gained from your own experience with coauthoring; Micki Browning; Pam Stack, thank you for offering honest feedback on an early draft; Kristopher Zgorski, thanks for your excitement and encouragement and hosting a wonderful cover reveal; and you—none of this would be possible without our wonderful readers—thank you for coming along for the ride.

While we did extensive interviews and research for the action sequences in this novel, some of the scenes stretch the safety boundaries of the real world and we wouldn't advise trying them at home—to learn more about diving or cave exploration, consult a qualified instructor. As always, any mistakes you might find are ours alone.

ABOUT BRUCE ROBERT COFFIN

Bruce Robert Coffin is the award-winning author of the Detective Byron Mysteries. Former detective sergeant with more than twenty-seven years in law enforcement, he is the winner of Killer Nashville's Silver Falchion Awards for Best Procedural, and Best Investigator, and the Maine Literary Award for Best Crime Fiction Novel. Bruce was also a finalist for the Agatha Award for Best Contemporary Novel. His short fiction appears in a number of anthologies, including Best American Mystery Stories 2016.

Sign up for the Turner and Mosley Files newsletter at
severnriverbooks.com

brucerobertcoffin@severnriverbooks.com

ABOUT LYNDEE WALKER

LynDee Walker is the national bestselling author of two crime fiction series featuring strong heroines and "twisty, absorbing" mysteries. Her first Nichelle Clarke crime thriller, FRONT PAGE FATALITY, was nominated for the Agatha Award for best first novel and is an Amazon Charts Best-seller. In 2018, she introduced readers to Texas Ranger Faith McClellan in FEAR NO TRUTH. Reviews have praised her work as "well-crafted, compelling, and fast-paced," and "an edge-of-your-seat ride" with "a spider web of twists and turns that will keep you reading until the end."

Before she started writing fiction, LynDee was an award-winning journalist who covered everything from ribbon cuttings to high level police corruption, and worked closely with the various law enforcement agencies that she reported on. Her work has appeared in newspapers and magazines across the U.S.

Aside from books, LynDee loves her family, her readers, travel, and coffee. She lives in Richmond, Virginia, where she is working on her next novel when she's not juggling laundry and children's sports schedules.

Sign up for the Turner and Mosley Files newsletter at
severnriverbooks.com

lyndee@severnriverbooks.com